Ripple

Ripple by Annie J Ryan
Publishing services by Australian eBook Publisher
www.AustralianEbookPublisher.com.au

2nd Edition 2017, pbk.
ISBN: 978-1-925516-43-2
Designer: Sharnai James-McGovern, Australian eBook Publisher
Editor: Alex Nahlous

National Library of Australia Cataloguing-in-Publication Entry

Creator: Ryan, Annie J., author.
Title: Ripple / Annie J Ryan
ISBN: 9781925516432 (paperback)
9781925516418 (ebook : epub)
9781925516425 (ebook : mobi)
Subjects: Families--Fiction.
Romance fiction.
Domestic fiction.
Western Australia--Fiction.
Dewey Number: A823.4

Also available as an ebook from major ebook vendors.

Find the author at anniejryan.com

Ripple

Some choices seem easy...

Annie J Ryan

Chapter One

Mel would have drifted in the warm gloop for longer but for the bright strip of daylight across her face. Still trapped in the thick syrup of sleep, she struggled to open her eyes, but when she did they widened in alarm. Saliva tingled on her chin and an ache pulsed across her neck and shoulder. Flat against the hot glass, her cheek raged with sunburn. And there was blood on her shirt. Had she fallen sleep?

Her eyes locked onto the moony head filling the window. The car rocked as the door handle was gripped and lifted.

'Jesus Mel, what happened?' His eyes hovered right above her face after she'd let him in. He grabbed her hand where blood had congealed and his eyes rounded as he took in the splatters of it on her white shirt.

'It's nothing. A savage paper cut.'

'Why are you in your car at lunch?' He looked around the car.

'I wanted to read the letter alone.' She saw the lines of concern. 'There's nothing else, truly Royce. I tried mopping it up, see?' She held up a bloodied wad of tissues and waggled the inflamed and crimson finger lined with a fresh tear.

'You had me worried.'

'I got it when I pulled out the letter.' On the floor by his feet were the shredded remains.

'The students really like you.'

'I love working with the students.' She held a tissue to her nose.

'And you give excellent career advice.'

'Actually a lot of them don't want to study business and accounting.' She blew into another tissue.

'I get that, but the point is to keep some of them in your course.'

'I know.'

They'd started in the business faculty at the same time, but Royce's genius with all things technological meant he was fast-tracked to a leading position and offered tenure with an enviable career path.

'You don't even like accounting Frodo.' He nudged her shoulder.

'I was never in love with it Samwise.' She offered him a thin smile before she gathered the tissues and tossed them onto the back seat.

'It might be why you didn't get your contract renewed.'

'I'm thinking you're right.'

'I can't understand why you chose accountancy instead of counselling or psychology?' The intensity of his gaze made her turn away. If she removed herself and pretended that it was someone else they were talking about, she'd have a hundred good ideas. Because, she wanted to say, it gets complicated when you're divorced with children and you're me. But she bit her lip, pushed stray locks of dark hair behind her ears and thought about a mature response.

'I didn't mind it in the beginning and I was good at it. Besides, I had no idea what to do and I needed to earn money.' It was confronting, examining herself from his perspective.

'Do you know now?'

'Yes, but I can't afford to go back and study with kids to support.' She wouldn't tell him because it sounded childish to moan about the guidance counsellor from high school. Mel had been advised to think about a more practical career. The counsellor said there would be only one or two positions each year for the thousands that applied in that line of work.

He patted her leg and shuffled towards the door. 'I'd better get back. Coming?'

'In a minute.' When her eyes landed on the shredded letter

her chest sank. 'Don't say it. You don't have kids, a mortgage and a fistful of bills.'

'I do as a matter of fact. Minus the kids and the mortgage.'

She managed a wan smile. He'd paid off his house with a family bequest and Linley, his wife, ran a hearing clinic.

'You'll—'

'No platitudes Royce, not from you or Samwise.'

'Right.' She attempted to ward off pricks of self-pity when he leaned over and squeezed her, but a bit leaked out of her eyes.

Inflated with pride at the success of their offspring or businesses, she observed colleagues and school mums shimmer with an inner glow. Their sparkler was definitely lit. The trajectory of her present life suggested hers was lost, spent or broken.

At the age of forty-two, she preferred to maintain a safe distance between herself and the crunch and grind of a pedestrian life. If she could pay her bills, feed her children, meet her mortgage and not look up, she wouldn't have to see what was headed her way. But once she saw the crisp white envelope, the fog-like mist she shrouded herself in fell away. A confrontation with the mess of reality was inescapable and it made her struggle to think and compressed her lungs; and much as she would have liked to push it all away and skip down to the river to become an unencumbered soul, she'd miss the children. Would they cope without her and still love her? If only she knew. No, she'd made the mistake of utterly falling in love with each child and they were inextricably linked forever and ever, or at least until they left home. Either way, they were not the responsibilities she wanted to escape. Not really.

Bright light bounced off the clinical walls of the staff bathroom and onto the mirror where large brown eyes stared back at her, dull and puffy, and her cheeks bore small red angry spots. Usually round and full, her curves sagged and pulled her downward; her five-foot-four frame seemed too big for her diminished self. She dumped each item of clothing onto the floor, kicking them aside to wriggle into the forgiving stretchiness of her running pants. She wasn't the only one to decline the after-work drinks. Royce confided to her that several more letters had been distributed during lunch.

At the beach car park, she closed her eyes and placed her head against the backrest. 'It's your own fault,' she told herself, but the desire to lash out whipped around and she wished she could blame someone else.

Cool ocean air slapped her face and an ache ran under her ribs. She pressed at it with the flat of her palm, pretty sure it was her heart, incandescent with rage.

Once out of the car, she slammed the door and took long awkward strides. Her thoughts swirled. Two of her credit cards were over the limit and one was close to getting there. What was she supposed to do now? Panic rose in her throat. The run was supposed to fill her with endorphins.

Toward the end of the run, a resounding pistol crack split the air. She flinched and looked around to locate the source. Beyond the moving strand of people she saw the front end of a car creased into concrete kerbing; plastic panel work and parts of a headlight lay scattered on the grass and road. A short distance away was the body of a boy.

'Mitchell!' A wail broke over the din.

The car door opened and a young man stepped out; one hand darted to his mouth before he jogged toward the family.

'Don't you come near us!' The father flicked him a look then kept his eyes trained on his son.

Phones slid from pockets and fingers tapped on screens. Mel caught thin curls of scorched rubber overriding the sea air.

The father ran fingertips all over the boy's face and picked up a limp hand, his voice soft and insistent. 'Mitchell, can you hear me son?'

'I'm so very sorry.' He collapsed to the ground near his car and sat with his head between his knees, his arms behind his head, and rocked. An older lady moved to stand beside the slight figure and placed her hand on his shoulder.

The path to Mel's car wound through the middle of the gathering crowd. She lifted an arm to mop at her face and tugged at her damp shirt.

'He's not breathing! I can't feel a pulse. Who can do resuscitation?' Several people shuffled closer and explained that they only knew what they'd seen in movies. He nodded. His desperation rose.

She longed to run to her car, close her ears, and not have the echo of the crack from the car bounce around inside her skull.

'I know how,' Mel said.

Heads turned. Wind ran over the sweat on her legs and she shivered. Once the words shot out she couldn't reel them back.

The father reached for her arm. 'Thank you.'

'Get everyone to move away.'

She opened the boy's shirt, placed her hands on his still warm flesh and looked up, hopeful that someone else would step forward.

'I've never had to do this.' Did people sue rescuers? She swallowed and took deep breaths to calm herself.

'He's only eleven.' The father pulled his daughter close and kept the small boy's hand in his palm. He twisted around to fix his gaze on the young driver.

'What the fuck were you doing driving like that?'

'I'm so sorry.' His voice came out thick and disjointed.

'Save it for the police.'

'It's Cam Robson. He plays for Rockforth Bay.' The flow of information rebounded around the crowd.

Mel tried to block it out as her palm descended into the frame of the little boy's rib cage. She gripped his chin and blew two strong breaths. After several rounds she paused; his chest didn't rise and she couldn't hear or feel his breath.

When she prepared to blow into his mouth again, the boy's eyes flew wide open and he lurched with a shudder. She quickly turned him on his side. His body quivered before a thick ball of undigested gummy chews hurtled out of his mouth, followed by several more sprays of fluid. Had he choked? The acrid reek unsettled her stomach.

'Mitchell! You're okay son.' His father wiped at his eyes with the back of his hand.

'I think he should lie still and wait for the paramedics.' Mel tried to prevent the boy from moving as he strained to push himself up with his arms.

'No Mitchell, the lady is right, lie down and we'll wait for the ambulance.'

'My leg! Dad!'

The father located Cam Robson and moved towards him; his fists tight balls by his side. Cam, pale and tight against the car, flinched with each verbal assault.

Mel heard Cam Robson's panicked voice alongside a softer one. She shook out her muscles, tingly and achy from being in the one position. Mitchell's cries upset the crowd and no one spoke.

Within minutes, the ascending and descending notes of the police vehicle rang out alongside the beat of the ambulance and the strobe of their lights added to the surreal evening. Mel stood and drifted back into the crowd.

The paramedics ran several checks over Mitchell before they placed him on a stretcher and attached a splint to one of his legs.

The father acknowledged Mel with a nod and jumped into the ambulance with his daughter.

A lady stepped forward and placed a hand on her shoulder. 'The father told me to thank you and asked for your name and number. Are you okay?' It was the same voice she'd heard comfort Cam Robson.

'I'm fine. Sure, I'm Mel Wilson.' She scribbled down her number but fought to control the pen. Her heart was still pounding with the adrenaline rush and the muscles across her shoulders were stretched tight.

The police collected information from her and others. 'I came after. I'm sorry, but I didn't see anything of the crash.'

'Tell us what you saw, what you did, your name and telephone number.' A young police officer formalised the interview and recorded their voices on her tablet.

The policewoman told her that no one had witnessed the exact moment of impact.

When the police left, Mel made her way to a bench. In the

cool wind and waning light she balled her body and bent her head into the crumple of clothes and flesh. She gave herself a few minutes before she pulled the phone from her back pocket.

'Do you want to watch a movie together, eat chocolate on the sofa and forget that you're fourteen and troubled and I'm forty-two and responsible? Oh Jack,' she sobbed to herself. There was no clawing back the days before puberty, but she longed for the time when it was just enough to hold onto her daughters. She pushed aside thoughts of her job, the toll of the accident, the unsteady beat of her heart, and pressed her eldest daughter's number.

'Jack, how are you?'

'Mum what's up? Are you drunk?'

'Why did you say that?'

'You get all gushy and weird when you're drunk, like at Christmas. You crush us till we can't breathe and your voice gets all thick.'

'No. I wanted to see how you are.' She coughed to disguise the thick voice and wiped away the tears that had appeared on hearing her daughter's voice. 'And because I'm your mother, that's why.'

'Right.'

'What did you do this afternoon?'

'I went to the beach with Danny and the others to hang out. I've only just got home,' and then she whispered, 'to mad Leah.'

Mel ignored that. She didn't need to hear how crazy her ex's partner was. 'Did you go surfing?'

'No there wasn't much of a swell. Dad and I are going to the football on Saturday, he scored box tickets.'

'Who's playing?'

'Cheswick and Rockforth Bay.' Mel's stomach gave a flutter. 'We're taking Danny, too and he's sleeping over. What have you been doing?'

'Nothing exciting. I wanted to hear about your day.'

'Dad's home and it's my turn to help with dinner. I have to go, bye Mum.'

'Bye Jack. I love you.'

'Me too.'

Mel hung up and swiped through the photo collection on her phone to the most recent one she had of Jack and Lil and bit at her lip. Jack had announced on her eleventh birthday that she would be known only as Jack and would no longer respond to Jacqui. She had inherited Tony's wiriness and height, and chose to wear her straight brown hair in the style of the male footballers she followed. She was the best goal scorer in her football team, and right now she preferred to stay closer to school and live with her dad from Monday to Friday. Jack had known Danny for years, and even though Jack was in denial about being female, Mel was pretty sure Danny had noticed. Should she worry about the sleepover? Lil on the other hand had thick wavy hair like hers, a smaller frame, olive skin and large brown eyes. She had always looked like more like Mel but right now she was all eleven-year-old bounce.

Her hands shook when she leaned over to untie the laces of her sneakers. Without the children, the house echoed, and she shivered in the cool air.

Standing under the warm stream she felt guilt rise because what plagued her wasn't the accident, it was losing her job, and like a compass her mind swung back to that point over and over. She knew what effect that would have on her relationship with the bank.

She trailed a fork around the plate then scraped most of it into the bin.

Unable to endure the ache of waiting until eight-thirty, she pulled on a jacket and grabbed her car keys. Only half an hour early, she consoled herself.

Chapter Two

Before Mel could knock, there was a snick and the door swung open. 'Hi Mum, we saw you on the security camera.'

'Hi Lil.' She leaned in and held her daughter close. 'Hi Eleanor and Sarah. Thanks for having Lil.'

'Anytime Mel.'

'Mum, you'll squash my project,' Lil said before pushing the poster away from her body. 'Are you okay? Is someone sick?'

What was it with her children? 'No. I'm just so happy to see you.'

'Well you can let go now, you're scaring Eleanor and Sarah.'

Eleanor came forward. 'Is everything okay, Mel?'

'Yes,' she cleared her throat, 'tough day at work.'

'Thanks for letting us have her.' Eleanor patted her arm and wandered back to the door.

Encumbered with poster board, they made their way to the car.

'Tell me about your project.'

'Eleanor had glossy card so we made grey buildings and building backgrounds. We used tiny bright-gold pieces of card for the windows, and more grey for the clouds.'

'What's it about?'

'Acid rain. When we get home I have to record the speech that you can hear on a QR code.' Lil yawned through the last few words.

'I can't wait to hear it.'

'You can't until the presentation evening in a couple of weeks. I love staying at Sarah's, her mum cooked the best cannelloni.'

'Better than mine?' Mel bumped her with her hips.

'You wish.' She bumped her back.

'Hey since it's late, do the recording tomorrow?'

'If you get me up in time.'

'Sure. What else happened today?'

Mel pulled into their driveway and they slipped out of the car.

'We start cross-country training,' Lil told her as they took brisk steps to the front porch. 'And I got chosen to sing in the choir.'

'Excellent news,' Mel said, unlocking the door. 'Does that mean I don't have to hear the audition song anymore?'

'Yes.' Lil dragged her bag and body towards her bedroom and Mel heard the mattress springs give.

'Shower,' she called from the kitchen.

'I'm so tired. Can't I skip it?'

'Nope.' There was a thump as school shoes were flung off. Books and other items clattered onto a desk and angry feet stomped into the bathroom.

Mel smiled. All of the evening routines with her child brought back a semblance of normality.

After reading one chapter of the latest must-read girl-with-powers book, Mel drifted off to sleep beside her. Lil didn't need to be read to, but she indulged her mother's desire to hang on to this ritual. The sudden and disturbing shrill of the phone forced her to sit up; blood drained from her head and she almost collapsed with giddiness. The headachy feeling was compounded by the pressing and urgent tone of the mobile phone and she made a note to ask Jack to change it for her.

She reached the lounge room too late. She stared at the number, but there was no name highlighted and it didn't look familiar. Before she headed into her bedroom, the phone trilled again. 'Hello?'

'Hi Mel?'

'Yes I'm Mel.'

'I'm calling to say thank you for...' the woman on the other end of the line began crying quietly. 'I'm sorry. I'm Mitchell's mother, the boy you helped today. My husband thought you should know about Mitchell. He had concussion, his femur has a fracture and he'll be in for observation. A few scans have been taken. We'll know more tomorrow. Thank you so much for what you did.' Her voice thickened and Mel could hear the tears starting up once more.

'It's okay,' Mel reassured, 'thank you for the call, and wish Mitchell the best from me.' The mother thanked her again and hung up.

Resting against the doorframe, Mel watched the gentle rise and fall of Lil's doona. She felt her heart squeeze.

Chapter Three

The next morning, Mel rested her head against her arms on the kitchen bench and kept an eye on the timer for the eggs. Lil leapt on to the stool and spread buttery honey to the furthest edges of her toast with her fingers. 'Why aren't you working?'

'I finished my old job yesterday and I'm looking for a new one.' Mel kept her tone even; it wasn't exactly a lie.

She ran the eggs under cold water and sat beside Lil. A quiet chinking of teaspoons, the crackle of shells, the aroma of a toast breakfast, and the backdrop of warbling magpies: it all smacked of her regular life. Still, the pit in her stomach and buzz in her mind remained.

She watched Lil's slight body bend over to tie frayed laces and tug at the zips on the gaping schoolbag. 'Here, have some money for lunch.'

'Thanks. Are you sure?'

Mel wilted under the gaze of her daughter's brown eyes. 'We're fine. Buy out the whole canteen.'

'With five dollars?'

She ruffled Lil's hair in response.

'Let's get you to school,' Mel headed to the front door.

It took Mel a few stunned seconds after she opened the door to realise the small group of photographers and reporters on the path in front of her house were there to speak to her. She gripped Lil's hand and covered her face with the other. She pushed through, kept her eyes down and fumbled to get to the remote unlocking button. A spasm in her stomach made the eggs want to launch right out of there as memories of Tony's scandal during his training for the Commonwealth Games flooded back. From the excitement of seeing herself in the picture alongside Tony when he was the darling of Western Australian swimming, to his demise under a cloud of suspicion, she'd come to loathe the presence of the media and it had nearly destroyed their relationship.

'Don't photograph my children or me, please. I have nothing to say.' She shepherded Lil and shoved her into the car.

A young reporter jumped in front of her. 'How are you feeling today, Ms Wilson, after yesterday's events? Can I interview you?'

'No, I have to go.' She slid into the driver's seat. 'They mean well,' she explained to Lil, whose face was a picture of confusion. 'They're only chasing a story.' *Breathe*, she told herself.

She heard shutters going off and blinked at the sudden glare from the flash. Someone shouted out to her as she put the key in the ignition and slotted into reverse. Television crews filmed.

'But why are they are here, Mum, at our house? Will we be on television or the internet?'

'God I hope not. It must be something to do with the accident.'

'What accident?'

Accidents made her feel ill, Lil had once told her. Mel hoped it wasn't because she had divorced parents. The endless puncturing guilt of that tore into her whenever she felt her children's pain, noticed their responses, tried to rationalise their behaviour.

She reversed out of the driveway and tried to focus on the drive to school. 'A boy about your age got hit by a car and I helped out.'

'That's awful. Why are they at our house though?'

'I resuscitated him.'

'You used your surf lifesaving skills?' Lil sounded impressed.

'Yes.'

'That's so great. What happened to him?'

Mel's knuckles were white with their too-firm grip on the steering wheel. She tried to relax, to inhale. 'He started to breathe and the paramedics took him to hospital. His mother rang last night to tell me he's okay, but he's still having tests. His leg has a fracture.'

'You didn't do surf lifesaving last year, did you?' She slid a glance at her daughter and she could see that Lil's eyes were wide with curiosity.

'No, it was a while back when I did it. Lil, it'll be okay. They're just interested in filling in a bit of news time.' She stopped the car when they reached the school. 'You have a wonderful day and good luck with the acid rain and singing.'

Mel helped her out of the passenger seat and they stood there for a moment, locked in a hug.

'Don't you worry either. Why don't you want to talk to them?' Lil asked.

Um, because your dad was involved in a doping scandal when he was nominated for the Commonwealth Games medley relay swim team, even though he ardently denied all knowledge of the coach's 'vitamin pack', and there was no real proof of complicity. We were hounded and photographed everywhere we went for a few awful months. After that, I had a mild to severe panic attack every time I thought I saw a reporter. 'I don't want to be in the news, you know I'm not like that.'

'I know. Aunty Georgie loves being in the news.'

'She sure does and it's important for her business.'

'Yeah. You can let go of me now, I don't want the poster to crumple.' Did Lil wish she *was* more like her events-manager sister?

'Mum!'

'Sorry.' Mel released her but held her hand on the walk to the school grounds.

'You don't need to walk me in, Mum, bye.' Her daughter looked up for a kiss, but Mel hugged her again.

'Bye.' Lil waved and disappeared, absorbed into the swarming mass of bobbing heads and high voices.

Her hands couldn't locate the car keys in the bag and she couldn't face going home.

Chapter Four

Mel sat in her car at the car park near the beach and waited to be put through to the right ward.

'Hi, my name is Mel Wilson. I'm calling about a young boy called Mitchell Drake. A car hit him yesterday evening and I was there. His mother said it was his leg mainly.'

'I have your name. He's scheduled to have several more scans this morning. He has to remain in hospital for a couple more days.'

'Please tell the parents that I'm thinking of them and Mitchell.' She hadn't meant to sound so plain and inconsequential when she knew they would be standing around the hospital feeling ripped apart, wondering whether their son could be put back together again.

Brisk walkers, joggers, breakfasting workers and boot campers had long since deserted the beachfront boardwalk. A few stragglers, retirees, pram pushers and dog walkers took their place along the beach path and struck up their own rhythm.

Perched on the bench with arms wrapped around her knees, Mel closed her eyes until a persistent faraway noise drove her to scrabble inside the voluminous sack of her bag. The screen revealed an unknown caller and she stared at it for a few seconds.

'Don't you hate that?' The timbre of a male voice echoed her own thoughts, but before she could respond her phone bleeped.

She popped her sunglasses back on her nose and squinted upwards.

'I'm not being personal, but do you come here often, to this particular area of the beach?'

He looked like he was dressed for office work, but the rude intrusion by the media earlier made her jumpy.

'Yes I do.' She pulled in the loose sweater around her.

'Only I'm interested in the story of an accident...'

She felt sick. A blast of trilling notes from her phone interrupted him.

'Excuse me while I get this. Hello? You're Daniel Arnott, I see. Yes it is Mel Wilson. No, I can't remember seeing much. Lunch? Today?' She pitched around for the right response. 'Not right now. This afternoon? Okay. Thanks. Bye.' She hung up and tapped the phone against her chin. The man was still there, waiting for her.

'You said you were here about an accident, which one?' she asked him.

He sat beside her on the bench, slid his glasses to the top of his head and looked at her with cool eyes. 'The one that happened here yesterday evening, when Cam Robson appeared to have run into an eleven-year-old boy?'

'I know about that accident.'

'I'm sorry, but I couldn't help overhearing some of your conversation.'

'Go on.'

'Someone else wanted to talk about it to you, too?'

'Yes.'

'Can I ask you how you're involved?'

'I've already had some reporters at my house. I don't have anything to say to anyone.'

'Here's my card. I'm Peter McIver, but I prefer Pete. I'm over here covering a range of issues in sport.'

She took his card—he was with a reputable paper. She was quite taken with his clean, smart look, but in her experience, men who looked like him were usually married, partnered or not into women. Why was she even entertaining those thoughts?

'I'm Mel Wilson. I happened to be near when the accident happened.' A faint nausea returned at the memory. 'I resuscitated the boy because I was the only one there who could.'

'I see.'

'He's in hospital with a fracture and they're running scans this morning.'

'That must have been pretty scary for you.'

'It was.'

'I've been investigating the football industry for a while.'

The sea sent up shards of reflected light, and despite the warmth of the morning sun, she shuddered.

'I didn't witness anything,' she told him.

'Do you want to go to that café and have a chat?'

'I don't think so.'

'Okay. Why don't you phone me if you want to talk? You have my card.' When he stood to leave she caught whiffs of his cologne.

'Sure. Thanks, Pete.'

He turned to walk away. 'Wait,' she called, 'just a chat?'

'Just a chat.'

'I don't want anything printed.' She wanted that clear from the outset.

'You're in charge.'

'No photos.'

'Can I record? Then you can listen to it and let me know what you want to do.'

'Maybe. I have some things to do. What about later, around eleven?'

She tried not to breathe in his masculine smell and reprimanded herself for allowing him to distract her thoughts.

'Eleven it is, I'll see you then,' he said, before giving her a farewell nod and walking away.

*

The street was quiet when Mel pulled into her driveway.

A message pinged on her phone; her doctor had a cancellation and could fit her in this morning. She abandoned the idea of a shower, changed her clothes, and figured she would make the doctor's appointment and arrive in time at the café.

'Do you think something's wrong?' she asked the doctor after confessing about her recent crying inclination. Frida Jacobsen had been her family doctor since Jack was born, and Mel felt safe to tell her most things.

'A few tears now and then is not a big issue,' Frida reassured her. 'You've lost your husband—unaccountable good luck, I'd say. I wish I could lose mine, he's such a worrywart.'

'I didn't lose him, we're divorced, and that was seven years ago.' Was she a worrywart?

'Same thing.'

'I'm not comfortable with publicity since Tony's episode,' Mel confessed.

'I remember that.'

'There were journalists at my house this morning and I felt bile. It was a horrible time back then when Tony was front and centre in the news. I hated it.'

'You're probably a little introverted.'

'Am I?'

'Only a little.' She busied herself with her notes and Mel knew it meant Frida thought she was a lot introverted but wasn't prepared to say. Years of visits had helped her read her doctor. She crossed her legs and tapped a foot. Introverted?

'Oh come on Mel, you're smart, healthy, and I've always envied your long wavy hair. Look at mine. You could have the world nibbling your toes.'

She smiled at Frida's Danish twist. 'Seems the world has other ideas.'

'A good man and lots of sex would help, but I can't write a script for that.'

She raised her eyebrows. 'My kids say the same thing, without the sex.'

'Smart kids. Accelerated heart rate, shortness of breath in a healthy body, a bit of emotional crying, these are some of the indicators of anxiety, and if you don't sort out a few things it will lead to more serious consequences. Many of my patients use yoga, meditation or tai chi. You like those doodling books?'

'I can't stay in the lines.'

'You non-conformist. Have you been having other symptoms? I don't think you're menopausal.'

'Me neither. Maybe it's the planets conspiring against me.'

'Even I feel like that some days, but let me know if it becomes every day. At least try yoga or meditation, or maybe a support group? You'd find many willing partners for horizontal gymnastics if you actually looked for them—think of all the health benefits it has! But come back soon if you're still having symptoms.' She reached over and clasped a warm hand over Mel's.

Chapter Five

Mel saw him as soon as she arrived at the café. He had his back to her and was speaking into his iPad. Before she reached him, he turned around and spotted her; warmth crept into her cheeks. 'This is simply an informal conversation,' she told herself, 'and we'll never see each other again.' She flushed all over when she recalled Frida's advice.

'Hi Pete.'

'Hi yourself.' He pulled out her chair and called over the waitress. 'What would you like Mel?'

'A flat white, thanks.'

'I'll have the same, please.' The waitress flicked him a smile and bounced away. 'Do you mind if I use this to record?'

'Go ahead. It must make life easier in your business. You won't print anything?'

'Not until you say so. I can't imagine life without these things and it stops me annoying people to crosscheck information.'

She couldn't imagine anyone being annoyed with him.

'Should I begin?'

'If you're comfortable.'

'I'd been running along the beachfront and was on my way back towards my car when I heard the sound of a collision. There was screaming so I stopped and headed over to the family to see what was going on. You think you go over to help and that you have good intentions, but all the while you hope someone else better qualified will be there. Turns out, there wasn't. I had no idea I'd end up resuscitating a child.'

Suddenly, an image of Cam Robson came to her, one she

hadn't previously recollected. In it, he was resting against the car door with a small item in his hands that he dropped and kicked under the car. Why hadn't she remembered this before? Any wonder the police had difficulty corroborating witness accounts.

'What's wrong Mel?' Pete asked, seeing her frown.

'Uh, I thought I remembered something,' she said, unsure whether to say it out loud.

'What was it?'

'Nothing important.'

She managed to relate the sequence of events in detail. 'After the ambulance left the police questioned me.'

They paused when their coffees arrived to take sips.

'Do you mind if I ask you a few questions about yourself?'

'If it's relevant. Can you turn that off?'

'Okay.' He flipped the cover and placed it into a case. 'Why were you at this beach?'

'I always come here.'

'But why were you here after work—I'm presuming you were at work?'

'I'd been at work. I wanted to go for a run and unwind.' *And release outrage at my inability to see that I would lose my job.* She had now joined the ranks of the unemployed, the not useful.

'I love running along the beach.' When Pete smiled at her, a little flutter ran inside her and made her smile bounce right back. 'What time was it when you first noticed the family?'

'After four.'

'What time was it when the accident occurred, do you think?'

'I'm pretty sure it was before five.'

'What do you think happened to the boy?'

'I didn't witness the accident, but I'm guessing the car came over the kerb and struck him. That's what the police said.'

'Your actions were heroic.'

'No they weren't.'

She turned away to look out to the horizon where she could see the familiar bright-white cone of the lighthouse on Rottnest Island. As awful as the event had been, it was not the only thing she'd had on her mind.

'Had you heard of Cam Robson before?'

'Very little. I've heard his name mentioned on the news.'

'He's quite talented and his skill set has whetted the appetite of the whole league. His team's public relations manager will probably contact you.'

'He's already contacted me.'

'That was Daniel Arnott you spoke to earlier?'

'Yes. Do you know him?'

'I know of him.'

'And?'

'I imagine he'll want to smooth things over and tell you some great things about the club and Cam.'

'I'll be honest with him.'

'When are you meeting him?'

'This afternoon.'

'I guess I'm lucky we had time now.'

Her phone rang. 'I'm sorry, Pete, but do you mind if I get this?'

'Go ahead.'

She walked behind the plastic café blinds, and stepped around the side of the building. 'Jack, shouldn't you be in class?'

'We have a break. Mum, you were so cool. Why didn't you tell me? I'm posting the link.'

'Tell you what?'

'What you did at the accident? Doing CPR?'

'How do you know?'

'I saw it on my phone. I'll send it to you.'

She felt woozy. 'Jack this isn't a cool thing. This is some child's life and he's in hospital with serious injuries. This isn't a playground spectacle.'

'I know that. I'm not dumb. I mean that it's great what you did. But the vomiting was a bit funny.'

'Not for Mitchell or his parents. Not great that someone filmed me.'

'That's why I thought I'd call and post it to you. It's only been on for a while, but it's gone crazy. I've gotta go.'

'Bye Jack and thanks, I'm sorry for jumping at you.'

'Bye Mum.'

She walked back to the table where Pete was waiting.

'Everything okay?' he asked.

'My daughter just told me about this clip and sent me the link. It's gone viral. Any wonder the cameras were at my house this morning.'

'What's on it?'

'Me. Some idiot filmed me performing CPR and posted it on Facebook and other places.' She went clammy at the thought of people watching the clip, watching her. After her experience with Tony, she would be happy to leave the world with no digital footprint.

'Mel, don't be concerned about this.'

'Of course I'm concerned. Why do people feel this is acceptable?' Her voice rose and she could feel the heat rising in her neck and face.

'Mel,' Pete said, 'it's not all bad. People are commenting, saying kind things about you. What *is* that?' He'd loaded the site and was reading the flood of comments.

'What do you mean?'

'It says the boy ate a whole bag of gummy chews and that's what stopped him breathing.'

'He wasn't choking before the car rammed him. A young boy has had a traumatic accident and that's what people focus on?' Her chest tightened; she took a few breaths. 'An idiot feels that he can film someone else's grief to satisfy some voyeuristic urge, but what about Mitchell and his family?' Several customers turned their heads and she wanted to duck in embarrassment.

'Let's go for a walk.' He paid the bill and stood up.

'I can't walk in these shoes.' Mel also stood, and they made their way to the exit.

'Maybe you should go home,' Pete suggested.

'How can I remove this?' There had to be a way to delete it.

'Not sure about that. I'll walk you to your car. Are you sure you're okay to drive home?'

'I'll be fine.'

'You have my card. Phone if you want, and off the record, please feel you can ask me anything.'

She wanted to split her life in two and stay with him, flirt, be a woman with a man, and he did seem very sincere. 'Okay, thanks.'

There was no one around when she stole into the driveway and raced to the front door. She examined the minutes of film. It showed her face, creased and pale, as she worked through several rounds of thirty compressions and two breaths.

The clip wasn't steady, showing that it was taken a little distance away and on a phone. However, it was distinct enough for everyone she knew to be able to recognise her.

Both her mobile and the home phone rang and she vacillated between them. She picked up her mobile phone and examined the long list of callers, most of whom she recognised. Explaining what had happened was the least she could do for her immediate family. Her mother offered to come over, but at eighty, and with her dubious driving skills, she thanked her and promised to talk to her later.

She had to see Daniel Arnott in the afternoon and was consoled by the thought that he would have professional advice. She turned off the phones and lay down for an hour.

Chapter Six

Mel drove down the highway towards the back end of a residential area, where market gardeners sold their wares. It was the route to Daniel Arnott's office.

Her car lurched, skipped a beat and shuddered. The engine vibrated and sent tremors throughout the whole chassis. 'Damn!' she exploded. She could feel the clamminess and nausea return. She brought it to rest on the white track reserved for emergencies. She plucked out her mobile phone and rummaged for her roadside-assistance card; after what seemed like an eternity, a reasonable human voice spoke.

'Where are you?' the operator asked.

She gave the location.

'Membership number please?'

When she rattled off the number, the smooth efficiency of the saviour-like being at the other end of the line calmed her.

'Pardon me, but could you repeat that please?'

She repeated the number.

'Your membership has lapsed.'

'Can you renew it for me?'

'Sure. Please give me your credit card details.'

There was about ten per cent of phone battery charge left when she shot out the numbers. They told her it would take about forty minutes for help to arrive. She phoned Daniel Arnott.

'No worries Mel. After you're sorted, let me know. I'll send a taxi and you can get the tow truck to take your car.'

'Thanks so much.'

A mother from Lil's school replied to her text and said she'd collect Lil and keep her until she could make it home.

She sat back for a few minutes, trying not to get caught up in the new problem. She couldn't afford a new car, let alone expensive repairs to the existing one, or to be without one.

She reached for the car radio and switched to a station with a soothing resonant voice and allowed the music wash over her. Drowsy from the radiated heat through the glass windows, and unable to use her phone in case she wasted the remaining charge, she closed her eyes.

A sharp rap on the window jolted her awake. The lurid colours of the road-assistance company made her almost yelp in delight.

'Hi, what seems to be the problem?'

'I have no idea. It just lurched a lot and hopped along on the road, so I pulled over. It didn't look like it would take me any further.'

'I'll have a look. Lift the bonnet please. Now start it up.'

The same jolted rhythm beat out from the sick engine.

'Okay, so it's one of several things, none of which I can fix here. You'll need a tow. I'll write a report and you phone,' he flicked open his file and scribbled down some information, 'and quote this number.'

'Okay, but...'

'He should be here in half an hour to an hour.'

'So I get it towed?'

'To your regular garage, if it's open now.'

'Yes it is.'

That was it. She had waited nearly an hour for that and faced another interminably long wait. She phoned her garage and a young mechanic told her that she could leave her car there until they could see to it and he also informed her that the courtesy car was booked out.

The sun baked the already worn plastic of the dashboard, sending up, she presumed, countless whirls of toxic dust no longer bound into the structure. She could feel the crumbling disintegration of matter throughout the car and wrestled open the door to escape the atrophying atmosphere.

She climbed the embankment and trod over layers of pine-bark mulch; her legs brushed past weathered plants clogged with road dust. A ring-lock fence separated the highway and suburbia where flattened acres of land lay divided by rivers of tarmac, and low-roofed brick houses on raised blocks of soil squatted, as if they had been dropped from the sky. She clambered back down.

No one in her family had a spare car and the school distances weren't close enough for her to either ride or walk. A hire car was inconceivable on the already overworked mortgage extension.

As though conjured by that very thought, the bank rang. 'Ms Mel Wilson?'

'Speaking.'

'Ms Wilson, you will need to come into the bank as soon as possible. Two of your credit cards have reached their limit and we noticed you are using the other one to pay them off. I think we may need to restructure your loan and see where you are. Can you come in tomorrow?'

'Yes,' she said, trying very hard not to sigh or kick something.

'Good. How does about ten tomorrow morning sound?'

'Okay. Sorry I have to rush, my phone is nearly out of charge.'

'No problem Ms Wilson, we'll see you then.'

She leaned her head on the dashboard. That wasn't all that was happening with her finances. They didn't know about the other mortgage against her property, the one she'd organised with the serpent-like Justin Gainsborough, the first and last fling she'd had straight after Tony's exit. Justin was a financier who worked in a firm that had business dealings with her ex-husband. He had a great strategy, he'd said, for dramatically improving her situation. It turned out that the shares were as flaky as Justin; something she discovered when she suggested a real relationship instead of bedroom calisthenics. He was a moral vacuum, she heard from another woman much too late, but she had other words for him. It was such a profound humiliation she lacked the courage to tell anyone.

The taxi and tow truck arrived at about the same time. She wiped away the smudged mascara and plastered on a polite smile.

Chapter Seven

Mel wasn't surprised to discover that Daniel Arnott's office was housed in a new complex close to the hallowed football grounds. Escorted by an officious male administrator, she was led into an office the size of her lounge room.

Daniel engaged her in a bit of banter.

'Mel, I can imagine how traumatic it's been for you. Young Cam has accidentally jeopardised the life of a boy. A young boy steps onto the road and into the path of a car. The driver doesn't take the corner well. A single moment of poor judgement can cause so many outcomes.'

'Mitchell faces the worst outcome,' she reminded him.

'Of course. It was lucky you were there to deliver the life-saving breaths. That was very brave and humane. We want to talk to you about what you saw and reassure you about legal representation, both yours and ours.'

That took her by surprise. 'I wasn't aware that I would need any.'

'You may not, but we can offer help if the court case proceeds and you need representing.'

'That's very kind of you.' She wouldn't be able to afford it anyway.

'We'll just go through what you saw if that's okay, because we need clarification and we'd like to have a chance to hear your version of events before the media gets a hold of you.'

She recounted the same information she had told the police, without the addition of what she thought she saw. It wouldn't be helpful to anyone if she couldn't be sure of her accuracy. She wondered if she should mention Peter McIver.

'So you didn't actually witness the accident?'

'No. As I said, I only saw what went on after because I heard some noises and saw people running towards the family, towards Mitchell.'

He looked relieved.

'You know we have to ensure everything is fair and look after our players. We would appreciate it if you could let us manage the media and suggest that you refuse to comment at this stage. They're fishing for a story that doesn't exist and will try to get as much mileage as they can, at least until something else catches their attention. But unfortunately, as Mitchell is a child, we're in for a lot of heat from them. Can we do that for you?'

She better contact Pete and tell him to definitely shelve their conversation. 'Yes. I don't want to talk to the media anyway. They were at my house this morning. You would have seen the clip doing the rounds on Facebook?'

'Yes. We'll try to get them to stop hounding you. We have some contacts, but we can't guarantee anything. I'm sure you'll be glad to get back to work.'

'I would but they haven't got a position for me.' At his look of inquiry, she added, 'Numbers were dwindling in my course and they're restructuring.'

'What do you do?'

'I'm an accountant by trade, but I was delivering some basic maths and accounting units at a college.'

'Let me think about this.' He walked over to the window where he pulled out his phone and tapped in a few messages. Texts sprang back and forth. More than five minutes passed, which she filled by reading the scant selection of magazines. He walked back over to a guest chair and sat on the one opposite her.

'Would you consider working here?' he said, to her astonishment. 'It would only be for a while until something came up. This last third of the season gets hectic. If I could release one more of the office team for media, and get you to attend to daily administration, that would solve our problem. What do you think?'

She couldn't believe it, but she wasn't exactly jumping up and down about this offer. Were conditions attached? She waited for him to elaborate but he only continued to look at her expectantly, awaiting her response. 'It would be great,' she told him. 'Are you sure about this?'

'I don't see why not.'

'Thank you. I need to work until something else comes up.'

'You're doing us a favour, too.'

He arranged for a driver to take her home. She wasn't sure what she'd just bought into, but she needed an income.

Chapter Eight

Mel groaned when she remembered where her car was. Lil had slept at Tony's for a dinner with his parents, relieving her of the school run. She phoned her garage and they told her that a courtesy car had become available and it would be delivered straight to her house.

She peered through a slit in the curtains but couldn't spot any reporters.

Daniel had told her yesterday that she should go to the bank at ten as planned and not change the meeting to lunchtime. The job, he said, was hers.

She made it to the bank on time, thanks to the courtesy car.

'I've seen you. That was an awesome thing you did.' The young bank clerk moved in front of the counter to stand beside her.

'Thank you.'

'You were great. Everyone is talking about you.' He led her down the corridor.

'Anyone would do the same.' She smiled and followed his youthful stride.

He opened the door to a spare, uninspiring office, where Wendy Bruker, the manager, stood as Mel entered.

'Mel. How are you?' Wendy extended her hand and Mel shook it. 'Please take a chair. You'd be aware that your finance needs restructuring.'

'I know.' Such a harmless word: restructuring. It was the same euphemism for utter destruction that the college had used in their letter. She'd like to do a bit of restructuring of her own, but she reined in her thoughts and rounded her eyes.

'We can't extend your loan or wave away the credit card debts,' Wendy said, her tone grave.

'I understand.' Her hands were sweaty and she knew she looked pale.

'What you need to know is that we also have the information about the other loan in shares, which is presently racking up interest. We've had queries about your credit rating.'

Mel's chest tightened. The two banks had merged a few months ago and she had hoped it would take a while for them to play catch-up before they discovered her embarrassingly large debt. Wrong again.

'How bad is this?' she croaked.

'Your current repayments will need to be increased to this figure.' She pointed to the large fortnightly repayment, which would have been a challenge on her previous wage. One glimmer of hope was that Daniel hadn't talked about money. How much would basic administration pay? She had to stop relying on hope.

'I was taken in by a great deal.' *And good looks and unbelievable sex*. 'I'm not all that savvy with shares.'

Wendy gave her a thin smile. 'You're not the only one.'

'I've started a new job and I can meet those repayments.' For a while she could manage, as long as she didn't do anything or eat much.

'Are you sure?'

'I think I can.'

'Because you do know that we will have to take action otherwise?'

'The action being that you'll have to force me to sell my home?'

'Precisely.'

'I realise.' She signed the documents and itched to be out of there.

She would die before she asked Georgie to bale her out. Grey clouds and a cool wind matched her mental fug. Concrete pavers pressed hard into her feet and made her wince as she wobbled forward in her uncomfortable but impression-making shoes. She wrapped her arms around herself and looked skyward to see if there were any silver linings.

When she made it into her new workplace, Daniel ushered her into his office.

'Mel, I'd like you to meet the lawyer who'll be advising you in the event of a court case, and a few members of the team.'

Did he have had them on standby? They appeared a couple of minutes later to shake her hand. Subtle waiters arrived with trays sporting a range of delicate food and champagne.

'Sorry to surprise you like this, but we always do this to welcome new staff.' His smile included the others. The men, and they were all men, were of a mixed age, but they shared a similar cut of suit and style of shoe. Their wrists flashed an assembly of watches and Mel guessed that they were the kind of watches she could pay off her loans with. Daniel introduced them as either members of the board or part of the administration team. A man of average height with greying wavy hair and a slightly rotund physique headed towards her with Daniel.

'Mel, this is Michael Widdicombe. He'll be representing you in any court dealings that arise as a consequence of the accident. It's not likely that you'll need representation at this stage.'

'Pleased to meet you.'

She felt his small but firm and warm hand in hers. He pushed his glasses further up the bridge of his nose and then clasped his other hand on top of hers.

'You have nothing to worry about. We'll work towards the best outcome for you and your family.'

She knew Pete's investigations were confidential and she didn't want to know about them. It was an accident and she'd heard others say the same. Everything hung on what approach Mitchell's lawyers took, and whether any proof of misdemeanour was discovered.

Football talk drifted about the room and with these particular men the conversation had currency. She could hear the buzz heighten as the empty champagne glasses cluttered the trays.

Daniel caught her by the arm before she left to begin work.

'Take a lunch break.'

'I've just been to the bank.' She tried not to sound as shocked as she felt.

'It's okay.'

'And I feel like I've had lunch,' she just wanted to work to fill her mind with something other than her predicament.

'Excellent catering company. We're one of its biggest clients. Up to you of course, but you don't have to rush back to your desk.'

'Thanks Daniel,' she forced herself to say because she still worried about the generosity.

She tried not to breathe in the headiness of expensive colognes, testosterone, and the smell of power and money, but she found all of it overwhelming.

Chapter Nine

With Tony away at a conference in Sydney it meant she could collect both girls from school, and she was excited to have them with her during the week. The smile fled her lips when she turned into her street and saw the house surrounded by cameramen and journalists.

'Quick, drive on Mum!' Jack slid under her schoolbag and collapsed deep into the seat.

'Get down Lil!' Jack yanked at Lil's arm and pulled her down. 'Cover your face!'

'You didn't have to hurt me.' Lil stayed low with her bag over her face and rubbed one arm.

'She didn't mean to Lil,' Mel soothed, 'but our privacy is extremely important. How about we head to a café on the river and call Grandma to see how she feels about some visitors?'

'I need my stuff. I haven't brought clothes with me from Dad's,' Jack complained.

'So do I. I've got sport tomorrow.' She could hear the irritation in their voices, saw the after-school tiredness in their limbs; belligerence was one stray comment away. She hoped food and some idea of a plan would restore them. She would feel a lot better, too, if she could actually think of a plan.

'We'll go back home tonight. They'll only hang around for a while.' She had no idea what their strategy was.

The children leaned back on the café sofas and completed homework on their computers and she tried not to panic. Jack was almost asleep with her headphones in.

'Jack, turn it down.' Jack looked up at her and swiped at the volume.

Mel called her mother.

'Mum, hi,' she said when her mother answered. 'The television crews and newspaper journalists are hanging around our house, and I was wondering if we could drop in soon and stay to have dinner with you? Would you like me to pick something up?'

She felt guilty. She'd been so caught up in her own trials that she hadn't made it over to see her mother recently.

'Of course,' her mother said. 'Come over as soon as you can. I'd love to see all of you and don't pick anything up. See you soon.'

*

'Remember, keep the towels Grandma gave you over your head. We'll walk straight inside. When you're inside, stay in the hallway till I close all of the blinds and curtains. There seems to be one vehicle parked on the roadside. I guess somebody is still hanging around waiting for their Pulitzer moment.'

'Their what?' Lil gave her a frown.

'Nothing. I'll tell you later, Lil. Keep calm, walk straight, and I'll hold your hand. Jack, follow behind.'

'Okay. This is so dumb.'

'Better than uncool photo shots, though, right?'

'Mel Wilson.' A figure appeared out of the shadows and she could see the sliver of red light on his camera. 'Can I have a few words with you please? Many people would love to hear from you and everyone thinks you were exceptional in saving that young boy.' He followed her along the steps to the porch. 'You should give an interview, you know. This is a big case.'

'Please respect the privacy of my family. I have nothing to say at this moment. I'll speak to someone later on. Thank you.' She shoved the children forward into the house and pushed the door shut. Her heart rattled. She bolted from room to room, pulled down blinds and secured curtains.

'Okay, done. Showers and bed I think for both of you.' She smiled at them, but couldn't mask her concern. Their faces looked pinched.

As the girls shuffled towards their rooms, she called the local police station to make a complaint about the media.

'I'm sorry, but they aren't trespassing,' the officer on the other end of the line told her, 'and they're not doing anything illegal. There's nothing we can really do, ma'am, unless they try to enter your property, of course.'

No, they weren't on her property, just surrounding it. She breathed out a sigh and called Daniel.

'Mel, hi,' he greeted.

'I presume you haven't been successful in getting the press off my back?' She couldn't hide the exasperation in her voice.

'They've been around again?'

'It feels like I'm being stalked. I think they're setting up camp around my house. I know they only want to talk to me and it's the hot topic of the day, but I don't want to be in the paper. Is there anything else you can do or suggest?' She hoped he didn't hear the anxious thud of her heart through the phone.

'There is something you can do.'

'What?'

'Have you got somewhere you could escape to for a week? A week usually kills off the initial blood lust and it'll give you some time.'

'I can't afford a holiday.'

'You'll still get paid. Call it stress leave.'

Mel opened her mouth to question him, only to stop herself. Really, she didn't have time to worry about what it might all mean.

She had one place she could go and Jill had offered it to her several times after Tony had left. 'I have somewhere and it's far enough away.'

'You should organise to leave tomorrow. Take the kids and have a break. You said your eldest was in Year Nine and your youngest daughter still at primary school?'

'That's right.'

'In that case they'd love a week off.'

It was mid-term, and she was pretty sure her children could catch up on anything that was covered in school in a week. 'It's a great idea,' she admitted.

'One tip though, leave really early. Whoever you tell, explain to them that they can't tell anyone else. That gives you complete privacy for a week.'

'Thanks, Daniel, I appreciate this help.'

'No problem Mel.'

Chapter Ten

Once she hit the main highway north, Mel's mood lifted. There were few cars on the road. Dawn broke with a dazzling pinkish blush over the Darling Scarp to the right, and on the left, the last stars winked.

'Mum, where are we going again? A whole week off school, I can't wait to tell Emma about it when I get back.' Lil reached forward and touched her shoulder.

Mel had asked her mother to phone the girls' principals to explain that the children would be away for a week. She backed this up with an email to each school and to Tony. He would be angry with her for taking the children out of school, but she didn't want to go away without them.

'All Jill said was that it was a shack.'

'Yes, but where?' Lil bounced on the seat while Jack looked down at her phone, quietly listening to her music. She hoped it was music.

'Uh-uh, I promised to keep that part a secret.'

'Can I guess?'

'Yes, but I'm not going to tell you if you guess.'

'Can we fish there?'

'Yes.'

'Swim?'

'Yes.'

'Watch TV?'

'Not sure.'

'Surf?'

'I didn't bring any boards, but possibly.'

'So, is it on the sea?'

'Information download complete! Let's play I-spy,' Mel suggested.

Jack groaned.

'Come on Jack, it's I-spy,' Mel said.

'She can't play, she's so mean to me,' Lil said.

'You're just dumb.'

'Jack!' Mel rounded on her. 'Can you give it a break and try a little normal conversation?'

'Okay. But I won't play I-spy.'

'I'd beat you anyway,' Lil said.

'As if.'

Before Jack could add anything else, she glanced up to see Mel's eyebrows raised and the tirade concluded. Jack plugged back into her music.

'I spy with my little eye something beginning with G?' Lil had an unquenchable thirst for games and conversation. It was fun, but for a long trip it could get tiring.

'Gravel?'

'Your turn.'

'I spy with my little eye something beginning with B.'

Mel caught sight of Pete McIver's business card in the console where she had deliberately placed it. She didn't use it in the game.

It was five hours later when she finally arrived at Jill's, exhausted, stiff-legged, and wearing the spillage from an iced coffee. Her body had assumed the shape of the car seat and she struggled to straighten it out on her walk over to give Jill a kiss on her cheek, before she fled to the bathroom.

'Hi Jill.' She said after she came back out with a fresh tee-shirt on.

'How are you? It's such a long trip,' Jill said.

'I wish I could have stayed the night,' Mel said, giving her friend a hug, 'but because of the clip, it's better if I make myself inaccessible. We'll have a few hours together before I drive back.'

'No problem, you know that. When you get there, use these

keys, but if the latch is a little rusty, jiggle it around or get some degreaser on the lock, okay?'

'Sure.'

'I've written down the instructions for the kerosene fridge. You might not need it if you've got a good icebox. See how you feel.'

'Thanks. Do I have to start the generator?'

'No. Kevin and John will take care of that. They're all still fishing.'

'Great, I hate starting it. The smell of petrol in that enclosed space makes me feel like it's going to explode.'

'I forgot you'd been across once before. Anyway, relax and make sure you keep your shoes on, the reef is full of blue-ringed octopus and cone shells.' Jill continued with the list of instructions about the shack. Lil and Jack had found Jill's boys in the games room and were glad of the company of other kids, even if they were ten-year-old twin boys.

Jill had prepared a lunch that really qualified as a gourmet sit-down meal. Months could go by without contact with Jill, but when they did see each other they lapsed into the thread of their friendship.

'How's your love-life?' Jill asked.

'Non-existent.'

Jill's warm and engaging presence had won her a devoted husband, Mike. The only disadvantage had been that his finance work had taken him away a lot. Jill had told her a while back that he'd quit that position in order to manage the properties and fishing vessels left by his father. His brothers, Kevin and John, ran the two fishing boats and worked at the Banderley Islands.

'I know you don't want to talk about it, but how are you going?' Jill lowered her voice.

'Okay. I think this time away will help me focus. Maybe make a few decisions.'

'Good.'

'I did meet one guy.'

Jill moved closer. 'And?'

'He wanted to talk to me about the incident and do an interview later. He's probably married or partnered.'

'You liked him though?'

'Yes, but I don't know anything about him.'

'Is he gorgeous?'

Mel smiled at that. 'He's got a nice face. He's fit, tall, can hold a conversation, polite...'

'Married or gay!' Jill dismissed.

'I was thinking the same.'

'Find out.'

'I thought I'd leave my thoughts on that matter for later. How have you been, how's country life?'

'This is outer suburbia.'

'You're five hundred kilometres away from the city!' Mel reminded her.

'True. There's been a new development at the islands. They're working on farming several species of fish, and two have been successful. Fishermen, government and local business are all involved. It could really go off and put us on the map.' She paused and put her arm around Mel's shoulders. 'Hey, we all saw the clip, you were so courageous.'

'Thank you. Even though I have a new job, things are a little tight for me.' She'd had to explain a few things when she asked Jill if they could use the shack.

'You mean money-wise?'

'Yes. Do you remember when Tony left and I went out with Justin Gainsborough?' Mel tried not to wince at saying his name.

'I remember one specific phone call. I thought it was what you needed at the time, wasn't it?'

'On a number of levels it was. He was very attractive but slippery.'

'And?'

'I trusted him on a financial decision.'

'I'm guessing it didn't do too well?' Jill frowned.

'Catastrophic. I don't know what I was thinking. I've never been into shares. I ignored all of the advice I would have given to someone else. I let him help me choose the shares and almost signed on my back, in his office. It's entirely my fault. You mustn't tell a soul. Tony would use it as grounds to have me committed and gain custody of the children.'

'He wouldn't and he can't do that. Don't be too hard on yourself.'

'Jill, it's so bad. I can hang on to the house for a while if this work continues, but I'll need a better paying job, and there isn't a lot out there at the moment. I feel so stupid.' She explained to Jill about the job she'd taken at the football club. 'I know the club is just shoring up its position by having me onside, and even though I didn't have any choice, I feel like I've been unethical in accepting the offer. Have you heard anything?'

'There's always speculation about corruption, the news is full of it. Mike talks about it with Kev. It's been rumoured that one or two clubs may have some of their finances underwritten by undesirable elements. That's all I know and it has nothing to do with you, how can it?'

'I'll try not to think about that when I get back to work. I don't think any of the clubs would want to risk being involved in anything underhand. That guy I mentioned earlier, he hinted at the same sort of thing.' She grew a little pink.

'The one you're not sure about?'

'The same. He's called Pete. He didn't tell me anything specific and I don't want to know. I've got enough to deal with.'

'They're rumours, and as if anyone would want those connections. You have to make your own decisions and you have to survive.'

'I know. The fish farming sounds great, I should have invested in that.'

Jill bumped her shoulder against Mel's. 'You look trashed. We'd better get all of you on the plane and then you can rest over there.'

'Sounds perfect.'

She dragged her body out of the chair, rallied the children and drove them to the floatplane at the marina. Jill offered to look after the car until they returned. Jill and Mike were entitled to several free return flights to the islands because of their business and Jill had insisted that Mel use one of them instead of risking seasickness on the carrier boat. She would think of a way to repay her later.

Chapter Eleven

'I know where we're going, to the Banderley Islands.' Lil hopped with excitement. Although the children had never been there, Mel had related her one and only experience of the islands to them a while ago.

'Cool plane.' Jack's first positive statement since they'd left home.

Mel became aware that the pilot had said something, but her headphones had slipped off and the roar and whine of the small plane made conversation impossible. 'What did you say?' She adjusted the headphones and spoke through the mouthpiece to him.

'Whales,' he answered, 'look over there, three or four of them. Do you want to get closer?'

He was young, it was his first season of flying to the islands, and she was not a fan of small planes. 'Um...' She turned to see the bright-eyed thrill on the faces of her children. 'Sure, why not.' Even though the pilot appeared confident, Mel's grip on the uninflated life jacket he'd attached to her waist tightened.

The plane banked and lowered into a sweep over the whales, near and long enough to see the massive bulk of the oceanic leviathans as they caroused around each other. She'd never flown this low over the ocean without land in sight. She glanced at the young pilot's face again and hoped her trust in him was not misplaced.

'Brilliant.' She heard Jack's quiet voice.

'Okay,' shouted the pilot, 'hang on, just bearing right again.'

Mel's gut wasn't cut out for that kind of three-dimensional

activity. She increased her grip on the safety belt. The engines whined with effort and she thought she could hear a tiny skip in the beat of the motor, similar to when her car had stopped on the highway. Was that just the way it was meant to sound? She studied the controls and the pilot in equal measure, with equal ignorance. Images from bad flight movies flashed through her overworked imagination.

Mel closed her eyes during the descent. As far as she was concerned, the speed at which the water was rising up to greet them was way too fast. She swallowed several times, felt herself grow pale and recognised the heady feel of a lunch about to evacuate through her mouth.

'We're here.' The pilot grinned at her. It was a very different kind of landing and it hadn't been that bad. The plane bobbed around. They stepped off onto a low-lying jetty and lifted out their bags.

'I'll see you in five days. I'll be here about lunchtime, say twelve o clock.'

After the bustle of a vibrant seaport, the coral island wilderness seemed heavenly in its cloak of muted sounds. Water swished and lapped against the island's edge, a low thrum of boat motors grumbled in the distance, and lines and chains chinked in rhythm with the tide. Fish bait mixed with diesel fumes and seaweed, spicing the air with pungent notes. There was something familiar about it all. Mel closed her eyes and sought the distant rumble of gargantuan waves far off at Long Island, at the south-west end of the island group, beyond which lay the truly big sea.

Mel and her daughters watched the spectacle of the floatplane take off before launching into action. Instructions in one hand and light luggage in the other, Mel called to Jack and Lil and the three walked past deckhands absorbed in fixing lobster pots, refuelling boats, hosing down winches and rinsing out their gloves and gear. They nodded as the trio passed.

Jill had organised stores and Mel knew the carrier boat that serviced the whole island group would have already labelled, stacked and delivered the food to their shack, called 'Squid'.

She remembered being delivered, along with the supplies, as she journeyed on a similar boat many years before she'd had children. She had spent most of her time heaving up over the edge of the railings in order to spend time with Tony, and she shuddered at the memory of one of the outings he'd taken her on. It had left her with the deepest respect for all those brave enough to venture off the edge, as they called it, where the distant rumbles became a crashing chorus in your head.

Once Lil and Jack had dumped their bags, they took off to investigate the island. Mel looked around at the shack. Timber bunk beds stood in two small rooms and a double bed was housed in a room directly off from the kitchen.

The view framed by each of the aluminium windows was of the Indian Ocean, tamed by fanning islands and flecked by reefs. The islands close by were flat, brown and crumbly, like biscuits; their size diminished by the expansive sea and a sky that loomed large.

She closed her eyes and a focused on the oceanic sounds till her body calmed.

Chapter Twelve

Mel abandoned regular underwear and slipped into comfortable bathers whenever she was on holiday. She had packed the ideal bikini with its elastic sufficiently stretched to hold on for one more summer; its stranglehold on her stomach and legs tempered by the fuzz of frayed edges. When she pulled the tee-shirt over her head, an earring flew underneath the bed. She crawled under the frame and hit her head on the unfinished timber edge. Her earring had settled amongst a few dry crab shells. She scooped them up in her hands, along with some of the bigger dust balls, and retreated, her legs and bottom wriggling out first. She heard a barely audible male voice.

'Hang on,' she called out. Sand and dust stuck to her skin in patches. As she stood, she noticed that not only had her tee-shirt rucked upwards, but also that the ties of her bikini top had loosened. Dumping the debris on the table, she yanked the tee-shirt down and turned, red-faced, towards her visitor.

'I brought the supplies over for you,' the man told her. 'You don't want the birds to get at them.'

'Thanks...?' He stood in rough dark cotton pants and shirt. They would have to be washed in brackish water because not much rain fell at the islands, and they matched his stubble and sleep-crumpled face.

'I'm Mark. I work for Kev.' His thick-set shape took up most of the doorframe and his hands and face wore the tan of constant exposure. His sunnies were on his head and his eyes were fixed on hers, a piercing blue. Did the ocean render them like that? She found them mesmerising and his sheer presence magnetic, animal-like. He was not city pretty, but she was drawn to him.

'I'm Mel.'

'I know. Keep the door closed when you're out and cover all the food because of the birds and crabs,' he instructed.

'Okay, will do.' She tried to prevent herself from colouring again.

'I'll be off. See you.'

'Thanks Mark.'

'No problem.'

Embarrassment had severed the connection between her tongue and brain.

The children were out and she knew she should use the time to think of a plan. She drummed a pencil on the shiny cover of a notepad.

She jotted down: job—tick, repayments—wobbly tick, and other opportunities—question mark. It was pathetic. She didn't have any other opportunities to explore or talents to mine. She was going to have to ask Tony to cover all of the school fees until she found the capital to restore herself to financial blackness. She wondered how that would go. It was why there was a brick lodged inside her gut. She considered whether her mother could cover the fees and help her out, but in her heart she knew she couldn't ask that of her. At least she now had employment and who knew where that would lead.

She was supposed to find positives to build on. She wrote down several points.

Number one: *I have a full employment.*

Number two: *I have a variety of administrative abilities and a degree. I will find a better paying position eventually.*

Number three: *I have beautiful children and look forward to them maturing and blossoming.*

Number four: *Mum probably can help out and we will organise a deal by reducing my share in the future inheritance.* She scratched out number four.

Number five: *I am healthy and the mirror doesn't crack when I look into it. I will find a loving partner, at some point.* Maybe.

Number six: *No problem is insurmountable and I can keep my home for the time being.*

Number seven: *I am at these stunning islands and have great friends who care for me.* She signed off and reclined in the chair.

A cool breeze washed over the island. She shrugged on a sweater and heard the generator start; it signalled the transition into evening rituals. She looked out through the salt-sprayed spider-webbed window to see her children pick their way over the coral near the edge. A slant of rays framed the profile of their bodies as the sun warbled blancmange-like, spreading a blast of orange into the sky.

'What's for dinner?' It was Jack's favourite meal of the day.

'Steak with salad and bread, but I've just got to turn the gas on first.'

'Do you know how?'

'Of course.'

'But we never have to, so...'

'Jill told me how.'

'Do you want me to help?'

'Sure.' Prising any conversation out of Jack was difficult. Maybe this holiday would give her more opportunities to figure some things out for herself. 'What do you think I have to do here?'

'Release this valve and turn this lever?'

She prayed that this was correct and that Jack could have her moment of triumph. A soft hiss indicated that all was well. It was a good sign. It was even better when after striking a match, the gas ring lit up. Daughter and mother stood in silent communion.

Lil bashed the TV a couple of times, but it refused to cough into life. They sat on the musty lounge chairs for a few minutes idly regarding the books that lay waiting to be read on the low packing-crate table. She'd banned the use of devices for a few days.

Jack grabbed her towel. 'I'm going to get ready for bed. How do we shower?'

'We have to boil the kettle for the bucket shower.'

The girls eventually went to bed, and Mel got ready to do the same. When she charged her phone, it kept beeping. She'd expected those but had decided not to deal with any of them, specifically those from the media. She pulled the phone from the charger and went to sleep.

At about three in the morning she stumbled out along the coral, sharp and rough on her unprotected feet, to the composting toilet. Startled by her presence, terns squawked and flew up against her legs and arms and jolted her into wakefulness. From then on she couldn't return to a proper sleep. A couple of hours later, she found the three hundred and sixty degree daylight overwhelming. Her hair sat stiff with salt, and, as she peered critically at herself in the triangular shard of mirror balanced on an exposed wall frame, felt she looked battered and worn by the elements already. She fell back against the bed.

A male voice called her name. She dragged herself out of bed, patted down her tufty mop of hair and ran her tongue around her dry and stale early-morning mouth. She threw on her shorts and top. 'Be there in a moment.'

'Thought you might like these.' In front of her were two fresh snapper.

'Thanks so much.' She looked up at Mark and met his eyes.

'I have to go. Your door was open again.' And then he was gone and she was left with a plate of fish. Even with early-morning woolly-headedness, she was confused about his manner, but she liked that he kept dropping by. She placed the fish in the fridge and stared into a mosaic mirror on the fridge door where she noticed her shorts were on back to front.

With a cup of tea, she stole down to the small jetty near the hut and basked in the spokes of light from the autumnal sun. Alongside the jetty sat an old aluminium dinghy. She'd been on many boats before and could figure out how to use the motor of this one, if she could lift it out of the shed where Jill had said it would be. She glanced down and saw the birds peck around in the sand amongst the mangroves; quiet and speckled like quail, they ran in and out of the protective branches. She found it absorbing and wondered if she could secure a job as a zoologist and watch speckled quail-like birds for the next twenty years.

She lay down on the jetty and peered over its edge into the shallow lagoon to watch the fish nibble at miniscule molluscs suckered onto the stout jetty legs. She couldn't remember the last time she'd had a chance to rest like this. Her usual life ran like clockwork with sports, dance lessons, music lessons, homework, her work, meetings, cleaning, cooking, shopping and exercise, each activity parcelled into neat slots of time. Even when the children were with their father, she scheduled her day and compiled endless lists of what had to be done.

When the inner voice called her to jump up, see to the children, organise the day and unpack belongings, she ignored it and chose to observe the damselfish, the blennies, and numerous blobby creatures drift by in the lagoon. She could almost hear the limpets suck and close their valves as mini-waves splashed against the poles of the jetty.

'What are you doing, Mum?' Lil brushed long locks away from sleepy eyes and plonked her warm body near Mel's. Mel drew her close and kissed her wild hair.

'Just looking.' Lil hung her body over the jetty and gripped the edge. Jack lumped over and stood; there would be no lying down on the jetty for her. Mel could see that her body was taut, ready for action.

'What are we going to do today?'

'After breakfast,' Mel said, 'why don't we putter around the island on the dinghy. What do you think?'

'Okay. I thought I heard a man's voice this morning.'

'Yes you did. That was Mark. We don't have to worry about dinner.'

'I saw them in the fridge.'

She raised herself and picked her way over the coral towards the hut.

'Can you come with me to the outside bathroom, Mum?'

'Of course. Jack, could you set up for breakfast please?'

'Sure.'

When they returned from the bathroom, a dark face greeted them at the door.

'What's wrong Jack?'

'You forgot the rest of the milk. Cereal with one carton of milk for the whole week?'

'Don't take that tone with me. It must have been shipped to another island or got left at the supermarket. Never mind, I'll ask Mark.'

'He's out at sea, Mum,' Lil said.

'You know what? I spotted some dried milk powder. Let' make our own milk.' Jack hated powdered milk.

'I'll help you,' Lil offered.

'I'll have toast.' Jack loved cereal. It was killing her to hold it in, but Mel wanted to giggle. This was about milk.

Mel stood beside her eldest daughter, not looking her in the eye. She swung her hips and nearly knocked Jack over. 'Sorry, didn't see you.'

In response, Jack dead-legged her mother's knees and Mel pretended to collapse. A fleeting smile lit up the face of her extraordinary child. With the breakfast catastrophe averted, the survivors would now move to the next challenge and potter around the island in a dinghy. They spent the rest of the day adjusting to a new rhythm. Mel spent the day wondering if it had been such a wise idea to come at all since the children were still out of sorts with each other.

Chapter Thirteen

On the second day, Jack took Lil out on a dinghy to explore around the edges of the smaller islands close by. They took crab nets to place in the mangroves on the island directly opposite called Stomizzi Island.

Mel watched as Jack tilted the motor around some of the lower-lying coral outcrops that became more prominent as the tide receded.

She didn't want to stay inside the shack with her thoughts. From a crate in the shack she untangled one of the handlines and attached new hooks and sinkers. If her previous fishing expeditions were a guide, the fish were safe but she enjoyed the ritual. The edge of the southern jetty, where the water dropped down to unfathomable depths, was where she hoped to observe some of the larger sea animals cruise by.

Mel followed the trail of crushed coral and breathed in the briny air, stringent with the taint of rotting salted bait and decomposing seaweed.

Grey-striped and mottled turban shells with their thick rubbery meat were ideal for bait. She hoped their unwitting sacrifice wouldn't be in vain and apologised when she bashed a piece of coral over one pearlescent home. When it shattered, sharp white splinters of shell rained down on the bleached boards of the jetty like confetti.

'You talk to molluscs?'

She missed the shell with the next bash and hammered the jetty timber with the shock of hearing a human voice.

'Sorry. I didn't mean to scare you.' He held out a large

slender hand. 'I'm Andy, one of Kev's friends. We were at school together.'

'I'm Mel, a friend of Jill's.'

'I know. I chatted to Kev before he headed out. We arrived this morning but were dropped over there.' He thrust out an arm to point towards the northern flank of the island, where there was another group of shacks and a jetty. Some distance away, bent over at the edge of the island, were two lanky children. He saw her look at them. 'They're my boys, Eli and Toby. We usually come over at this time of year.'

She hadn't counted on having to make friendly banter. Dangling over the edge of the jetty, she pulled out the moist muscular foot and threaded the slippery flesh onto her hook. 'You probably know more than me about fishing off this jetty. What are my chances?'

'Depends on the tide. I think you may be in for a bit of a wait until the tide turns.'

'That doesn't surprise me. I'm not such a great fisherman. Are you here with the boys on your own?'

'No, my wife came too. She's lying down suffering from seasickness, possibly for the day. The idea of the holiday is for me to spend more time with the boys and give her some time for her art.'

'Great place for art.'

'Every year she takes photos and sketches in a few ideas to take back to her studio.' He sat down near her and they both watched the tiny blennies nibble at her bait. 'I saw what you did for that boy. That must have been tough.'

She gripped the line a bit tighter. 'Yes it was tough, especially for the family. And no one wants their privacy invaded like that.' She knew she sounded short.

'I work in the media. I know what you mean, but I don't think it came across like that.'

'You're only saying that because it's not you plastered all over the internet.'

'True,' he conceded.

'What do you do?' she asked.

'Cameraman.'

If a camera suddenly appeared she knew she wouldn't be able to restrain herself. She placed another turban shell on the jetty and hammered; shards of its pearly interior showered over him. She would never have done anything like that ordinarily.

'Sorry.'

After a few minutes, he made his way back around the island, but it had shaken her to realise how much she reeled in the wash of those emotions. She felt her line grow taut. It had snagged on the coral.

Chapter Fourteen

Jill had explained the rules of island life. If Mel went out on a boat, she was to leave a note in the hut detailing expected times and locations.

The next couple of days rolled into each other as Mel and the girls tinkered around the edges of the island, fishing and fossicking. Mark continued to drop by unannounced, and nearly always caught her by surprise. They had unimaginative conversations about the weather, boating and the day's catch.

May was by far the mildest of months with its tempered winds and balminess, and she wished it would last forever after the intensity of summer heat and howling winds of the previous months.

The day before they were due to leave they chose to venture further afield to see other islands. Jack was engrossed. 'I've primed it and filled the tank. We should be good for ages.' She'd taken over the management of the boat.

'Okay, but I don't want to be out for more than a couple of hours,' Mel said when she noticed the milk-washed sky. Further away, on the edge of the horizon, there was a white lining of blossom-shaped clouds.

'Sit down Lil.' The dinghy was small, and it felt even smaller when Mel looked out at the water around them. The sense of isolation made Mel feel vulnerable when she realised the mistake she'd made.

'I forgot to scrawl a note,' she told Jack, a flicker of alarm running through her. No one would notice their absence for hours or maybe longer.

'Mum! That was your job!' Jack's voice exploded.

'I know, I got busy with the food and water.' And, she added to herself, the life jackets, sun block, hats and toilet paper.

'It's okay, we won't go too far. They'll work it out.'

She bit her lip because she was supposed to be the adult, so how could she have forgotten the note?

'Okay, but we won't motor far away from those small islands.'

'Look a fin!' Lil pointed towards the bow.

In the bow wave glimmered the velvet-grey body of a young dolphin. Jack hammered the dinghy to keep the dolphin interested and soon two more dolphins joined in.

'Jack, slow down,' Mel called, but her daughter couldn't hear. 'Jack, slow down!'

'What? Okay.'

They puttered along, quieter.

'Did you bring fishing gear?'

'Yes.'

They made their way towards a small island the size of a hockey field. 'I think they call this Seal Island.' Mel was pretty sure because she'd seen a vague outline on a rough map back at the shack.

'Oh really, and that would be because of the seals. How many Seal Islands do you think there are in the world? They could have been a bit more original.'

'Since you're so smart, you name it, then. If it was my island I—'

'Who wants to know what you think?' Jack interrupted.

Mel glared at her. Jack apologised.

'Can I have the orange line? I think it looks lucky.' Lil sidled closer to Mel and shot her sister a foul look.

'Sure.' Lil chose distraction. Mel wondered, was it all hormones with her teenage daughter, or was Jack a tortured individual? She had to stop picking at the scab of if-we-hadn't-divorced-she'd-be-different.

Lil and Jack devoured most of the picnic before lunchtime and their lines hung limp in the water. She could see their bodies twitch with restlessness.

Jack scanned around. 'Let's move to another island.'

Mel took in the view out towards the horizon, where a massive bank of frontal clouds covered a third of the sky. 'Perhaps for a little while because the weather might change.' It was hard to see how, since only a light breeze scudded over the wave tops, and because a huge fringing outer reef protected it, the waves wouldn't amount to more than a chop. She consoled herself with that thought. Jack started the outboard and she could see her try to disguise the thrill of the adventure.

About fifteen minutes later Jack said, 'Will we stop here?'

'I think so.' It was in deep water, close to the fringing reef.

'Why don't we drift fish, it saves dropping the anchor?'

'But Jack, someone needs to stay on the look-out if we do that.'

'I can see deep down. What's that?' Lil peered into the depths where a sea turtle made its way to the surface.

'Jack don't drop your line yet, and Lil, sit down.'

'I just want to see where it goes.' Lil said. 'What if I swim around it?'

'Not a good idea.'

'But why not?' Mel bit her lip, scanned.

'I don't know why not.' Mel said. 'Go on, jump in.' She turned to Jack. 'Jack, do not put that line in. Let Lil swim for a bit.'

'I wasn't going to.' She pulled her cap low.

'I'm scared, but I want to go in.' Lil slipped her a sideways look. Big ocean. She knew what was expected of her; she was supposed to be the grown up.

'Why don't I come in with you?' Very big ocean.

Mel shrugged off her shorts and top, ignored the rapid beat of her heart and heaved herself over the edge of the dinghy with Lil. Jack balanced the other side. With their snorkels on, they floated above the cauliflower-shaped coral outcrops. Turquoise water on each side of the coral gardens graduated in shade till it was the deepest blue, and the water clarity enabled every shade and shape of coral to stand out in a colourful montage. They lost sight of the turtle when it turned and swam out to the deeper channel, where Mel did not wish to venture. Lil was intrigued by the myriad life forms and spectacle of the coral outcrop. Mel hung by her side and kept a wary eye out above and below when they dived to swim over the expansive coral lumps.

She felt a nudge. Her eyes grew in alarm when she spotted a dark shape below her. She grabbed Lil's hand and flurried against the coral with her flippers, creating an instant soupy suspension. They darted upward. She broke through the surface and screamed, 'Jack, pull us in quick!'

Jack scrambled and paddled with her hands to get closer to them. She reached out and grabbed their arms.

'Quick Jack!' The dinghy swayed and nearly tipped with the sudden lurch of their bodies. They squelched and spread on the bench seats, cold and gelatinous. She peered over the edge to see the dark sinuous outline of a long creature cruise below them.

'Mum, you're bleeding!' Mel saw that her legs sported only minor grazes, but she was more impressed that they were still attached to her torso. Thankfully, Lil was unscathed.

'What was that?' She could barely speak.

'It was just a seal, you guys. I saw it after you dived in.'

'It must have been the coral that gave me these grazes. I'd better get something on them.' She didn't want the children to see just how relieved she was. She bent over and fossicked in her bag for something to clean the wounds with.

'That was so amazing! Wait till I tell Dad.' At least Lil had enjoyed the drama.

'Jack, let's go back,' Mel told her.

'What about we try one more spot?'

'I think I'd rather get back now, Jack.'

Jack pulled the cord and nothing happened. She pulled it repeatedly. The motor wouldn't catch. 'Must be something simple.' She lifted the lid and tried again.

Large waves started to wash and spill over the outer reef into the deep channel where they had been fishing. 'Let's drop the anchor here.' Mel thought she sounded confident and hoped that it would stop the small dinghy from battering into any coral protrusions.

Oh God, she thought, no phone works out here; there

would be no seaside assistance to render help.

'Why are you looking under the benches, Mum?' Lil's voice slid a smidgeon higher.

'Checking for flares.' She was also hunting for evidence of rowlocks, oars, supplies of anything. She didn't want her actions to worry the girls, but they weren't fooled. 'Jack, leave the motor for a while or else it will flood with fuel.'

'I can't believe you didn't leave that note.'

'Nor can I.'

'So stupid.'

'I agree.'

'I mean, really dumb for a grown-up.'

'I get it Jack.' Mel gritted her teeth.

'They'll never figure out where we are since you—'

'Jack!'

'Maybe the dolphins will help us.' Lil spoke each word carefully in an attempt to hide a wobble in her voice.

'You're so stupid,' Jack cut in.

'Jack!' Mel turned to Lil. 'Actually, Lil, dolphins have helped people before so you never know.'

Jack muttered under her breath.

It was after lunch so Mel calculated they still had four hours of daylight. She found one oar, no rowlocks and no flares. Six apples and two litres of water were left from the picnic and they were wearing only light day clothes. She wasn't sure what to do next.

'I spy...'

'Ocean coral fish sky!'

'Jack!'

Mel sat with Lil's head rested against her and slung her arm around her youngest daughter's slight frame.

They'll know we're here, she thought. She remembered hearing how the fishermen always knew something was wrong when the visitors' shack was mysteriously quiet. Jill's voice echoed and she was disgusted to realise she had become one of those stupid visitors.

Why had she been so forgetful? What was the outcome of

this running away? Who said she had to talk to the media? If only the image of Cam Robson didn't bang around in her head so much. The pointless circular nature of her thoughts creased her brow.

'Mum!' She looked up. She heard a deep constricted breath. Oh no, not here, she prayed. She looked closer at Lil. Only several times in Lil's childhood had this happened, and on each occasion they'd been mere minutes from the hospital. It wasn't great to be here with Lil having an asthma attack; her eyes bulged, she struggled for breath and the wheezy breathing scared all of them.

'Lil,' Mel said, 'we'll soon be out of here. Where's your inhaler?'

'I forgot it.' More wheezing.

'It's,' she said with not much breath, 'just...' A hard sucking-in sound was followed by a rasping sound, like someone had winded her.

She looked into Lil's eyes. 'Don't talk anymore,' she told her. 'Jack, look again at the motor.' Mel stripped off her top and grabbed all the towels and clothing to wrap around Lil, who was still cold from the dive. She knew she should have checked, but Lil hadn't had many attacks and she had seemed to have it all under control. She felt sick with fear and guilt.

'Just nod. Is it at the shack?'

She shook her head.

'Did you leave it back at home?'

With frightened eyes and blue lips, she nodded.

'It's no good, Mum, I don't know how to fix it,' Jack said.

'Just give it another go, Jack.' Lifeless and dull, the motor droned as Jack pulled the cord. Her cheeks grew red. Tears rolled down Lil's cheeks. Mel held her close and drew her bony shoulders into hers, yet her breaths continued, raspy, shallow and alarming.

'Mum! Look!' Jack pointed at the horizon.

'What?' Her eyes swept around the thin edge of inky dark sea against the lighter blue sky, but she couldn't see anything.

Jack became excited as she pointed in the direction of the

horizon again. 'I think its Kev's boat.'

They could see the grey outline of the cabin, the frothy tail of wake, and then heard the rhythmic whine of an engine. The hum grew louder.

In only a few minutes Kevin's boat drew alongside. Mark was navigating on the fly bridge. Their small dinghy rocked in its wake. Mel threw a rope up and they tied it to a cleat towards the back of the boat.

'Kev, Lil can't breathe properly.' Whatever irritation and annoyance they had about rescuing her disappeared when they laid eyes on Lil. Her blue lips and rasping breath rattled them. Mark left the bridge and leaned against the railings to pull at the rope. He stepped down on the transom, pulled on the dinghy rope so he could grab Lil and move her into the cabin, while Kevin shored up the dinghy. After securing a towrope to the bow, he helped Mel and Jack climb aboard.

'I can organise a chopper to take you and Lil back. There's one due at Stomizzi. It's dropping off a parcel. I'll call through and tell him to drop over and pick you up,' said Kevin.

'I'm so sorry, Kev.'

'Is it asthma?' Mark asked.

'Yes.'

'I have a puffer on board. I keep it here for when my son Dylan comes out.'

Mel felt the painful knot in her stomach ease. In that moment she could have kissed him. He banged about in a cabinet and pulled out the Ventolin inhaler. They watched Lil draw in the lifesaving vapour.

'Thanks so much, Mark, she left hers at home and I forgot to check.' She wiped away tears as she watched Lil.

'Don't even think about it.'

'Yes, but...'

'It's okay.'

She turned to face Kevin. 'Thank you, Kev. Sorry, we should have discussed this with you. We were all too keen to get going.'

'It's a not such a dangerous place out here behind the reef, but without a note no one will know for ages that you've gone, or where you are. A good motor helps, too.'

'I should have written that note.' *If only I wasn't such an idiot.* Jack glanced at her.

Kevin flattened the motors and drove them back to Mary Island. She looked up at the two men standing in the cabin, their thick forms shaped by the repetitive exposure to the demands of fishing in a wild environment.

'Mel, that outboard wasn't a good one. I've got a better one I could have given you. But I guess you weren't to know. My deckhand, Jake, spotted that you'd taken the wrong motor. Everyone heads in this general direction. Why didn't you come and see me before you left? I could have fixed you up.' He wasn't accusing her, he just sounded hurt. She knew he felt some responsibility for her since she was Jill's friend.

That was a very good question. 'I should have, I'm sorry.'

Mark emerged. 'You'd better take her straight to hospital.'

'I plan to.'

'We can throw your stuff on the next supply boat back to town. Just take what you need.'

'Thanks Mark,' she called after him, but he had already jumped up to the fly bridge to navigate the boat around the shallow outcrops until they were back in the safer passage that led to Mary Island. Kevin spoke to Jake on the radio.

'Yep, we've got them. Chopper organised? Good, see you in ten.'

Mel's teeth chattered. Lil had most of their clothes draped over her and she sat in her bathers. She held Lil and heard the rattle of restricted breaths. Mark jumped down from the fly bridge to hand her his wet-weather jacket. Was he annoyed or was that his manner? She took it from him and gave an involuntary shudder.

The twin jet engines almost lifted the boat out of the water and it would have been a thrilling experience on a less catastrophic day. Mark came down and checked on Lil. Mel had consistently demonstrated that she was not a native of island life and that bothered her.

'Someone's been trying to contact you,' he said.

'Mum was on the internet because she saved a boy. Now everyone wants to interview her.'

'Thanks Jack,' Mark said, 'but I knew about that.'

Mel was surprised. 'You did?'

A brief smile ran over his lips. 'Yes, we're not totally in the dark out here you know.'

'No one is meant to know I'm here.' She presumed it was Tony.

'Jake took the call on Kev's boat, said you were out and that Kev was about to go looking for you.'

She couldn't wait to have that conversation. He probably phoned her mother after he received the email. 'It may have been Tony, my ex-husband.'

'Look, if you need help...'

Jack interrupted Mark and stood between them. 'We'd better take Lil quickly, Mum.' Lil's breaths were less harsh. The inhaler had worked, but she had fallen asleep and Mel hated to shift her.

The deckhands on the jetty tied up the boat. Kevin sorted out the dinghy and Mark leaned down and gathered up Lil in his arms without looking at her. 'Let me know if you need anything,' he said, before striding off in front of her. Mel carried what she could of their gear and headed out towards the helicopter.

After depositing Lil into the aircraft, Mark stood near Mel and she got the sense that he wanted to speak, so she looked up at him, almost holding her breath.

'Mel, can I drop by when I'm in Perth?' She could see that it was a struggle for him getting those words out, but he'd had to shout over the helicopter and that had probably made him uncomfortable. His arms hung by his side like he wanted to do something useful with them. She could see through his sunnies to his direct gaze.

'Of course.' With the thrumming whoosh and deafening beat of rotor blades, she took a moment and scrawled her number and address on a receipt she found in her bag.

He moved away from the helicopter once she was inside and

she found herself watching him as he waved them off.

A few moments later Lil awoke and appeared fine.

'The hospital has to check you out,' Mel told her gently. 'You haven't had one that bad in a while.'

'Okay. Do we have to leave now?'

'Yes. We only had one more day anyway.'

'Buckle up Mum.' Jack's cheekbones wore fine red clouds of humiliation over the boating incident.

Chapter Fifteen

The helicopter journey was brief. She was grateful that the pilot could take all of them. She hated the thought of leaving Jack behind, even though Kevin and Mark offered to look after her and send her on the next supply boat.

'Jack,' she said and then waited as Jack pulled out one earplug, 'I've organised Jill to collect you and take you back to her house because I'll have to stay with Lil in the hospital. Is that okay?'

'Sure.' She saw the raw emotions flicker around on her daughter's face. She looked at Lil, then back at Mel. 'I want to go to Dad's as soon as we're back.'

'Okay.'

'I want to go for a while.'

'All right Jack.' Nothing Mel could do would draw her out once she'd retracted into her teenage shell, and secretly she worried that she wouldn't ever get it right with Jack.

*

Although Lil's condition had stabilised, the doctor wanted to keep her overnight for observation. 'I'm just ducking out, Lil, I'll be back.' Her daughter nodded, engrossed in a movie on her iPad.

She called Tony to let him know about Lil's situation and emphasised that Lil was completely recovered and in capable hands. After a few minutes she managed to beg off saying that the doctor wanted to talk to her. There'd be more to that conversation when she got home. Had she made everything worse by going away?

After checking in on Lil, she called Pete because he'd left a couple of brief texts. 'Pete, hi.'

'Hi Mel, I've been trying to catch you.'

'I went away with my kids. I'm working for Rockforth Bay and Daniel told me not to talk to the media and I didn't tell him about meeting you straight after the accident, so you can't use any of that conversation we had, I signed an agreement.' Her words came out in a rush.

'I said it would be up to you. You're working for them? That was quick.'

'I had to, I needed a job. I had no idea how the whole incident would affect us. I was advised to take a week off till it cooled down and took up my friend's offer of a shack at the Banderley Islands.'

'I hear they're spectacular for diving.'

'They are. We rushed back today because Lil had an asthma attack. I'm in hospital.'

'Sorry to hear that.'

'She's fine. I forgot her inhaler.'

'You might like to know that the parents are pressing ahead with a court case.'

'I figured they might.' She slumped in the hard green plastic seat.

'You'll probably be called as a witness and be questioned about everything.'

'I realise that.'

'How are you feeling?' He had lowered his voice. It sounded intimate and warm and she wondered about him again, reflecting on the conversation she'd had with Jill. She didn't know that much about him, only that a faint buzz trickled through her whenever she heard him speak.

'I've had better months,' she said after a few seconds passed.

'Understandable. I'm in town, why don't we catch up? I don't know that many people in Perth and I get sick of hanging around newspaper people. When are you back?'

'I drive back tomorrow, but I'll be too worn out to do anything. We could catch up, but not for any more of those chats.

Are you here Saturday evening?'

'Yeah I'll still be here Saturday. I can just talk you through what could happen. It may help to hear an insider's perspective. Lock it in. We'll have a meal. I'll text you with details and I'll search for a place near your home so you don't have to go far.'

'Okay. See you then.'

Next, she needed to phone Daniel.

'Hi Daniel. You wanted to talk to me?'

'Hi. How was the break?'

'Wonderful. It was great advice and we only had a slight hiccup with my daughter forgetting her inhaler. I've had her checked her out at the local hospital and she's all right now.' She wasn't going to tell him about the boating incident, either.

'That's good to hear. You'll get more attention next week and you may need to stay with your mother because there will be a court case. Michael will advise you on what to say and on how to deal with the media, so don't worry.'

She wasn't worried before, but since speaking to both Pete and Daniel, she could feel her chest tighten. The court case did concern her. 'Thanks Daniel, I'll see you on Monday.'

'Take care Mel, see you then.'

Chapter Sixteen

The trip home was quiet. Lil slept off and on and Jack wouldn't respond to anything Mel said. Mel ached with weariness.

Tony said he'd be around in the evening to pick the children up. There would be a conversation, he said, when he dropped by to take Lil and Jack for the weekend. She could hardly wait.

She pulled into the driveway and the girls filed out. As she let them in and brought in their bags, she saw the red light of the answering machine pulsing in the hallway. She ignored it.

When she tuned into the news, stories floated around about Cam. Some hinted that he might be involved with gaming and drugs and there was even a suggestion that he had been on the phone to someone connected with this when his car collided with the kerb and Mitchell. She thought again about that flash of memory.

'Dad's here.' Lil had positioned herself on the sofa to watch for his car through the curtains.

She heard the car door close and the crunch of his familiar gait on the gravel driveway. He banged on the door. Lil skidded on her socks to the hallway to open it.

'Dad!' He swept her up in his arms, kissed her and stroked the wavy hair away from her eyes.

'You're okay?' he asked.

'I'm fine. It wasn't a big one. I should have packed my puffer.'

'I've bought a couple of spares for home.' He had an angry shine in his eyes when they locked on Mel. He leaned in and continued to hug Lil. When Lil left to gather her bag and put her shoes on, he strode into the lounge room. His eyes were cool, his lips tight and unsmiling. Tension rode on the tsunami he had stormed in with.

'Where's Jack?'

'Hi Tony. How are you? She's in her room. Where else would our teenager be? I'll call her.' She wandered towards Jack's bedroom and tapped on the door. 'Jack, your dad's here.'

'Okay, coming.'

When he finished greeting the children, he suggested they have a quiet word.

'Jack and Lil, I need both of you to go the supermarket to buy a couple of cartons of milk,' Mel told them.

'Can't Jack just go?'

'Lil, please.'

'Okay. Can we have a milkshake, too, at the café?'

'Sure Lil.' Tony gave the girls a few notes. 'Only a milkshake guys and bring back the change Jack.'

'Sure Dad.'

Mel gave them money for the milk and they left. Jack didn't say anything. She kept her eyes down when she passed them.

'What were you thinking, taking them to the Banderley Islands? For Christ's sake, Mel.'

'The media, in case you haven't noticed, are on a feeding frenzy. Do you think I want our children's photos plastered on the front page of the newspapers or worse, on the net and television? I took them away to protect them.'

'You should have sent them to me.'

'I wanted to take them away. I thought they deserved a break, too.'

'You're supposed to consult me.'

'I did.'

'Not after the event.' He threw his arms up in exasperation.

'It hasn't been easy, Tony. I was made redundant.'

'I'm not surprised.'

'What do you mean?'

'You lack passion for your work.'

'Yes, I did take a job to fit in with parenting, not the other way around. My children are my priority. And for your information,

I was pretty good at my job, but they have new online courses. There's less money for sessional lecturers. I wasn't the only one made redundant.' If only there wasn't some truth in what he said. She felt her face redden, her voice rise. 'I have another job, so I'm fine.'

'You exposed our kids to a potential disaster. Anything,' he snarled as he moved closer, 'any fucking thing could have happened to Lil. You know that. You didn't check that she had her inhaler? Yeah right they're your priority!'

'I know I should have checked. You know how thorough I am about the medical kit when we go away. It was just this one time.'

'It only takes one time.' She hadn't seen him this worked up in a while. 'And you were miles away from help.' He stormed around the room. 'What possessed you to take a dinghy, go far out to sea and not have a good motor? Jesus Christ, Mel, you're at the bloody Banderley Islands, anything could have happened. I can't believe that you placed our children, your *priorities*, in such a dangerous situation.'

'They weren't in danger.'

'I heard through a friend, whose son was chatting to our daughter, that you didn't leave a note and that the motor was dodgy. You're unstable, that's what you are.'

She exploded. 'I am not! I took our kids away from public exposure—'

'And straight into the open ocean so they could drown, die from an asthma attack or be mauled by sharks.'

'You're over-dramatising. Kev and Mark knew where we were.'

'That was luck. God knows what else could have happened. I'm having them for a week. Both of them.'

'Tony, sit down and stop berating me for a minute. You know how much I love our kids.'

He snorted but sat in the nearest chair.

'I'm ignoring your outburst. I have something to ask you.'

'What?' He pushed back his hair, his lean frame tense, his cheeks inflamed. She thought that they wouldn't become like that, that they wouldn't be reduced to open hostility and squabbling, but then she'd never been divorced with children before.

'You can have them for the week, but I need help for the rest of this year.'

'In what way? Oh, let me guess, in the money way.'

'Yes.' She couldn't have felt smaller.

'No fucking way.'

'Listen, to cover my share of the school fees for this year.'

'Why? I thought you were smarter than this. You shouldn't need any money, not how you're set up.'

'Tony, I wouldn't ask if I had any way of paying, you know that. I'll pay you back next year, as soon as I can.'

'There's something not right here. You should be able to pay.' He sat forward in the chair. 'I heard a rumour about you, several years ago.'

'What?'

'It was about you and Justin Gainsborough. But, in your defence, I said no way, not Mel. She wouldn't go near that predator. Judging by the colour of your face, they were right. Jesus Mel, what did you do?'

'Whatever I did, it isn't any of your business.' She glared at him. 'Forget it. I'll sort it out another way.'

'You'd better. You need to grow up, be responsible. You're pathetic.'

'I'm pathetic! I didn't run away with long-legged Leah and her family-law company. No, that was innocent romance. No convenience there. Helped you out with your accountancy by suggesting you to her clients? Right.'

'At least she has a zest for life, a passion and interests. You're like someone on autopilot. You're so disengaged. I needed to move out to feel alive. Maybe this is the kick in the arse you need.'

He'd never spoken to her like that. She recognised tiny chinks of truth in what he said. They'd fallen into the monotonous years of marriage, but she had thought it would segue into a mature and sustaining relationship, over time. She could see now that no amount of time would have resurrected it, and she had been equally to blame.

'Anyway,' he sneered, 'the rumour was, he said you weren't that good, a bit too desperate.'

Whatever she felt, whatever string had tethered them together, snapped.

'Tony, bring Lil back in one week and we'll continue with our usual arrangement. Don't worry, I won't be asking you for anything ever again. Oh, and next time Leah's chatting with her girlfriends about her antics in the bedroom, I suggest she check whether Jack is at home. One whiff of her sordid words in Lil's ears and you won't be seeing that much of her, either.' She stood up. He'd never know it was a version of the truth. 'Our children are walking up the driveway. One week.' His entire face was red now. 'We don't have to battle. And they had fun, real fun, at the islands.'

It took all of her self-control to hold herself upright while the children packed and left. 'See you at the netball courts at nine, Lil, and I'll be at football at one, Jack.'

'Bye, Mum.' They kissed and hugged. She could feel them sense that something had happened between her and Tony. She hated that.

Chapter Seventeen

'How's it all going?' Pete pulled the chair out for her. When he wandered over to the other side of the table, Mel caught drifts of his cologne.

'I'm real cosy with the media now. My children have taken to wearing towels over their heads to protect their identity. Daniel has warned me not to speak to anyone or give any interviews because he said everything will be handled by the club.' *And my ex-husband thinks I am parent of the year for submitting his children to a near-death experience at the islands.*

'Is it okay working there?'

'At the moment. I don't think my future lies in college education anymore. They want many more students per lecturer so fewer courses will run. Anyway, the online courses are replacing a lot of what's offered.'

He leaned over the table. 'I doubt they could deliver it with your personal touch.'

She tried not to breathe him in. 'I don't think it factors in the college's return on investment.' She still didn't know much about him, but flirting felt acceptable. Her confidence was so low after her conversation with Tony yesterday, she felt transparent. 'What do you do back in Sydney, on the weekends when you aren't working?'

'I run around Coogee. It's where our townhouse is. However, my partner has recently left to have a break from "us" and is staying at her parents' house in Rose Bay. I swim and do a bit of amateur woodwork. My grandpa was a carpenter, and with great optimism, he left me his tools. I've graduated to small tables with curious legs of varying heights. Flat surfaces and uniform legs are vastly overrated.'

Little bubbles rose inside her. 'I run and sometimes swim. I used to be a coach at the surf club, the one close to the scene of the accident.'

'That's why you administered CPR.'

'Yes.'

'I was a nipper and then a cadet at my local club, but it became too hard to keep it up with work. Even I've had to pluck the odd tourist out, and that's in the shallows at Bondi. They get all picture-postcard gooey-eyed, but most of them can barely swim.'

She listened and watched his lips. She would have liked to drown when he was around, though she controlled the urge to tell him.

'What about you, what else do you like to do? Let me guess. You are a superb mother, a brilliant cook and have a rare talent with DIY?'

'You'd have to ask my children about my parenting skills. I'm an ordinary cook. I've studied pieces of reticulation in my hand but can never work out how to put it back together again. I'm still searching for my true calling.'

He raised his eyebrows. She blushed.

'What's it like working in a football club?' He forked a mound of quinoa into his mouth.

'Like any other administrative office, except there's a lot more talk about the season.'

He paused between mouthfuls. 'They haven't mentioned the case to you?'

'Only that I am to say nothing.'

'How do you feel about that?'

'Pete, I didn't see anything and I didn't do anything wrong, so I feel fine about that. They've been great. It'll be my first full week beginning Monday and it will give me a chance to direct my focus on something else.'

'I'm sorry, part of my job the cynicism. Being employed is very important. You have to raise a family. I admire anyone who can do that with the ridiculous cost of living.'

'You have no idea.'

'It's why I'm taking you out.'

'I didn't mean that.'

'No, I have an expense account when I travel. It's also my pleasure. I don't laugh at my jokes nearly as much dining on my own.'

Although she knew he was still interested in the story, she was enjoying his company and playing this game.

As they ate, she found his undivided attention heady and more than once she felt the brush of his leg against hers under the table. She felt a tingly sensation spread all over her skin; it had been a while. She hoped she didn't appear desperate and her cheeks burned when she remembered Tony's snarl as he delivered the blow of those words.

She swirled the last of the wine in her glass and watched him as he rested his knife and fork tidily on the side of the plate.

'Tell me again, why are you single?'

'Something to do with the massive sign on my head that says, "Divorced woman, likely to be desperate. Has kids".' She hadn't meant to say desperate.

'Oh that sign. I was reading the other one, "Gorgeous woman, smart and cute, not easily taken in by goofy guys".'

'You obviously need glasses to read the subtext.'

'No I don't. If you're fishing for compliments, I think you are sassy, brave and,' he whispered as he leaned in towards the centre of the table, 'pretty hot. Love the dress.'

Uncontrollable things happened to her stomach. 'I have been taken in by a guy, but it turned out I was the goofy one.'

'What happened?'

'Good-looking, rich financier wandered into my path after my husband left. All sense evacuated my brain and he offered me a deal. Like him, it was too good to be true. It was not my finest hour on a number of levels. My shares plummeted not long after he left me.'

She recalled his physical presence and the way she wanted to lie against his crisp shirts and breathe him in. A car would turn up to collect her if he was running late, and his bedroom suite was more than worthy of the over-the-top imported underwear she'd started wearing. He was an excellent lover and she'd been furious later about her finances, and about his cavalier attitude to women, but it wasn't entirely his fault. 'Anyway, now that I have this job I can survive.'

'I'm not after your assets, but I would like to see you again. You never went out after that?'

'Justin the financier cauterised my fledgling interest in dating.'

'What about online dating?'

'I tried it a couple of times, but I found it hard. I thought I would leave it to chance.' She reddened.

'Works for me. Some friends of mine met online and are happily married now.'

'It works for some. Do you think you and your partner will ever get back together?'

'Right now, no. I'm too short on family estate for her parents. Her mum and I got along quite well, but her dad was often caught up with business conversations that were too important to leave to chat with me. Can I see you again?' he asked abruptly.

'That would be nice.' Divine and sensual was what she thought about seeing him again.

They walked out of the front door of the restaurant together.

'Thanks for dinner,' she said, feeling almost shy.

'Next time I'm here I'll have the whole weekend, but tomorrow I have to catch the obscene early-morning flight back to Sydney. When I come back, why don't we go for a swim or run together after a night out?'

'Have you swum in the ocean this time of year? It's freezing.'

'There was I thinking you'd be up for anything.'

'I'll watch.'

He walked her to her car.

'I'll see you in a fortnight, Pete.'

Mindful of his role and her position, she was glad she'd chosen to drive to the restaurant. She trailed her hand over the side of her face that he had kissed as they'd parted and she lingered in the afterglow of his presence. He said he had to be in Perth a lot over the next few months. She wished she could quell the quivering traces of excitement she felt about that.

Chapter Eighteen

The following fortnight it was Tony's turn to have the children and Pete was back in Perth. His work commitments had changed and he asked whether Mel could go to dinner on Friday night and he suggested they go for a run together on Saturday morning. Her insides bounced whenever a text blipped. She kept the tone of her texts friendly. She avoided any symbols, even though he had started to appear in her dreams.

There was a rap at the door. Thinking it was Pete, Mel was delighted and surprised when she saw who it was.

'Mark! Come in. What brings you to the city?' He'd shaved, he was wearing cologne and he looked like a startled faun. It was like he wanted to see her but now thought that it was a mistake. She took in his shoes, smart shirt and clean jeans.

'My son. They have this father-and-son weekend in Year Ten. I thought I'd drop by.'

'That's great.' She wished she'd known that he was planning on being in town.

'I wanted to see if you—'

He was interrupted by another knock at the door.

'Sorry Mark.' Mel felt embarrassed. 'I'm expecting someone.'

'Sure. I'll be off.' His face clouded. She could see he was out of his usual comfort zone; no boats.

'Don't go.' She held his arm.

'No, I've got to go and see my son.'

She used that line all the time.

'Okay. Come by when you can again, I mean it. It would be great to catch up.' Catch up? What else did you say to a new male friend you hadn't spent much time with?

He mumbled a goodbye.

On his way out, he passed Pete. Both men did the male shuffle of grunt-and-nod acknowledgement.

'Hi, you're early. That was Mark, a friend of mine from up north.'

'Quite the talker.'

'He was in a hurry to go and see his son.' She wasn't sure why she felt she needed to defend Mark, but for some reason she didn't want Pete to think badly of him.

'Right. I think he had something else on his mind,' Pete said, his eyebrows shooting up in exaggeration.

She coloured. 'We met at the islands when I went over.'

'I see.'

'There's nothing to see, but he's a nice guy. I said to drop by if he was ever in Perth.'

'Which of course he would do because you are gorgeous.'

'I don't think he thinks that.'

'I think I can guess what he thinks.'

She reminded herself that Pete wasn't going to be available on tap. He lived on the east coast and she told her wayward mind to stop imagining anything else about him. He leapt down the driveway in a few easy bounds and opened the hire-car door for her. She stood in the hallway and bent over to secure her strappy shoes.

'Like the shoes. Shall we go?'

She ignored the warmth that ran all over her. 'Yes.'

He took her to the newly opened bar and restaurant on the ocean front, where they were guided by a waiter to table with a large window facing the breaking waves lit by moonlight.

After they ordered, he relaxed into his chair, undid the buttons on his cuffs and flipped up the sleeves. He gripped the wineglass by the stem and rocked it gently.

'How was your week?' he asked.

For a moment she'd forgotten. This wasn't just a meal with a handsome man.

'Fine. They've gone through the scenarios with me, and

since I didn't witness anything, there isn't too much more to add. The rest has been all football talk. We also re-examined the contract I signed, which lists the reasons under which my employment may be terminated. Basically, I don't say anything to anyone. Not that I'm privy to any secrets.'

'That's pretty much what I thought would be going on.'

'And you how has your work been?'

'I'm also contracted to keep my investigations confidential. There's one club under the microscope and a large web of people are rumoured to be associated with underhanded dealings. That's it. Are you happy with the offer still?'

'I think I'm happy. It's a pretty good offer and it takes care of some of my financial considerations.'

He leaned his head on his hand. 'This has been a pretty hideous time for you. It must be a relief to have work. I would love to do a longer interview with you when they let you talk. It may be after the court case though.'

'I don't know, it depends on what Daniel says. It was horrible when the media kept showing up on my doorstep, but we got used to ducking for cover. They seem to have dropped off lately. Other stories must be about to break.' She forced herself not to stare at his kissable lips.

He took a sip from his wine. 'I'm on your side and you did what all our fellow countrymen would like to believe they would do in similar circumstances. It's a strength they can build their credibility on, since you're working with them.' He rested his hand on her arm. She tried to ignore the sparks that flew from his touch.

She was weary. The children had been a bit testy over the media attention and were not immune to the hostility that had materialised between her and Tony over the trip to the islands. They were used to a more amicable situation.

All through dinner, her body gradually relaxed, and his company lit her inside like she was spritzed with bliss. It had been ages since she'd felt like that. His stories were compelling and the crazy situations he'd found himself in all over Sydney made her laugh. She was so glad he was staying another day and she could spend the next morning with him. It was only when she yawned that she realised just how late it had become.

'Come on, I'll take you home.' He signalled for the bill, and when it arrived, he paid and helped her out of her chair. 'I should have said earlier how great you look in that dress,' he whispered as they were walking out of the restaurant.

Her cheeks, already warm with the afterglow of wine, disguised the additional pink.

'Thanks. I thought your dress was pretty neat too, only I think you should wear the strapless next time.'

'You'd like me to wear a dress? Kinky.' He arched one eyebrow and shoved her lightly against her shoulder. She shoved him back. 'What about the food?'

'Wait, were we eating?'

'I'm sure there was food there somewhere. Maybe I distracted you with my sparkling repartee?'

'Could be. I just remember laughing. Now that you mention it, um, it was very earthy.'

'It was a crap, overpriced uber-trendy bar. I'll find somewhere else next time.'

'I thought it was me, I don't get out that much.'

'You're still a bit worried by the whole case aren't you?' He pulled out his keys and unlocked the car.

'With all the attention I feel like I'm being attacked, but I don't know why I'm the target.' She went to go inside but he turned to her and held both of her arms.

'You're not a target. This is the press, they sniff out a possible contentious court case and this is what happens. It'll fizz out. Once you've spoken in court, you'll be fine and then we can celebrate.' He released her and opened the door.

When they arrived back at her house, he walked her to the front door. 'Goodnight and thank you for having dinner with me.' He went to kiss her lightly on the cheek, but she turned and they ended up kissing on the lips.

'Sorry,' she said, though she didn't feel sorry at all.

'What for?' He grabbed her and folded her into a hug. She relaxed into his arms.

'You'd better go, but I did need that.'

'Are we on for a run tomorrow?'

'Yes, if you're still up for it.'

'I'll pick you up at...?'

'It's so cold at the moment. I think eight is early enough for Saturday.'

'Agreed. See you then.'

Chapter Nineteen

The court case loomed. It was no longer top billing, as Pete had predicted. Financial doom, natural disasters and terrorism, in some form or another, displaced most other news. Mel knew that when the court case took place the press would attack in a feeding frenzy.

Saturday afternoons at her house were about time out after the hectic round of Saturday-morning sports. Jack drummed a regular rhythm with the ball and hoop. Lil had retreated to hang out in the garden to climb a tree. Mel took a chair and a book outside to be near them and to bask in the warm winter sun.

Thoughts about Pete bubbled in the background and she recalled their last encounter. She had wanted to invite him in, but there was still the news reporter—client distance she thought wise to maintain, even though her imagination had other ideas.

There was a knock at the door.

'Mum!' Lil yelled. 'Someone's at the front door.'

'Okay, I'm going.' She was still in the grip of a sensual fogginess.

Lil clambered out of the branches and slithered down the rope to swing on the tyre below. 'Mum, I love you.' She blew her a kiss.

Mel smiled as she headed indoors. 'Love you too.' She blew her a kiss back. Jack kept up the beat with the basketball and glanced over to her and rolled her eyes. Mel blew her a kiss as well.

She took the steps two at a time. As she sped down the

hallway, she planted one foot on the hall rug, but it slipped beneath her and she fell on her bottom, before skidding along the polished wooden floor. She picked herself up quickly and opened the door, trying not to rub her backside where a large bruise would surely flourish.

'I brought some fish for you and the kids.' It was Mark in what she was getting to know as his style: no greeting, no affected hugging and kissing; he simply appears at her doorstep out of the blue. Despite this, she was pleased their last meeting hadn't put him off. He also looked like he'd just stepped off the boat and driven down.

'Thanks so much. We love your fish. Why don't you come in?'

'Can't. I'm in fishing clothes and I've got to see Dylan.'

'Don't worry about fishing clothes.' She smiled to encourage him.

'I've been called to Dylan's school. He broke his arm in footy training. Thought I'd bring you this.'

'It's so great to see you.'

'I'll be staying with a mate. I've got to be with Dylan at the hospital tomorrow.'

'If you have time on your way back, you're welcome to drop by.'

'It'll be too hard this time. I've got some business to sort out. Maybe next time.'

There was an awkward few seconds before he leaned forward, gripped her arms, and kissed her lightly on the cheek.

'I'll see you soon, Mel.'

She wasn't sure what to make of him, and then there was the fish. That made her chuckle.

A face appeared at the back door flyscreen.

'Hey, Mark brought fish!' Lil shouted back to Jack.

Jack raised her eyebrows. They seemed to be saying, 'So, Mark... fish... Mum...'

Even in thought, teenagers had spaces between words, or it could be Mel was misreading her.

Chapter Twenty

Over the next couple of months, Mel eased into the pattern of her new work. It seemed to involve rehashing badly written minutes into reports for the members and producing documents for the public domain. An office was an office, and it was like many she had been in, but the main difference was the atmosphere. The place vibrated with a palpable buzz about the weekend games, and even she had taken to watching the highlights because a place for the club in the top four was likely. Everyone talked statistics and probability and patted each other on the back, their voices loud with barely suppressed elation. She excused herself most evenings from the extracurricular drinking to make it in time for after school sports or music lessons, all located on the school's site.

The one thing that continued to bother her was the fleeting vision she'd had of Cam. If it was a correct image, she wondered if it would make a difference to the decision of the court. How could she be a reliable witness after the event, if she had this image and hadn't reported it? The only thing holding her back was her lack of conviction about her own memory of what she had seen and she clung to her belief that it wouldn't make any real difference to the outcome.

Pete phoned her. 'Hi Mel.'

'Pete, hi. I'm guessing you're in town?'

'Yes. Do you want to go out for dinner date with me? I can't seem to get you out of my mind when I'm home.' There was a warm whispery tone to his voice.

A glow spread through her insides. 'Of course.' They made

arrangements for later that evening, and Mel was distracted by the memory of the last dinner and the heightened sensuality he brought out in her.

'Are you okay Mel?' Jodi, the administrative assistant, asked when she caught her re-reading the same notes.

'Yes fine,' she answered and flushed, 'just wondering where I left those reports. I'll check the other office.' She trotted out, smiling. The children would be with Tony and the weekend held promise for once.

Did it compromise her work agreement? It was dating and she wouldn't say anything about work.

The afternoon flew by and she rushed home to shower and dress and wait for Pete.

He was on time, and when she opened the door the first thing she noticed was how incredible he smelled, although she was getting used to some amazing colognes in her new job.

'Hello,' he said, giving her a singularly sexy smile.

'Hello yourself.' She hoped she wasn't glowing bright red as she suspected she was.

'Shall we go?' He slipped his hand into hers, just like that. It caught her by surprise and made her heady. He held open the door. 'There's a new place that's just opened in the city. It's had excellent reviews, if they're to be believed, and its speciality is seafood. Much better than the last place.'

'I love seafood.'

'Good, so do I.'

He told her he was over for the continued investigation plus some new work on an inquiry in the mining industry.

When they arrived, she noticed the subtle lighting reflected on the river. She knew that this was a great restaurant because the club's board used it for meetings and raved about the food.

'Mel,' Pete said after they had been seated, 'you look gorgeous tonight. You should know that I'm finished with Lou. The removalists took away her things during the week.'

'I'm sorry.'

'Don't be.' He rubbed his thumb around the stem of the

wineglass and swirled it before he drank. The evening got better after that. Pete seemed to cheer up and they talked non-stop until it was time to leave.

Stepping out of the restaurant, he pulled her into the shadow of a portico and drew her close for a kiss. It was the one thing she'd been thinking about ever since she'd taken up watching his lips. Pete suggested they go back to his place, the apartment owned by his company for employers when they were on the west coast. She knew after the kiss that she wanted to spend the night with him.

'I'm not a teenager, I can wait if you're having second thoughts? I want to keep seeing you,' he told her.

It was the last bit of indecisiveness Mel had. When he offered his hand she took it. She slid close to him in the car on the drive to the apartment, and they remained close all the way up to the apartment.

Later, lying in his arms, she savoured everything that was happening to her body.

A phone flashed and lit up the room. Shards of light emanated from its upturned surface. They ignored it. When Pete upended it, it persisted.

She traced her fingers over his exposed torso when he slid over her and moved towards the phone; the tenderness of flesh on flesh left a trail of fizz in its wake.

A change crept into the atmosphere of the room as he took that call. He looked back at her and stepped away with the phone into the living room of the small apartment. She leaned into the place he had been sleeping to breathe in the masculine smell of him.

It was a short conversation. When he came back into the bedroom, his movements were polite and he tried not to disturb her. His eyes dipped and his whole body slumped.

'What's wrong?' Goosebumps appeared on her flesh.

He didn't speak for a few seconds. 'Mel, I'm so sorry. I can't believe this has happened now.'

'What?' She sat up.

'They've released the interview.'

'What interview? I haven't done one. I'm under a contractual obligation not to. What's going on?'

'Things are tight at work. They've culled positions lately because of falling readership. My boss asked me what I'd been up to in Perth.'

'You told him about me? After I asked you not to?'

'I showed him the transcript, plus we've got our other work. It was too good not to run. But I didn't run it.'

'Pete, I will lose my job!'

'He just took it and put it with some other information. I'm so sorry. You didn't say much, remember?'

'What does that matter? I signed a contract. The club had rights on my words, my interviews. They had the right to make money on this and everything else. What have you done?'

'My editor did it. He took the file and wrote the report. He said I needed to print a teaser article because the ongoing investigation wasn't substantial enough without printing something. They needed this to validate my position, to keep me employed.'

'So your job over mine!' She drew in the covers and grabbed some of her clothes. Her head was spinning.

'Mel, I didn't authorise anything.'

'That's a cop-out. It didn't need your authority. He took it. I can't believe you showed it to him. Don't touch me!' she practically yelled when he tried to take her arm. 'I'll lose my home too. You have no idea how important it was for me to have this job.' She was hysterical.

'I'm so very sorry.'

'I hope you are. You promised me. I should never have sat with you at the café. I'm sorry I ever trusted you.'

As soon as she was dressed she ordered a taxi, and when it arrived she slid into the seat and fixed her eyes on the road ahead. A hard ball of pain settled in her gut and her fists were white and tight around the straps of her bag.

When she got home, she switched off her phone and jumped into the shower where angry tears joined the stream.

Chapter Twenty-one

Early the next morning Mel responded to Daniel's seventeen missed calls.

'Hi Daniel.'

'Hi Mel. Just read the front covers on the main newspapers in Melbourne, Sydney and here. We need to talk. I presume I can come around in about half an hour?'

'Yes. I know what's happened.'

'Save it. I'll see you soon.'

She looked at her phone and switched it to vibrate. Pete had tried to call and had left numerous texts. There were other people with unknown mobile numbers trying to contact her. The media would soon be at her door.

Daniel rang again.

'You'd better meet me. Come down to the car park near the Clifton Park medical centre. I'll look out for you.'

'Okay.'

'The press will be outside your house and also at the club. It'll be easier to have our meeting in my car.' If she was feeling nervous before, she was terrified now. 'Come as soon as you can and don't speak to anyone.'

'All right.' She peeked through the blinds and saw the vans. Several young guys stood around with cameras, and a few smart young women in skirt suits had microphones at the ready. She prayed for rain. There were low grey clouds and it had been forecast.

Mel stormed out, furious and hollow.

'I'm sorry, no comment. Thank you.' She leapt into her car

and tried to calm the pace at which her heart pulsed. She hadn't eaten anything, her head was pounding and her stomach had contracted. She'd dressed in her smartest long-sleeved running clothes as a guise. When she slotted her car into reverse, she could see them back away, but the young camera crews mobilised into action, hooked their cameras onto shoulders, and took awkward running steps after her. One reporter tried tapping on the window. Mel gave her a scowl and indicated for her to move away.

Once she was seated in Daniel's car, he gave her one of the papers to look at. 'It begins simply, the same words you told us, the same thing you told the police, but, for added colour, just towards the end of that section, it says,' and he read this part out to her, '"She indicated that she may have seen something that day, and when pressed, Ms Wilson said she may have seen Cam Robson with a second phone in his hand." Jesus fucking Christ, Mel, you never told us that! I gave you a job, I took you in, you signed a contract, and I trusted you. What were you doing with Pete McIver?'

She remembered precisely how it had happened. After a couple of wines a fortnight ago, she had told Pete what she thought she might have seen. He had pressed her in that way he had of making her talk; while he leaned back in his chair, his sexy body all loose and inviting. Later on, his lips were all over hers. It was the teaser evening to last night.

'I didn't mention it because I wasn't sure. I said I might have seen that. At first I thought it was a cigarette packet.' She tried to keep the tremor out of her voice.

'The report continues with hints about corruption in the clubs, money laundering, gambling, and the suggestion that the less-than-salubrious members of the international community are investing heavily into the code. I can't tell you how this positions our club in relation to this smear campaign. And we are involved in none of those things.' His voice spilled out, granite hard and loud.

'I met him before I met you that first day. I told him to shelve the conversation. He knew that I didn't want it used, I was firm about that, especially after meeting you and then signing the contract. He gave me his word. Over the last few months, we've been seeing each other.'

'It just gets better.'

'He's not often here. He only flew over once a fortnight for work. I told him what I had seen because I needed to tell someone. I told him it was unclear and likely to be inaccurate.' Now that her thoughts weren't clouded in a sensual miasma, she didn't know why she had confided in him.

'Why didn't you tell us?'

'I needed a job and I knew what you wanted.'

'How did it get out?'

'He must have made a note of what I told him and filed it with the report. His work computers and files are accessible to his editor. He mustn't have filed it very well.'

'Naïve and wrong. I heard he showed his editor to keep him off his back and said that it would come out soon. Editors are concerned with getting reports out while the public has an appetite for them. Timing is everything, so he printed it while Pete was on his back with you.'

She winced at that. 'What do you want me to do?'

'Nothing. You've done enough for us. I can't offer you severance, because the contract is null and void now. You have some sick days and a small number of pro-rata holiday days that you'll be paid for. We are in a mess because you couldn't close your mouth or legs. I'm sorry, but you have no idea how this is going to look for our club, and my job has just become a twenty-four-hour one.' He opened the door for her to step out.

She leaned and spoke to him through his opened window. 'I did nothing wrong here except maybe sign up with you. I think that was my real mistake. I agree, I should have said what I thought I'd seen. Goodbye, Daniel.'

When he drove off she sat in her car, pale and shaken.

Chapter Twenty-two

'Mum?'

'Mel? I've seen the paper. How are you?' Rosemary Jane Cruthers didn't view her daughters through rose-coloured glasses, and never ceased to offer advice whether it was solicited or not, but she would defend them with her last breath.

'Can I come around?'

'Yes, you know you can.'

'See you in half an hour.'

She parked on the road in front of the house and almost cried at the familiar figure of her tall elderly mother by the opened front door. She raced in. Beside her mother on the sofa, Mel wept. Her mother fetched two mugs of tea and sat with an arm around her.

'I've lost everything, including my job.'

'No you haven't.'

She held onto a fistful of tissues and spoke in a strained voice. 'Mum, I made a financial mess of myself with a stupid investment that compromised the house. Yes, I have lost everything. What is everyone going to think? The great heroine of the day has been sleeping with a newspaper reporter, and, what a coincidence, she was offered a position in the same club Cam Robson plays for. The press, already buzzing both with my statement and at the hinted link to corruption, will go into overdrive when they know of my relationship with Pete. People are going to draw their own unsavoury conclusions about me. I had no idea what I was getting myself into. I'll lose people's trust, credibility, respect, and God knows what

Jack and Lil will think.' She leaned against her mother's thin shoulders.

'They're more interested in the allegations about the clubs. They're not interested in your relationships, or your employers. I don't think they'll pursue that line.'

'You're kidding, right? This is a bit like public flogging. There'll always be people out there keen to read about it, so long as it's not them. They'll drop that in as soon as they have confirmation of it.'

'Mel, you're stronger than this. Give an interview and give it right back to them. Tell them the truth.'

'I'm not like that. I can't stand this.'

'Phone that man...'

'Pete?'

'Yes, phone him and tell him you'll sue him for breach of confidence. Make it up if you have to. Get him to secure your information and deny everything about your friendship with him.'

'That would be easy if there wasn't security film footage of us in about seven restaurants around town.'

'He manipulated you, preyed on a vulnerable divorced parent. What about that line?'

'He did and I am. Nothing surprising in that. I think I'll lie down for a while.'

'It won't be as bad as you think, I'm sure of it.'

Mel gave her mother a tight hug and wandered towards one of the spare bedrooms.

'You always worry too much, my darling,' her mother said. Mel paused by the bedroom door.

'I wish I had your calm easy grace, Mum,' Mel said. 'I guess I take after Aunty Lola in more than just looks, hey?'

Her parents had often told her she was like Aunty Lola, but she'd never met her. What was this aunty really like? Too late now, she'd died apparently.

Unexpectedly, a distant memory pushed its way to the forefront of her mind. It was the only time she remembered there being any discord between her parents.

It was when Mel was about four and only her sister, Georgie, went to school. Her mother would take Mel to Mr Angelopoulos's store to buy their groceries. Her mother didn't know that Mel could see her and the grocer from where she stood on a fruit crate. As they weighed items on the shiny steel scales, Mel watched her mother trail slender fingers over Mr Angelopoulos's upturned wide fleshy palms.

'Mum, did you have a thing with Mr Angelopoulos?' Mel said, suddenly wanting to know.

Her mother's face pinked and she became still. 'Why do you ask?'

'I saw your hand on his at the shop one day.'

'Oh. I was going to tell you anyway.'

'Tell me what?' She walked back towards the sofa and sat down. Her mother blew her nose. 'Did you have an affair?'

'Yes. But I was saying goodbye when you saw me. He and his family were headed to New South Wales where his brothers had bought some land. They were going to establish orchards and large-scale market gardens.'

'There's something else isn't there?' Mel pushed, a strange understanding dawning on her. 'I'm not like Aunty Lola, am I? I'm like him.'

'Mel, it isn't what you think. We'd finished before you were born. It was a brief relationship and he was a lovely man.'

'I can't understand why you wouldn't tell me about my real father. Any wonder I don't fit in. It would have helped so much to know where I came from, it would have made a real difference.' Her loud, heated voice hung in the air. Her mother's face collapsed.

'I'm so sorry, but I promised Michael I'd never tell you because he adored you. Your father and I married late in life. We struggled to fall pregnant and we wanted another child straight after Georgie because I wasn't young. We had difficulties.'

'What was wrong?'

'I loved your dad and he was my best friend, but I think if he'd been born today he wouldn't have married a woman.'

'He was gay?'

'He was in nature but not in practice. He tried a few medical solutions but gave up. He stayed with me because he loved me in his way, and he idolised both of you.'

'I can't imagine him like that. That would've been very hard for you and for him. Is that why you fell for Mr Angelopoulos?'

'He delivered the fruit and vegetables during the day. We both felt guilty and it lasted less than two months.'

'Do you regret it?'

'No. I desperately wanted another child, but of course I never thought it would be with someone else. Your dad wasn't surprised because of how he was, but he was hurt. The absolute thrill of being a father again won out and we worked at our marriage. Our friendship endured where many marriages broke up.'

Mel remembered the numerous occasions when she'd sit with her father on the bleachers watching Georgie play netball or swim in competitions; her pudgy olive-skinned arm against his lean fair, freckled one.

'Is he alive?' She knew she should feel greater astonishment at the surprising revelation, but the dull ache of the weekend's news had deadened the impact.

'He passed away a few years ago and I was going to give you this at some point. Perhaps it's that time now.' She noticed for the first time that her mother's gait had become laboured and she struggled to push herself up from the sofa. Mel winced at this deterioration and at her lack of awareness of it. Her mother stepped over to the cabinet and retrieved an envelope from a drawer.

'By the time he passed away he had quite an estate to leave to his wife and children, and you were bequeathed a small portion. They phoned me to get your details because Christos had stated that he wanted it sent to me to give to you, when I saw fit.'

She looked at the large creamy envelope and then at her mother's face.

'It's okay, it was so long ago,' her mother said.

'I'm sorry for your loss,' Mel said, and wrapped her arms tight around her mother. 'I bet you haven't shared this and it must have been hard, carrying that burden for so long. He always seemed like a generous man to me when I was young.' Tears streamed down her mother's soft, lined face. 'I still love you, Mum.'

She could feel her mother's eyes follow her hands as they opened the seal. She drew out the letter drawn up by the solicitor, and within it she was named as one of many beneficiaries from the estate of Mr Christos Angelopoulos. The cheque slid out and she saw several zeroes.

'Seventy-five thousand dollars, you're kidding.'

'I wanted this to be special for you and that's why I waited. It could be a deposit on a small place?' Her mother blew her nose again.

Mel watched her mother; with her dad long gone and Christos deceased, her mother must have begun releasing her hidden store of memories.

'I'll leave it here with you and bank it later.' She sat for a little while, still in shock. The cheque gave her a tiny flicker, a small seed of hope, and she sat in the lounge room holding her mother's hand for a bit longer. She had more immediate concerns than a biological father to deal with.

'I need to phone Tony,' she told her mum.

'Go ahead, love.'

Mel steeled herself in preparation as she located her phone. 'Tony, hi. Yes, I have seen the papers.' She was relieved to discover that journalists had been fleshing out information on similar issues in other sports. Maybe, she hoped, she wouldn't be of any importance. 'I'll bring everything around to your house at five. Is that okay? It'll only be until Friday. Thanks.' She hung up and turned to her mum.

'Mum, I'm going to drive back home and collect a pile of things. After I see the bank and the house is sold, the children and I will need a place to stay for a while.'

'You know you can stay here.'

'Thank you.' They had almost emptied one tissue box between them.

'How about I make an early lunch?'

'Sounds perfect.'

She hoped the sale would cover the mortgage, the loan she took out on the shares, and leave enough to add to the amount from Christos for a deposit on a home. Were there homes that cheap?

She wanted to spend time with her children first and sort everything out before looking for a job. It didn't feel right to be her age and marooned.

Chapter Twenty-three

'Mel, you know you can come and spend time up here anytime you want.'

'Thanks Jill. I needed to talk to someone.'

'Do you want me to come down?'

'No. I've got a lot to do and just knowing that you know is a great help.'

'On another note, I heard Mark dropped by a while ago,' Jill teased.

'He did, but if he reads the newspapers I don't think he'll come around again. Anyway, it seems like he's busy with Dylan and fishing.'

'He's got a lot going on in his life. I'll leave that for him to tell you about. How are the kids?'

'They seem fine. Jack will probably disown me once the house is sold and she decides I'm a lame parent. Lil will be devastated to have to move in with her grandma because it's cramped and she'll have to share a room with me. Can't wait to share this special time with them!' She tried not to let the anxiety take over.

'Kids are tough and it's only temporary,' Jill's voice was all calm confidence, and Mel wished she had some of it. 'I can see you getting yourself into a much better place, once you find a new job. And what a start, a biological father who left you with something more than your olive skin and wavy mane.'

'I feel like such a stupid idiot, but thanks for your support.'

As soon as she hung up, a text from Jack appeared on her screen. *Check out the news, Mum.*

Mel quickly logged on the internet and scanned the daily newspaper. There was a report on Mitchell. It stated that he'd been knocked over by a child who ran into him at school. In the melee, he'd lost his crutch, banged his head on an aluminium bench and then cracked his skull on the concrete path. He was in a coma in hospital with a blood clot on the brain, and the report said that it was unclear whether the blood clot was from that accident or from his previous collision.

Mel rested her head in her arms and closed her eyes. She couldn't move for a few minutes.

Chapter Twenty-four

Over the following months, Mel put the house on the market and explained about her loss of employment to Wendy Bruker at the bank. Wendy encouraged her to consider other alternatives, but without a job it was too risky. She gave herself one school term to find employment and make headway with a plan for her life. It looked easy written down as a goal on a piece of paper she had attached to her mother's fridge.

When she dropped by her house to collect clothes after the first couple of days of the initial newspaper article, the media had stopped hanging around. She ignored calls from anyone she didn't know. The papers stated that Mitchell was still in a coma and that a court case was imminent, but there was no further mention of his condition.

She packed the house and resisted her mother's offer of help with the cleaning. The removalists took the bulk of their possessions to a cheap storage facility, leaving only a few things to take to her mother's diminutive home. When it was empty, Mel tried not to run her hands over the walls in each of the children's rooms.

Lil loved all the time Mel was able to give her both at school and at home. In contrast, Jack was scathing of her losing their home and of being with Pete. She'd had to tell the children everything to prepare them, in case anything further was released. Both children were less than impressed at having to share their grandmother's small house but enjoyed having their grandma around. Mel's mother took the edge off the new reality.

With a soft thud Saturday's paper ricocheted along the

driveway. Her mother had driven over to Georgie's house to be with the boys and would remain there until the evening to enable Georgie and Dave to work on a large government event.

The familiar sound roused Mel and was followed by the intrusion of the alarm on her phone. Fingertips of light lit up the room as it burst through chinks in the roughly drawn curtains and a bright-skied morning lured her out. Saturdays usually began with a jog along the beach, but with Lil still asleep in the room with her, she crept out to collect the paper.

A cool, fresh brightness in the air made her gather her dressing gown tight as she whipped out and raced back in. Lil's netball team had no game this week and Jack's match would be on in the afternoon. She relished the peaceful hush and put the kettle on.

A photo on page seven of her attending to Mitchell made her put her cup down with a bang. It was linked to the upcoming court case of Cam Robson. She scoured the article but found no connection to her and the club or to her and Pete. How long, she wondered, would she be put through the agony of waiting to see whether that would crop up in the news? Every morning she felt the lightness growing, but it didn't take much to wind back into the fear and unease of being exposed to the public eye.

With a steamy cup in one hand, she swiped through the employment listings on her iPad, though she felt her hope of finding some nameless opportunity ebb away. She ran her eyes over the last of the employment choices, closed it down and picked up the paper again to glance at the headlines. She shoved it to one side and held her head in her hands; she didn't want the children to be confronted by the image in the paper. The classifieds slipped out on the way to the recycling bin. To support her mother's recent purchase of a compost bin, she brought that section inside for the peelings. With a second cup of tea, she browsed through the properties, none of which were within her price range.

It was her turn to provide the fruit tray for Jack's team. She grabbed the bowl of apples and oranges and began peeling them. Spreading out the paper to catch the peels, she cast an eye over the listings in the 'businesses for sale' section. Curls of apple skin dropped onto the paper.

One business caught her interest, mainly because of its price. It was an advertisement for a postal service at Pelican Point. She pushed the peel away to study the short notice. It said that it had to follow the standard rules of the postal-service agreement; she had no idea what they were, but that was incidental to what really held her attention. She'd been in that area for holidays when she was a young child. She remembered the air thick with the eucalypt spice of the ancient forests, and the wild windy coastal strip. Its distance from the city and cool climate kept most people away. The actual postal store was in a region a bit further south. When she looked it up on the web, she noticed it was located on an inlet shaped like a horseshoe.

To even think about it was preposterous as she knew nothing about running her own business, but she couldn't stop her eyes from locking on it. She pulled out scissors from a kitchen drawer and cut out the advertisement. Her stomach fluttered and a minute tendril of excitement flooded her body.

With the money she had from the sale of the house, about fifty thousand dollars, and the money from Christos, she figured she could secure a loan. It said it had reasonable annual earnings. They couldn't state what they were, but it would be easy to check and she could at least inquire. A nagging voice insisted that Jack and Lil would not welcome the idea of moving, yet she couldn't stop herself.

She rang the number. A viewing was organised for the following weekend.

Chapter Twenty-five

'But, Mel darling, it's so far away from Jack's school,' her mother said.

'I know Mum.'

'You've never actually run a business.'

'I realise that.'

'You could lose everything.'

'Not quite.'

'You could.'

'Not sure how you figure that.' Mel huffed out a frustrated breath.

'By getting yourself into serious debt, of course.'

'I know. Been there, done that. I need to,' she cringed as she said, 'move forward into a new situation and see what I can really do. I need to make some changes to my life.' She found she was talking to herself. Her mother looked unmoved.

'It sounds like you'll be working full-time and then there's Lil...'

'There's a fabulous school close by. I've done a bit of research, Mum.'

'Oh Mel, I don't know.'

'Guess what? I don't either, but I'm scared about staying here and never finding out. I'm old enough. We both know there's not much I can afford.'

'I'll miss you.'

Mel drew her in and hugged her tight. 'I haven't gone yet and they could have sold it already. Stop with the dramatics.'

'Okay.' Her mother brightened. 'Yes, it might already be sold.'

Mel gave her a look.

'For you, obviously I hope it hasn't.'

'I can see you crossing your fingers behind your back. Anyway, there might be a spare room and you can come to visit and maybe help me. What do you think?'

'I'm not young.'

'Isn't eighty the new seventy? Let's get Lil from school. Tony has them this weekend so I'll drive down tomorrow.' She squeezed her mother's hand when she saw the little pinch lines cross her brow.

Chapter Twenty-six

With the radio on and a long country drive ahead, Mel relaxed. A growing thrill took over her body. Although she was completely unsure about the whole prospect, she enjoyed the sense of abandonment. It was like the first day of a holiday as a kid, when the day could hold such promise because a whole unchartered territory lay before you and your body hopped on the inside. It never felt like that as an adult, but today that's exactly how she was feeling.

With a mouth full of apple, she sang wildly along to an old rock song on the radio but it soon gave up to crackle when she reached the halfway mark. She'd never bothered downloading any music on her phone and now wished she had. She was about to fling the core out of the window when a white four-wheel drive cruised by. It was only for the briefest of moments, but she thought the silhouetted shape in the driver's seat looked like Mark. Although, with window tinting, sunglasses, and the speed at which he passed, it could have been any man in a similar age range. She pushed the thought aside and made a pact with herself not to consider men for a while.

She chose to listen to someone ramble about the price of wool, wheat and other farm produce, instead of allowing the soupy mix of furious thoughts she'd been having about Pete and the media to crowd her mind. She hoped the long drive would give her time to file them away.

It was a few hours later when she pulled into the major town of Bettong. After ten minutes on a side road, she arrived at the small community of Pelican Point. She parked in a bay facing an inlet and felt a shiver of pleasant delight when she stepped out of the car. It had more natural wilderness than the photos on the web had shown. A flat blue inlet basked in the midday spring sun. It was, as the pictures had shown, a huge horseshoe shape with gently sloping hills behind it. A large hill or small mountain was on the left flank of the inlet, poised like a gargantuan sentry. She faced out towards the ocean entrance on the low sandy edge of the right side.

It had the sleepy beach-town flavour she remembered, like other places from her childhood, places now flooded with wineries and punctuated with development. Their laid-back seaside atmosphere long gone as few could afford the kind of housing that now replaced the shacks of her childhood. She stood transfixed by the natural rawness and splendour, entranced by the juxtaposition of the impossibly calm bay, and beyond, the outer rumble of reef ripped rolling tubes.

She turned to walk across the main street, where tucked on the corner, a rather small, unimposing and shadowy building sat. A bright-red door lit up the plain look of tired bricks. This was the postal store. Presumably, the house lay behind it. Along a dusty red-brick wall, two small but long windows sat. The whole building wasn't much wider than a double garage. A worn cherry-red door was propped open behind a grimy flywire door, and when she stepped inside, it creaked and sprang back with a loud clanging ping.

Inside, the walls were uniform creamy white and freshly painted. It was festooned with the usual postal paraphernalia, with white shelves and mountings along the wall. Small box-shaped tables held goods for sale. There was the ubiquitous grey counter with all of the stationery, accessories and technology for efficient service. Behind the counter sat the owner of two enormous ginger eyebrows sheltering pale-blue eyes, and they were divided by a sunburnt thick nose held in place by a jowly freckled face. It took her by surprise. 'You'd be Mel?'

His voice broke her study of the place. 'Yes I am. Are you Mr Terence Robertson?'

'Call me Red.'

'Red, hello. I made it.'

'We've had a few offers, just so you know.' A woman appeared beside Red and gave Mel a nod.

'This is my wife, Joy.'

'Pleased to meet you,' Mel said, all the while thinking, *damn*.

'But we've not settled yet. The wife's a bit tired of,' Red waved his hand around to drive home the point, 'working and everything.'

'I see.'

'I want to move, to be near the grandchildren.' Joy wiped over a counter and stood, hesitant.

'To Perth?'

'No, to Bettong. I'll see you inside, I've got a few things to do.' She scuttled through an open back door.

Mel thought it was strange to want to move about ten kilometres away to Bettong. Pelican Point looked like a place for retirees, although she understood the tiredness. You had to stop work sometime.

Red and Joy, she sensed, were keener than they wanted her to believe. She was conscious not to appear eager about the sale, despite their statements of others being interested. She had a feeling that she was the only one who had actually come with intent. However, it hadn't been on the market long and anyone looking for a small coastal business was sure to snap it up.

'The books show a decent turnover,' she said, to begin gathering more information about the place.

'Yes it does well. Of course it can be quiet sometimes, but it gets busy during Christmas and all of the other celebration times. The regular business of the postal service is what drives the income.'

'I see.' The business was closed on Saturday afternoons and they had opened it only to show her. When she looked about, she thought she could make improvements to the overall look.

'There's talk of a boom down here. A new estate will be ready soon. You would have seen the signs on your drive down? That's to match the new college they built a few years back.'

'I might have, but I was pretty tired by then.'

'Anyway, that means plenty more people wandering around town and this is the only store so far, apart from the café at the caravan park.'

'That's great.'

'This shop has exclusive access to the tourists and there aren't plans to build any more. I had it checked out when I bought it several years ago.'

'A new estate usually has a brand-new shopping complex built right in the centre of it,' Mel said.

'Yes, but who likes complexes? This has a unique location and exclusive rights to the customer market.'

'How so?'

'They can't build any more shops down here because of restrictions around the coastal environment. This used to be the general store. It has rights to sell whatever the owner decides, as long as it doesn't offer the same as any existing shop, and of course, there aren't any existing shops, apart from the café. If I was younger, I'd be doing a lot more with this store, but with my arthritis and with Joy being needed by our daughter for the grandchildren, we have to hand it over to someone else.'

Mel listened to Red describe the stock, the town and the trade.

'There are a few decent-sized storerooms out back. Come and take a look.'

It was deceptive. From the front it looked small, but she could see that if more room was needed the walls in the storerooms could be knocked down, except she didn't have any money for renovations. She thought the overly crowded storefront could be made better use of.

'These storerooms are largely empty.'

'Since we hope to sell, we didn't want to stock them with too much. In the next few weeks all the Christmas stock will arrive and you should see how it fills up then. We're always surprised at how much walks out the door over Christmas.'

From what she'd seen, it didn't look like Red and Joy were selling anything that exciting, but Christmas would be their peak period. Mel knew what would be stocked. She'd always enjoyed browsing in her own local post office around Christmas time.

'May I take a look at the house?'

'Of course. It's an old house and we aren't home renovators.'

Since reading the advertisement, she had steeled herself to have low expectations about the condition of the house.

'Hi, come on in,' Joy told her.

Mel could smell the blossoms of star jasmine that clung to the side palings of the timber fence, and noted other small shrubs spearing the spring air with buds and blossoms of native and other species. She recognised a few plants.

The house was a different matter. Her nose ran almost immediately and she sneezed several times, lunging into her bag for the small tissue packet.

'Oh dear, it must be our cats. Sorry Mel, we have two inside cats.'

'It's okay,' she said between sneezing and blowing her nose. Her eyes became itchy and her nose ran, but she'd never had that kind of reaction before. It may have been because there were two of them, or maybe because the house needed a lot more fresh air. As they walked through the entrance to the lounge room, the afternoon sun entered in skinny shafts between the blinds and lit up the dust motes. It smelled musty and light didn't reach most of the interior.

'Would you like a cup of tea?' Joy was keen to bustle around. The house was full of oversized modern furniture.

She wanted to say no. 'I'd love one thanks, Joy.'

'As you can see,' Red said, 'the previous owners did up the big bathroom and toilet a while ago, but not the kitchen.'

'It's nice.' She struggled to find a sufficient word for the apricot-tiled bathroom. The paintwork was something that could be attacked and in budget, but not the kitchen. The bedrooms were basic and roomy, crammed with Red and Joy's beds and drawers.

She finished her tea and they sat around the kitchen table. The vinyl floor and carpets didn't match the earnest bones of the 1940s brick home where timber floorboards lay beneath.

'So,' said Red, 'what do you think?'

What did she think? Even though she liked it all she wanted more time. She'd planned to drive back straightaway but at the last minute had thrown in a small overnight bag.

'Would it be all right if I slept on it and came around tomorrow morning before I head back?'

They didn't look that happy. 'You do what you need to do. The caravan park at the Point has little chalets, if they're not all booked out with the retirees.'

'I'm very interested and would like first offer. Can I come see you both tomorrow at about ten?'

Joy took over for a minute. 'Certainly. You need to think it over. It's a big decision for you.'

'Thank you for showing me around. I'll see you tomorrow.'

Chapter Twenty-seven

A buxom, well-groomed and attractive woman about her age greeted Mel when she checked into the caravan park. 'Hi, how can I help you?'

'I'd like a room for the night in one of your chalets, please.'

'Sure. They're not five star but they're fine. On your own?'

'Yes.'

She gave her a sly grin. Her skin glowed with a light tan and her eyes were round, blue and warm. 'I'm not prying, there's an extra cost if there is someone else.'

'I understand.' Mel smiled back.

She pushed over a form for her to fill in. 'Down here for business?'

'Yes.'

'The post office?'

How did she know? She couldn't very well lie to her. 'Sort of.'

She laughed and her whole body moved in a gentle wave, sending out a tiny wash of perfume. 'It's okay, I saw you step around the side of the house as I drove past this afternoon. Everyone knows it's on the market and there isn't a great deal of other business going on down here. Here,' she said as she reached down and pulled out a bottle of red wine, 'you'll need this if you're doing business with Red and Joy. Friendly enough people, though I think they didn't exactly have their heart in it. New blood will be welcome.'

'I haven't made my mind up yet, and thank you, but I can't take this wine from you.'

'Yes you can. I'll have a glass with you in a minute. I don't normally work here.'

'Oh?' She handed back the form.

'No. I own it, but my manager is off sick this afternoon. Come on, I'll take you down to your unit. My name is Sally and I can see by the form that yours is Mel. Welcome to Pelican Point.'

'Thanks.'

As they wandered down the path, Mel discovered that Sally had a daughter the same age as Lil. Her daughter attended the local new school and loved it.

'I can't stay long.' Sally pulled up a vinyl chair and grabbed two glasses. 'I'll only have half a glass because I've got to work a bit longer. What about you?'

'I'll have the same.'

'Here's to your decision.' They toasted and took a sip. 'If you do decide to come down, give me a call, we'll have coffee.'

'That would be great. You own this?'

'We have a house in town and we have another caravan park out by the river. We do the books, Brian and I. I've lived around this area all my life. Brian is the import from the big smoke, but we forgive him.' She drained her glass. 'I'd better make a move to the front desk, although I think you should enjoy another glass with dinner. I think you'll need it to help with your decisions. I hope to see you around.'

'Thank you Sally. I'll call you if I move down and thanks a lot for the wine and company.'

'No problem. The manager should be in tomorrow, but if not, just drop the keys into the slot in the front door.'

'Okay.' Sally left. Her waves of thick blonde hair bounced just lower than her neckline and the elegant shirt and long flowing skirt suited her frame. Mel stood in her wake. If she moved down, there was now one person she knew. She pulled out the documents and examined them again. A slight shiver ran through her when she considered the enormity of the decision she faced.

She lay on the bed to rest her eyes. A couple of hours later she sat bolt upright, disorientated, and squinted around at the chalet. Seconds later, the mental fug cleared and she realised where she was. The coolness of the late afternoon made her throw on jeans and a long-sleeved sweater. She hoped a walk around the inlet on foot would give her a feel for the flavour of the town.

She loved late afternoons. Only a few wanderers and idle cyclists intervened between the view of sand on one side and the blue-green mountainous headland on the other. The inlet lay between, heavy, quiet, a silken cobalt mat, shadowed by passing clouds. It seemed like the expanse between was swimmable, but distances on water could be deceptive.

She followed the curve of the horseshoe in towards the inlet, and was again captivated by the sheer majesty of its size and the beauty of its undulating backdrop. The calm, glassy water ticked a low beat of small waves that broke softly against her feet. Small groups of pelicans glided past, and as she wandered further along, she saw the marked boards where they had chosen to flock. A small floating jetty with a tether of fishing vessels struck out from the sandy edge. Pelicans sat behind the locked mesh-wire door on the other side, at home with the sardine flavour of the boats.

On the left side of the jetty was a sculpture. It was a blue whale reduced to about half scale. The artist had positioned it semi-submerged, near the fishing jetty. A plaque stood on the shoreline documenting that an anonymous benefactor had both commissioned and donated it to the community of Pelican Point. A short dedication called for conservation and preservation of wild places for marine creatures. It was in an entirely different class to other town sculptures she had seen.

Further along, few in number and small in size, was a clatter of sheds. She presumed it was to ensure they didn't detract from the view. A timber cabin housed a small boat shop with a smattering of watercraft for sale and hire, behind a secure fence. The other buildings had similar chain-mail fences secured with padlocks, and all shed doors were closed. She imagined the inlet would be busy and colourful with all the little boats in summer. The sandy shore decreased in size as it gave way to small bays and personal jetties. Well behind, on the road that wrapped around the perimeter, sat an assortment of houses.

An hour had passed. She reasoned she had another hour of light and headed back the way she had come. Little evidence of the marine life below could be detected on the shoreline. Out beyond the mouth of the inlet and to the left, she saw the signs of a surf break. Great hammering waves bit into the flank of the headland and the white wash of foam formed a brilliant frill hard against the vibrant blue. Binoculars would be needed to get a clear view from where she stood.

Small children squealed at the water's edge; the only intrusion in the quiet air. She could imagine the tease of cold water against their warm bodies, fired with the thrill and temptation of falling in.

A lone fisherman stood on the rocks near her chalet at the mouth of the inlet.

'Hi.' Mel smiled at him in greeting.

'Hi. Herring aren't biting today, dolphins probably scared them away.'

'Too bad.'

'Still, I'll come back tomorrow.'

'Is it a good fishing spot?'

'Not especially. I have better ones I drive to, but I live close by. I spend one week on the mines and one week here, feeding the fish.' He smiled.

'A great way to unwind on your week off.'

'Exactly, one day I'll be here full-time.' He closed the tackle lid, spun in his line and attached the hook to the rod. 'Bye.' He waved before he gathered up his equipment and left.

'See you.' She paused by the rocks to take in the dying light of the tangerine sun as it slipped into the sea between two islands further out. They were mountainous looking, like the headland.

Her stomach announced that it was time for dinner and she winced at the thought of driving into Bettong. Pelican Point only had the nine-to-five café. In the chalet, she located the visitor's guide for restaurants and fast-food outlets.

It was dark by the time she arrived back with her dinner and sat down at the diminutive dinner table. Once she had consumed her meal, she re-examined the ledger. She wouldn't become rich, but it appeared she could eke out a decent living.

Several texts and missed calls were on her phone. She phoned her children for a quick chat but wasn't going to fill them in on the plans until she'd signed up. Her mother had left a message wishing her well with her decision. Her sister's text said that they were hosting Christmas and asked that she call back to discuss it. Georgie liked her events organised well in advance, and she could almost hear the clack of heels and strident voice rattling off the 'to do' lists through the text's command. There was also a missed call from Pete. There was nothing she wanted to say to him that was in any way civilised.

Her eyes became bleary examining and reconfiguring the budget scenarios. She brainstormed the consequences of a move to Pelican Point. In its favour she wrote: on beach front—love beach, own hours, Lil's new school, own boss, role model for children, new start, not rubber balling, could have Jack for whole holidays, can eat fish that I catch—possibly, relearn boat-handling skills, close to stunning natural environment, rural and relaxing. The negatives she listed were: Jack at school in the city—I will miss her, have never run business—may not understand how, could fail, could get into debt, would have Mum say 'I told you so' ad infinitum, confirm feeling about lack of business acumen, could be insular town that excludes single mums, naively purchase infested property that slowly sinks below earth, Lil could hate me forever because of leaving friends. Then she considered the possibilities: could be a great change to our whole life, could meet new friends, will learn how to run a business and other skills, potential for unplanned exciting things—but she couldn't think of any specific exciting things.

Tony, she knew, would need to be consulted due to access agreements. Rumour had it that they were thinking about trying for a baby and she figured that could work in her favour. She felt no closer to a solution. When she lay in the bed, her body slumped into the basic but clean linen and her breathing slowed.

Chapter Twenty-eight

The next morning, Mel's weary mind yearned for another eight hours of sleep and it was too befuddled to contemplate an answer. The morning light on the landscape, tinged with peachy-rose hues, even found its way through the salt-etched windows of the chalet. She tugged on shoes and went outside. To be a hundred metres from the water's edge sent a quiver of excitement throughout her body.

The dedicated pathway on the right that ran all the way through to Bettong, was filled with walkers and cyclists, and on the left, it snaked away to follow the scalloped edge of the inlet. She saw several joggers take that route. She chose the Bettong way, with the idea that she would jog a couple of kilometres along it and turn back around. The risen sun glanced over the backdrop of hills to reveal a panorama of exposed granite patches and green forest. Further in that forest, she had walked amongst ancient tall trees with her parents when she was small.

Along the Bettong route, the open ocean was gentle, cornered by a protective bay. Less than a kilometre straight out from there, as well as all the way past the inlet opening on the left, she could see the untamed southern ocean. The further she jogged along the path the more overgrown it became. Towering bushes joined up overhead and shut out the light and she shuddered at its unfamiliarity. She turned to strike out to the beach and continued her run on the sand.

On the way back, she caught a glimpse of something in the ocean. Silver trevally burst through the waves. Several silky grey fins broke the surface behind them; spouts exhaled and puffs of fishy breath were taken, leaving skinny plumes of mist. It was a small pod of dolphins. A few people on their morning ritual paused to view the display. In response to some instinctive signal, the dolphins stopped fishing in the waves and swam further out. Their time below the surface lengthened. She could only just make them out as they continued to track towards the inlet. Circular waves were all they left in their wake.

The same fisherman from yesterday stood balanced on the rocks.

'Hi again. Still no bites?' Mel called.

'No, a few nibbles, but it's a bit like meditation this time of the morning.'

'It sure is.'

She took in the light cloud dusting softly against the blue sky. With the morning's exercise, she felt crisp, awake and eager to be doing something.

'Come for a coffee?' She must have made a funny face because he quickly added, 'I don't mean anything by it.'

'No, but thanks,' she said gently. 'I'm going to jog on a bit more and then head back. If you're still here, I'll join you then.'

'I probably will be.'

'Okay. See you soon.'

After her run, she waved and caught up with him and wondered if it was wise to accept a coffee with a complete stranger. He was a solidly built young man with a small bushy beard. He didn't look threatening.

'Hi there Brad.' The waitress at the café greeted him.

'Hi Stephanie, can I have the usual and...?'

'I'll have a latte, thanks.'

'Sure, be ready soon.'

'I come here for breakfast most days when I'm back from a tour up north. What are you doing here?'

'I'm looking at an investment.'

'That sounds interesting. I'm on my last leave day. It's a long couple of flights to where I'm headed tomorrow, but they pay so well it means my home will be paid off soon.' He stirred sugar into his coffee.

'So what's it like to live here, in your alternate week?' Mel asked.

'I like it. It's peaceful, but I'm not married yet and I don't have children. I guess it would change then. Do you?'

'Children yes, marriage not anymore.'

'Having children means you would meet a lot more people than me. I have friends from a fishing club.'

'Are there any problems around town?'

'None come to mind. The closest police station is in Bettong and there isn't much need for them out here.'

'That's good to hear.'

'It's hard to describe. I spend my time off heading down four-wheel-drive tracks to get to remote fishing spots. I feel removed from the problems going on elsewhere in the world when I'm here.'

'What about the locals? Is it a friendly kind of place?'

'There's a lot of older people and they seem to know each other. It's hard to say how friendly though because I haven't lived in many other places. I guess I'm friendly.' He raised his eyebrows at her as he drained his coffee. 'I know Bettong has a small youth problem, but I read that they're establishing a marine college and an agricultural research centre. I don't know that much about it.'

'That sounds promising.'

'I think they're anticipating the building will take a few years.'

'What about around Pelican Point? Do you know if anything is planned for here?' She hoped not, at least not until she could properly establish the business.

'There is that new estate near the college and a new shopping complex tipped to be built in a couple of years. I get all my news from the local paper. Who knows how accurate it is.'

If only he knew. 'I heard the same from some people I was chatting to.'

'How long have you been here?'

'Only since about lunchtime yesterday.'

'On the other hand, there are people like me who love the

place and want it to stay this way. I happen to know that some landowners with money are snapping up any property available to slow down development.'

'That's interesting.'

'It's not an exciting place and can be too quiet. You have to make your own entertainment.'

'Like inviting strangers for coffee?'

'Exactly. Plus you're about thirty years younger than most of the women I greet on their walks and jogs.'

'I think you're being generous about my age and I'm glad you asked me for coffee. It's tricky when you don't know a place.' He had no idea how attractive it sounded. She started to imagine a life where the roar of the ocean replaced the drone of traffic, and where possums, instead of the press, might hang around your home. She pushed her chair in. 'Thanks, Brad.'

'Bye Mel, and good luck with whatever you decide.'

She had already decided, and when she told Red and Joy, they struggled to suppress their delight. Their obvious happiness was understandable, but nonetheless she felt niggles of anxiety as she frowned into the rear-view mirror in the car on the drive home. The small matter of explaining this to her ex-husband and children wasn't something she looked forward to. However, she was resolute. The deal had been struck.

There was a lot she needed to achieve before she could leave. She itemised the numerous tasks on the long drive but stopped when the list started to take on monumental proportions.

Chapter Twenty-nine

'I'm not going with you.' Jack's face was all belligerent teenager.

'Jack, I wasn't going to take you out of school. You'll get to stay here with your dad and Leah and attend school, but instead of going to Grandma's house, you'll fly down every second weekend. Lil will fly up every second weekend, too. Not much will change there.'

'What about sports?'

'Summer sports will be over when we move there, but you can fly down afterwards. I'll respect your decision if you choose not to come some weekends because there might be something you need to stay for. But you will be coming down. You'll be a bit like a boarder. I'll drive up for some events. You can let me know which ones you want me for and I'll do my best to get there.'

'If you hadn't been so stupid this would never have happened,' she sniped.

'Agreed, but that isn't for you to worry about. That's the downside of world economics.'

'That's not what I meant.'

'In that case, hold your tongue and remember I'm your mother and I have never let you down and I'm not about to start. Save your criticism, Jack, you're only fourteen. You have another seven more years at least of finding everything wrong with your parents.'

Mel wasn't sure if there was a slight movement from belligerence to a glint of a smile, but she'd take what she could. She left Jack scowling and plugged in. Lil was next. When she'd announced it as lightly as she could at the dinner table, Lil had fled into their shared room in an angry burst of tears and hadn't come out since. Her mother had driven over to Georgie's for the evening to allow Mel to have this private conversation.

She knocked on the door.

'Don't come in,' Lil yelled.

Mel stood by the door. 'Lil, it's my room too. You'll have your own room at Pelican Point and it's a nice big one. Maybe we could fit a small couch in for you and your friends.'

There was silence. Mel opened the door and saw Lil on her bed, clutching her bear. 'I don't have any friends down there.'

'Not yet.'

'Not ever!'

Mel refused to engage on that one. 'All your friends are moving on from school this year and will be going to different high schools and colleges. It's that time anyway. This is a good time for a move.'

'They're not leaving Perth.'

'I happen to know some are leaving for England, America and Indonesia. They have to, it's where their parents have work. Some are leaving for boarding schools, too.'

'I don't want to go.' She was sobbing and it was hard for Mel not to join in.

'Change is scary at first. I know you feel like this now, but we have to go. If you want to, you can look at the school online. It's pretty interesting and it has animals. If you do look it up, you'll see what I mean.' She left the room. She hoped the equestrian centre on site would create just the tiny spark of interest she hoped for.

She sat in the kitchen, her own doubts now doubled.

*

'You're just going to move down south?'

Mel had lined up a time with Tony when he came to collect the girls for the weekend, to sit and talk. The children had gone for a walk with her mum.

'You know why.'

'What will you do when Jack needs you?'

'I'll come if she needs me, of course. It's not perfect, but I'm giving this a go. I've got to build something for my future and the children's. I can't afford to do this in Perth, and you don't need to mention anything else because you can't make me feel any worse. I was hoping you'd understand. It won't change your time with the children because Lil will fly up to see you on your weekend and Jack will fly down for my weekend, after sports.'

'I don't like this idea. I hate the idea of Lil being down there.'

'I hate not being near Jack and being unable to secure a future for myself. There aren't many jobs here and real estate is beyond my means. Not everyone has a lot of choice.'

'You had some choices.'

'I've dealt with that, Tony, I don't need a reminder. I'm taking this chance to have my own business and it's a huge step for me. If I fail, you can do the loser dance.'

A brief flicker of a smile swept across both of their faces.

'I guess you've made your decision,' he said, his tone softening.

'Yes, but I wanted to talk. I know it'll be difficult in the beginning for you. I understand that, these are our children.'

'Difficult? You have no idea how I feel. When are you thinking of moving?'

'I'll head down in December for a week by myself to get to know the business. The children will come after school finishes, and then we'll revert to our usual Christmas holiday time split. I'll be back in Perth for Christmas Day. It's at Georgie and Dave's this year.'

'Right. Jack has that trip first.'

'Yes I do know about that. She'll come with me after Christmas.'

He was agitated when he left with the children.

'How did that go?' Her mother passed her a mug of hot chocolate.

'Oh super. He can see how I need this business to provide for my children now and in the future.'

'Not so well.'

'No. You know, I don't care. I'll just have to wear it. Ever since Lil's episode at the islands he's been more hostile. Something mustn't be going his way, but I've signed up and the bank details are being sorted this week. With Christos's money and the small residual from the house, I can get a loan for the rest based on the turnover.'

'I'm proud of you Mel.' Her mother placed a warm hand over hers. She stifled the welling of tears and pushed the image of the store and Pelican Point to the front of her mind.

Chapter Thirty

When it arrived, Mel was busy writing a list of jobs she had to get done that week. It was delivered in person to her at her mother's house. She felt the envelope and noticed the legal stamping. Her heart sank. She knew what it contained. She was to appear in court as a witness in two weeks.

*

On the morning she was due in court, Mel was sick with apprehension. Pete had texted to wish her luck. Everything attached to Pete made her feel raw and edgy. She told him to stop sending her texts.

Her feet found the snappy leather heels tight following the past couple of months in a variety of sports shoes. She continued to pace around on the wooden floors of the court. Since the accident, her life had taken a less-than-impressive path. She reflected on Jack's detachment, Lil's tears, and her own bundle of disasters. Perched on one of the varnished timber benches outside the courtroom, she examined the growing welts where the shoes bit into her flesh. When she pressed her shoulders back into the bench, she caught sight of Cam. She was ushered into a small room to wait for the time until she was called in.

*

Inside the courtroom, the prosecutor hammered Cam Robson.

'Was it true that you had alcohol in your blood?'

'No.'

'Did you take energy drinks with caffeine?'

'Yes.'

'Why?'

'Everyone does after a night out.'

'So you went out?'

'You know I did. It's in the records. I did drink but had finished drinking at about six in the morning.'

'A pretty big night out. Most people wouldn't drink that late.'

'We're not supposed to, and I was celebrating with some friends, not with my team.'

'It says here that you were incoherent and had your car keys confiscated. A close friend drove you home and you collected the car at about one in the afternoon. Is this correct?'

'Yes. But I was sober when I drove in the afternoon.'

'I put it to you that you were not in a fit state to drive.'

'That's not true!'

'Were you on your phone while driving?'

It was all conjecture. They had very little to pin on Cam. He slumped into his seat.

'It's bluetooth. I can talk and drive. Everyone does.' His voice was quiet.

'Was there another phone? It was printed in the paper that someone believed they had seen you kick it under your car?'

Cam's lawyer leapt to his feet. 'Conjecture, Your Honour. Nothing has been proven and we haven't heard from the witness.'

The whole court became more attentive. They watched as Cam sat in his chair, head bowed, not answering.

'Mr Robson, was there another phone?'

Cam straightened and looked around. 'Yes.' He was almost inaudible.

'Yes,' he restated, 'I had a phone and I was talking on it when I shouldn't have been. The accident was my fault.' He looked squarely at Mitchell's parents.

Michael Widdicombe picked up his phone and spoke into it quietly. Daniel Arnett blanched. Cam's lawyer dropped his head and rubbed his brow. Confusion took hold of both sides of the courtroom. A slow perplexed rumbling gave way to a growing din, but Mitchell's parents and Cam remained still and silent.

*

The court attendant told Mel what had happened and explained that she was no longer required. She felt queasy with the roiling and pitching in her stomach; she had intended to state that she did believe he had kicked a phone under the car. Mitchell was still in a coma after the fall at school, and the doctors didn't know if he'd ever recover.

Standing back with photographers and camera crew surrounding them were Mitchell's parents, and nothing the court could achieve would alter what was in store for Mitchell.

Chapter Thirty-one

Through some unexpected lining up of the planets, because Mel couldn't imagine what else it could have been, Tony phoned her and said that he thought he would cope with Lil living down south but would come down to be with her in her new environment from time to time. She was suspicious but grateful not to have his hostility needling her. Leah, she knew, would have had something to do with the decision. She wanted a baby and Tony all to herself, even though Jack would still be around. Jack, she knew, would disappear to friends' houses a lot, and that bothered her. Nothing would be easy.

Dates and jobs were ticked off. The swiftness of passing time didn't seem to reduce the inexorable list of tasks required for the move. The school took up her time with its share of end-of-year events. She was always astounded at the plethora of things children had to be in, organise, or take to school during the silly season.

She went to the storage unit with the removalists to collect the bulk of the furniture, before driving back to give them the smaller items from her mother's place. By the time the removal truck left, she collapsed on the spare bed. She was grateful that Lil and Jack had a week more of school and were staying with Tony because it gave her a week to work and learn the ropes from Red and Joy. She wouldn't have coped with disgruntled children and a new business in a new town.

'Mum, it'll be fine.' The worry lines on her mother's face the next morning matched what she felt in her heart. 'I'll phone when I arrive, or text if I'm very tired. Lil will call you if she needs anything that Tony can't organise. She'll be emotional.'

'It is a big move.'

'I need you on my side. This is harder than it looks.'

'I know. I don't think I could run a business. Drive safe, Mel.'

Mel stood and gripped her in a hug but she wouldn't risk speaking. She slipped into the driver's seat and waved; in the rear-view mirror she could see her tall frame planted on the verge, waving back at her. She blew her nose and wiped away her tears. What awaited her?

Chapter Thirty-two

The house looked neglected already. Red and Joy had moved into Bettong, straight into a new home in a new estate.

When she opened the door, her eyes itched and her nose ran, again. In Perth, she'd made the decision to postpone the removalist truck's arrival till she had a tradesman work on restoring all of the timber floors. She held onto the doorframe and pushed through her suitcase and blow-up mattress, but the whole house was a daunting prospect. Without Red and Joy's furniture she could see just how much work would be required to bring it back to a neat old home. After her initial visit and signing over with the bank, she had phoned to secure the service of a tradesman who specialised in stripping and sealing timber floors. He would arrive after her first day at work and give her a quote. She had told him to be prepared to start straightaway. She didn't want to poison the children with fumes.

She couldn't wait to remove the cat smell from the carpets and window fixtures. The dull grey lace curtains emitted a strong mustiness, and could easily be removed. Decent timber blinds lay behind them. They would have to do. The walls would require extensive painting. The pink, grey and apricot shadings would have to go, but painting would have to wait for the weeks when Tony had the children. All of the walls were scuffed where chips of plaster had been gouged out from years of furniture moving.

The kitchen cupboards, now that she could inspect them without appearing to be rude, were old plywood ones, shiny with a film of grease. Their creamy surface was long overdue for a new coat of paint. The oven could be replaced, as could the exhaust above it. The linoleum would be stripped off, and the warm glow of the planks of red jarrah that lay below would have a chance to shine. Inside the kitchen cupboards, raw timber shelves had been covered over with adhesive vinyl. There were changes she could do that required painting and hard work, even though painting had never been her strong suit.

Exhausted from the move and the long drive down, her sleep that evening had been sound. Even so, she awoke early to enjoy a quiet ramble along the inlet. After breakfast, and bolstered by the knowledge that Red and Joy would soon be joining her, she dressed in a simple summery dress and comfortable sandals, only the third outfit she had tried on that morning. She was well aware that she would be looked over by a smattering of townsfolk and that there would be only one chance at a first impression. Checking herself once more in the mirror, she braced herself for her first day as manager and owner of her store.

To walk the thirty steps to work made her feel buoyant, despite the waves of concern that she had over the whole venture. She opened the back door and unlocked and unpacked the till and work spaces. She had already tidied, cleaned and organised the store the night before, but she found plenty to occupy her time in becoming familiar with every item and doing the undesirable but extremely necessary rodent check.

'Mail arrives at ten-thirty from Bettong, on Mondays, Wednesdays and Fridays, but there is some talk it will become daily. Thommo delivers it,' Red announced, when he arrived with Joy.

'Thommo?'

'Yes. You'll meet him soon. He'll be here to check you out since you're taking over.'

'Do I employ him? I didn't see his name in the books.' She frowned, trying to remember if she'd missed it.

'Oh no, he's employed by the postal service and his motorbike is managed by them, too. They own it and he manages his own affairs with them.'

'That's good, then.'

'Except...'

'Yes?'

'He's very handy and you'll probably find you may be glad of his help on Tuesdays and Thursdays.'

She wasn't about to employ someone on the strength of the books she had seen, but she appreciated the offer. 'I'll know who to call, then.'

'Right,' he said, 'let's open up.'

Gleaming in the morning sun, the newly scrubbed cherry-red door looked inviting, and Mel ran her hands over it before she drove the bolt into the concrete to prop it open. When she glanced down the street, she wondered if there'd been a mass evacuation.

Red and Joy spied the look on her face.

'It's a quiet town, but we have regulars and there are really busy times, you've seen the books,' said Joy,

'Of course.'

Red and Joy busied themselves with setting up the Christmas displays and goods and suggested to her that she get to know every single item and the ordering procedure on the computer. As they each buried themselves into chores, a steady trickle of locals wandered in, although their purchases hardly warranted it; curiosity, she guessed.

At ten o'clock, a little motorbike puttered down the driveway and parked around the side of the building. A slightly built older man strode into the store; bright-blue eyes animated his sun-weathered face. He ignored Red and Joy. 'You're very welcome, Miss?'

'Just call me Mel.'

He shook her hand. 'I'm Thommo and no doubt Red and Joy,' he said when he turned to finally acknowledge them, 'told you about what I do.'

She wasn't blind to her predicament. She was short on staff—a solo operation would do that—so an ally and workmate like Thommo would be helpful in her new environment, and anyway, he was quite compelling. She flashed a thankful smile at him.

'I've lived around these parts most of my life, except when I travelled with Margie. If there's anything you need doing, call me.' When he scrawled his number and details on a sheet of paper, she didn't mention Red and Joy had already done that.

'Thanks. Red and Joy have given me excellent advice, but when they go I'll have plenty to ask.'

Red held the door open for Thommo. 'I expect you'll be taking the mail now, Thommo, the truck has arrived.'

'See you later Mel.' He winked at her and walked out.

Red and Joy hadn't relaxed around Thommo. Was she developing small-town paranoia already?

'Hello Mrs Dickson, this is Mel Wilson, the new owner. She'll be helping you from now on.'

Mel noticed the slight stoop in Mrs Dickson's back and thick cane by her side. Was it really a retirement village? She remembered that she had met Sally and Brad, who were both much younger than Mrs Dickson. She would give Sally a ring and see if she was interested in a coffee.

'How do you do Mrs Dickson? What can I help you with?'

The old lady studied her through glasses too large for her small face. 'It's lovely to meet you, Mel. Do you think you'll be staying in Pelican Point?'

'I hope so. I've bought the shop and house.'

'You'll be here for a while, then. The market's not great so you won't get your money back for years. I read the financials. Could I have a packet of ten stamps and this calendar for my sister in Queensland? I only spotted one and I'd like another. Have you got another one?'

'Umm...?' So the old bird wasn't so doddery after all.

'It's okay Mrs Dickson, we have them stored underneath the display. I'll get one. Mel, you stay by the till.'

'Thanks, Red.' She scanned the items and Mrs Dickson dug around in her cavernous bag to present her with her card. When she tapped in her pin number, Mel wondered how this operation would go when the shop was full. Would they all take this long? It must be hard for them as their sight failed, and their fingers don't work so fast, she sympathised, reflecting on her own mother, but prayed that their banks issued them with swipe cards.

A kaleidoscopic blur of faces, names, new routines, paperwork and cleaning meant the days passed rapidly. After the first night, Mel left the house to spend four nights at the caravan park while the floors were stripped and sealed, but she didn't see Sally. When she rang, Sally told her that she was in Perth doing a bit of Christmas shopping and that she would have a coffee with her as soon as she got back. The floors were ready to be gently stepped on by the fifth day.

Every evening when she went for a jog, she delighted in recounting how little she'd used the car. When finances improved, she would buy them all new bicycles.

She was excited on the Friday to have her furniture arrive and directed the removalists, between ducking in to manage the shop, with the positioning of the big items. She couldn't believe how different the place looked without the carpet, linoleum and dusty curtains. With the cleaning and scrubbing, her eyes and nose had stopped running, and she could hardly take her eyes off the floor. The removalists were just a bit tetchy with her fiftieth reminder to be careful with it.

After they drove off, she stared at the pile of unopened boxes and wondered how they'd managed to accumulate so much despite an enormous donation of clothes and books to charity stores before she left Perth. When she examined their labels, she took the least needed and carted them into the back room of the store. 'And,' she addressed the boxes, 'if I don't open any of you within one year, you're going. Don't make yourself at home.'

The flywire door sang on the stretched springs and heavy footfalls echoed dull on the timber planks. Mel wiped the sweat off her face and took a tissue to dab at the dust and grime from the shifting and hefting of boxes; she'd only just opened the store and the air hung thick, warm and still, and the back room wasn't air-conditioned.

'Coming,' she said. She waved the front of her shirt and blew into it to stop it from sticking with sweaty dampness. When she switched on the air conditioner in the shop, cool air belched out and descended in waves. A man in a faded blue shirt and light-brown shorts browsed behind the card stand, but she could only see thin strips of him through the crowded metal carousel.

'Mark?'

He moved in front of the carousel. 'Mel, hi.'

'What are you doing down here?'

'A bit of business, a bit of family.'

'Right.'

'Jill said you'd moved down.'

'And here I am, trying not to get overrun by the morning rush hour.' Her face reddened. What was she even saying? His quiet grumpy air had her overwrought and over thinking.

'You should do all right, the community is growing.'

'Seriously? They've found the elixir of life for the octogenarians?'

'New estates are popping up everywhere.'

'Yeah, but new estates, new-estate shopping centres.'

'Climate change. People are moving down here in increasing numbers. Anyway, build the business and the people will come.'

'In the meantime they do come, every pension Thursday.'

'I'm off to Perth, but when I come back, would you like to go fishing?'

Was that the Mark version of an invite out? 'That would be great, except I get sick on big boats.'

'Who said anything about boats?'

She laughed, but it came out as a strangled snort. 'In that case, yes, I'd like to go fishing.'

'I've got to leave now.' He moved toward her and stood beside the counter.

'Merry Christmas Mark.' She leaned over the counter to peck him on the cheek, but her lips ended up on one of his eyes and it was open.

He blinked rapidly.

'I'm so sorry, Mark.' She was mortified.

'It's fine.' He wiped and blinked, but his eye became splotchy and red.

'Must have been the lipstick.' She thought about its toxic components, and how it would also be tainted with ancient dust remnants from the storeroom; a cocktail of who knew what.

'It'll be okay.' He put one hand over the eye and waved. 'I'll see you around.' He nearly bumped into the flywire door. The melody of the flywire resonated after it bounced several times before catching on the latch, and Mel stood contemplating her ridiculous conversation.

*

'So,' Sally said, blowing over the steam of her coffee in a new café in Bettong overlooking the harbour, 'you survived the week, how did it go?'

'It was great having Red and Joy's support, but I'm a bit scared about being on my own next week. It's become quite busy.'

'Christmas will give you a feel for the financials. Christmas is the litmus test for business survival. When your children are around you'll feel more settled.'

'I was thinking the same, but I'm glad I had this week without them, and thank God for the precedence of a four-o'clock close. I'm a blithering wreck by the time I hit the pillow. How about your business, this must be the peak season?'

'Both caravan parks are booked up ages in advance and we get the odd heated flare-up from our regulars if the managers stuff up and double book. We had one new manager close to tears when one of our less savoury regulars came in ready to tear the place apart because he didn't get his booking.'

'What did you do?'

'We found him a spot, not his favourite one, which by then had been taken by another family, and didn't charge him. He accepted and grumbled. We said that if he chose that kind of behaviour perhaps he didn't want to respect our kind services in the future. Sadly, he's booked again for next year, and we're obliged to take his booking. We're keeping an eye on him.'

'The silly season begins.'

'You have no idea, that's why we try to employ managers who can handle it. Brian and I oversee and do the bookwork, leaving all other issues for the manager of each site. Thank God. We've installed new computer software that doesn't seem to make any errors and a local computer guy manages our site. We give thanks for regular power and a reliable internet service to keep everything smooth. Surprises still happen though.'

'I guess you don't really know what's going to happen until it does.' She hoped the electronic funds machines didn't break down or the wi-fi went on the blink, or some difficult person ended up in her shop. She gave an involuntary shudder.

'What?'

'I haven't got a worst-case scenario plan.'

'You will need one. How's the security?'

'There's a camera running footage all the time, but it's a low-budget kind. There's a panic button that goes to the Bettong Police Station behind the counter, and I have a storeroom I can hide in.'

'Don't worry, there're plenty of people around and heaps are always walking or out enjoying the bay. You're in an open place.'

'It does feel safe like that. I'm such a newbie.'

'Everyone is when they begin something new, that's what wine o'clock is for. If you weren't driving down early tomorrow morning, we could watch the sun set and have a glass on my balcony.'

'That sounds wonderful. Sign me up.'

Chapter Thirty-three

Mel's time back in the city for the final school assemblies and farewells, and to collect Lil for the start of the Christmas holidays, had been far more emotionally draining than she'd expected. She saw Jack only briefly as she was to leave on a tour with Tony for a community-service visit to Vietnam. She wouldn't see her until Christmas Eve. She hoped Pelican Point held some attraction for Lil, or else it was going to be a glum break. There were some softeners to the trauma of moving school: the new school for Lil had a purpose-built world-class equestrian centre and state-of-the-art dance centre. *Two strikes to me*, she thought, as she cast her eyes upon the slumped body of her sleeping daughter. They pulled into the driveway at Pelican Point early Sunday evening.

Lunch and tears with her mother before they left hadn't helped either. Not the tone she would have liked as she left Perth. Jack had been reserved, her face a mask and her lips a thin line. So much for the brave new start; Mel would have to be the cheerleader and team.

'Is this my room?' Lil said in horror when Mel opened the front door to let her in. 'Orange?'

'They used to call it apricot.'

'It's awful.'

'I agree, but paint can be changed. During the week you can think about it and let me know what colour you'd like.'

'Isn't there a family room?'

'Not exactly, but we live by the sea and there are so many things you can do outside.'

'What do you mean?'

'It's a great environment, we don't need a family room,' she said. 'Look, Lil, we have to make do with what we've got. Whole families with six children used to live in houses like this.' That's what her mother would have said to her. Personally, she thought that would be hideous.

'Where will I take my friends?'

'I gave you a huge bedroom. We'll organise it better.'

'Are there any kids my age around here?'

She paused. 'Of course there are, my friend Sally has a daughter.'

'One! You know one kid?'

'There's bound to be more. I'm still new here, too.' She thought about all the retired people she'd met in the store and didn't confess to Lil that she hadn't actually seen many children about.

'It looks like a boring old place. I'm going to my room, my ridiculous orange room!'

'You can go to your room later because we're going for a walk right now. My legs are itching to stretch.'

Lil's eyes thinned to black slits and blazed with annoyance. She wasn't used to getting those looks from Lil; they were Jack's speciality.

Not only was Lil catapulted into a new environment and school, but also she was at an age where all kinds of changes were about to assail her, and Mel fretted about that. She whispered into her ear that she would be able to take her to school, or let her catch a little bus to school, and that they could catch fish every evening if they wanted. They followed the easy path towards the inlet and she could sense her daughter's body relax.

'We live this close to the water? And look, there's an island over there.'

Mel didn't correct her. The way the headland jutted out on the other side of the inlet did make it look like an island. As she predicted, the walk around the inlet, the magnificent blue whale sculpture, the companionable pelicans and the airy breeze, had brightened Lil's outlook.

As much as she was trying to remain upbeat about the move and its consequent changes to their lives, Mel recognised there would be many trials ahead for all of them.

'I saw the tree in the yard.'

'What do you think of it?'

'I think I could build a tree house in it.'

The tree's boughs had been worn smooth in places and there had even been evidence of previous tree houses. Lil squeezed her hand. There was room for a trampoline, if Mel could order one in time for Christmas, and the bit of concreting around the back shed could support a basketball ring. She would try to have both ready for when the children came back after Christmas to make up for the lack of inside space. She considered purchasing two large umbrellas to give a little festive and social feel to the garden.

They were still near the water's edge when she saw something glimmer in the evening light, far over on the lower reaches of the headland opposite. She'd ask Thommo about that tomorrow. Thommo, as she'd anticipated, was only too willing to enlighten her on everything to do with the town and the local folk.

'Can I invite one of my friends down, like Emma?' Lil asked.

'Yes, but because I have to work at the shop it's a bit tricky for me to supervise. They could come for a weekend break. Buses run down here from Perth.'

'I'll phone her tonight.'

'Make if for later in January. Christmas time is chaotic and I want to spend some time alone with you and Jack. I know you'll miss everyone, but when you're with your dad you can visit your friends and have sleepovers.' She could see Lil struggling. 'You know that friend I mentioned? Sally? Her daughter is Bronte, and Sally is lovely. They own the caravan park over there.' She pointed with her free hand because Lil was holding on to the other. She had to remember that Lil's world was spinning and not all changes were welcome.

'Can we have a trampoline, like we used to?'

'I'll see what I can get down here, or what Santa delivers.'

'Yeah sure.' Lil nudged her, a little playfulness returning. 'Where are the shops?'

'There aren't many. Bettong has heaps of shops and it's only ten minutes away. We can drive out there and go for a walk near the harbour. There are a couple of cafés in Bettong and market stalls on Sunday.' She'd heard about the markets but so far she hadn't done anything other than get her house and shop into vague order.

'Can we have an ice cream from the café at the caravan park?'

'Sounds like a plan.'

A lush green apron of grass lay on the rounded edge of the point in front of the café, where picnic things sat in cluttered disarray. A few children scavenged and dug around at the edges of the shore. Lil dropped her hand. Their parents, she presumed, sat on the edges of the low limestone wall at the back of the grassed area with a pair of golden labradors on leads.

The children, three boys and a couple of girls, glanced over and spotted Lil. Lil pretended not to notice. They continued walking towards their new home. Lil turned around to give the kids one more look, and as she did, one of the boys stared back at her. She blushed. Since when had she begun blushing at boys like that? Mel had difficulties contemplating Lil ever leaving childhood. Her slight frame, variety of interests and enthusiasm for all things physical, meant Lil spent most of her time in shorts and tee shirts.

*

Edwina Quentin-Jones, the principal of Lil's school, was diminutive, with bright intelligent eyes. Edwina was married, Mel had already heard on the communal grapevine, to a local town planner, and was also an active council member.

When they walked around the grounds with Edwina, Mel took in the quality and extent of the school's resources and knew school fetes, cake stalls and quiz nights didn't add up to the kind of money that had been spent on Bray College. The enormous and well-equipped equestrian centre won Lil over. On display, in two enormous frames, were photos of the two current age champions in show jumping and both were students of the school. The remaining walls were adorned with countless banners, ribbons and medals.

They entered the expansive dance studio. Even Lil's old dance centre didn't have such a wide sprung floor, or floor-to-ceiling mirrors, or such an enormous stage for rehearsing.

'You said the school had a sponsor, is it a corporate body or individual?' Mel asked the principal.

'We have an anonymous benefactor and I'm afraid that's all I can say.'

'It's amazing.'

'You weren't expecting this in the country?'

'No.' She figured Edwina probably got this jaw-dropping response from most new parents.

'We don't advertise the fact, but we're probably the highest funded school in this hemisphere. Now, Lil, the first Monday of term is orientation day for our new students. I'll leave you here at the uniform shop. And welcome to our school.'

'Thank you very much, Ms Quentin-Jones.'

When the principal left, Mel asked Lil, 'What do you think?'

'I like that we can do horse riding at school.'

'What about the dance centre?'

'I wish Emma could see it. I wish she was coming to this school too.'

'When she comes down we can show it to her from the outside.'

'Not the same.' A little wobble began in her face. What was Mel expecting? It would be ages for the changes and friendships to assert themselves. Hollowness rang in her own stomach.

'Let's get a milkshake at the café after?'

'All right.'

She added spiritual healer to her personal skill set.

At the uniform shop, Mel ushered Lil into the change room to try on a variety of uniform ensembles just as a text pinged from Sally. She wanted to know how it was going with Lil. Leaving the lady in the shop to fuss around and collect the requisite sprawl of uniforms for the different sports, Mel stood at the back of the shop and texted her back. Sally invited them to drop over after five. Somehow that simple response made breathing easier and she smiled at her daughter, who twirled in front of the mirror with jodhpurs on.

'Now all you need is a horse and we'll be set. I didn't see them in the uniform shop?'

Lil rolled her eyes.

With the paperwork sorted, and, despite the extensive resources and the wide-ranging curriculum, the school fees were very reasonable. Tony would be happy. Could that be another result of the support from the mysterious benefactor?

In the café, she held back on admonishing Lil as she slurped the dregs.

'Oops. Sorry Mum.'

'I'm officially giving you the assistant post mistress job today.'

'Why?'

'You can earn pocket money. But it won't be huge because this is a small business in a little town, and we've only just started.'

'What can I do?'

'We'll go into the store and you can get to know where everything is kept. When some of our customers are looking for specific items, you'll know where to find them. That will save me a lot of time because it's going to be busy. You only have to do what you want, though. I've set up a little table and beanbag in one of the storerooms as your chill-out zone. I don't want you in the house on your own.'

'Why not?'

'Your age and my responsibility. Not negotiable.'

'Okay.'

'Even though I need to run the store each day, there is still a large chunk of Monday to Friday for us to do whatever we want.'

A small queue had formed outside the front door of the store. Going to the school had meant a later opening, let alone the trip to the café for a milkshake. Mel was almost breathless when Thommo arrived. 'Hi, Thommo, this is Lil, my daughter,' she said as she tidied one of the vertical display shelves.

'Hi there Lil.' He removed his helmet and leaned on the counter. 'Hey don't make it too nice, you'll never get rid of the customers.'

'And here I was thinking that keeping customers would be the way to improve business.'

'You've got it all wrong, Mel,' he teased. 'Don't tidy up, sell little, and sit all day in the sunshine moaning.'

She realised he was having a dig at Red and Joy.

'At the rate you're going, you'll need a second-in-charge. Wait a minute, I know the perfect person, and he's cheap.'

'Thanks for the offer, Thommo, but I prefer slave labour. That's why I had children.'

'Yes, I'm just a slave here.' Lil waved.

'Oh, you poor tyke. Hey, have you met young Eddie?'

'No.'

'He's about your age and only lives around the corner. Though he might be away in Perth at the moment. His granny looks after him when his mum's at work. If I see him, I'll tell him to drop by and say hello.'

Lil grew red patches on her cheeks. 'Thanks for that, Thommo. We'll just take it one day at a time here. We may bump into Eddie in our travels, but don't worry about telling him to drop by just yet.'

Thommo winked at her as he went out, oblivious to her eye-widening and throat-cutting gestures.

'If you want to ride your bike and join me Lil, you can, if your mum lets you. Only when I do the few streets close to here, then you can cycle back home.'

'Okay, thank you.'

'She might be able to do that when I buy her a new bike. See you Wednesday.'

The rest of the day saw the steady trickle of regulars who left with a large selection of Christmas stock. Mel didn't think much of what was on offer and knew that she could organise to purchase a better quality range for next Christmas. She would have to figure out what sold and what the population would buy.

Chapter Thirty-four

'Do you think I should wear this?' Lil asked later that afternoon.

'You look perfect. Sally has just sent a text saying to bring bathers. I would stick with the tee-shirt and shorts and bring a big towel and jumper.'

Mel drove the few streets to Sally's home. She had limited knowledge of the layout of the residential area and hadn't had any reason to venture to this section of town, where the houses that straddled the small hill were in an altogether different class from the older ones on the flat. The blocks and houses were larger and designed by craftsmen, and they were nearly all two-storey with wide balconies to capture the impressive view out to the inlet and beyond.

Sally's house was built of limestone blocks with timber windows, and a large timber-and-steel balcony ran around the top. Sally leaned over the railing to wave at her. Her blonde hair jerked around with her waving arm and a layered ocean-blue dress fanned out behind in the gentle breeze. Sunlight bounced off an assortment of bangles. Mel squeezed Lil's hand as they hopped out of the car.

'Bronte!' She heard Sally calling out to her daughter.

The door opened and Bronte stood like a mini-Sally, only with glasses and braces. She had the same warm eyes and healthy glow to her skin as Sally. 'Come in. Mum thinks I'm deaf.' Mel was relieved when she noticed Bronte's shorts, canvas shoes and tee-shirt.

'Hi Bronte, I'm Mel and this is Lil.'

'Hi. Mum's upstairs. I'll take you there.'

They trotted up the timber stairs to the top storey, where the main living space was located. Sally came over and greeted her with a hug. 'Hi Mel, and you must be Lil?'

'Yes. Hi Sally, I love your house.'

'Thank you. Did you bring your bathers?'

'Yes.'

'Bronte will take you to the pool area. She's been waiting to have a swim with you. I hope you like warm pools because we use a pool blanket, an absolute must if you live this far south.'

Bronte and Lil left. Bronte chattered away to Lil.

'They'll be fine,' Sally said.

'I know. I'm just realising how many changes Lil and Jack will need to make. It's really kind of you to invite us around.'

'Not at all. I would have to eat all of this food and drink all that wine by myself otherwise.' She waved her hand to where a selection of cheeses, smoked salmon, pickled and fresh vegetables, crackers and baguette slices lay, swamping a large low table on the balcony.

'You shouldn't have gone to so much trouble, but it looks fabulous. This is for you.' She pulled out a bottle of local red wine.

'How was today?' Sally invited her to move through the opened timber doors that lead out to the balcony, and with little effort, removed the cork from the bottle. Plumping down on the thick cushions on the outdoor sofas, she poured them both a glass.

'It was great. I was worried there for a while, but the season has cast its magic spell over the wallets. I needed Lil to help out today and will need her help all this week. It's the crazy week before Christmas. I couldn't afford someone else at this stage.'

'How did Lil find the school?'

'I'd say she was impressed, who wouldn't be? But she's still very concerned about missing her friends. It was lucky she was about to move into middle school anyway.'

'I haven't had to do too much moving in my life, but I can imagine it wouldn't be easy. Make sure you come to all of the parent social events, especially the cocktail evening. Occasionally we party on afterwards. If we do, don't let me near the karaoke machine because Bronte said she'd leave if I ever sang in front of the school parents again.'

Mel sliced a bit of the tangy crumbly cheese and tipped it onto a slice of sourdough. 'That sounds like the kind of evening I need. Cheers to us, Sally.'

'Here's to your new business and your life down here with us hick country people.'

They clinked glasses and admired the last blast of light in the evening sky.

'Where's your husband?'

'Brian's staying with his mum because he's taking his brother and family to the airport. They're moving to Indonesia for work for a couple of years and he knew his mum would need a bit of support saying goodbye. She lived near them and now the children are teenagers. It's a big deal for her. It's too busy for us both to leave and I said goodbye when I went to Perth to go shopping with Bronte. We go to Perth before Christmas and stay with Brian's mum every year. It's our little tradition. Bronte loves the lights and Christmas displays, but I love manhandling all of the new-season colours and I normally come back with far too many clothes. I keep the charity stores in the style to which they've become accustomed. I like to do my bit for town aesthetics.'

'I know where to go when I need a new outfit.'

'You'd need a bit more meat on you to fit into my rejects. Here, have some of this salmon. I'm addicted to it.'

A calm and pleasant ease took hold of Mel. The food, the wine, but chiefly Sally, made her relax, something she hadn't done since she'd moved to the town. Chattering voices could be heard floating up the stairwell and footsteps echoed on the wooden staircase.

'Bronte, pop those pizzas under the grill for a minute.' Sally turned to Mel. 'Bronte and I made a few homemade mini-pizzas before you came. It was her request for tonight. Lil's not allergic to anything?'

'No. A bit of asthma, but no allergies that we know of and she's been surrounded by nuts and seafood all her life.'

'Bronte's been surrounded by a few nuts all her life, too, mainly on her father's side.' Sally's eyes glinted wickedly.

'Good for building resistance, I suppose.' Mel laughed.

'Absolutely, you have to live with nuts to build tolerance.'

'Then my two should be epic survivors.'

'Here's to surviving.' Glasses clinked again and Mel lit up with a smile that began in her stomach and rose up to her cheeks.

'Can we take it into the theatre room?'

'If you each have a tray.'

'Thanks Mum.'

'Thanks Sally.'

'How did you find the pool, Lil?' Sally asked her.

'It's so warm. I loved it.'

'Glad it got used.'

Lil sidled over with a towel skirted around her and a hooded sweater on top, to give Mel a pool-smelling hug, then slipped back to the kitchen to be with Bronte.

When the girls had filled up their trays and wandered into the theatre room, Sally leaned over. 'I may be loud, Mel, but I want you to know, your business is your business and I am not in the habit of letting people know my own affairs, let alone anyone else's. It's a small town so starting a business and getting to know people will take time. When I left for home after meeting you at the caravan park that Saturday, I crossed my fingers. Pelican Point needs a bit of new blood, although lately we've had a few move down for the sea and tree change. Some stick it out.'

'I hope I'm one of those who does.'

'I'll drink to that.' They leaned back in the chairs and watched the view over the inlet. Canoeists and paddle boarders headed for the banks to pull in their craft.

Easing into her own driveway later in the night, Mel looked back and saw Lil's head loll around. She looked tired but content. For most of the evening, Bronte and Lil had chatted and laughed. When she'd gone to fetch Lil, Mel saw them on the couch relaxed and comfortable, talking. She didn't want to hope for too much too soon, but it had lifted her spirits and given her a flicker of warmth. Sally had said she'd drop by to see her during the week. With Sally, Bronte, Thommo and Brad, plus a few regulars at the shop, her circle of known faces had increased. She felt less like a shipwreck.

Chapter Thirty-five

Although Mel had called them several times, Red and Joy appeared to have vanished. 'Sorry, love,' Red said after her fifth call got through, 'we've been in Victoria visiting our son. What can I do for you?'

'I wonder if you could drop over and help me for a couple of days? I'm still unsure about a few things. I'll pay?'

The line went quiet. 'Of course, you need to get used to it all.'

When Red arrived, he was animated and cheery; it seemed the break from work had given him a spark. A large parcel of supplies wrapped in thick brown paper and heavily secured with wide strong tape had been delivered. Mel left it in the store-room because it didn't appear to match with any of the orders.

'Did you find a packing slip?' Red rubbed his beard.

'I couldn't find any paperwork.'

'Should we open a bit of it up? It looks like a whole heap of packages lie underneath.'

She took a knife and sliced through one layer of tape, hacked through several layers of brown paper and prised open the newly made flap, under which lay dozens of smaller brown paper packages. These were labelled.

'Dolls? We don't sell dolls. This must be for the toy store.'

Red's face blossomed shades of crimson and he reached for her hand before she tore open the package. 'I don't think you want to open that one up.'

She met his eyes. 'We don't sell these sorts of dolls, tell me we don't, Red?'

'Of course not, but there's a shop in Bettong that does. The truck driver must have presumed these were for here. I'll give them a call.' He winked at her on his way out.

She slipped the small package back into the flap and walked into the store.

'All fixed. The owner will drop around later this afternoon and collect it. And while we're on that subject...'

'I wasn't aware we were.'

'Old John Bouros collects his magazines from here.'

'We don't sell those magazines.'

'We don't, he orders them in.' He grinned and it annoyed her. 'But he likes them in a paper bag when he arrives.'

'This is a family post office.' A sharp edge crept into her voice.

'Keep your hair on, they're pigeon magazines.'

'Right. Why the subterfuge?'

'His wife has a fit if she sees them, so he buys them on the quiet. I think he trades them with his mates from the pigeon club. The pigeons are a sore point in their relationship.'

'He could get information online.'

'Not everyone can afford the internet on their pension.'

'What about the library in Bettong?'

'He's lost his licence. Things deteriorate and get tough as you get older.'

Her fingers drummed on the counter as she reflected on her mother's issues; her mind whirred when she considered potential ideas for the business, but the solutions had to meet her customers where they were, and she wasn't sure she had the resources to tackle that. Anyway, she reminded herself, she hadn't met everyone and she knew some customers were definitely under seventy.

'I'll make sure his magazines are ready for him.'

Red assisted her with the remaining administration tasks and introduced her to a few more locals during the two mornings he stayed.

The week before Christmas flew by, but Mel made time to head to the beach for a swim in the evening with Lil. On the evening before they were due to drive to Perth, Bronte and Sally joined them for a swim at the inlet. After a light meal, the girls rode scooters along the path around the bay.

'Only until the sun goes down. Okay?'

'Yes.' Two voices chorused followed by a refrain of rolled eyes and swinging ponytails.

'I'm not keen for their next phase.' Sally said, before taking another sip of wine and stretching out her legs.

'Me neither. One adolescent is enough.'

'What's Jack like?'

'A teenager. Loves her sport, the beach and her mates, not so keen on completing school work until the night before it's due, and gives us a few headaches.'

'Jack's a girl?'

'She was Jacqui, but prefers to be called Jack, and is, as she tells me, not gender defined.' The truth was, Mel was still figuring out Jack, and Jack was still figuring out everything.

'Good for her. If Bronte is anything like me, I'm leaving town. My mother says I was a mouthy handful in my teenage years and she's glad Brian has to put up with me now. How did you go with your Christmas food shopping?'

'Thanks for the tip about Salt Flake. I could have stood and drooled all evening, but Lil pushed me around to get the lobsters, berries and a few other treats for Christmas. They had samples out on trays throughout the store. We were starving by the time we got there, and we might have been a bit too enthusiastic in helping ourselves because we scored dark looks. Everything's packed inside the fridge ready for the big drive to take to my sister's place. What about you, what are you doing?' A light breeze made her pull a towel around her shoulders.

'Brian's mum will come down and my parents will come around, and that's it. It'll be hard for Bronte being the only child with the cousins in Indonesia this year, but there are kids down the street who'll play outside for a while. We'll eat too much and drink all day then sit around the pool on floating chairs getting burnt. Everyone collapses on a bed or sofa for a couple of hours and then revives in time for the evening, when we head down to the inlet and toast to the dying rays of another Christmas Day. Every year we say we'll do something different, but we don't. And you guys?'

'Similar. This time it's at my sister's place—Georgie and her husband, Dave—instead of Mum's, which is great because they have a pool, a magnificent guest suite, and a huge dining room. I love my sister, but I can't spend more than a couple of days there with teenagers. I hate the idea of it, but I'll drive back on Boxing Day. I'm taking the Christmas to New Year week off.'

'When you get back, we'll have a barbecue.'

'Sure, but we can just catch up here. No need for big meals.'

'Agreed.'

'We both have enough to do. Anyway, you'd beat me hands down in the cooking department.'

'Unlikely, but you're right, life is too short to spend it in the kitchen, when we can be talking, drinking and eating. Will Santa be bringing anyone special down?'

'Not unless you know something I don't.'

'I had to ask. I get this feeling about next year.'

'I think it's the wine and the food.'

'Yes. Not the season of mellow fruitfulness. What is our summer, then?'

'The season of reclining, dining, drinking and whining?'

'That works.'

Chapter Thirty-six

Mel loved Christmas but dreaded the drive back to the city in her old car in the stifling heat of December. The trade had become brisk before Christmas and she'd got the hang of beefing up the supplies to match demand. An income was being generated and it plumped up the bank account. She was keen to see Jack and bring her back to Pelican Point. In her fantasy of ideal life, she pictured Jack and herself at work in the store, after which they would head out with Lil to a favourite beach to surf and boogie board. It wasn't a huge stretch.

Newly poured tarmac ran smooth under her tyres after hours on the long, grey, flat highway. Glimpses of ocean, leafy trees surrounded by trimmed verges, sweeping driveways, sheltered porticoes, and the requisite sprinkling of European cars told her she was close to her sister's house. Her car crunched lightly over the crushed limestone where she parked next to a smart black four-wheel drive. At about the same time, Tony arrived in his low-slung sports car to collect Lil, and to let her see Jack. They would be reunited at lunch on Christmas Day. She'd been longing to seeing Jack and wanted to enfold her thin frame in a tight embrace, and because it was Christmas Eve, Jack let her. Lil joined the hug.

'I'll bring them back at twelve tomorrow,' Tony said. For Mel, Christmas didn't really happen until her children were there. She didn't have long to stare after the vigorous waves from Lil in the back seat before her sister swept out from the house.

'I was hoping to catch the kids before they left.' She caught Mel's slumped face. 'But we'll see them when they come at lunch tomorrow, anyway.'

Georgie lived an amazing life and looked annoyingly well for it. She was perfectly positioned as manager of a corporate events company. That was how she had met David. It had been a successful and prosperous marriage and business partnership ever since, and even their tall, athletic teenage boys seemed to shine with a winning glow.

Sweaty and tired from the long drive and the fairly weak air-conditioning system, Mel was desperate for a shower. Wealth and prosperity had enabled David and Georgie to build a fabulous home, complete with a stunning guest suite. The bathroom was larger than her bedroom at Pelican Point. After the hugs and general chat, she excused herself to enjoy the luxuries of a well-stocked bathroom, where she couldn't wait to indulge in the fluffy towels and fragrant skin-care products.

Mel ran her hands over the massive bed and sighed; any thoughts of a siesta had to be postponed so that she could join in with the traditional Christmas Eve activities in the kitchen. There was always a great deal of fooling around and competition during the preparation of various parts of the meal. She towelled her hair and marvelled at the house. Out across the balcony past the tasteful garden and pool, beyond the treetops, she caught glimpses of a glittering ocean.

A few hours later, her eyes felt gritty with tiredness. When she thought it would be about the right time, she excused herself and nearly skipped with joy towards the huge bed.

'Mel?' It was her sister's voice. 'Can I come in?'

Rather than risk dribbling out toothpaste froth in reply, she opened the door. She and Georgie weren't that close, but they had shared a lot over the years, especially regarding their mutual concern for their mother since their father had died, although she hadn't been Georgie's confidante. She held in awe the sister who had enjoyed reasonable success all her life. Georgie entered the room a little drunk and not so well put together.

'Can I talk to you, I mean really talk to you?' She slurred her words.

'Of course.' They sat down on the sofa facing the balcony. Georgie pulled out a cigarette.

Mel was gobsmacked. 'Why don't we sit out on the balcony?' The guest suite was quite a way from the main section of the house and they were in no danger of being overheard.

'Don't worry, I haven't started smoking.' Georgie put her feet up on the low table. 'No, I'm definitely not smoking. This is a joint. It's perfectly legal in some places of the world. You want some?'

Mel examined her sister's face and saw shadows beneath her perfect lashes; thin lines furrowed her forehead, and fanning out from the corners of her eyes were soft wrinkles. It surprised her to see Georgie as fallible.

'No thanks. Is this a good idea?'

'It's my new thing. I needed a new thing, because…' A grimace turned down her otherwise perfect lips. Mel thought they were probably enhanced, but that was being petty. 'Is it a good idea? I know something that's not a good idea. It's not a good idea to sleep with your personal assistant. No, not a good idea.'

'You slept with your personal assistant?'

'No,' she said as she inhaled, 'David did.'

'David slept with his personal assistant?' Mel knew she sounded as astounded as she felt by this revelation.

'Yes. Oh, Mel, you just don't see stuff.' With this Georgie tapped her nose. 'But I love you for it. You're up front with who you are, but around here,' she said and pointed all around with a wavy movement of her arm, 'it's different. The world I work in has shown me a whole new side. It was Kim.'

'Kim was his personal assistant?'

'Yes. I wasn't supposed to be dropping home, but I had to pick up something for Xandy. He'd left his epipen at home and I was driving down with a bunch of other mums for a mother-and-son sleepover at the school campsite, about an hour away. That's where David thought I was.' She coughed a little before she continued. 'Anyway, when I came in, I heard a noise and pushed open our bedroom door. There they were.' She paused and closed her eyes, her voice thick. 'I couldn't believe it. Kim, the PA.'

Mel put her arm around her sister. 'What did you do?'

'It was pretty horrible. I still went to camp because I'd

promised. I can tell you, that vision hasn't left me. I didn't tell anyone. It happened over a year ago, but recently I've started on these.' She held up the burning stump.

'You guys must have patched things up because things look pretty normal around here. You both seem much the same to me.' Was that because she didn't really see stuff?

'We are and he said that it was a one-off and he never wanted to do that again. He loves me, he said, and our boys. But it's so hard,' she nestled against Mel's shoulder, 'when you find your husband like that. I mean they were clothed and they were talking, but still, who goes to a bedroom to talk?'

'So nothing actually happened?'

'No. But I think only because I came home, and they both said nothing happened.'

'Is Kim still around?'

'No. We wrote him a good resume and he left.'

'Kim is a he?' David had never struck her that way. Suddenly, she could see why this had such a profound effect on her unflappable sister.

'Yes, he's a he. He is so gorgeous, I wondered why he never flirted with me. He's a very masculine guy and competes in triathlons. Apparently, he swings both ways. That's what I heard.'

What could she say?

'I would have understood if it was a woman, though I'd have sacked her, too. No marriage is perfect. I've had several very generous offers in my time. You're getting on with your life, and I know the effect of the accident and all that coverage couldn't have been easy, but I think it's great the way you've taken up this little business challenge. Good for you.' Mel gave her one last hug before she left, but Georgie paused at the door.

'There's something else?' Mel asked.

'Yes.'

'Is it about Mum?'

'Yes.'

'Are we going to play twenty questions, because I'm pretty tired?'

'Mum's getting a little down.'

'Okay. Is she seeing someone?'

'If you ask her, she will say she is *seeing* all of her friends and us. You know she won't *see* anyone else.'

'Right. Thanks for letting me know. I'll keep phoning and make sure she comes to Pelican Point soon.'

'She seems to need both of us right now.' She turned towards her again. 'And thanks.'

Mel was struggling with what she'd heard. Again her mind flitted out to consider Mitchell lying in a coma and wondered about the kind of Christmas his family would be having. She collapsed onto the substantial bed and slept. David. Really? It wasn't the greatest last thought for the night.

Chapter Thirty-seven

Mel couldn't conceive how the hours had evaporated so quickly and was distraught when the brilliant summer morning threw blinding daggers across her eyes. She longed for more hours in the heavenly bed but allowed her nephews to drag her out for a morning dip in the quasi-warm pool. When her mother arrived and bustled around, she helped her put the final touches to the lunch, all the while trying to banish thoughts of last night's conversation with Georgie. After hanging onto and swamping her children with hugs and kisses when they arrived, she sat down with the rest of the family to eat.

She enjoyed preparing the fresh lobsters, goat cheese flan, and berry coulis. All of the purchases had been made at Salt Flake and were sourced from areas around Bettong and Pelican Point. It was important to her, the idea of provenance. Everyone enjoyed the food and commented on the lobsters. Having gorged themselves on a variety of oceanic bounty, they trailed out to sit in the shade to while away the afternoon and sprawl on the pool lounges. After several hours of swimming, the children disappeared into the well-appointed games room.

Occasionally she'd meet Georgie's eyes, and Georgie would smile back at her. She wondered how David felt.

A small collection of David's cousins joined them in the evening. They dished out another meal. Jack and Lil dived back into the pool with the arrival of more family and revelled in the bigger group after spending Christmas morning with Tony and Leah and Leah's parents. The adults reclined on the many outdoor settings surrounding the pool with drinks in hand, food on trays, and a sense of festive relief at the end of the craziness.

'Mel,' David said, 'met any men down at the Point?'

'Only the postie and a smattering of retirees. You know, pick a town and spread out the camper trailer for ever.'

'You never know, country towns are famous for city-girl-meets-country-guy scenarios.'

'Thanks Dave, I'll bear that in mind when I see the next flannel shirt and manure-clad boots stomp through the door, but you've been watching far too many reality shows.' She considered the conversation she'd had with her mum about Christos, and what her mum had said about her dad maybe not being as straight as he appeared. Could there be any more revelations this Christmas?

Despite the complete opulence and comfort of her sister's house, Mel couldn't wait to bundle her children back into the car and take them to their new coastal home. David helped attach the surfboard she had bought Jack and the boogie board she had bought Lil, to the roof of the car. As she drove away, the grand scale and magnificence of the homes surrounding Georgie's left her with a sense of disquiet.

Chapter Thirty-eight

Driving back was a grind; the air conditioner struggled to do its job and the heat was jarring. The children lolled with over indulgence. In this less-than-salubrious environment, Lil vomited into a bucket; previous experience had ensured there was always one in the car. A journey stop was called for and Jack gave up the hallowed front seat for the remainder of the journey to try to avoid a repeat performance from Lil, but Jack didn't complain. Mel found the drive long, torturous and too quiet.

When they pulled into the driveway, she could see Jack take in the rather small, insignificant and dowdy house. It was a complete contrast to where they'd been and way more down scale than Tony and Leah's place. Whatever she thought about it, there wasn't anything Mel could do that would transform it. Jack's impressions were important to her and she felt like she'd let her down, again.

They each stumbled out of the car and the heat rushed at them, dry and stinging.

'This is it?'

'Yes. Our beach house.' Mel continued to grab bags out of the car.

'The beach is just around the corner and the inlet is down there. You only have to walk and you're there.' Lil had had a week's advantage. 'Mum gave you a big bedroom and painted yours first.'

'Come on you two, let's take our bags and gifts inside.'

'And there's a pontoon you can swim to. I'm going to swim

out with Mum.' It was news to Mel, but she could see Lil rallying.

'Are there any surf beaches?' Jack said when she reached up and grabbed her new board.

'I believe so.'

When she opened the front door, the gleam of the floorboards and the Christmas tree added a warm festive air, but she'd been close to tears when she spied the look on Jack's face. Before she left, and while Lil had already buckled herself into the car for the long drive to Georgie's, she'd spread out a few more presents under the tree for this very moment.

'Mum, you already bought us some presents.'

'I know, these are just a few things for here.'

Jack took the board to her room and wandered back into the lounge room.

'Do you like your room?' Mel asked her.

'Yeah, thanks. I saw the magazines.' There it was, the beautiful Jack smile.

'There's a pretty good surf shop in Bettong and they had a couple of surf magazines that you got for free if you bought a new board.'

Lil ripped into a few presents. 'A thermal rash shirt?'

'Yes, you both got one. It's not so warm down here and I know you'll want to keep swimming.'

'I love the new bathers and shorts. Thanks for the pin-up boards. I can't wait to decorate them.' Lil gave her an extra squeeze.

Jack found her gifts. 'Deodorant?'

'It's a cologne deodorant. Year Ten is a sweaty year.'

'Ah well, thanks for the new board shorts and cap. Not sure about the sunnies.'

'If you're going to spend a lot of time in the surf, it gets pretty glary on the sand. Come around the back, guys.'

They dumped their bags and left a trail of torn Christmas paper.

'You did manage to get a trampoline and basketball ring!' Lil clambered up and started bouncing straightaway.

'You can thank Thommo for putting it up when you see him.'

'Who's Thommo?' Jack flicked her wrist and scored a basket each time.

'Thommo is the local postie.'

'He's a nice postie,' Lil called out between flips and somersaults.

Lil bounced for a minute more, and Jack brought in the basketball. It was too hot for any more.

'Banana smoothies and a rest. I'm beat.' She called to both of them.

'Sounds good.' There was some kind of grunt from Jack; her cheeks bulged with something she'd taken out of the fridge.

'I'm lying down for a while,' Mel announced.

No one complained.

A couple of short hours later she mustered sufficient spirit to take them to a local surf spot she'd found on the town map. Immense granite boulders flanked the edges, the creamy white sand squeaked noisily when they walked on it, and the ocean was a shade of turquoise that simply didn't exist at any of the beaches in Perth. She draped a shirt over the milky skin of her torso when she spied the panorama of lean tanned bodies parading along the shoreline. This was a summer and a town to develop a more uniform hue.

'Come on, it's so nice in.' Lil stood over her and dripped.

'That's cold!' Mel picked up the spare boogie board, Jack's old one, and wandered down to the shore. The coconut-and-chemical smell of sunblock smeared on the sprawled bodies hit her in drifts.

'Let's get this wave together.' Lil reached over and grabbed her hand. Mel tried to steady the board with the other, but they both crashed and tumbled through the waves.

'Let's get another one.'

'Not if you're going to try to drown me.'

'Let's not hold hands this time.' This time they caught the wave together and bounced along it till it spent itself on the shore. Their boards came to rest on dark, damp sand.

'And again.' Lil raced back in. Mel scanned out further to the wave break, to see if she could locate Jack.

In the city, Jack would often go with a couple of friends to surf at the local beach, but Mel hadn't seen anything remarkable in those previous expeditions. She spotted her out on the break riding most of the waves that came her way.

By the time they left, the wind had shifted and the breeze made them shiver.

'Can we go there again?' Lil asked between chattering teeth.

'Yes.'

'Can we go tomorrow because the guys I talked to at the back think the swell will stick around all week?' This was from Jack.

'Definitely.' The business was closed and everything could wait. This was her time with her children in a town that felt like a summer holiday.

Chapter Thirty-nine

When she thought it was about the right time, Mel tiptoed to Lil's room the following morning.

'Lil,' she knocked and whispered, 'want to come down to the beach?'

'Why? It's early.'

'Dolphins cruise around the beach and inlet to feed.'

'Dolphins?'

'Usually every day.'

'Okay.' She could hear Lil's voice dry and thick with sleep, the rustle of sheets and a stomp.

'Wear sneakers, we might want to jog.'

Mel squeezed three orange juices and left Jack's one in the fridge.

Lil padded through to the kitchen, a wash of wavy hair tumbled around her shoulders and back and she grabbed at it to tame it into a ponytail. 'Thanks Mum.' She almost drained the glass in one gulp. 'I forgot to put a glass of water in my room. What about Jack?'

'What do you think?'

'Yeah. She won't want to come with us right now.'

'I'll leave her a note.'

The sun had already risen, but the air was morning fresh and the sky held traces of pink and peach.

Mel looked up and down the inlet. 'I can't see them so let's head right, out towards the beach area.'

Cool air made them take quick steps and they followed the beach path, where the waves rolled and the shore widened into scallops of mini-sandy bays.

'Can we go back to that surf beach and go boogie-boarding again today?'

'Of course.'

'Tomorrow?'

'Yes and every day this week and every day after work in the holidays. We have to make the most of summer down here, it doesn't last as long as Perth's summer.'

'Can Bronte come over?'

'Later. Let's get Jack used to Pelican Point first.'

Silver flashes exploded from the surface behind the breaking waves.

'Watch there, behind the jumping fish.' She pointed so Lil could spot the dolphins.

'I can see them!'

Mel gave her hand a squeeze and they ran down to the wave's edge and paddled to their knees. They tied the laces of their sneakers together and swung them in their hands.

When they turned into the inlet, the dolphins followed their quarry further out. Many more people had gathered to stand and watch from around the edge of the shore. Mel sat back on the limestone wall surrounding the grassy expanse, while Lil ventured further down to where bunches of children and parents were already about.

Someone walked up to Lil. She was close enough to hear their voices.

'Hi, I'm Eddie.' A thin dark-haired youth with a board attached to the back of his bike, introduced himself to Lil. 'You're new. Does your mum own the post office?'

'Yeah. I'm Lil. How did you know?'

'Thommo told me, but I wasn't sure if it was you. Do you have a boogie board?'

'Yes.'

'Do you want to go get it and swim out to the pontoon?'

'I'll see if I'm allowed.'

'Sure.'

They walked towards Mel. 'Do you swim out to the pontoon a lot?'

'All the time. But I've only been allowed to go by myself since I turned twelve. Before that, my grandmother or mum would sit on the wall to keep an eye on me. Mum says she'll be coming down later to see that I'm okay.' At that he made a face. Lil giggled.

'Mum, this is Eddie. He asked if I could swim to the pontoon with him on my boogie board.'

'Hello Mrs...?'

'Ms Wilson.'

'Hi Ms Wilson.'

'Can I?' Lil asked.

'Sure, but I'll be lying on the grass with my book because there aren't any lifesavers down here. Let's go get your gear. Do you want to come, Eddie?'

'Yes. I know your shop, I have to get stamps for my grandmother.'

It was only a short distance to the house. She could hear Lil and Eddie chat about schools. Lil raced into her room to get changed.

'Eddie,' Mel said, 'what school are you going to?'

'Bettong High. I'm in the special select music and maths program. Mum wanted me to go to Lil's school, Bray College, but I was offered the music program and one free tour. A lot of my friends are going to Bettong.'

'You must be good at your music.'

'I do all right on the piano, but I'm hoping to pick up another instrument. I was thinking of saxophone.'

'Lil sings and she wants to start guitar.'

'Singing is good.'

She pulled out a couple of towels from the linen press. 'You mentioned your grandmother. Does she live in town, too?'

He pushed a sweep of dark hair back from his face and revealed his fine olive skin. 'She lives with us. Since my grandfather died in Japan, she decided to come over and stay with us. Mum's her only child.'

'She must love being around you guys.'

'She does. When Mum works late at the nickel mine she

doesn't have to worry about me. Dad flies in and out of a gold mine up north. He looks after me when he's home and gives Grandma a break.'

Mel picked a cap off the hat stand. 'Here Lil, wear this,' she told her when she entered the room.

'Yuck. It's one of Jack's.'

'I washed it and it's old so if it falls off it won't be such a big deal.'

'Okay. Where is she?'

She saw the drained glass in the sink. 'She'll be talking to her friends. Breakfast and surf beach when we come back. I promised Jack. You can swim around on the pontoon for about an hour.'

'Okay.'

Lil and Eddie went ahead. Eddie pushed his bike and kept up a commentary on Pelican Point or quizzed Lil about herself. They'd only just met, but he had none of the awkwardness of other boys around Lil's age.

So, Mel thought, Eddie. She'd get his mum's number and invite her over another day.

Back at the water, Mel said, 'Don't jump if someone else is in the water and...'

'I know, Mum.'

'Right. I'll be here.'

They tossed their towels on the grass and slipped off their shoes. Eddie rested his bike on the limestone wall and they made their way to the calm edge. When it was deep enough, they pushed their boards ahead and jumped on them. Lil turned around to wave at her. The pontoon wasn't far and in a couple of minutes they were there. Eddie held the edge of a ladder with one arm and Lil's board with the other, so that she could steady herself and grip the ladder. When she climbed up, he passed the ankle rope of her board to her and then leapt up to join her. He appeared to be telling her where they should jump.

Mel watched them on the pontoon, legs dangling, observing the older children. When the main diving area was clear, they jumped in with a backflip. She nearly choked. It wasn't the safest dive to do in an unknown environment.

A slender lady came to sit further along from her. She walked over to her.

'Hi, I'm Mel Wilson. My daughter Lil is out there with Eddie. I'm thinking you're Eddie's mum?'

'Yes I am. I'm Kyu Jameson.' She had Eddie's smile and warm eyes.

'He's a nice kid. He introduced himself to Lil. It seems Thommo mentioned to him that we're new around here.'

'Thank you. He's our only one, and so far, we think so, too. Eddie told me that there was a new family at the post office.' She turned to watch the children. 'I told him not to do backflips.' She waved and indicated for him to stop. He waved back and nodded.

'Isn't there an island where you can leave children and collect them after their teenage years?' Mel joked.

'I wish, but how boring would that be.'

'True. Anyway, I have to blame my wrinkles on something.'

'I better go now. I said after he turned twelve that I wouldn't stay for the whole time. It was lovely meeting you, Mel.'

'And it was nice to meet you, too. We're not down here for longer than an hour because I promised to take both Lil and my other daughter to a surf spot.'

'Eddie will probably hang around the pontoon after you take Lil. See you later Mel.'

*

'See you Lil.' Eddie waved to her. He'd chosen to go home at the same time. His board wobbled in the holder at the back of his bike as he took off.

Lil's eyes were bright. 'That pontoon is so much fun. You'll have to come out with me one day.'

'I'd love to when there aren't so many children around.'

'Did you see Eddie? He's amazingly gymnastic for a boy.'

They paused to dust off by the front door.

'Yes I saw you both. I'm not convinced back-flipping is safe off the pontoon.'

'We stopped when Eddie's mum told him not to.'

'I noticed. We had a little chat. Her name is Kyu, pronounced *queue*. At least I hope that's correct.'

'Yeah we saw you. Eddie told me her name and that sounds about right. Can I go out there every day?'

'If you promise not to backflip.'

'Okay. I can't wait to tell Emma about it. I hope she can come down in the next week I'm here. Can she, for a couple of days?'

'We'll talk. Maybe Jack might like a friend, too. But let's wait till the third week we're together.'

'Eddie invited me around after we come back from the beach this afternoon. He told me his address and it's the street behind us, Sandpiper Lane, number forty-six. Can I go?'

'That's kind of him. I'll walk around with you, but Lil, we don't know them yet,' Mel cautioned.

'I know what you mean.'

'I trust you to be sensible.'

'Of course. I'm starving. Can we have breakfast?'

'In a minute. Tiptoe to the bathroom. These floors cost me a fortune and I am in love with them. Hang your wet gear outside.'

'Okay, I get it.' She exaggerated her steps to the bathroom.

Eddie had improved Lil's outlook and rounded out her number of new friends to two. Mel counted Sally and Thommo as her new friends, with Brad and Kyu moving into the band of people she hoped she would get to know. The customers increased the number of known faces.

'Jack, how are you?' Mel asked, when her daughter waltzed into the kitchen. She reached into the cupboard to retrieve the frying pan.

'Okay.'

'We're having pancakes.'

'Good.' She slumped over and before she could resist, Mel grabbed her in a morning hug. Jack groaned and hugged her back. She opened the fridge and pulled out a milk carton.

'Thanks Mum for the orange juice.'

'I was going to say that.' Jack looked sheepish.

'Here, use this glass.'

'I was going to.'

'Right.'

'What?'

'Nothing. You seem to be taller this morning.'

'You say that all the time.' Jack squinted her eyes.

'Sorry. Beach after breakfast?'

'Yeah. Same as yesterday?' Jack leaned against the counter and drained a glass of milk.

'Sure.'

'The guys out the back with me yesterday said it should be good this morning.'

'It was calm at the inlet.'

'Offshore breeze. I looked it up. And a two-metre swell.'

'You told me it was called Jet Spa?'

'That's right. Mainly older dudes yesterday.'

'There should be more young people out today now that the official Christmas family days are over. I thought I saw some about your age yesterday.'

'Not where I was. Have you got lemons?'

'As if I wouldn't, and the sugar, bananas and mascarpone.'

'Great.'

Mel shoved Jack with her hips as she pulled out the butter.

'Can you throw shorts over your boxers before breakfast?' Mel told her and watched as she loped off to her room to slip into some clothes.

The butter wafted and sizzled in the pan. The whisk was a blur as Mel blended the flour, eggs and milk together. She sliced the lemons and bananas and poured brown sugar into a small bowl. She spooned fat creamy globs of the mascarpone into another. Taking a small spoonful of batter, she ran it around the pan and watched the creamy edges fritter against the buttery sides. Every holiday she cooked pancakes for breakfast. She felt a return to some familiar place.

Chapter Forty

It was hard saying goodbye to her daughters at the airport at the end of the Christmas week. Mel filled in the time by working longer hours when they were with Tony, and found that the weeks they were with her flew by. When she had to work in the shop, the children would pop in. Jack would wander in to check it out then she'd retire to her room or mess around on her skateboard till she could be taken out to surf. Lil preferred to be near her mother. A good swell meant Mel would drop Jack off early in the morning and dash out to collect her at lunch. She always hoped she hadn't missed too many customers when she left.

On days when the children were with Tony, she would dig around the base of the big tree at the back to remove the forest of weeds. One morning, her small spade shuddered when it hit a solid object in the soil. Mel stopped and scooped soil out with her hands until she unearthed an oversized metal teapot. Once inside and rinsed through, she saw its robust appeal. It might have served tea in a hospital once as it was big enough to hold about fifteen cups, or else it had come from a farm. She took it into the store.

The post-Christmas trade was slow and the takings pitiful, and despite anticipating this, Mel was still disappointed. She hadn't realised how few customers would be around and wondered if she hadn't been naïve about the whole venture. Dark thoughts about the possibility of Red and Joy gilding the lily entered her mind. She was grateful for the company of Thommo. His general cheeriness and conversation on both the useful and inconsequential, added colour to her otherwise quiet days. While she didn't expect to live in luxury, she hoped to provide enough income to sustain them and pay the bills. When she calculated the present takings, it appeared they would barely cover that.

Tourists started to trickle in on a quest for souvenirs, but apart from some standard stationery made overseas and a scattering of tea towels other tableware, there wasn't much to be had. A few ideas spun around in Mel's head.

One idea kept on resurfacing and when Mel looked into it properly, she found it could all be done online. She applied for and was granted the option of selling some local foodstuffs because the store had historic precedence in that area. The main condition stipulated that she could go ahead as long as it didn't involve extensive food preparation. She only wanted to serve tea, not prepare food. Once she held the enormous no-nonsense teapot in her hands, she knew she would use it. She decided to fill it the next morning.

Beside the glowing teapot, she wrote a sign announcing that the tea was free to customers till it ran out. She found an old round table in the back storeroom, spruced it up with one of her tablecloths, and dusted down a couple of old chairs. The look was enhanced with a trimmed-down display of bush plants.

A couple of local ladies she recognised from previous visits came in to organise their mail and purchase calendars. Margaret spotted the teapot. 'What a great idea, I'd love a cup of tea. What about you, Barbara?'

'I'll bring the tea over,' Mel told them with a smile.

Pouring the tea was easy considering the enormous size of the pot.

'What have you been up to over the holidays, Mel?' Barbara put her cup down.

'The kids and I spent most of it at a few surf spots. The beaches around here are stunning.'

'Best time of year, but they can dangerous. Every year there's an accidental drowning because we have hardly any lifesavers and they can only patrol one beach.' Margaret let Barbara do most of the talking.

'I noticed.'

'Do you play tennis?' Margaret spooned in some sugar and swirled it around.

'I used to when the children were little and I didn't work.'

'You should come down and play. The club is about halfway around the inlet.'

'I may do.' The children had good racquets, but hers needed restringing.

'We're off to pennants soon.'

Margaret wasn't as tall as Barbara, but they both bore sun-browned, weathered faces. 'Barbara has had to put up with me a bit more since Trevor died.'

'Nonsense, it's what mates are for.'

'Trevor was your husband?' Mel moved over towards the shelves to tidy and organise the stock of children's school stationery.

'Yes. He passed away four years ago now. I have a son in London and a son in Canada, but they can't come home much because of their work and young families. I have a couple of nieces who love to come and spend some of the summer here. It's never that quiet at home.'

She left them to their tea to serve a few more customers when a familiar shape entered through the front door. She waved to Sally to indicate that they could talk once the last few customers were served. It was a slow day.

'What are you doing?' Sally slid over, leaned her arms on the counter and whispered, 'Are you hosting Senior Citizens' Week?'

'They'll hear you.' She whispered back and coughed. 'No. I found that teapot in the garden.'

Her brows shot straight up. 'On an archaeological dig?'

'It was under the big gum tree at the back.'

'If you serve tea you might need to offer a toilet.'

'I hadn't thought about that. No one's asked yet, but good point. Two are attached to this building, one at the back, which would be the one I'd suggest. That leaves the inside one for me.'

'Good idea. Some places make customers use public toilets. There are some near the barbecues at the Point.'

'Even better. Well done you. I keep running away with ideas. But I've checked the conditions of service and I can serve tea so long as I'm not preparing food.'

'How have you been?'

'Pretty good. The kids like it so far. Even Jack likes surfing at the beaches here. It'll take a while for her to get to know people.'

'I came over to find out if you want to join a few of us for tennis on Thursday evening, purely social.'

'I'm hopeless,' Mel told her. 'I haven't played for ages.'

'Doesn't matter. I decided to resurrect the idea with a bunch of parents because we used to do it a few years ago. It's only a few of us and I think you'll like them. Bring some money for the lights and a plate of food for supper. Starts about five and I think we'll be done by seven.'

'Sounds good to me. Thursday night is perfect.' She was free every evening. Her social life flat-lined when the children were with Tony. She would have to use Lil's racquet.

'Hello Mrs Dickson. How are you? How's the new puppy?' Mel greeted the elderly woman.

Sally moved to browse through one of the bookstands.

'That puppy chews everything, not like Tina, our old dog.'

'Isn't there a puppy school? Is that all you'd like?'

'Yes thanks. I love the discounts after Christmas. I suppose I could take her to puppy school.'

'They send down a lot of interesting products for Christmas,' Mel explained. 'Eighteen dollars fifty, thanks.'

She watched Mrs Dickson pull out her card and caught Sally's eye. Sally held up one of the calendars of firemen with their fire equipment. Mel ignored her.

'I see you have a teapot?' Mrs Dickson said.

'Yes. I'm filling it for my customers. Would you like a cup?'

Sally flicked through the calendar behind her and animated a few actions with her hands. 'No thanks. Not today. But I'll be back for one another day.'

'Thanks Mrs Dickson. See you later.'

'Bye Mel.' Barbara and Margaret waved and left. 'Loved the tea.'

'Bye ladies.'

She wandered over to Sally. 'I see a particular purchase has caught madam's eyes, you know if you salivate on the products you have to buy them. It's marked down.'

'Tempting. I'll buy it if you can give me their phone numbers.'

'And what would Brian have to say about that? I'm sorry, but you're confusing me with another kind of shop.'

'Attractive, aren't they?'

'They're pretty neat.'

'No harm in window-shopping. Anyway, better get back to Bronte. I put her in swimming lessons at the beach. She's finishing her junior bronze. I'll see you Thursday at tennis?'

'For sure. I hope the nets around the outside of the courts are high. I haven't had a hit in ages.'

With the store empty, Mel scribbled down a couple of ideas in a book behind the counter, and wondered how she could source local sealed food items to sell with the tea. Were there tea plantations around the state? There were dairies around Bettong, so she could authenticate the provenance of the milk, but she didn't even know where they sold their produce. She made a note to inquire and to investigate more food items. Her mind developed a little whir and a spike of glimmering light entered her world again. It was the rush of excitement of possibilities. She smiled to herself when she reflected on Sally's face with the calendar. They were very gorgeous-looking men and she recognised that it had been a while since she'd even thought about them.

An attractive couple and their two young boys burst through the door. The children were buzzing and one small boy looked at the teapot.

'It says free tea!' one boy enthused.

'You don't even like tea,' his mother admonished.

'Yeah but, Mum it's free.' The parents examined the small range of gifts and stationery.

'Can we have a tea please?' the boy asked.

'It says free for customers, Jake,' his father told him.

'What does that mean?'

'It means,' said the dad, 'we have to buy something.'

Mel smiled at them.

'Okay.' The small boy looked at the stand full of discounted Christmas gifts for children and dug around. 'Will you buy me something, then?'

'Jake, we've just had Christmas and Santa was very kind to you. You have plenty of toys. Mum and I might find something we need in a minute. We're going canoeing in one hour, so you can be a bit patient here.'

'Okay, Dad.'

Mel felt a little embarrassed, but she didn't want a crèche in her store anytime soon. The parents walked over to her and bought a few items of stationery. 'Would you all like some tea?'

'That would be great.' There weren't many cafés or sit-down places at Pelican Point. People had taken to wandering into her shop out of festive idleness.

'How about,' she addressed the parents, 'I load the children's tea with a lot of milk to cool it down?'

'That would be lovely.'

Mel poured the tea. 'Do you come to the Point often?' she asked them.

'We drive down a couple of times a year to visit my parents.' The wife spoke while the father extracted a tissue and mopped up a bit of milk spillage from Jake's cup. The other boy read his book and looked bored.

'Do you see a lot of people down here visiting their families, this time of year?'

'Quite a few. We catch up with some of my old school mates who arrive for the summer holidays. You're new. Mum told me about the other owners leaving. I like your tea idea.'

'Thanks. Enjoy your holiday.'

Thommo arrived and noticed the teapot. 'Do you mind if I have one, Mel?'

He liked his in a large mug and lamented about the lack of

cake. Mel informed him that he was only the hundredth person to state that.

'Tea and cake, it's like bread and butter, bacon and eggs. You need to have tea with something.'

'I'm working on a few ideas.'

He winked. 'Only teasing you. It's better than how it used to be in here.'

'How's that?'

'Red and Joy made the shop look boring. You seem to have livened it up and it feels better.'

'I appreciate that, Thommo. It's easy to do new things when you first arrive. I hope I keep it fresh in here.'

'I think you will. You already have good ideas.'

The pot ran out of tea at about eleven in the morning and she had done her best to keep it hot. A sweaty group of mature ladies swanned in, and after making a few purchases, emitted a collective sigh after noticing that the teapot was now empty. She saw an opportunity, broke with her plan of only filling it once, left the shop in their care and dashed inside to refill it. She also grabbed some of her folding chairs. They were in the same tennis team as Margaret and Barbara. The grapevine was definitely in working order.

What Mel hadn't learned in a month was gleaned in one day. She was left with invites for tennis, free bridge lessons, recipes for teacake and an assortment of unsolicited but kindly intended business ideas.

Before she left to wait for Lil, a lady bustled inside and, after sitting down to enjoy her second cup of tea, shifted her bulky frame and enthused, 'I love the tea idea. You know you could be onto something.'

It was the end of the day so Mel joined her. 'I'm Mel, and you are?'

'I'm Gemma,' she said, then she glanced around the store, 'this place could be a lovely teashop.'

'I was hoping to do more than sell tea.'

'I think you could. I belong to a knitting group and a photography group. We don't have many nice places to sit and knit or to talk to others about our special interests. You don't want to invade people's homes all the time. It would be nice if there was a different kind of place because the café at the Point gets crowded with teens and families eating burgers and drinking milkshakes.'

'I see.' Mel didn't see how she could make much money out of them, but it was an idea. 'What about the new shopping complex? Won't that have a few cafés?'

Gemma wrinkled her nose and turned down her mouth. 'There's no atmosphere at those new centres. Your place has something about it. It could become a special place.' She drained the last of her tea.

'I'm thinking of rebranding it into a new kind of store. I just haven't worked out what or how yet.'

'You've made it look attractive already. I'm glad I stopped by. What about asking other people for their ideas?'

Mel thought about how she might do that. 'Nice to meet you Gemma, and thanks for the encouragement.'

'See you soon Mel.'

Mel's spirit rose and she resurrected the image of herself as a successful business manager. A rich spirit was one thing, but to stay viable, she knew she would have to come up with a few financial brainwaves.

Chapter Forty-one

When Lil found out that Eddie was going to a different school she'd become concerned about finding new friends. On the morning of her first day at school, she resisted a kiss in the parking lot, before joining the sea of shiny shoes and white shirts. Mel's own heart thumped at watching her youngest child swim out into the unknown, but then she saw Bronte sidle up to her and walk through the gates with her and she sighed, relieved.

In the car park in the afternoon, she watched clumps of children splinter off to shuck bags and leap into their parents' cars.

'Hi there.' She smiled at Lil.

'Hi Mum.'

'How was it?'

'Okay. I'm not in Bronte's home group, but we have maths and dance together.'

'That's good.'

'Can we go to the beach after?'

'Yes, Pontoon or Jet Spa?'

'The Jets. That's what the kids call it. Will you come out boogie-boarding with me?'

'I'd love to. It's way too hot to sit on the sand.'

They drove home. The car was quiet until Lil pulled out her phone.

'Hi Dad.' Mel had forgotten that Tony had bought Lil a new phone for starting middle school. 'Yeah it was okay. I miss my friends.'

She eased the car into the driveway and grabbed Lil's schoolbag.

'We have a horse-riding school and I'm going to try out for the dance squad. Okay, bye. I love you too.'

Lil walked briskly up to the porch. When the door was unlocked, she tore straight into her room, flung herself onto the bed and cried into the covers. 'I suck at horse riding and the maths is twice as hard. I hate this school. I don't know anybody and they all know each other. I hate it here!' she cried.

Mel hung back in the kitchen. She wanted to comfort her daughter—she felt sick listening to her crying—but at the same time she didn't want to make it a bigger drama. A swim and fresh air would be the best things to make Lil forget about her difficult first day at school. So she called out from the kitchen to say that they might take the boogie boards down the beach in half an hour. She poured icy water into a glass with a lemon slice, and left it on Lil's bedside table. Lil had curled her body to face away from her, her hands gripping a pillow, and her face was red and pinched. She walked out quietly but the sobs tore holes in Mel's heart.

She needed to call Jack to check on her as well.

'Jack,' Mel said when her eldest picked up the phone.

'Hi Mum.'

'How was your first day in Year Ten?'

'Okay.'

'What are your plans for the evening?'

'Dan and I are going down to the beach to hang out with a bunch of other guys and swim. Dad said he'd pick us up later and take us out for dinner.'

'All right, be safe, wear sunblock. It's even stinking hot down here.' She could feel Jack's eyes rolling. 'And don't roll your eyes, I have extra parental sensory organs.' She waited for a response. 'You know the drill, Jack. Have a great rest of the day.'

'Yeah I know. I'm not stupid.'

'Lil and I are heading out to Jet Spa. The kids call it the Jets. I'll take you back there next time.'

'Okay.'

'Bye Jack. I love you.'

'Me too. Bye, Mum.'

Mel hung onto the phone and flicked through to a recent photo she'd taken of her daughter. She stared into the closed-up teenage face, every bit more boy than girl. She moved over to the kitchen table, leaned back on her chair, closed her eyes and prayed for a time when it would feel like she wasn't in a boxing ring.

She waited for about twenty minutes. She could hear Lil talk to Emma on the phone and heard some light laughs sprinkle the conversation and let out a breath, not realising she'd been holding one in.

'Lil, do you want to get ready for the Jets?' she called.

'Can I say goodbye to Emma first?'

'For sure.' Mel resisted any lectures on phone use and let her finish.

Eddie arrived and banged on the flywire door.

'Hi Ms Wilson. Is Lil home?'

'Yes.'

'There are dolphins down at the Point. I thought she might like to come and see them and swim out to the pontoon with me.'

'Um...'

'Is that Eddie Mum?'

'Yes,' she said and pulled open the door. 'Come in Eddie, it's too hot to stand on the porch.'

'Tell him to come in. I'll be out in a minute.' She heard a thump as school shoes were dropped. She gave a little prayer of thanks.

When Eddie saw Lil, he noticed her eyes. 'What's up?' With bathers underneath a hastily dragged on tee shirt and shorts, she looked every bit a carefree child, but the face was still undone.

'Allergies.' She cast a brief look up to her mum, before they blazed out of the door.

Mel tidied away the chopped fruit and walked to the inlet. It was warm with only a flicker of a breeze. She loved how she could close the store and walk down to the inlet or beach straight from home. It was one of the best changes from her previous life. The air was fragrant with salt spray, seaweed musk and fishy overtones from guano laid down by the pelicans and cormorants.

She saw Lil and Eddie with a small splatter of other children on the pontoon. The Jets could wait for another day.

*

'So the horse riding was a bit of a challenge?' Mel asked later that evening.

'All the other kids have been on horses for ages. I'm so bad at it.' Lil's mouth turned down.

'Really? All the other children could ride well?'

She picked up a corncob. 'Not every single kid.'

'Maybe we could get some extra sessions on the weekend to help build the skills you need?' There had to be some compensation for leaving her friends.

Lil put the cob down and forked a piece of chicken. 'That's exactly what the instructor suggested for anyone wanting to enter this year's competitions.'

'I'll look them up tonight and book you in,' Mel suggested.

'It's run at the school, but you better get in early.'

'Yes ma'am.'

'Thanks.'

'Did you meet any other kids who are also new to the area?'

'A couple.' Even though she hadn't intended to probe, she could see Lil tiring of the conversation. 'Can I talk to Emma again and tell her about the dolphins?'

'Yes. Why don't you phone your dad too? I'll clean up.'

Lil wandered over to sit on her knee and they hugged. It wasn't fun watching the pain lines on her little face as she wrestled with the newness of it all.

Each day that week, Eddie banged on the door and the two children skittered out of the house. Lil still said she sucked at horse riding and maths. Eddie found everything easy.

Chapter Forty-two

'Be nice to Jack when you get to your dad's.' Mel helped Lil pack her clothes for the weekend flight to Perth.

'She's the mean one.'

'It's the first time during the school term that I won't be around to drop you off. She'll be missing us.'

'I doubt she misses me,' Lil said.

'Maybe that's the case right now, but it won't always be. Promise?'

'Okay. I'm so tired. Why does it leave at six o'clock in the morning?'

'People have business to do. Usually you'll catch the Friday-evening flight.'

'Good.' Lil tipped her body over the case and closed her eyes.

'Come on. You can rest on the plane.'

After the plane took off, Mel stayed until it traced a path into the northern reaches of the sky. The sky domed over, morning bright, and she felt a fine trail of sweat slide down her back. If she left it any later she wouldn't be able to jog and she wanted to move. It was the best time for ideas to unfold in her mind and it would numb some of the ache she felt about missing Jack.

Empty nesters had packed out both of the caravan parks, Sally told her, so Mel had made the decision to open the store till lunchtime.

She tidied the shelves and worked on a display of discounted Christmas goods. Thommo slipped into the store. 'Hi Mel. I knocked on your front door. I didn't expect you'd be opening the shop on a Saturday. Another of your new ideas?'

He stood still. His hands went in and out of his pockets and he pushed thin hair back from his forehead, where a sweaty red streak had formed from the helmet. There was a serious line to his lips. 'Yes. I'm going to give it a go, see what happens. Are you okay?'

'I've got something to tell you.' There was no one else in the shop at the time, yet he seemed to waver. She was used to him dropping in, but today was a bit unusual for both of them since it was a Saturday.

'Yes?'

'I have a medical situation.'

'I see. I guess you'll be away then?'

'I have to have a couple of months off the bike while I have some treatment.' Tony's dad had prostate cancer and had pulled through, and Mel was guessing Thommo had the same, but it was only a hunch.

'How will I survive without you? Though I'm sure they'll send a replacement.'

'I already have one.'

'That was quick.'

'I know. It was good timing. It's my son. He's come back to work on his other business.'

He looked pleased with himself. Mel, on the other hand, thought that a young man zooming around the neighbourhood wouldn't necessarily be up to Thommo's universal appeal, and would lack the capacity to solve her various problems. Nor would he have Thommo's ability to buoy her up in her fledgling business. She realised just how much she had come to rely on Thommo, as Red and Joy had said she would.

'He's been away,' he continued, 'but he grew up here.'

They'd built up a great camaraderie, though the topic of his son hadn't featured that much. Thommo had amused her with endless stories of the town and its people because of his many decades of history, and she wanted to hear more. Now he and his font of information would be gone for a while. He'd also become a friend. She felt guilty thinking only of herself and grabbed him in a hug, taking them both by surprise.

The store echoed with his departure, but she rounded on herself and snapped open her computer. She enrolled in an online marketing course. Her nights had to be filled with steps towards something.

The Saturday-morning trade gave her no time to dwell. Sally was right, there were sufficient idlers on holiday to warrant a big change of stock type, plus the tea was an outright winner.

The new week began with less of the harsh weariness of the first week of school. She expected a gradual ease as they slid into their new routine, but Thommo's illness and impending departure unsettled her.

Chapter Forty-three

Thommo organised lists of things that needed attending to for PJ. 'Paul John Thompson, but we call him PJ,' Thommo had said as they'd sat with a tea after his last morning round. Mel knew PJ was returning from a position of coach and mentor to some up-and-coming professional surfers and had a part-share in the surf shop in Bettong.

'Mel, I've come to say goodbye.'

She rushed over and embraced him one last time. Tears pricked the corners of her eyes.

'You'll be okay. You've got the shop going and you have PJ.' He was comforting her. She stood back and wiped her eyes.

'Mel, this is PJ.'

The first thing she noticed was that he wasn't as young as she thought he would be. He was easily in his mid-thirties. He was tall, broad-shouldered, sun-browned, and his short brown hair was fuzzed blond by too much sun. He stood regarding her with his sea-green eyes.

She was trying to think of the right thing to say without seeming like she was star struck or starved of male company. She was spared when he stepped forward to shake her hand.

'Hi Mel. Dad has told me what to do and you're not to worry, he's pretty good like that.' He had some of the same manner as Thommo. He continued, 'I'm just glad to be able to help him because he hardly ever lets me.'

'Now that's sorted,' Thommo interrupted, 'just keep him busy. He's almost as useful as me with the tools, but chances are if the surf's up he'll be off.'

'It'll be great to have you on board, PJ,' she said. 'I'm still so new around here. A local will be a real asset.'

'No problems Mel. I'll just go and get changed for work and I'll be back around ten.'

When they left, she stood and swayed, captured by the thought of how pleasant it would be to have PJ around. He probably had a fleet of gorgeous women in tow. She decided he was a tonic, like Thommo, and there was nothing wrong with medicine like that.

He appeared as the mail truck arrived and it seemed strange to see him astride the motorbike she had considered Thommo's. He didn't linger. When he returned after the mail run, he looked hot. 'I'll see you Monday Mel, just taking the old man to the airport.'

'Okay PJ, see you Monday.' He smiled up at her as he turned to leave. She tried not to watch the motorbike as it disappeared around the corner. The smile made her stomach flip-flop.

*

After she deposited Lil on the six-o'clock Saturday-morning flight the following fortnight, Mel headed out for an early run and swim. With the recent tennis and jogging, she noticed an improvement in the muscle tone in her arms and legs.

The only time she could work on the house was when Tony had the children. She had a few ideas about what she could do to the massive amount of land alongside the store, but she tucked those away for a time in the future when she hoped she had some money. In the meantime, painting was her only affordable upgrade option.

Thommo had helped a lot when she'd tackled Jack's room. The other rooms all begged to be brightened and changed. She'd come to rely on his advice about her home renovations and he'd taught her how to mask up for a paint job. In his texts, he told her the food was hideous and the view out the window was of another ward in the hospital. He missed the sea.

She shut the shop at noon and slipped on an old linen shirt

of her mother's. Her mother's timeless cologne wafted when she pushed her arms through the shirtsleeves and she smiled. The morning's takings warranted opening every Saturday during the tourist season.

She prised open the wooden door of the shed where she'd stored the paint. All of the walls needed to be in a light creamy colour to go with the bare wooden boards and to add warmth and brightness. Latte, it said on the paint card. She'd allowed each child to have one feature wall.

With Jack's room done before Christmas, it was Lil's turn. Her non-existent social life, apart from Sally's invites, gave her plenty of time to paint. She looked forward to the family night and parent cocktail evening at Lil's school to get to know a few more people other than the customers she'd met so far. Eddie's mum, Kyu, worked and then looked after her own mother; it limited their opportunities to get to know each other.

Painting was not a skill she had ever mastered. Within a few minutes she'd streaked her hair, splattered her shoes and speckled her face. Drops of paint seemed to find their way onto the floor and stuck to the soles of her shoes—luckily, she'd covered her precious floorboards—but from then on she tried to be more careful. She only just heard a knock on the door when her headphones slipped and became another redecorated casualty in the paint zone.

She wiped her hands on her shirt and pelted down the hallway to unlatch the door.

'Dad suggested I drop around.' It was PJ, looking fresh and gorgeous and smiling at her. 'He told me about the painting.' He ran his eyes over her paint-splattered clothing. 'He also told me that it wasn't your strong point.'

She wiped strands of hair from her eyes and spread more paint onto her face and wondered if the paint masked her astonishment at seeing him on the porch. 'He's right, but I'm getting the hang of it. He gave me some excellent tips.'

'I'm not brilliant myself, but Dad and I have done a bit of painting together. We did the painting during the refit of the surf shop. It saved a lot of money.'

'I bought my daughter's surfboard there. It has a great atmosphere.' She wasn't sure if she was deliberately dumbing down her language because he was a surfer or, because she had so little conversation with good-looking men she had become dumbfounded. 'To be honest, PJ, I'd love a hand. Are you sure this is what you want to do on your time off?'

'I had nothing on. I've seen the guys at the store and been for a surf.'

'I know it's your dad's suggestion, but you don't have to.'

'Don't feel you have to be polite, you can say no.'

She swallowed. 'It would be fantastic to have someone with a bit of skill help out, but the agreement is I'll pay you what I paid Thommo, okay?'

'Deal.' They shook and some paint ended up on his sea-cleansed hands.

'How is your dad?' He followed her into the laundry, where the painting equipment was temporarily housed. She suggested he begin with the edging, since she couldn't edge without getting paint on the cornice work or skirting boards. They walked into Lil's room, where he put paint on the edger and leaned down close to the skirting boards to start, while she picked up the roller.

'Okay. He's responding to some of the treatment.'

'That's great.' She used the rollers to do the big sweeps, he worked on the details and edging, and followed her as she completed each section. 'What did you do overseas?'

'I was part of the support crew for an Australian group of surfers. I took them out on jet skis, coached and fixed boards. I'm a bit of a go-get-everything kind of guy, plus I did some junior coaching in the quiet times.'

'Were you ever on the circuit?' she asked him.

'Only when I was a Junior in Australia. I travelled for a while after that. A few years later, I came back. Three of us pitched in and opened the surf store in town. They run it when I'm out of town and I direct a bit of traffic there with my contacts. I pour a lot of my earnings into it. We keep in touch all the time.'

'It sounds like you've had a fabulous life.'

'Some of it was, but the constant moving wears you down. Nothing is as glamorous as it looks.'

'Is this where you plan to live?' She tried not to sound too hopeful.

'I don't know. I've always thought of it as home because of Dad and the business. I haven't lived with him for ages though. I usually drop in and then move on. Now that I'm hanging out in his cottage, it seems a bit strange without him around.'

'I'll get the pistachio paint tin for this wall.' She lifted her roller up to wash, only to pause for a few moments to watch him. He reached up with his arm, the muscles in his back taut and pronounced as he ran the edging tool along under the cornice, and his tee-shirt, unlike hers, had barely a fleck of paint on it.

'Pistachio?' He turned and caught her studying him. She fussed with the roller and the tray.

'Yes, it's one of her favourite colours. I'll wash this out and come back.' She hoped the blossoming red of her cheeks was suitably disguised by the splatter of paint she was freckled with.

'I love pistachio ice cream.'

'Me too. A French café near my house in Perth sold pistachio macarons with pistachio ice cream inside. I really miss them.' She hoped she wasn't gushing.

He stopped and examined his work. 'I better come with you and rinse this out for the pistachio edging. I'm done here.'

'You are so neat. There's not a drop on you.'

They went to the laundry room to soak the rollers and edger. She left him there and took happy light steps to the shed to collect the other paint tin, and on her return she caught herself breathing in his oceanic scent.

'Do you want to stop?'

'No. Let's wait till we've finished your daughter's room.'

When they went back in, the heat from the afternoon had almost dried all of the paint. 'I'm glad I'm doing this in summer.'

'Much too wet here in winter.' He scooped a little of the paint on his edger and continued. She dipped her roller in the tray and found that the creaminess of the other walls did make the pistachio pop. It also popped, splattered and dripped onto her shoes, shirt and face, but she decided to ignore all of that.

Sweat ran and soaked their clothes, despite Lil's overhead fan.

'You have an eye for colour,' he said. 'I like the look of the other room, too.'

'That's my eldest daughter's room, Jack. She's the surfer.'

'It looks great. Where's your phone?'

'I don't want Lil to see the room yet. It's to be a surprise.'

'I wasn't going to take a shot of the room. I want to take one of you. You need to see yourself and your kids need to see how you look.'

'Right.' She found her phone in the lounge room. 'This can be a lesson in how not to paint.'

'Or that,' he said. She let him take her photo then excused herself to strip off her paint gear and remove some of the paint from her face. She suggested he head to the kitchen.

They stretched out on the chairs at the kitchen table with a glass of iced tea and sliced watermelon. The last rays of light lit up the evening sky and sent in filtered beams through the dust and salt-speckled windows. PJ looked to her like some kind of sports star, while she felt she looked like the hard-working, middle-aged woman she was. She found everything about him easy and time ran away from her.

'What brought you down here?' he asked.

'I wanted to start a business and this came up. There's not much like this in Perth.' She felt the colour rise in her cheeks again.

'Sorry if I'm being personal.'

'No, it's fine. I thought a move away from the city would give me a chance to live a different kind of life.'

'And have you? What do you think so far?'

As he ran his hand through his thick hair, she could see that he only bore the tiniest dots of paint on the sandy-coloured shafts of hair that ran over his arms. He looked up at her.

'It's been very different and not without challenges. I miss Jack the most and I'm too far away to drop in on my mother and sister, but I've made a few friends and Lil has, too. The business is another issue. I'm still figuring out what I'm going to do about that. I like being so close to the bay and beaches. I love not needing my car so much.'

'Me too. I've realised how easy it is to live here since I've come back.' He drew himself up and jiggled the ice around in his glass. 'But it can be quiet. I have my surf shop in Bettong, so I'm always going into town to talk to the guys about new developments with that, and to have dinner with them. My other mates are scattered on farms or they've moved away. There aren't that many people my age around here.'

'You would have seen so much in your travels.'

'Enough to know that people are similar everywhere, and that we are lucky to have so much unspoilt coastline. I've been privileged to see some of the world's best beaches and some dodgy cities.'

'Jack loves to surf,' she told him, trying not to get too caught up in looking into his eyes.

'It's a mecca down here, and because of the distance from Perth it should stay that way. She'll love it, but she'll need a thick wetsuit once summer is over.'

'I hadn't thought about that.' She bit her lip.

'Lucky you know someone who can give you a discount at the local surf shop, then.'

'You don't have to do that.'

'I'm insisting. Is she keen to compete?'

'I'm not sure.'

'It's become a bit heated, the whole junior surf competition. Too many people want their child to be the next big surf legend and Australia does produce the rankings, but it's not like when I was a kid.'

'Not just in surfing.'

'The ugly parent syndrome.'

'It's everywhere in my children's sports, but I don't think Jack or Lil want to be that competitive. They'd have to want to do that for themselves.' She knew Lil had it in her to be good at a few sports, including dancing, but she hoped she didn't want to follow anything to that point of devotion. Jack was the real unknown quantity. Mel wasn't sure what she was passionate about or where she saw herself in the future. Adolescent metamorphosis was a long process.

'I can't see you being an ugly parent,' he said suddenly.

She blushed under the remaining scabs of dried paint.

'Sorry Mel, I have to leave now. Robby and Macka, my business partners and mates, have invited me to dinner with their wives.'

'Hang on.' She darted into her room to pick up the notes and raced back. 'Here you go.'

'I didn't do that much,' he protested.

'It was a deal.'

'Okay, this time.'

'I can't wait to see Lil's face when she arrives home.'

'They're lucky to have such a thoughtful mum.'

'Thank you. I should get you to market me to my kids.'

When she brushed alongside his arm as they walked through the hallway to the front door, it sent a small tremor throughout her body. On the porch he turned towards her and flashed a brief smile.

'See you later Mel.'

'See you PJ.' She hoped that came out as casual friendliness and not as drooling. She peeked through the lounge-room blinds and watched his four-wheel drive reverse onto the road and drive off.

Chapter Forty-four

The lounge room required extensive preparation, but after an early-morning run along the beach, Mel felt she could handle anything. The memory and scent of PJ lingered in the house.

The paint was puckered in places from old water damage and other sections were powdery. A new roof a couple of years ago meant the water damage would have happened some time back, but she knocked on the walls to check.

She scraped, filled, sanded and sugar-soaped the walls until she heard someone at the door. When she whipped off her dust mask, a ghostly visage stared back in the hallway mirror. She pulled open the door and wiped away at some of the paint dust with the back of her hand. PJ was on the porch with two takeaway coffee cups in a cardboard tray in one hand, and a brown paper bag in the other.

'I have a roll of indeterminate quality and moderately acceptable coffee from the café at the Point. Interested?' He lifted both arms slightly to show her.

'Sure, but you do know it's Sunday? You don't have to feel sorry for me and my painting is improving.'

He looked at her.

'Okay.' She invited him in. 'Not surfing?'

'I was but so was a white pointer.'

They walked into the kitchen, where they sat down to drink the coffee. They demolished the roll and polished off some mangoes she'd bought.

'I needed that, thanks PJ.' Did he go out with girls with real appetites? Why was she thinking this?

'Not much fun eating on my own. The lounge room today?'

'Yes. I've done the prep and covered everything with drop sheets.'

'You want me to do the edging again?'

'If that's okay? I've put the ladder in the room.'

'Sure. One thing these old places have going for them is their high ceilings. The floor looks great. Did you get it done recently?'

'As soon as I could because the carpet was hideous and choked up with cat dust and hair.'

'Not pleasant.' They moved to the laundry, where she kept the painting tools and tins from yesterday. 'No pistachio today?'

'No, going for boring beige, as Lil would say. Anyway, the shop calls it latte.' Intelligent conversation deserted her and she was mortified.

'This won't take long with two of us.'

'Could you sand off any lumps that I've overlooked as you go?'

'Of course. Don't undersell yourself, you've done a good job on the prep.'

If she'd had a tail it would have wagged. She rolled the spongy roller in the tray, collected too much paint, and then spent an age rolling it back and forth over the tray to achieve the consistency she wanted. Despite her best efforts, a lot of it oozed back along the handle and through the tube. When she worked the roller on the wall, the splatter freckled her hair, face and any exposed body part with a fine shower of paint drops. A small giggle escaped.

'What?'

'Amusing myself with my incompetence.' She continued rolling.

When he stood on the ladder, she glanced at his legs, back and arms, and became mesmerised by his expert motion. 'Painting isn't that easy. You've got the messy end of the job.' He turned and caught her watching him again. She reddened and went to reapply paint to the already sodden roller.

'I know, but I'm sure this didn't happen to Michelangelo.'

'No. He did have underlings to do his tasks.'

Like me, Mel thought, *I have you*. It took a lot of energy to stop thinking about him and to focus on the painting.

They finished half the room's first coat, which would dry by the time they finished the last wall. She looked forward to a break with him.

'What about a swim after?'

'I have to leave to pick up Lil at about five because her plane lands at six, and by the time I drive out to the airport...'

'We'll have plenty of time. It's the best thing for getting rid of the paint, and by then, you'll have a lot to get rid of.' He stepped down the ladder and leaned over her tray to recoat the edger. He was so close she could feel the warmth of his body and the gentle wave of air he created as he stood back up. He rested the edger on the tray.

'Want a drink now?' he asked.

'I better.' She wiped strands of damp hair away from her forehead. 'It's pretty hot.'

'Here.' He passed her one of the iced water bottles she'd placed in an old cooler bag in the centre of the room, and leaned back to drink. She watched his lips and the trail of water drip down his light stubble, course down his neck and soak some of his tee-shirt.

He took the bottle from her, and when his hand brushed hers, she tried not to quiver. He placed them both back in the cooler bag. 'You're improving.'

'How can you tell?' she said.

'The cooler bag hasn't got any paint on it.'

'It's in the centre of the room.'

'Just saying.' He shrugged.

'I haven't finished yet.'

'And I can still see your face. Wait. You are Mel, right?'

She felt tickled from the inside.

'I'll take you.'

Her heart thudded at the unexpected words. 'Pardon?'

'I'll take you to a beach where we can rinse off.' He collected the edger and stepped up the ladder. They were only new friends, but it was a small town.

'Thanks. Is it one of your secret surf spots?' She tried to roll out a clog of paint.

'Not really. It's not in town, but not too far away. We'll be back in plenty of time.'

'Okay,' she said. It embarrassed her how little persuasion it took.

They washed out the painting gear and Mel ran to her bedroom to throw on bathers and a simple dress for the trip to the beach. With a towel and bag in her hands, she locked the front door and stepped down the porch into his waiting car.

'You were quick,' he said, and she wished she had longer to tidy up properly.

On the drive to the beach she shared her limited knowledge of surfing gleaned from Jack and Lil, and he spoke about the surf spots he used to go to as a kid.

The beach was secluded and only a handful of young adults clustered in small groups up and down the shore.

Mel took off her dress and was glad she'd been boogie-boarding with the kids. She hadn't been this close to a man for a while with so little material on, though her bikinis were not like the tiny scraps of fabric she noted on the long-limbed bodies of the young women further along the beach. She ran into the cold slap of water. PJ secured his phone and keys after talking to one of his business partners.

Mel drifted and swam but turned to watch as he removed his shirt. His lean musculature shone with sweat and the sun glanced off his blond edges. When he faced her, she spun around and swam. He looked like summer. All day as he'd painted, she felt him create a current of air in the still lounge room, like a breeze, which she'd catch as it ran soft and light on her skin. It was a new experience.

The strand of bikini-clad young women raised themselves on their elbows and didn't take their eyes off him till he dived under the shore break to swim towards her.

'Here.' He took long, easy strokes and offered her a mound of wet sand. 'Rub this into your arms and legs where the paint is, it'll come off easily.'

She took the sand and started rubbing, and the paint sloughed off. 'That was a good idea.' There was so much going on inside her.

'How are your body-surfing skills? Want to catch a few waves?'

'Sure.'

'Come on then.' They stroked out and treaded water. 'Now!' he instructed.

It nearly caught her, but she pushed her hands forward, clasped them and kept her head low as she rode through. For a moment she was held there suspended, his body so close in the tumble of wash. They stood in the shallows and fought against the onslaught of steady waves.

'Let's go again.' He pushed his way forward with her. The water clutched and pinned their legs as they took awkward steps against the rush and pulse of waves. When it was deep enough, they dolphin-dived and headed out behind the break.

When they were back on the sand, she wrapped a towel around her body and apologised. 'I better get back, but that was so much fun. Thank you.'

He draped a towel around his waist. 'We should do that again.'

She had an urge to run her hands over his chest, arms and shoulders, but instead she focused on her feet and slipped her sandals on. 'It was the best way to get the paint off.'

'I meant I'd like to take you to the beach again, not just after painting. Only if you have nothing on and your kids are away for a weekend?'

'I'd really like that.'

He drove her home and pulled over beside her house.

'Wait, I've got some money for you.' She started to open the door, but his hand on her arm stopped her.

'No Mel, I don't want any money. I came to help. Come here, you've missed a bit.' He leaned over and removed the last dot of paint from near her eye. 'You don't want that on your face when you go to the airport.'

He was so close it was intoxicating. 'I had a great day, PJ. I'd still be painting if you hadn't turned up.'

'No problem. I'll see you tomorrow at work.' He waved and drove off. Mel leapt up the steps of the porch and floated to the bathroom. The living-room walls beamed at her and she peeked into Lil's room on the way to the bathroom. It all looked amazing and it wasn't even close to how she felt.

Chapter Forty-five

Lil was almost asleep by the time they reached home.

'What did you get up to?' Mel asked.

'Dad and I spent about four hours at the beach. It was so warm.'

'How's Jack?'

Lil snorted and collected her bag to walk to the porch. 'She hardly said hello and spent most of the time in her room. Dad made her.'

'Why?' They went to the kitchen for a drink.

'Because she isn't getting some of her school work done and has been spending a lot of time hanging out with Danny.'

'I thought your dad liked Danny?'

'He does, but Danny's getting Jack to join up with a bigger group of boys and girls. This group just hangs around and does stuff.'

'Oh,' Mel said, not really knowing what that meant. She should phone Tony and find out what was going on and then talk to Jack.

'Did you catch up with Emma?'

'And Sophie and Sarah. They all wanted to catch up with me. Dad said that we should all meet at the beach. That's why we were there for so long.'

'How are they?'

'They're great. They miss me, but they were jealous of the horse riding and they loved the photo of the dance centre. They all want to come down and swim at the pontoon, too. I hated saying goodbye to them.'

'Every holiday you'll spend half the time with your dad and that way you can see all your friends, plus you have every second weekend.'

'It's not the same as being at school with them.'

'I know.' They finished their iced water. 'Why don't you take your bag to your room? I'll make supper.'

'It smells like you've been painting.'

'I have.' Lil took off with her bag. 'Unpack and put your grubby clothes in the laundry.'

'I know already.' Mel heard the door open. 'Mum! It looks so good.' Lil ran back into the kitchen and wrapped her arms around Mel. 'I didn't think you'd get that much done. My room is awesome and it looks way better than apricot. The doona cover and cushions are great.'

'I had help. PJ has taken over from Thommo and he helped me out. I'm not that great on my own.'

'You're okay at painting. And I saw the lounge, too. It looks so new.'

'Thanks. I loved painting your room.' Mel leaned down to hold her and for a moment they stood locked in a hug in the kitchen.

'I'm going to take a photo and show Em and Dad.' Lil whizzed away, a blaze of pre-teen bounce.

Once Lil drifted off to sleep, Mel called Tony.

'Hi Tony. Can we talk for a minute?'

'Mel, hi. Sure. What's wrong?'

'Is Jack okay?'

'Why?'

'Lil said she's been hanging around with a bunch of kids and got into trouble. I just wondered if there was anything I needed to know, that's all.'

'You're not here, Mel and I'm not going to document every stray teenage moment Jack has. Just accept that things are being dealt with.' His voice prickled.

'I may be down here, but she's still my daughter and I wanted to discuss her with you.'

He huffed out a breath. 'She's been hanging out with her

mates and doing more socialising than homework. I slashed the socialising this weekend, that's all.'

'Okay then, thanks. Bye Tony.' Not a very satisfactory conversation, but Jack was coming down next weekend and Mel could hardly wait to see her. Maybe then she could unpack a little of what was happening in her world.

The next day she waited a little off the main route of the bus stop, until she saw Lil emerge from the school gate.

'Hi Mum. I'm working on my horse riding this weekend. And guess what? Mina—I'll tell you about her later—invited me back this weekend for extra horsemanship—that's what she calls it—with her private instructor. That is so amazing. Imagine having your own private horse instructor!'

'That's really kind of her. Mina lives nearby?'

'Yes. Well I think so. You'll need to use the parent contact list and phone to find out. Mina says that the address isn't listed, just a number. You can get the address when you call. I can go can't I?'

'I'm sure there won't be a problem. But you know the rules, Lil, I have to know them and your safety is important.'

'I know. Her grandma looks after her because her dad travels away. He's an international businessman.'

'What about her mum?'

'She didn't say anything about her.'

'Oh.'

'I know. I thought she'd tell me when she wanted to.'

'Good move.'

'She's so smart and she's going to help with some of my maths because she's a maths genius.'

'Excellent. You mean she's better than me?' Mel teased.

Lil shoved her with her hips. 'You're okay.'

'Gee thanks.'

When they stepped inside the house, Lil bounded to her room. Mel went to the living room and looked around at the fresh, clean walls. She couldn't be in the room without reliving the pleasurable sensations that coursed in her veins about everything from that Sunday. She dug around in the drawer of the cabinet where she stored the parent list and found Mina's name. It was Mina Derijaweer, and only the father was listed, a Mr Moqutat Derijaweer.

'Hello? I'm Lil Wilson's mum, Mel. I believe Mina is a new friend of hers?'

'Oh wait please.' The grandmother had limited English and called for the nanny. A young woman with a soft accent spoke.

'Hi, I'm Suraya, Mina's nanny. How can I help?'

Mel explained about the horse riding.

'Of course she can come. We'd love to have her.'

'I'll bring her on Saturday afternoon and can you let me know about how to get there? I'm new to the area. Also, what about horse-riding safety?'

'Mrs Wilson, Mina's father is very protective of his only daughter. We've employed a really wonderful lady to instruct Mina and you'll see this when you come out. Your daughter's safety is as important to us as Mina's. Please come and have tea with us when you drive out here. Mina isn't allowed on the horses without a lot of protection and adult supervision.'

'Thank you, that will be lovely. I won't stay long because I'll have my other daughter down from Perth.'

'That's fine. We look forward to meeting you both on Saturday afternoon.'

'See you then.' Mel was left wondering. Should she know who Moqutat Derijaweer was?

Chapter Forty-six

The likelihood of PJ going surfing rapidly increased with the weather that rolled in and the mail often had to wait until he returned. It didn't bother Mel because his customers were eager to talk to him about his day when he did his rounds and they didn't care when that was.

An international professional surf competition was to be held soon. PJ told her he had to keep out on the surf break both for his own personal development and to maintain a presence for the surf shop. Bettong had been chosen to host it for the first time and that meant that the town and the outlying areas were donning more tidy and glamorous facades. Pelican Point would be near the epicentre. Ripples of its effect would be felt, even in her small shop.

After his round later in the week, PJ stepped over to confide in her. 'Dad's not doing so well. He's suffering with the treatment a bit more than expected.' He slumped into a chair and wiped his damp forehead with the back of his hand. When his legs brushed against hers, she wished it didn't make her body quake and she could just be his work colleague and friend. 'I'm worried he's giving in. He's had to be the tough guy for me, since my mum left. Then his second wife had issues and left, too. The old hippy and surf culture left Dad stranded in its wake. I may surf, but I draw the line.'

The shop was empty and Mel was about to close. She rested a hand on his shoulder.

'I'm so sorry to hear that about Thommo. He's so strong I doubt that he'll give up. It's the treatment. It knocks everyone around.'

'Thanks Mel.' When he stood to leave, she had to control an impulse to hug him. When he puttered away on the motorbike, she tried not to gaze longingly after him.

Jack was due for her first weekend after the holidays. Whatever chaos her teenage heart was experiencing on its path through puberty and beyond, Mel vowed she would weather it with her.

She reflected on her sister, David, her mother, Christos, the accident, Pete McIver, and herself; adolescence was only the beginning.

Chapter Forty-seven

PJ breezed into the store on Friday. 'I spoke to Dad last night and he's feeling better.' He tapped the counter and smiled. 'What are you up to this weekend?'

'Jack's flying down tonight.'

'That's right, you said. No body painting this weekend?'

'Ha. No. I'll take Jack to the beach and Lil to horse-riding lessons. What about you?'

'Surfing and filming. The whole focus of the comp will give amazing exposure to this region. Are you going to paint the following weekend?'

'I may do. The house needs a lot of work.'

'I won't be available in the immediate future with the comp coming up, but after it dies down, I'll be glad to help.'

'You mean you'll be glad to let me splatter while you tidy up and finish the job.'

'You're fun to watch.' She could say the same. 'Mail truck, I better go. See you later.'

When he came back from his delivery, he was drenched with sweat. He dismounted from the bike and poured water from the hose over his head and shirt. Mel locked the shop and flipped her sunglasses down from her head. She caught the full blast of the garden hose and shrieked. PJ laughed. She grabbed the hose and squirted him back.

'I knew you had it in you,' he teased.

'What?'

'This.'

'I don't usually get squirted by postmen.'

'You haven't lived.'

She threw him a towel from the washing line and grabbed one for herself. She felt the colour glow and spread around her face and neck when she saw the look on his face.

'How come you don't have a man?'

'Divorced, in my forties, impoverished, and I have teenagers. Not sure that is a most striking feature.'

'A bit harsh.'

'A bit true. Also, I may have accidentally ended up in a town where the average age is seventy.'

'Not for long. There's a lot of development happening.'

'That will help.' She soaked up some of the water with the towel. He took off his shirt and shook his hair. She had trouble breathing.

He let the breeze run over his bare skin. 'You're an attractive woman, Mel. I'm sure other guys have noticed.'

'Thanks.' She wiped the towel over her arms and neck, trying not to blush. He stepped towards her. He stayed close and lifted his hand up to her face, traced over it, and worked over the outline of her lips. Mel held her breath but felt brave enough to run her fingertips over his chest, shoulders and arms. He kissed her.

'I have to go,' she whispered, her throat thick. Her hands ran all over his shoulders, and when they kissed again she knew there would be more. 'Lil's due back in a few minutes. We're going out to collect Jack from the airport.'

He brushed hair from her face and planted his feet outside hers, his body close, warm and enticing. 'I'll come over next weekend then. You'll be on your own, you'll need help.'

Yes, she thought, I'll need help breathing when you're around. She couldn't move. She felt delirious with the delicious rise of sensations long buried under her adult soul. There was a gentle eruption of sensuality, of what it was like after that first kiss, the simple pure ache and longing of her younger self.

'That will be great.' She didn't say anymore because his lips had closed around hers and he ran his hands up her arms and cupped her face to kiss her more deeply.

Even though Mel wanted to bask in the delectable thrill of him, she had many balls in the air to juggle. It didn't stop a hot flush running through her when she thought about the prospect of being alone with him, and not painting.

*

Lil greeted her with a bubble of her own euphoria. 'My extra lesson is at ten tomorrow. Mina said to come around one in the afternoon and stay till dinner. Is that okay? I can't wait to have two horse-riding lessons. Mina is so nice. You'd really like her. She's so interesting.'

'How so?'

'Her stepmother lives in London with her two brothers. Mina flies to England for Christmas and then they all go to Oxford Street and Paris to buy Christmas presents. I don't know what's so good about Oxford Street, but she said it's got great Christmas lights along the street and on the shop fronts, and they have a public ice-skating rink in winter. How cool is that?'

'Pretty cool.' Lil bounced along the footpath to the front door. The sun was punishing, but the line of thin sapling peppermint gums planted by their neighbour lent some coolness and a fresh fragrant air, as they bent and flicked around in the light sea breeze behind the palings. Mel effervesced in private deliciousness.

'Mina's dad set up this horse property and decided to live in Australia with Mina before he met his second wife, but Mina never got on that well with her and the stepmother preferred London. That's all Mina told me. She's so lucky. She can fly anywhere in the world in her dad's private plane, but she loves being here with the horses and her grandmother.'

'Her dad must miss her.' They entered the kitchen, where Mel had left some fruit chopped up on a plate. Lil picked up a small wedge of watermelon.

'He does, but they talk every day. He spends time on his business and flies between London and here. Isn't that exciting?' They sat on the kitchen chairs and forked tangy slices of mango onto their plates.

'Sure is.' She wondered what kind of business Mr Moqutat Derijaweer was in, and hoped it wasn't anything illegal or dangerous.

Chapter Forty-eight

Mel collected Jack from the airport and chatted to her as they drove out to Lil's school for the family-picnic evening.

'Why do I have to go?' Jack's voice slushed with the impact of her new braces.

'It's a family picnic. Did the dentist list what you're to avoid?'

'I know what to do with my braces. I won't know anyone at the picnic.'

'That's the point, we meet people.'

'I'm tired.'

'Too bad, we're going.'

Games were organised and sport equipment was set out for the children. Senior students managed and coordinated all of the activities. Mel had never really enjoyed outings where parents sat with picnics and the children ran around in a wild undisciplined herd. It usually gave her a headache, but this was quite a different experience.

Jack sat plugged into her music, off to one side on a picnic chair, happy to let Mel wander and meet other families. Lil had made friends with a wide circle of children and introduced her to them and their parents. The youngsters left to join in with the games.

There was something aesthetic and tasteful about the whole school construct. Her curiosity about the benefactor grew.

'Mel, hi there.'

'Hi Sally, hi Brian. This is my eldest, Jack.' She nudged Jack and she removed her plugs and shook hands. After polite chit-chat, she plugged back in.

'How have you been?' Sally asked.

'Okay. Business is ticking along. I'm sorry I didn't get to tennis this week, Lil and I have been out and about at the beach.'

Sally parked her folding chair next to Mel's and had a picnic basket that would have put most catering companies to shame. Mel's chicken and salad seemed to wilt against the backdrop of extravagant pickles, cheeses, cold meats, breads and crackers, all of which would have been sourced from Salt Flake.

'I didn't go either. It was way too hot for tennis. I stayed by the pool.' Brian wandered off to chat with other dads and Lil joined in a game with Bronte and the students from her class. 'How's the new postie?'

'He's very nice.'

'And?' Sally gave her a look.

'What?' Mel pretended she didn't know what Sally was after.

'You haven't noticed how he is more attractive than the firemen in the calendars in your shop?'

'I might have.'

'And his car wasn't parked in your driveway last weekend?'

'It's that kind of town?' Mel flushed a couple of shades of crimson.

'Just letting you know. Small town.'

'Nothing is going on and he's helping me paint, like Thommo did. We went for a swim on Sunday to get rid of the paint.'

'I wondered why I hadn't heard from you.'

'Trying to get the house look a bit decent takes up most of my time,' Mel argued.

'It's okay. Anyway, you're a single woman, what you do is your business, but yes, eagle eyes are everywhere and I thought you needed to know.'

Mel groaned. Everything they did, being the new family on the block and owners of the postal store, would be up for gossip. A fact she hadn't even considered. 'Thanks Sally. Let me know everything you hear. It isn't anything and he's painting. I pay him.'

'Of course and that would be why you're blushing,' Sally poured her a little champagne from her bottomless basket.

'Don't worry. I'm your mate. Here's to you, cheers.'

'Here's to friendship.' She clinked her glass against Sally's. The two elegant champagne flutes were not like any she owned. 'I agree though, he's nice to look at.'

'Good for you on a number of levels.' Sally nudged her. Mel nudged her right back. Thank God she'd made friends with her first.

Jack sat glued both to the chair and her music. Eventually, Mel felt that they'd stayed long enough to make small talk with several parents and become roped into the essential parent network. Mina wasn't there, but Lil had several other buddies that she seemed close to. Mel felt conspicuous as a single parent. Perhaps there weren't that many of them. She knew she had to make an effort to untangle the hidden social subtleties of the parenting scene and that would happen over coffee.

'I better take Jack home.' She packed away the plates and remaining food.

'Let's catch up later,' Sally said.

'I'm busy with both of them this weekend. Later in the week sounds good. See you Brian and Bronte.'

She struggled to get much conversation out of Jack.

'School's fine. Dad and Leah are fine too.'

'Good. What about your mates?' Mel pressed.

'They're all great, fine. What are we doing this weekend?' She didn't look all that interested.

'I thought you might like to go surfing down at the Jets when I drop Lil off for horse riding. I'll stay while she has her lesson and then pick you up. There's been a good swell these last few days.'

'Sure. Sounds good.'

'Do you have homework?'

'Yes and before you ask, I'm organised with that.' Mel knew Jack's approach with homework and projects. She got by with an incredible memory and a sound intellect, but her attitude was a different matter. Mel cringed every time she read one of her school reports.

Sally told her about a parent gathering in Bettong for coffee on Friday morning. It would be the only way she'd get to the bottom of what was going on and maybe it would stifle the gossip about her, once she was part of the pack, and she really did need to widen her circle of friends. She just had to figure out how to do that and keep the shop open.

*

The surf was huge when she dropped Jack off. 'Don't worry, I'm not going to do anything stupid.' Jack turned her thin wet-suited frame towards the reef and hunkered down against the wind. As she approached the wave line, she threw herself onto the board. With swift strong sweeps of her arms she paddled out to the break: her attention narrowed to the onslaught of waves. Mel wasn't sure it was a wise decision to leave her there.

The thunderous crash of the waves reverberated along the shore. The view of her slight black form became more eclipsed by precipitous seas and wild foam, the further out she paddled. In the car park Mel noticed a familiar four-wheel drive and exhaled. PJ was out there, too.

She and Lil drove in companionable silence and tuned into the local radio station. Her outer calm was a thin membrane over her decision to leave Jack on the beach. Lil looked sideways at her. 'Check out this goofy hat.' She perched the riding helmet on backwards.

When they arrived at the horse-riding school, Mel observed that Lil had exaggerated her horse-riding difficulties.

Straight after the lesson, Mel drove back to the beach. Jack was nowhere to be seen. She saw her towel and jumper strewn across the sand where she'd dropped them, untouched. Mel trawled the ocean and scanned for her familiar shape, although from where she stood, they all looked like thin sinuous seal-like creatures. Lil sidled up to her. Several times she thought she saw her amongst the bobbing shapes.

Lil's voice was quiet as she spoke. 'I have to be at Mina's at one, but that's only if we find Jack first.'

'Of course we'll find her. She's probably waiting behind the break with those others out there.' Pricks of tears began building in Mel's eyes. Many of the riders were still in the water. There was no one she could ask. She felt foolish, but she started waving at the surfers. No one seemed perturbed. The swell was big, the ocean noisy, no one would hear her, and there was no way anyone would even know who Jack was.

'Hey Mum, look!' Lil pointed to a dark form paddling in towards the shore. Mel could barely stand for the relief she felt when she saw her daughter.

She rushed over to her.

'Hi Mum.' She frowned when she saw her face. 'What's the matter?'

'Jack, I couldn't tell you from the others and I...'

'She nearly flipped Jack. We thought you might have been eaten by a shark or something.'

'I was a bit worried.'

Lil's eyes rolled. 'Mum, you had a panic attack.'

'Do you think you might need a waterproof watch so we can organise our times a bit better?'

'Maybe. Tell me roughly when you're coming so I know when to get out. Hey, I met PJ out there. He's in for Thommo right? He's pretty cool on a board.'

'That's right. He's been a great help.'

'How sick is Thommo?' Lil asked. She had formed a bond with Thommo. In the holidays, he brought in new jokes for her and she fished some out for him. PJ finished work before Lil came home.

'He's recovering from his operation. PJ thinks he's coming along fine.'

'Anyway,' Jack said, 'can I stay a bit longer?'

Mel hated to disappoint her, but with Lil going out to Mina's, who lived in a different direction, she would be out there on her own in a rough swell for a long time.

'Come on Mum, I'll be fine.'

Yes, she thought, if the universe could bestow upon you the superhuman powers you think you have, you'll be fine. Lil was keen to get home, have lunch, and head out to Mina's for her additional horse-riding session and dinner. Why didn't they take up a safe hobby like table tennis or knitting?

'Okay Jack. I'll be back as soon as I've dropped off Lil, at two. Please don't go far out or do anything risky. Got that?'

'Sure Mum.' She shivered and walked back in with her board under her arm. Mel tried not to watch.

Lil gathered a few more clothes and downed a hasty lunch. She would be out riding again and dinner was a long way off.

They were both astounded when they pulled into the winding limestone driveway. Mel wasn't too familiar with the equestrian side of things, but a few of her friends had been involved and she'd gone along to watch them at the odd gymkhana. This, however, looked like the gold standard in equestrian facilities.

They rounded the driveway and headed towards the large car-bay area. A short distance away was the elegant and well-positioned house. It was a one-storey traditional wide-flanked home oriented to capture the view of the undulating valley with landscaping that bled into the natural bushland; wide-girthed trees stood surrounded by bench seats. Off to one side, swings hung from tree branches, a trampoline was sunk into the grass and sport paraphernalia sat beneath a concrete apron near a shed. In the private garage beside the car bay sat a couple of new four-wheel drives.

An olive-skinned, long-limbed girl leapt down the steps and ran toward them. 'It's Mina!' Lil enthused. 'What a cool house.'

'It's a beautiful home. Mina looks lovely.'

'She is. I really like her.' Lil unbuckled and leapt out. The two girls embraced and then Lil introduced her mum to Mina.

'Hello Ms Wilson, thank you for bringing Lil here. Come over and meet Suraya, my nanny.'

'Thanks Mina, it's kind of you to invite Lil.' Mina's oval face was striking, and her deep-brown eyes, warm. They walked over the grass that lay below the sweep of limestone steps. The house had a wraparound verandah and a grand wide entrance at the top of the limestone steps.

'This is Suraya, and Suraya, this is Lil and her mother, Ms Wilson.'

'Nice to meet you Suraya.' Mel extended her hand and they shook. 'Please call me Mel.'

'Welcome Lil and Mel. Do you have time for tea? I know you said you had your other daughter here.'

Suraya looked like a recent graduate from university. Her English was softened with a faint accent.

'I'd really like to, but I've left her out at the beach and it's a bit rough today. I'd love to stay for tea another time.'

'Of course. First, I have to apologise. Mina's grandmother wanted to come out and meet you, but she's resting after lunch. You mustn't worry about Lil's safety because Moqutat is very strict about it.'

'This place looks perfect for horses.'

'He's keen on horses and the instructor is a lady with high standards. Lil will be perfectly safe.'

'See you later Mum. I'm going inside with Mina. She's showing me her room while we wait for the instructor.'

'Okay. I'll see you after dinner.'

'Nice meeting you Ms Wilson.' Mina and Lil bounced up the steps and then disappeared behind the folding timber doors.

'Would you like me to drop Lil home? I know Mina would like the opportunity to get out and see where Lil lives.'

'Only if that's not an inconvenience?'

'No, I need to get out.' She could see a spark of youthfulness in Suraya's eyes. 'Later tonight, I'm going out with a couple of the guys who help out on the property for my first open-mic night. It's my night off.'

'That could be fun.'

'I can't wait to get out and try some real Australian experiences. I'm staying until September before going back to university. I'm a second cousin of Mina's.'

'Where are you studying?'

'America, Harvard Business School.'

Mel tried not to look too surprised. 'This must seem pretty small town compared to America.'

'Sometimes. I miss my family and friends. I'm from Iran originally, from French and Iranian parents. We had to live in several countries as we grew up. They always encouraged us to make new friends and enjoy the experience that each new place brings. I'm still adjusting to the quietness, but I love horses. Moqutat wanted someone who loved horse riding to accompany Mina at all times.'

'Lil said Mina spoke to her father every day.'

'He's devoted to her, especially since her mother died in childbirth.'

'That must be hard for her.'

'That's why her grandmother stays with her all the time.'

'Thanks for having Lil and for your offer to bring her home, Suraya.' They wandered towards her car. 'I'll see you later this evening.'

'That's fine Mel.'

Mel wondered if Mina's father was the sponsor of the school.

On her return to the surf break, Jack was waiting for her with blue lips. She was grateful she didn't have to scan the horizon again.

Once inside, Jack raced into the shower while Mel prepared a late lunch for both of them. Jack was ravenous and more relaxed than when she'd arrived. She told her mother all about the surf and revealed the source of blight on her teenage life. 'Dad's got Leah pregnant. Aren't two kids enough? I don't get it.'

Mel didn't answer. She didn't think it was a fantastic idea either, but her opinion on their decision would not help Jack get past it. 'Is PJ a good surfer?' she asked instead.

'Are you kidding? You know a bit of his history, right? He's amazing. I'd love to surf like that. I'll be down when that big surf comp is on and I can't wait to see all of those guys out there. That'll be awesome.'

'There's no reason why you can't surf most of the time you come down to visit, as long as you get your homework done.'

Jack bit into the chicken-and-salad roll and chewed. 'Yeah okay, I can do that.'

'It gets really cold I've been told, and you'll need a new wettie for the winter.'

'Maybe we can get one off thc internet?'

'I hadn't thought about that. PJ offered me a discount at his surf store.'

'Cool. Let's see if we can get a second-hand one first. Heaps of people take up surfing but don't follow it through.'

'You're smarter than you look.'

'Everyone does it at school.' Jack shrugged.

'This is why I have teenagers.'

'Thanks for lunch.' Jack took her plate to the kitchen sink. Before she loped off to her girl cave, Jack wrapped her lean arms tight around Mel in a hug. Mel blinked back the soft happy tears that burst out whenever Jack surprised her.

From her room she called out, 'I'm thinking of getting a little camera for the front of my board.'

'Save up then.'

'Can I work in the store?'

'Yes, but I won't be paying much. Why not try for a job on a Thursday night back in town when you're at Dad's?'

'I'll talk to my mates, see what's out there.'

Suraya dropped Lil home in the early evening.

'Mina's grandma cooked the most amazing dinner.' Lil came in and sat down beside Mel in the kitchen with her bag of horse-riding gear.

'Maybe she can teach you and you can cook for us?'

Lil screwed up her face. 'I don't think so. It looks a bit tricky. The horse-riding instructor was very bossy, but I've learned so much. We taught the horses to weave between barrels, canter, trot and everything. You should see the horses. They're so well groomed. They're nothing like the ones I had in my morning session.'

'Mina is very lucky to have all of that.'

'Yes she is, but she's not spoilt. She has chores to do and we washed up after dinner and we thanked her grandma for the meal. She's very respectful towards adults.'

This was even better news than the horses. 'You're fortunate to have such a kind friend. I hope you were polite too.'

'Of course. After horse riding, we sat on the swings and played on the trampoline and Suraya brought out iced rose water with chopped fruit on a plate.' She yawned and Mel detected a slight horsey smell.

'How about you dump your dirties and have a shower. Have you got any homework to do?'

'I did it when I got up this morning, and I finished it.'

'I'm going to read in the lounge room, unless you want to join me and we watch something together?'

'No, I'm tired. Can I chat to Dad and Em?'

'Yes, not for ages though.'

'I know.'

Lil went to bed exhausted. Jack came out and together they watched one of Mel's favourite movies.

Chapter Forty-nine

Both children awoke earlier than usual for a Sunday morning and elected to have breakfast in the garden. The proximity of the coast and the realisation that summer days were coming to an end meant they didn't want to miss out on anything. There was a rumble in the driveway.

'Hi Mel!' PJ called to her from his cab as he jumped out.

Mel tried to quell the shiver of delight that ran through her on hearing his voice. She didn't want her children to pick up on anything, and it already looked like the year would be ringing in the changes. 'Hi PJ.'

'I met Jack yesterday on the water and thought I'd drop by to see if she wanted to come out again. How are you Jack?'

Jack leapt up and smiled back with a gob of food in her mouth. Mel could see her throat swallow the large lump of toast before she found her voice. 'I'd love to go out today.'

'That's really great of you to offer, PJ, but she was out for a long while yesterday.'

'Mum.'

'It's okay. I don't plan on being out for more than a couple of hours today. Things to do back in Bettong with the shop.'

'Come on, Mum.'

'Okay,' she caved.

PJ and Jack left, but not before PJ flashed her a smile. Her arm brushed his when she handed over some food and water bottles. Warmth cruised through her.

She left with Lil for a morning run. 'Apart from Mina and Bronte,' she said between breaths, 'how are the rest of the kids?'

'They're okay. I'm invited to a party next weekend, but I said I'd be at Dad's.'

'That's a shame.'

'Mum, it was Matthew. He's nice, but I don't mind because only two girls have been invited and I don't know any of the boys.'

She grinned. 'All good then.'

When they rounded back towards the inlet, Lil spied Eddie. They paused and dangled their legs over the edge the limestone wall.

'Hi Ms Wilson. Lil, do you want to come out for a swim to the pontoon?'

'Yes. Can I Mum?'

'Sure.' Mel and Lil walked back to the house. Eddie waited at the inlet with his bike and board. Mel lay on the towel on the grassy bank and opened her book. Even though she pulsed with a little joy in her soul, she missed her mum and the company of her friends.

Time had diminished the ache of the events of the preceding year, but the memories still rattled when she held each newspaper before opening it.

She read her book but paused at the end of each page to scan the area and spot the kids. They waved back at her.

A few hours later, PJ deposited a shivering Jack home. Lil had gone to Eddie's for lunch.

'Thanks PJ.' Jack's teeth chattered and she patted the car door before she bolted for a shower.

'She's good Mel.'

'Thank you for taking her out.'

'I'm heading over to Macka's. We've got a heap to do for this comp.'

'I'll see you later in the week.'

He waved and gazed up at her for the briefest of seconds. She was all jelly and blushing.

The blistering intensity of the afternoon sun justified her position on the sofa with her computer, where she worked through her notes on the online course. The children worked on their homework or spoke to their friends.

'My board is brilliant, I love it,' Jack said.

PJ had told her it was one of the better boards in their store. It was a rare triumph and Mel glowed with Jack's praise. They exchanged smiles before Jack gulped down another toasted sandwich, headed to her room, and became immersed in her homework. She hoped.

*

When it was time for her to board the plane, Jack didn't appear to relish the idea of flying back to Perth.

'Next time you're down, the comp will be on,' Mel told her.

'I know. I can't stop thinking about it and I wonder if we'll get to meet any of the competitors.'

'You never know, maybe they'll drop by to pick up a parcel or two at the store.'

Jack thinned her eyes. 'Yeah sure.'

Mel gripped her in a hug. 'Bye Jack.'

'Bye Mum.'

Mel pulled out of the airport road and watched the taillights of the plane in the mirror.

In the quiet of the evening, a text bleeped. It was PJ and it was a line of kisses.

Chapter Fifty

PJ told her he couldn't wait for the weekend. Big-name surfers were due to arrive in a couple of days to prepare in the local conditions for the following weekend of competition. Mel hoped PJ might realise she was on her own on the weekend and offer to 'help' her with the painting again. He seemed excited about everything lately but toned down his flirting with her when the customers were present. Mel leapt out of bed every morning.

The week coasted by and she took Lil for her Friday-evening flight. Tony promised horse-riding lessons for the Saturdays she was in Perth.

She watched till the aeroplane's lights were indistinguishable from the stars that flecked the night sky. It was the night of the parents' cocktail evening at Lil's school. It was hard to step out as a single mum, but it was time to enter the wider social arena of Pelican Point.

It was fortunate that little black dresses were dateless and de rigueur. She was pleased to discover that her trimmer figure meant that even an old cocktail dress looked fairly acceptable. With a last glance in the hallway mirror to check for stray blobs of makeup or wrongly fastened jewellery, she felt ready.

She pulled open the door to find PJ on the porch, poised to knock. 'You look amazing. Have I caught you at a bad time?' he asked. His eyes travelled slowly along her body.

The flirty woman blazed inside. 'The school-cocktail evening.'

'What an idiot. I forgot.'

'It's one of those events I have to make an appearance at.'

'Sure. I'll see you later?'

'Perhaps. It finishes at nine.'

'Okay.'

'If I come home early I'll let you know. I thought you were chasing waves and surf pros this weekend?'

'I am most of the weekend. Macka and Robby have lined up a dinner tomorrow night with a couple of the competitors.'

'That's what you were hoping for.'

'It's pretty exciting.' He nodded. 'There's a real buzz in town at the moment.'

'Jack can't wait to come down next weekend,' she told him.

'She'll love it—small country town becomes surf mecca for a couple of weeks. I thought I'd drop by to check out the painting.' He took a step towards her on the porch. She could feel waves of heat roll off him.

'I can show you the painting later, but right now I have to go.' She swallowed.

They stood on the front step facing each other. After a few breathless moments, he leaned towards her and pressed his lips against hers. She wanted to tear his shirt off.

'I'll phone you tomorrow,' he said as he pulled away.

Mel couldn't wipe the dopey grin off her face as she drove.

*

The vapour of champagne and wine hung in the air. Bright voices rose and bursts of laughter punched into the calm, star-studded night. A small local jazz band played on a stage in the corner. She scanned the crowd after collecting a glass of champagne from a waiter, and located Sally amongst a band of parents, many of whom she could now name because of all the standing around at various after-school events and sports.

'The lady with the teapot,' said one slightly slurred voice. Mel recognised her from the shop.

'Gemma?'

'Yes. This is my partner, James.'

'Hi James.' They shook hands.

'I've been telling them that Pelican Point is about to get a fresh look with our newly flavoured postal shop sporting a teapot, and who knows what else is in the offing.'

'It's early days yet. I'm working on re-imaging the business.' Mel could feel pink blossoms flourishing on her cheeks. She hoped she sounded more confident than she felt as she addressed the small crowd clustered around Sally.

'Oh God this place could do with a kick in the arse. It's like nothing has changed for a hundred years.'

'Yes and that would be why people move here. Not everyone wants a city landscape, Angie.' Gemma, of the knitting and photography clubs, did look like laid-back was her preferred state.

'I know, but a few cafés would be great. Maybe we could have an art gallery. I don't know. It needs something to liven it up and add a bit of class and flair to its tired old front.' Angie tilted her empty champagne glass. 'Damn, but there goes another one.' Her husband looked over at her and grinned.

Mel thought the same and she was encouraged by their honesty. 'I'm doing a bit of research. Feel free to drop by and give me some ideas and have a cup of tea.'

'I'll drink to that. I'll drink to anything!' Angie winked at her. This was fun. Mel made a mental note to herself to get out a whole lot more.

She sidled closer to Sally. 'How's it going, Sal, with the caravan parks?'

'You mean because of the comp? We could have packed in twice the number of people. We've been knocking back bookings and that's totally unheard of this time of year. This is becoming much bigger than everyone anticipated. People who've never watched a surf comp in their lives are venturing out of their safe suburban enclaves to come and spectate. I think it's gaining momentum like a bucket-list item. Who'd have thought? We're thinking of extending our licence for sites next year.' Sally and Brian had the Midas touch. All Mel hoped for was to sell a few more wares, whereas they would be looking at raking in the kind of money that made her business look like a lemonade stall beside a supermarket. Maybe some of Sally's business smarts would rub off on her.

'Does that mean now that Bettong has hosted it once it will come each year?'

'I don't know. Ask PJ when he drops over to do some painting.'

She raised her eyebrows and glared at Sally. She did not want the school tongues wagging. Sally had mentioned that his unmistakeable vehicle had been spotted at her house by several town observers. It was the kind of town that didn't need drones or street cameras to deliver damning exposes: people opened their front doors and drew their own conclusions from what they saw in your driveway.

Angie leaned over, her voice a loud wine-flavoured whisper. 'Mel, coffee in Bettong Friday, after school drop-off. Can you make it?'

'I'll try. Maybe I can get someone to man the store.' She knew the man and trusted he'd be obliging for an hour and a half.

'Good. It's the new café on the harbour, Foam. All shiny oiled timber, big fans, uber cool, and views that make you want to sit for hours. Some of us spend whole days there.' She cackled and added in her winey breath, 'Sally will fill you in on the details. Also, some pretty hot waiters. Backpackers down for the surfing.'

'I love the sound of the café already. Thanks Angie.'

At the gong of nine, the principal thanked the parents, gave a brief welcome to new parents and closed the evening.

Sally caught Mel's arm as she was leaving. 'I'll drop by and pick you up on Friday and take you to coffee, if you like? Don't forget tennis Thursday if you can make it.'

'Sure. Thanks Sal, a lift would be great. I'll call later and we can sort it out.'

'I expect details at some point,' she whispered as they hugged goodbye.

Sally winked at her as she was leaving, and Mel tried to ignore it, but she couldn't shut down the smile that had started on the porch and now ran all over her.

When she got home, she leaned against the frame of the

unlocked door, slipped off her shoes, and rubbed one foot on the other; she wasn't used to heels. Her thoughts about whether to contact PJ fluctuated. It wasn't that she didn't want to see him; it was more that now she knew her driveway had beady eyes trained on it.

A text bleeped. *You still in cute dress?* Delight soared through her. Another text followed. *You hungry?* She was starving.

She texted back. *Is this a good idea?*

Hell yes, I'm hungry and I need an eating partner. I've been busy on financials for the store. I'll bring some fish I was given. You got salad ingredients?

Within a few minutes she heard a knock on the front door. She opened it and went out towards him on the porch. He put down everything he held in his hands and lifted her up. She wrapped her legs around him and when they kissed this time, she felt barriers tumble. She didn't waste time leading him into her bedroom. The food could wait.

'You looked stunning in that dress, I didn't want to leave,' he told her between kisses.

'Words like that will ensure you won't have to. Like most women my age, I'm a sucker for flattery.'

'Stop with the women my age—you're no age, and,' he said as he traced the outline of her face with his hands, 'you're gorgeous.' He slipped his hands over the length of her shoulders, and then ran them along the inside of her arms towards her fingertips. She tried not to pant in shivery excitement. The kissing supplanted words and he lifted her onto her bed, threw his shirt off, and that was when a groan escaped her lips. His chest did that to her.

He slipped off his jeans, lifted her dress above her head, and ran his hands lightly over her body. After unhitching her bra he breathed into her, 'I knew this body lay beneath the painting shirt.' Her body craved the pressure and scent of him.

Afterwards, she ran her hands over his arms, his chest, his face; it was such a contrast to her curves and post-children breasts.

He turned towards her and brought her hands to his lips to

kiss them. 'Let's cook, if you're still hungry?'

'I am.' She tipped out of bed and slipped into a thin shirt.

He pulled on his boxers and grabbed her against him. 'Did I tell you you're gorgeous?'

'You might have mentioned that.' He gave her a hard kiss on the lips and carried her to the kitchen.

Mel watched a pat of butter sizzle in the pan while PJ threw a few salad ingredients together. When he wasn't looking, she watched him: the serious intent of his movements as he sliced and diced, peeled and scooped ingredients, and threw them into the glass bowl.

He turned towards her. 'Have you got some coriander and a lime?'

'Yes. Limes are in the fruit bowl and the coriander is in the little drawer in the fridge.' She flipped the fish over and grabbed two plates. 'Have you done a lot of cooking?'

'Some, but in a lot of the places I've travelled to it's easier and cheaper to eat out. When I'm back home, I cook for Dad. Not many eateries down here, but,' he said when he slipped his lime-zesty hands around her waist from behind, 'I can't wait to do a whole lot more cooking in your kitchen.'

His lips and tongue found hers and they sparked with lime-juice when they kissed.

'Ms Wilson of the painting school, what's next? Do you need a hand with your technique?'

'Stop it, I'm trying to eat.' Under the table he placed his feet alongside hers and she found it ticklish. He forked a sliver of fish and popped it into his mouth. It was a mouth she had an unnatural interest in.

At some point in the night they fell asleep.

'Stop it,' his voice low and thick with sleepiness.

'What?' Mel trailed her fingertips along his arm.

'I can feel you staring at me.'

'I haven't had someone sleep over in years. Besides, I like looking at you.'

She reflected on his many attributes—he even smelled right—but he wasn't handsome in a regular way. His overt enjoyment of life and overall physical fitness manifested itself in the way he held himself and it spilled into his smile.

'It should be a magnificent day out on the water.'

'It's already off to a stunning start.' He leapt out of bed and put the kettle on.

Mel flopped back onto the bed. Today her life was not the stuff of mere mortals. He was heading out to do some more filming for his shop and then to surf with the big-name surfers. His excitement was palpable and he tumbled back in beside her as the kettle boiled.

From the cab of his car he turned towards her. 'I'll call you later, let you know how it's all going.'

'Great.' She went back to bed, lolled around in the rucked-up linen, and savoured the heady feeling of not enough sleep and quite a lot of everything else.

*

With the buzz in town and extra tourists around, Mel couldn't afford to waste a Saturday trade. The teapot was given special prominence and she decided it was time it earned an income. She bought locally sourced biscuits and positioned a sign near the teapot; it made it sound a little more exciting than it was.

By the end of the morning, sales had been moderate, but the tea and biscuits had made a substantial return on investment.

All through the morning, at odd moments, her skin tingled and her cheeks flushed.

PJ reported that Thommo had responded well to treatment but needed to stay in the city for a couple of months. Mel sent Thommo frequent texts about what was going on in Pelican Point.

That night PJ was wining and dining with his surf-shop partners and a collection of surf professionals.

At her desk, the sun found its way through the gaps in the slats of the blind as she tried to capture the ideas floating around in her head.

The warm sun drew her outside to the beach. She longed

for some female company and she missed her mum. The children and business kept her busy and exhausted, let alone her new distraction. Her mum had always dropped by, usually with something for the children. Mel called her.

'Mum, hi. How are you?'

'Hi Mel, I'm fine. I miss you and the kids.'

'I miss you too.'

'I'm around Georgie's a lot. With the international festival and major tennis tournament, they have so many extra events to organise. I had no idea that kind of money existed in Perth. They need me to be there when Xandy and Clayton come home. I think there's a bit of tension between them.'

She sounded flat. 'There's bound to be tension, they both have very demanding jobs and they try to be great parents, too.' Mel promised Georgie she wouldn't say a word to anyone about their problems.

'Still, something doesn't seem right between them.'

'Their marriage is like every other marriage, Mum. Georgie and Dave will work through their challenges, and it's a hectic time for them. Their business always settles down during winter.'

'I suppose you're right.'

'How about you come down to visit me in a month?'

'I'd really like that.' Her voice lifted and Mel winced. She'd been so busy she hadn't made time for her either. 'Have you got room?'

'You can use Lil's room and she can put a mattress on the floor in my room. Easy to do.'

'Will you call with a date?'

'Of course. I'll make sure it's when the children are both here. I'll get back to you when I check with Jack's sports schedule. I can book you a flight, unless you'd prefer to take the bus?'

'We'll see what's available.'

Her mother had never liked flying, but she despaired of long bus trips and was beyond driving that kind of distance on her own. 'When I get back to you, we'll book in your flight.'

'Thanks Mel. How's your business going?'

'Not too bad at the moment. The pro-circuit surf competition in Bettong means crowds are milling around all over the district, even out here.'

'I can't wait to work with you in the store.'

'It'll be great to have help.' She was thinking about the average age of her usual customers. 'How's book club? How's June?'

'Oh my God,' her mum said through a little chuckle, 'even more insufferable since her son Anthony published his three ebooks.'

'That's great though.'

'But we have to listen to her describe them in microscopic detail at each meeting. I'm glad we only meet once a month.'

'What has he written about?'

'One is about the six most prevalent moths in the wheat fields of the mid-west.'

'A fascinating read, I'm sure.' Mel laughed.

'For birds maybe.'

'What are the others?'

She could hear a little giggle build in her mother's voice. 'The second is about the four most destructive ant species found in the mid-west. Wait till I tell you what the third book is about.' She struggled for breath.

'Let me guess, it's about the three types of cockroaches most likely to invade your home in the mid-west?'

'Close. It's about helpful beetles or harmful bugs and how to recognise them.' It took her mother a few moments before the laughter ebbed.

'After three meetings you'll be fine. What's the group reading?'

'A lot of us have ebook readers and we don't read the same book. We talk about whatever we're reading.'

'Technology in your book club!'

'I know, but it saves paying for books you don't want to read and I love how many I can put on my reader.'

'You have one?'

'Yes. Georgie bought me one because of the amount of time I'm spending with Xandy and Clayton.'

'That was a great idea.'

'I love it, especially with my arthritis. I'll talk to you later. Bye Mel, see you soon.'

'Bye Mum.' Small wisps of tears wetted the corners of her eyes. She would make the effort to phone more often.

Tugging out a few weeds amongst the lawn in the evening light, her phone bleeped with a text.

Hi, Mum, it said, *you should see how Leah has decorated the baby's room. It's so beautiful. Lil xxx*. She hoped Tony knew how to manage his more complicated family situation.

With no one to cook for, Mel prepared a light meal and put her feet up on the lounge-room coffee table.

A couple of hours later she awoke. Her book had tipped out of her lap and was splayed open on the floor, and her plate sat unwashed on the coffee table. A noise outside the front door shattered the late-night stillness. A glance at the clock told her it was one in the morning. Her mind raced. She'd forgotten to organise a plan for a home invasion. A soft rap at the door had her hunting through the sports gear stashed in the hallway cupboard. She drew her dressing robe close and peered through the window with a hockey stick in one hand and her phone in the other. It was PJ.

She opened the door, relieved.

'Had the best evening. They wanted me to stay, but the thought of last night with you...' He noticed the hockey stick. 'Sorry Mel, I should have rung. Can I come in?'

PJ told her he'd been asked to film additional footage, and one of the competitors had agreed to support the business in an advertising promotion. So much good news had to be celebrated.

When PJ left later that morning to film and surf, Mel remained in bed. She slid out to the kitchen and looked at the bright arc of sky. She took her tea to bed and lay back on the pillows. She traced over her lips to feel a tingle of PJ's last kiss and listened to a new artist he'd introduced her to. She longed for a day when they could stay in bed, with nothing to rush out for. Right now he faced a huge week and an even bigger following weekend.

PJ had invited Jack to spend most of the following Saturday out at the competition, and Jack had tried not to show how impressed she was about that when she spoke to her on the phone later in the day.

Throughout Sunday, PJ dropped the odd text. Mel spent a while drafting her tentative ideas which, no matter how she tried to factor in cheaper timber cuts or lower employment rates, exceeded her tight budget. Small changes to the tearoom could be accomplished with a handyman. Her drawing, drafting, planning and daydreaming was brought to an abrupt end by the resonant tone of the landline.

Chapter Fifty-one

It was Tony.

'Hi Tony?'

'Mel, it's about Jack.'

Tony's serious voice caused her stomach to spasm and she could feel the weight of his tone. 'What about Jack?'

'She's been expelled.'

'What? Why?'

He paused, his voice dry and weary. 'A few boys and girls on afternoon detention had vodka in their water bottles. She was one of them.'

'She was on detention? What for?'

'Repeatedly not handing in an essay on the history of one of the local suburbs, and for not completing most of her maths assignments.'

'Term's hardly begun, how can she have missed so many things? She's always been great at maths.'

'They were given the homework and assignment schedule. She chose to ignore it.'

'Did you ask her why?'

'Of course I did. She says the maths is easy and she doesn't need to practise several thousand questions on the same thing. I pointed out that practice is what means it'll be easy when it comes to other assessments. She disagreed. She has been really difficult lately.'

'What's with the vodka?'

'She's hanging out with a few other girls and boys who think it's fun to lose it during the school week. Two boys hung around the trees, unseen by the teacher, while the others did the gardening clean up for detention. When no one was watching, they handed the boys and girls their water bottles. One of the boys is the deputy's son. The deputy is moving him to a boarding school over east and I suspect he blames Jack for influencing him.'

Mel felt sick that she had missed what was going on with her daughter. 'Why didn't you tell me what she's been up to?'

'I'm telling you now.' He was getting short with her. 'And another thing.'

'There's more?'

'She's taken a few random days off this term to spend with that particular boy.'

'Don't they text you to tell you she's absent?'

'Yes and when I phone Jack she blocks my calls and goes out.'

'Do you confront her after?'

'Of course I do. Then she gets all mouthy about me and Leah.'

'What do you think we should do? Get a counsellor involved?'

'I suggested that. The school doesn't want her back and she doesn't want to go back. She said that she doesn't want any counselling. She said she wants to live with you.'

That would have stung. She could hear it in his voice. 'If that's what she wants, she can live with me. She'll still have to go to school.'

'She knows that. She wants to go to Bettong High School, not Bray College.'

'That figures.'

'I'll pay for Lil's schooling since Jack has chosen this option and I'll cover their flights home every second weekend. This isn't going to be easy for you.'

'Thanks. You should have communicated more with me.' She was scared by his offer of money. What exactly was she facing with Jack?

'Right,' he said, 'before or after you shunted our children out of the glare of the media and into your mother's house? Before or after you lost your job and moved down south? When, for

God's sake, were you in a good state to handle anything?'

His words lashed at the flickering tendril of hope she'd started to feel about herself and the children. Busy as she had been with her predicament, she had put any concerns she had about Jack down to regular teenage hormones and now realised that Tony had shouldered the issues with Jack, alone.

'I've managed to survive and make a go of a new business without compromising my care of our children,' she shot back.

'I know.' He paused. 'Lil keeps us informed and she seems to be settling in.' He sounded apologetic. He sounded like he was a hundred.

'Should I come up? Should we get some mediation? This is so awful. I had no idea.'

'I think she's smarter than that. So long as you and I present a united front, I don't know what else we can do, other than let her start school in Pelican Point and hope she makes wiser decisions.'

'Hey, we've been good parents and there's no excuse for some of her behaviour. She can't go playing the blame game. She needs to bear some of the responsibility.'

'I agree, just not sure how we do that.'

'Firstly, no money unless she earns it.'

'Agreed.'

'Remove her phone and suggest she buys her own and funds the calls.'

'That will be the hard one.'

'Stop paying the account but tell her why. It's abuse of privilege and there has to be room for negotiation or else we've failed.'

There was a longish pause. 'Okay. I'll talk to her tonight before I put her on the plane, and you won't find Lil all that cheery either. She was really annoyed with Jack. I think she thinks that she might cramp her new life and she told her that you don't need a stupid teenage idiot, or words to that effect, to look after.'

'Let's hope she remembers that in a couple of years.'

'Exactly.' Tony had teenagers, a newly pregnant hormonal wife, and a busy accounting business to run. The sympathy she felt for him was overlaid with a little glee that he would now be out of the honeymoon phase with Leah. She shouldn't delight in that, she knew, but she couldn't help it.

After they hung up, she called Sally.

'Hi Mel,' Sally said when she answered.

'What do you know about Bettong High?' Mel asked without preamble. 'I know Eddie goes there and he seems to like it.'

'Why? You're not moving Lil?'

'No, it's Jack. She and her father haven't been getting along and she wants to move down here to be with us. She wants to go to Bettong High.'

'It's full of a mix of kids, a typical country high school. They've received massive government funding over the years, so the music, sports, drama and academic programs, I've heard, are probably equivalent to Bray College. Of course they don't have the dance, equestrian or agricultural facilities of Bray.'

'I don't think Jack cares about that. Do you have any friends who send their kids there or know about enrolment?'

'Bec's kids go there. She's my neighbour. I see each of her kids lug around a laptop. Because it's the local state high school you can enrol straightaway and they have to accept you.'

'I was thinking the same thing. She'll be starting tomorrow, but I'll check on the website.'

'That'll be a bit of a change for you and Lil.'

'I'm looking forward to it. I always wanted to spend more time with Jack. Right now, she thinks she deserves adult privileges and freedoms.'

'Can't wait for that time with Bronte.'

'Remind me why we had them?'

'Mild alcohol-induced concussion and a weakness for handsome men with silken tongues?' She heard Sally move onto one of her kitchen stools and take a draught of something.

'Young and naïve?'

'That too.'

'They say puberty now lasts from eleven to twenty-two.'

'What happened to military school where you could sign them up at eleven?'

'Yeah, I think they might have stopped that due to the effect it had on the children.'

'Shame.'

'I think kids need to learn other understandings apart from what's offered in an academic program.'

'Bray is hoping to work with the new aquaculture and marine science college when it gets started, and is building its agriculture program on sustainable farming practices. Still, I'm not sure about employment in those fields in the future. It's tricky isn't it, thinking about the future for the kids. It was much simpler for us.'

'Was it really? I didn't know anything about the numerous careers out there. There are so many choices for them to consider.' Mel moved to the kitchen window, placed her cup in the sink, wandered back to the chair and stretched out her legs. Her hand rested on a surf magazine Jack had left on the table from her previous visit.

'She could end up like PJ, surfing and filming,' Sally said.

'That's a thought, though I bet even that will morph into something different in time.'

'Surely kids will figure these things out like we did.' Sally said.

'I hope so.'

'Coffee in Bettong at Foam, later in the week, when the girls are doing dance squad? I can ask Brian to pick them up.'

'Sure. See you later, and thanks, Sal.'

'No problem. Bye.'

Her chat with Sally made her feel better, but Mel was uneasy about Tony's unsolicited offer of money. That had never happened, so she had to ask herself: how well did she know Jack?

She went on Bettong High's website and checked on the enrolment information. Sally was right, she could enrol Jack since she lived in the district, and it said that the uniform and bookstore were on site. She emailed the principal about her intentions and requested a meeting. She planned to take Jack straightaway in the morning, after Lil left for school. The enrolment could take place with or without a meeting with the principal, but she hoped he might have time for her.

PJ arrived in his four-wheel drive late in the afternoon, straight from the beach. 'Filming was excellent.'

He leapt out of the car, dusted down his shorts and shook his head. Sand sprinkled onto the porch. 'Sorry about that. What's up?' He moved towards her and held her chin in his hand while he kissed her.

'Jack. She's been expelled and I'm collecting her in a couple of hours when I pick up Lil.'

'Wow. She didn't strike me as that kind of kid.'

'Me neither and I'm her mum. She wants to live here and go to Bettong High.'

'I went there. I heard it's really improved. Could be a great thing.'

'I hope so.'

'Come here.' He lifted her up and carried her inside, buoyed with his morning's work. Nothing would dampen his spirit. 'With her love of surfing and this surf comp, she'll be fine. Teenagers like to test the ropes a bit. Maybe that's all it is.'

'Sure. My plan is to keep her busy and see if she can find a little job. My ex and I are drying up the cash flow.'

'Good idea.' He pressed his chest against hers and she breathed him in. She had to drive to the airport, and he had to edit, load and show his film at the shop with Macka and Robby.

'Next fortnight we'll have more time.' His reply was another kiss.

*

Lil did not gallop down the steps of the plane and breeze over to her. Jack followed Lil's clumping pace.

'Hi Jack.' She held her in a hug. She grabbed Lil and kissed her cheek.

'Hi Mum. I don't want to talk about it.' Jack was quick to shut her down.

'I was going to say that we'll both be going to Bettong tomorrow morning, to your new school.'

'I know.'

'They have rules, too.'

'I get it.'

'Okay then.' It was going to be a long week.

'Mum, Leah couldn't help me with the right board for my project.' Lil's voice teetered and she looked spent. 'I'm going to have the worst project now.'

'I think I have some poster board in the shop. How about you let me know what it is you were meant to do. You'll feel better tomorrow and you can finish it off when you wake up.'

'You always say that. The morning won't change anything.'

'Maybe not. Give me what you've done and I'll see what we can use from the shop.'

Jack continued with monosyllabic answers and Lil was still teary when they turned into the driveway. The sheer physical and mental strain of the weekend's events meant everyone left for bed early. Mel lay in her bed and hoped that they could all get through the week.

She left a corner of her mind to think about PJ. *Can't wait to see you again.* It was his last text for the night.

When the morning sky still blushed pink, she ransacked the store for anything that could help save Lil's project from becoming the disaster she believed it would be. Lil walked into the kitchen to see what she had done and became delirious with gratitude.

'Thanks Mum and I'm sorry for being a grump. I'll finish it off.'

'I enjoyed putting it together and it's made me think about becoming more creative in the shop.'

She looked over at her children. One was arranging the last photos and display components on her poster in between bites of toast and the other, slunk over a cereal bowl, was reading her phone and texting. Should she ban phones at the breakfast table? She kept finding herself caught in the fray of parenting with new technology. Maybe she would leave that till the next morning and work on getting through the day for now.

Chapter Fifty-two

Jack stood in the uniform shop at the new school. The casual sports shirt and shorts that passed for a uniform billowed around her lean frame. Jack noticed the passing traffic of students and Mel could see her take in the view of the diverse range of students that paraded before the window. It was a very different mix from her previous school and would offer a whole new perspective. Mel prayed she didn't gravitate towards the same kind of students she had begun to show a penchant for. The next few years weren't going to be easy for Jack and Mel wasn't sure which way her daughter was going.

'Don't stare at me,' Jack said as they walked back to the principal's office.

'Okay.' Jack tugged at the shirt and she saw that she had worn the more weather-beaten canvas shoes. Mel figured she put on the older ones to counteract the newness of the uniform. Her hair flopped over her eyes; her daughter's tiny vanities of coolness made her smile. 'You have bus money?'

'No, I have a card.'

'Right. I'll see you when you get home.'

'Okay, but don't stand and wave.'

'See you then.'

'I'll take you to your first class,' the young principal said.

'Bye Mum.' Jack strode off with the principal and tried to hide her newness by not gawping. It would be a long, tough day in a school where everyone else knew everyone else.

The principal had time for a chat after he had delivered Jack to her class. 'Ms Wilson, you've completed all of the forms, do you have any questions?'

'Not really. You have a very comprehensive website and you've given me a parent login. Is there anything I should know?'

'We do expect homework to be completed and we have a strong mentor and guidance system in place to track students in Year Ten, to help prepare them for the senior years where important decisions have to be made.'

'That sounds great.'

'Jack's records, apart from this year, show that she's a strong student with potential.'

'I bet that's never been said before.'

He smiled. 'I guess they all have a lot of potential. It's our job to build on it and to give them opportunities, but it becomes their responsibility to take advantage of what's offered.'

'I agree.'

'Don't worry, we'll keep an eye on her and ensure she settles in. There are some great kids in Year Ten similar to Jack with interests in surfing, music and football.'

'She didn't say that she was interested in learning?'

He grinned. 'That was what she told me when we walked to class, but she'll be filling in a survey right now. It's one of the things they have to do after enrolment. From it we build a profile on every student that changes as we gather more information about them. Every few months we ask them to modify their profile, depending on what they believe they can add to it. Anyway,' he said as he stood up, 'feel free to keep in contact, Ms Wilson. The school texts parents instantly if there's anything important they need to know.'

'Thanks.' They shook hands and she drove back to the store, praying that vodka and anything harder would remain off Jack's agenda for a while.

Chapter Fifty-three

'How'd it go?' Mel unlocked the door at the back of the store. PJ leaned against the back wall beside the door after securing his motorcycle, and trailed his fingers over her exposed arm.

'She's enrolled.' Her heart thumped with the quivering sparks his fingers left as they tracked back and forth along her skin.

'Kind of glad I may have missed the whole parenting thing.'

'You're young, there's still time.'

He studied her. 'You want more kids?'

'No. But you may meet someone after me…' He crushed her to his chest and sank into her lips. It was a whole body kind of kiss.

'Let's leave it,' he said.

'Okay.'

'I don't think past you.' Did he sound hurt?

When he took off on his motorcycle, she was left with a frisson of sensual euphoria. She wanted to waltz up to someone and say, 'Hey, I'm the woman he wants.' If only she could hold onto the feeling that throbbed within her. It was like the beginning and end; she could live on it. If she didn't keep her emotions in check, she was in danger of frightening the customers away with her glowing cheeks and body heat.

She waited for Jack's return. Lil hung around to be near her.

'Can you see her yet?'

'No.' She removed the spider webs from the outside chairs. She hadn't noticed them before, or the rings left over from mugs of tea, or the crumbs and trails of grease from peanut-butter sandwiches.

'I had a great day.' Lil observed her mother's flurry of domesticity and swung her legs on a chair. She listed the numerous birthday parties coming up, the school events and the funny things that a few of the boys did to the toilet paper. Lil also reported that Mina would soon be due a visit from her father. 'Are you even listening to me?'

'I heard everything you said.' Mostly. 'Mina and her father have a very special relationship. She strikes me as being a smart girl.'

'She is, but she must miss having her own mum. Can I keep going to Mina's on Saturdays for horsemanship? Mina says I can and she says her dad says it's fine, too.'

'I guess so, but I feel like we should do something for them or pay them.'

'Mina told me to tell you not to worry. The lessons are paid for and her dad prefers it if she has a friend to do them with. Mina says it's boring at her place without other kids anyway. They don't mind. Please?'

'All right.' She would think of a way to thank them later.

The chairs and table couldn't take any more scrubbing. She glanced up and down the street for the familiar lanky form of her daughter.

'Mum, she'll see you.'

She rearranged the outdoor furniture, snipped away dead heads from the plants, swept the path and wiped down the salt-and-sand flecked palings of the front fence.

Jack sauntered up to the gate and watched her mum de-cobweb the cross-section of timber posts behind it. Mel straightened and wiped away the grime and beads of sweat that had collected on her brow and took in her very masculine-looking daughter. Sweat bled dark-grey patches against the light grey of her new uniform. 'How was it?'

'It was okay.' Jack grinned and thumped her on the arm as she went past.

Mel punched her back and said, 'The kids?'

'Yeah, they're okay.'

All the waiting, cleaning and concern had worn Mel out. Lil

peered around the front door after Jack had passed through. She would go to her room, dump her things, make something to eat and then lie on her bed with one or more pieces of technology.

'See? She didn't even say anything,' Lil said. 'Let's go down to the beach and have a swim Mum.'

Mel welcomed the distraction. Monday was the only night in the week when there wasn't dance, music, horse riding or swim training.

She grabbed a towel and a hat and called out to Jack to say they were going.

'Where are you going to swim?' Jack wandered out from her room to return a plate, and followed them down the hallway where their shoes lay.

'At the main beach, around the corner.'

'Can you swim in the bay?' Jack asked.

'Why?' Mel wanted to know.

'Are you going to the beach with some of the high school kids?' Lil asked.

Jack stood in the hallway and glared at Lil. 'No.' Then, ignoring her sister, she said, 'Lil can show you how to swim out to the pontoon.'

'We wanted to go to the main beach first!' Lil's eyes blazed challengingly.

Jack raised her eyebrows. Lil threw her sister a squinty look. Mel ignored the both of them.

As they struck out on the path to the inlet, Mel noted a small cluster of teenagers make their way down the street towards her house. Jack appeared at the gate and blended into the group. She tried not to stare at them for too long or Jack would be furious with her.

Jack had new friends already? If only she would apply herself to the learning program with as much speed and enthusiasm. Mel was going to have to use the parent network to find out what was happening at the school and see what Sally knew about the local teenagers.

PJ arrived at the store an hour before closing time the following day. He scanned around to ensure there were no customers before he spoke. 'Since it's going to be a busy week and your weekend is going to be tied up with children, and I'll be out with the comp, I thought you might like to come over to Dad's place and help me with a little "painting" this afternoon, after you close up?'

'That could be interesting.' A flurry of thoughts bounded around her head, all of them good.

'You said Lil has dance then horse riding tonight? What do you think?'

She could get Lil picked up after dance and taken to horse riding with one call to Sally, but that meant Jack would be alone. 'I'll check with Jack and text you.'

'See you later then.' He kissed the back of her neck and wandered down the hallway. She heard the putter of the little motorcycle but remained within the store. Beady eyes would be watching.

She quizzed Jack when she sat at the kitchen eating a sandwich she'd prepared. 'What are you planning to do after school today?'

'Go to the beach.'

'Same group every day?'

'Come on Mum, I'm not doing anything wrong. We just talk, swim and sit around on the sand. I'm just hanging out with them. They're my friends.'

'Okay, I know. But one thing can lead to another...'

'It's not like that. I know what you're thinking. It was dumb what I did at my old school. This is different. We're all interested in the surf and things. I can't explain it to you.'

'I have to be able to trust you, Jack, that's all I want to be able to do.'

'You can.'

Mel gave her a shove. 'All right then.'

Jack shoved her back, and allowed a flicker of her light to shine with a smile. It didn't stop Mel worrying about her.

'Be home by seven, no later.'

'Sure.'

Mel felt like a guilty adolescent as she engaged in the

subterfuge of going to paint. From the shed she collected a paintbrush, and in her bedroom she rifled through drawers to find her painting shorts and shirt. There was something incredibly tantalising about the private nature of her relationship with PJ.

Chapter Fifty-four

Thommo's home was more like a beach shack. Weathered clapboards held the remnants of the original buttercup yellow paint, but most of it had peeled off. The window frames and door had been recently coated in cornflower blue, the colour bold and fresh against the faded look everywhere else. It was a small building with a steep tin roof, and the cracked and dry timber decking on the front verandah simply made it look homely and worn rather than neglected. It sat at end of the street deep into its pocket of land, nestled at the bottom of a hillock.

Mel breathed in air tinged with damp rubber from PJ's wet suits; their dull black carcasses hung over the balustrading on the verandah. The front door opened.

Behind the wooden flywire door stood PJ, a paintbrush incongruously in his hand. She grinned. Once the door was closed, she ran her hands over his warm skin. He held her hand and pressed it close to his heart.

'Feel what you do to me.' Then he took both of her arms and wrapped them around his waist in the shadow of the hallway.

He placed his hands over her shoulders, ran them down the length of her arms, where he caressed her fingertips with his fingers. Taking her hand in his, he led her to his bedroom, where candles cast flickering shadows, and surfboards stood propped in the corners.

A few hours later, she wanted to lie back in his bed and savour the sensation of his body beside hers. They hadn't run out of things to say or minded when they just nestled against each other wordlessly.

'So,' he said, trailing a finger over the insides of her arm as he leaned up on one shoulder, 'you have to go.'

'I like your lips.' She shook out her hair and began dressing, while he threw her various items of clothing.

'When they're attached to yours?' He tugged on his shorts to walk her to the door.

'Yes.'

She gave him a final kiss and coasted in a pleasant haze to collect Lil.

She arrived in time to see Lil dismount and do the post-care of the horse before turning him into the paddock. An unfamiliar, tall and distinguished man was smiling at her daughter. Guilt flooded her. What kind of mother was she leaving Lil alone with horse lessons when all kinds of people or parents could be there? She flew over to the stables.

'Hi Mum. Meet Mina's dad, Mr Derijaweer.' Realisation dawned on Mel: he'd been watching both Lil and Mina. Mina was behind the horse, out of her range of view. He'd been smiling at Mina, not Lil.

'Please call me Moqutat. I am Moqutat Derijaweer, and you must be lovely Lil's mother, Mrs...?' He held out a smooth light-brown hand and clasped hers in a warm handshake.

'I'm fine with Mel.'

'I've heard so much about you.' His smile was easy.

'And we've heard a great deal about the horses at your house. I've been hoping to have an opportunity to thank you for allowing Lil to...'

'There's no need to thank us. My daughter, one of my many blessings, is delighted to have Lil's company. This is truly gratitude enough. We thank you for allowing her to come.' He concluded with a warm smile and she found his rich, slightly accented voice enchanting to listen to. His linen shirtsleeves were folded back along his athletic arms. 'And now please excuse us as I have some riding to do at home. Also Mina, I think,' he said, looking at his daughter's upward pointing face, 'has homework. It was such a pleasure to meet both of you and I hope to see more of you in the future.'

It was like being in the presence of royalty. When they were in the car, Lil was gushing. 'Wow. Mina told me he just flew to Perth on his private jet yesterday, and then flew down from the city this morning. Mina doesn't even need the after-school lessons. She only comes to be with me. Isn't that so nice? I really like Mina.'

Mel let the clouds of euphoria they were both enveloped in bubble around in the car. Just as they pulled up outside their house, Lil said, 'I got into the dance squad and we're doing a performance at the autumn concert in Bettong with all of the schools, a whole troupe of us.' The joy meter cranked up. 'Why have you got that smile on your face? It looks weird.'

When she was young and smiled, people thought she looked great. Now when she smiled she frightened her daughter. 'Hey you, I'm just happy. Sorry for scaring you.' She reached over and grabbed her daughter till she writhed and shrieked.

That was when Mel noticed that none of the lights were on.

Chapter Fifty-five

There was a little light left in the sky, but if Jack had come home when she'd said, the lights would be on. Black thoughts about teenagers fooling around in the ocean and drowning erupted into Mel's parental consciousness, and for the second time that evening she felt pangs of guilt for swanning off to be with PJ. She raced around the house, checking rooms. Lil watched her.

'She's probably still hanging out with her friends.'

'That's what I think too.' She noted the time and buried herself in dinner preparation. She'd give her a few more minutes.

Halfway through tossing the salad, she heard the flywire door creak open, followed by the stomp and slap of beach shoes on timber floors.

'Hi Jack.'

'Hi Mum.' Jack gave her the I'm-going-to-my-room voice.

Mel decided that she would catch up with that conversation at the dinner table. She used to love the free ranging, wide and deep nature of dinnertime conversations, but Jack hadn't been joining in or playing that game for a while.

'In future please stick to the time, okay?' Jack sat opposite her on the sofa after dinner, phone in her hands. Mel insisted they had at least an hour together before bedtime.

'I'll try. Kirby and Tyler said their dad might pick me up to go surfing with them sometimes. Can I go?'

'If you bring their dad in first to meet me.'

'Mum, we don't do it that way. He'll drop by and pick me up.'

'I need a phone number or else no.'

'Okay, I'll get it for you.' Her hands were a blur as she texted.

Mel could imagine the tone of the request. 'Even though he's the police sergeant at Bettong.'

'Then he'll appreciate a phone call from me. There's been a huge advertising campaign by the police telling parents that they should know where their children are at all times.'

Jack shook her head. 'So lame.'

'Don't mutter and no, not lame. Tell me about Tyler and Kirby?'

'Kirby's a boy.' Lil piped up from her book.

'Who asked you?'

'You tell me,' Mel cut into the bickering.

'Tyler and Kirby are twins, brother and sister. They're my friends.'

'They surf a lot?'

'Yes, and their dad Matt, sometimes surfs out on the back break with them. I'm going to bed.'

Jack leaned in and gave Mel a quick hug. She heard footsteps on her passage to the kitchen for a last graze before Jack disappeared into her room.

'The modem is going off in half an hour and please leave your phone charging in the kitchen thanks.' That had been the deal they'd struck for her move down. A muffled agreement was garbled through a half-full mouth.

Lil hopped onto her lap. 'She's such a grumpy toad.'

'It's her age.'

'Why did I have to have her for a sister?'

'To make you appreciate me more?'

'I don't think so.'

'Bed for you too.'

'Goodnight Mum.'

Throughout the following week more tourists dropped into the store. Lil came in to help when she could, but Jack was yet to make an appearance. Anything souvenir-like was snapped up. She made a list of what the customers bought and quizzed them about what else they thought they would like to purchase if they could, when they stood around the displays. Her journal filled and plans began to take shape.

PJ took the rest of the week off to film at the beach and to help out in the surf store. It was paying off, PJ confided to her, and it eclipsed some of their Christmas season trading days. The huge screen in the shop ran all of the footage he'd stitched together; it had captured the attention of the customers.

Later in the week, after work, PJ manoeuvred her into a storeroom for a quick embrace and kiss. She locked up on their way out.

'Does Jack want to come out with me on Saturday?'

'What do you think?'

'Is she home?'

'I think so, let's go find her.'

'Jack?' Mel knocked on her bedroom door.

'Yeah?'

'PJ's here to ask you something.' Mel didn't comment on the lightning way Jack flew out of her room.

'Hi PJ.'

'Hi Jack. You want to come out on Saturday? It'll mean a before-dawn pick-up.'

'Sure. That would be great.'

'I'll see you then.'

Mel followed him out to the car where he mouthed her a kiss. A blaze of warmth raced through her.

She rinsed through a couple of glasses and spoke to Jack. 'You'll have to apply sunblock more than once and keep in touch.'

'I know Mum, but don't pick me up too early.' She put down the milk carton after tipping most of the contents into the blender with frozen bananas.

Mel often wished she had Tony alongside her to add his parental weight. It wasn't easy implementing the 'you-shall-nots' on your own.

'Okay. I'll collect you after Lil's finished riding at Mina's.'

'You don't need to look for me on Saturday, I'll find you.'

Chapter Fifty-six

Mel collected her notes, and after a search on the computer, found what she was looking for. She contacted Sally.

'Hi Sally. Can you escape to come for a drive with me tomorrow afternoon? I'm closing early. There's something I've got to do.'

'I can wing it with Brian. What are you thinking?'

'You know I've been looking at what else I can source in the local community to sell to tourists?'

'Yes.'

'I searched to see what's selling but not everything came up, so I went to the local business pages in Bettong's community news, and all of these names popped on the screen with a list of their products.'

'I'm listening.'

'There's a whole community of people making things out there in the hinterland. They're selling things like olive-oil products, wool beanies and scarves, recycled wood-pallet furniture, vintage goods, recycled timber photo frames, handmade paper products and pottery goods. No one is showcasing these products in town. I want to offer the craftspeople an opportunity to display their goods and invite them to talk to the public. I also want to have a large screen running with footage showing their process of production. I'm bursting with ideas.'

'I'm home. Why don't we meet at the café to talk some more.'

'Okay. See you in five.'

A spray of gravel made people turn to watch the large four-wheel drive pull into a car bay, their eyes drawn to the colourful swish of fabric as Sally descended the cab. Her swirling locks, larger-than-life personality and liveliness were magnetic. She wandered over in a vaporous wave of expensive perfume and caught Mel in an embrace. They made their way into the café and ordered. Within a few minutes they were seated with their drinks. It wasn't a busy day.

'What else are you thinking?'

'I could advertise and be the meeting place for guided historical, marine and scientific walks. Talks on those topics and screens with clips documenting the walks could feature in one of my back rooms. As for the local producers, I thought they could offer me between one to three items to sell in the store, products that can't be purchased online. Customers would have to use foot trade to get them.'

'Smart.'

'What do you think about book signings?'

'Know any authors?'

'No, but people love that sort of thing, especially if the writer is a local. Wait a minute.'

'What?'

'Even short papers could be signed. Oh no, I've had a brain wave, what about, "Meet your Favourite Blogger"?'

'I think we should stop the brainstorm.'

'My mum's in a book club and her friend's son has written about insects in the mid-west region. I think there might be an audience for everything.'

'I love reading science articles about areas I'm familiar with.' Sally wiped a few strands of hair from her face and spooned up the cinnamon-topped froth on her coffee.

'You do?'

'I do.'

Mel popped a marshmallow from her hot chocolate into her mouth. 'You'd even read about the four most destructive species of ant found near homes in the mid-west?'

Sally's eyes widened. 'Yes. My uncle had a farm out there and we went every winter holidays. I would read that.'

'Who'd have thought?' She spooned the remainder of the

creamy chocolate sauce at the bottom of her cup into her mouth.

'Underneath these bottle-bought golden locks lurks a real science geek.'

'You're full of surprises.'

Sally nodded. 'I like that about me.'

'Modest too. I'll pick you up tomorrow at about two. I've been emailing and phoning them to see if we can drop in. A few have replied.'

She pulled into Sally and Brian's driveway the following day.

Sally looked at her car. 'No offence Mel, but if there are some dodgy tracks we'd be better off driving in my car.'

'I was hoping you'd say that.'

*

'You know your store's not a charity?' Sally squinted at her over the roof of the car.

'I know.' Mel looked back at the diminutive house, discarded tumble of toys, and neglected plants. 'But did you see her face?'

'Mel.' She turned the ignition on and faced her.

'It's okay Sally, but I'll stock her goods.'

'Okay, it's your business. Yes I did see her face.'

'Her beanies and scarves were pretty special.'

'Not that unique.'

'Maybe she just needs someone to have faith in her.'

'So you are a charity.' Mel squeezed her friend's arm and leaned her head briefly against Sally's shoulder. 'You could use her, but if you want my advice, not too many beanie makers.'

'Okay.'

'Or sob stories.'

'I'll try.'

They drove to the next location.

A tall young woman in her late twenties with a sparkly stud in her nose and eyebrow piercings, opened the door after they knocked; faded navy workpants hung loose on her thin frame. She took an unadorned hand out of a pocket and offered it to each of them in turn.

'Hi, you're Meg? I'm Mel Wilson and this is Sally, my friend.' Mel quickly scanned through a page in her notebook.

'Yes. Hi Mel and Sally, welcome.' Her face relaxed a little.

Over a mug of tea, they settled into a couple of worn sofas covered with clean, bright throw rugs, and examined Meg's work.

'Your recycled timber frames are great. I love the artwork of discarded pieces of tin and glass inside your frames, too. You have a real gift.'

Her smile was fleeting. 'My dad drives down from Perth and helps me, but he can only stay one day and night with us. My mum isn't well. He has to go back to be with her.'

'I can see these frames selling quickly. If you and your dad think of anything else you'd like to make, email me and I'll see if I can make room for it in my store. Think about prices, and think about a couple of products that you can offer me as unique items for foot trade only, as we discussed on the phone.'

Meg had an unhurried way of speaking. 'I have a couple of ideas. I thought I could build a pattern for one specific frame with a light scratching of a pelican in the corner and stamp it as bought in your store. That was one idea.'

'That would sell. So many people want one unique thing to take away.'

'Thanks Mel.'

'Thank you Meg. I look forward to having your woodwork in my store.'

'Nice to meet you too, Sally.'

Everywhere they went they bought about ten items and ordered more. The stack grew in the back of Sally's car.

'She's talented. I wonder what her story is?' Sally said about the young woman they'd just visited.

'I don't want you getting involved Sally,' Mel said. 'This is a business remember, not a charity.'

'Don't steal my lines.'

'It's concerning, this absence of fathers in the lives of young children. How many single mums did we deal with today?'

'It's like that movie, the guy moves on like a bee pollinating the flowers.'

'And the flowers once with seed, wilt and die? Oh bad analogy. Maybe they grow into a tall, strong tree afterwards.'

'Not sure we can generalise like that.' Sally eased the car onto the main road.

'I'm buying everything she makes.' Mel underlined her name and wrote notes below it. Sally pinched her in the shoulder.

'What's that for?'

'Reality, it bites.'

'Very funny.'

They took the route back to Pelican Point. 'We better get my car from your house and drive both cars to the store so I can unload.'

'Good thinking. Can I come with you when you visit the four surfing buddies who are building surfboard art?'

'So shallow.' Mel shook her head.

'You need a bit of fun in life, as you would well know.'

'Stop hinting. Yes it's going well.'

'It's your business.' Though Sally couldn't quite hide the pleased glint in her eye.

Chapter Fifty-seven

With Jack and Lil's help, Mel dug out and tidied several old packing crates, an unusual dresser, an old chest of drawers and a couple of plain wooden boxes. They disguised them all with tablecloths and sheets and stood back to admire their handiwork. On each of them they arranged the sample of goods.

'The shop needs a new name,' Jack said.

'Write down any suggestions and we'll keep them in a bowl. I'll need to do a bit of building and redesigning before we go that far.'

'It looks great.' Mel tried not to let Jack see how pleased she was about the changes she'd noticed in her in the last week.

Mel tingled. She couldn't wait to show PJ or see the reactions of her regulars.

*

'Come on Mum, guitar lesson is at quarter to eight.' Mel was still lumpy with exhaustion and found it hard to move from the kitchen chair.

'Okay Lil. Bye Jack.' Jack lifted her eyes from the phone and smiled. Mel leaned around and hugged her from behind as they headed out.

Before the start of the competition, the overseas and out-of-town surfers spent time out on the surf break to familiarise themselves with the local conditions, a filming opportunity that PJ took advantage of. With PJ out for the week, the mail delivery was left up to Mel and it had to be done after work.

Amongst the mail in the bag left by the mail truck, Mel

spied a parcel for Beth Hawthorne. Beth, she'd heard, was the lady who lived in a shack across the bay, but that was all she knew about her, and it accounted for the winking lights she'd noticed in the evening. Thommo used to deliver Beth's mail by dinghy. Her last spectacularly unpleasant dinghy experience at the Banderley Islands hadn't given her confidence in her abilities with a boat.

This week could be one of the busiest of the year in the shop with the competition and tourists. Mel was annoyed about having to use valuable time to drive over and deliver mail later that evening to a possibly intractable old woman.

For the first time since she had opened up the shop, Mel was run off her feet. The locals picked over items on the display but didn't buy much except tea and biscuits. Curious tourists bought everything. Their buying veracity was astonishing and she fantasised about being financial enough to employ an assistant. Her legs and feet ached and she longed to sit with a cup of tea.

Lil arrived home and didn't look like she would be much use in the shop. Mel closed the door at the end of the day and ran her eyes over her mail-delivery list. It wasn't too bad, she thought, except for the trip across the bay. She scanned out across the inlet where a light afternoon breeze built the water into a short chop. She knew it would strengthen. When she considered that she would be heading against it in the fading light, she decided it would be better to go visit Beth the next day and do the delivery in town tonight.

'Stay by the pots when you have the stove on.'

'I know Mum.'

'Use a chopping board and wipe up after everything.'

'Okay. I have cooked spaghetti bolognaise before.'

'Thanks for cooking tonight. I'll be about an hour.'

'See you Mum.'

The string of warnings would vaporise before Lil had time to think about them.

The locals loved a chat and didn't notice the size of the bags below her eyes. However, they were not only her neighbours but also her customers. Halfway through, she notified Lil of the expected later return.

'Don't worry I'll be fine. Eddie's come over and he's helping.'

'That's fantastic.' She refused to think about the state of the kitchen.

'And Eddie said there's a raft building competition. It's for a race to the pontoon. He wants to build one with me and we're entering and designing ours tonight.'

'Sounds like you'll be busy. Maybe Jack will help you?'

'I haven't even seen her. She's in her room talking on her phone.'

'Tell her I'll be home in little while.'

'I'll call through the door.'

'See you later.'

On her way home, Mel spotted a faint light at the other side of the bay and wondered about Beth.

'What do you think of it?' Lil asked when she served dinner.

'I love this variation of spaghetti bolognaise in lettuce cups. It's very creative. Not to mention the spaghetti in a capsicum half. Who would have thought of that?' Mel turned and raised her eyebrows at Jack. She didn't mention the aphids crawling out of the lettuce. She gave them an eight. Lil and Eddie seemed pleased. Jack wrote a two on her paper napkin and walked off.

Mel entered the kitchen, at least that's what it was before they cooked.

Lil looked at her. 'It's okay, we'll help clean.'

After a vigorous assault on the countertop and stove, Eddie left. Lil slid off to bed and Jack demolished another bowl of spaghetti before she slipped into her room to complete some more homework.

Mel tossed around ideas for the store. The application to the council to secure sole rights to a souvenir store had proven fortuitous.

She sat in the lounge room and worked on her bookwork. PJ kept in touch with texts but was absorbed by the events on the beach because the competition had started.

Before dawn on Saturday morning, PJ pulled into her

driveway and she raced outside to be with him for about five minutes while Jack ate her toast and juice. PJ whisked her off to the side of the house and they kissed. It was like learning to live in a new body, speak a new language.

The house was quiet and Mel's muscles rebelled at the thought of a jog. She fell back onto the bed and ignored the dusky-pink streak of early-morning light. In a couple of hours she would be at work. The tourist trade was going to become her bread and butter and she had to put all of her energies into meeting the market with only a hiatus of eighteen months to establish her business before the complex opened.

She sprang out of bed when she realised she'd forgotten about Beth's mail. If she took Lil over with her, she figured she'd get a better reception as she'd heard around town that Beth didn't welcome many people.

She found the neglected aluminium dinghy tethered to a bollard on a small jetty by a worn and shredded rope. Mel and Lil looked at each other. The motor was at least quite new and not too powerful for her to handle. Frowning, she re-read Thommo's instructions.

'Mum it's okay.' Lil touched her arm. 'I'll be fine. We're surrounded by people here, not like last time.'

Mel pulled the cord and turned the throttle, and was surprised when it started on the first try. She let out a whoop of joy. They both checked the fuel gauge. Lil untied it from the bollard on the small pier, and sat down with a lopsided thump on the bench beside her. The boat wobbled as their weights adjusted in the dinghy. Mel pointed it roughly in the direction of Beth's place.

Lil chose to move up to the front, her body dwarfed by the faded yellow life jacket. In her hands she held Thommo's binoculars and pressed them close to her eyes; her long hair streamed behind, buffeted by the wind.

Mother and daughter perched on the cold metal seats. Cool air drilled into them, but at that time of year it was refreshing. Mel could just make out the rough shape of a low and simple jetty. Lil scanned the horizon, and kept up a running commentary about the real and speculated marine life that leapt into her view.

Mel felt smacked awake in the rush of wind and thought how much she loved the shape of her new life. With one hand on the throttle, she reached over the edge with the other, and pushed it low enough to feel the neat soft slap of water on her fingertips.

As they neared their destination, Mel spotted a figure walking around the jetty. It had to be Beth. Calm and intent, she flicked, gathered, and released ropes from the barnacled bollards, years of experience told in the way her hands moved. Mel cut back the throttle and was thrown a rope but was unsure of where to attach it.

'Just there by the rowlock, that's where Thommo puts it.' A voice dry and clear shot out at her.

'Thanks, I'm Mel.'

'I know. You know who I am, too since it's written on the package you've brought.'

Not going to be a long stop, then.

As she leaned over to help tie up the stern rope, Beth's otherwise impassive face creaked into a smile. 'And who are you?'

'I'm Lil.'

'So you are. Thommo mentioned you.'

Mel had bargained correctly on the cute factor.

'How do you like it at Pelican Point?'

'I love being beside the sea and my new school is okay, too. It must be great to have your own island with your own jetty.'

Beth smiled. 'Not quite an island, but yes it's like an island. This is just a headland though. Would you like a cup of tea?'

Even though Mel knew the question was for both of them, it had been directed at Lil.

'I'd love one, but unfortunately we won't have long, I still have to open the shop.'

'On a Saturday morning at the Point?' Beth's tone was incredulous.

'Tourists are everywhere because of the surf competition. Have you heard about it?'

'I caught wind of that. My boys used to surf when they were young.'

They crunched along a meandering path of sun-bleached shells and coral towards higher ground. A timber beach shack sat at the end of the path, hedged in by walls of tough coastal bushes. Shells, coral and fossils were mosaicked on walls or sat perched on timber framing, and above, mobiles of glass and shell dangled and tinkled.

Lil assailed Beth with endless questions about the various facets of 'island life' and the curios she had scattered throughout the homely shack. Mel surveyed the small collection of old photos taped onto the ancient fridge, their edges nibbled by years of salt and dust. The yellowed and peeling tape, despite its age, still stuck them firm to the fridge door. As she brought the strong, hot tea to her lips, her eyes lit on an image in one photo. It seemed like a familiar face, although it looked like a much younger version of the man she knew. There might come a time when she could have a talk with Beth, but it wouldn't be now. She tucked the idea away to ask Thommo about when he came back.

When their short visit ended, Beth gazed at her for a brief moment. Being in Beth's presence was quite an experience for her. Lil felt it too.

Chapter Fifty-eight

A steady stream of tourists arrived in Pelican Point, drawn by the excitement of an international surfing event. Bettong was the closest big town, but the actual competition was at a surf break south of Pelican Point and many travellers chose to venture off the main route into the small town. Mel reaped the benefits of her budding entrepreneurship.

Lil had gone to her horse-riding lesson with Bronte, and Suraya had offered to pick her up to take her back with Mina for the afternoon. Mel spent a couple of hours in a small alcove in her dining room, against which she had rammed her desk. If she could execute all of the ideas she'd discussed with Sally, the future would hold promise.

She was about to text Thommo with a question regarding Beth, when her phone blipped. A couple of texts arrived. The first was from her mother wanting a date for a visit. The second was a photo from PJ showing Jack on her board in the surf with a text saying that he couldn't wait to spend a whole day with her. That message threw all other ideas out of her head. Her mother would have to wait until after she had time alone with PJ. Things were looking up.

Chapter Fifty-nine

By the final sale on Friday afternoon of that week, Mel's stock had been depleted. She could have sold a whole lot more of Meg's frames, and the recycled wooden chopping boards built by the surfing buddies were popular. Items needed to be transportable, but she did notice people looking at the photos she had on a computer screen exhibiting the larger products for sale. She couldn't wait to have the large screens up to market and showcase the artisans, and to fill the back room with guest speakers. She planned to drive around on Saturday morning to purchase more stock.

'You don't know what she's like.' Jack yanked at the zip on her bag for her trip to Perth. She'd seemed happy this past week, having settled into a routine, but she was back to being grumpy this morning because she was heading home to Tony and Leah.

'It's not fun being pregnant, it makes you tired,' Mel tried to explain. And when she was pregnant, she hadn't had to contend with teenage stepchildren.

'Then why get pregnant?'

'I'm not answering that Jack, but the human race is based on this process. How else would you have mates?'

'We have to be quiet when she's tired and that's all the time. We don't do much except when Dad takes us to the beach. She complains when we're there and she complains if he's not around doing things for her. It's a pain.'

'When the baby is born, you'll have a little brother or sister to enjoy and you can teach him or her things.'

'I never wanted one.'

'It doesn't need your permission to enter the world.'

'Shame about that.'

Two faces peeked out of the aeroplane window for a final farewell.

Mel's phone sang out just as she watched the taillights disappear on the horizon.

'Do you want to come to dinner with Macka, Robby and their wives?' It was PJ.

Instead of feeling happy at the offer, Mel was conflicted. What would other people think? What if the children found out?

'Are you there Mel?'

'Yes.'

'It's just dinner. I've mentioned you several times. They know about our "friendship", but they're my mates.'

'You know I'd love to...'

'It'd be fantastic if you could come. Think about it and let me know in a few minutes. Macka's wife, Lisette, is cooking, and she wants to know how many are coming.'

She stood in the car park of the airport and watched the winking trail of stars begin to fill out the late evening sky. 'I'd love to come,' she decided, 'thank them for me.'

*

Mel took in his clean, fresh look as he leaned against the doorjamb on the porch. He was dressed in jeans and a collared shirt. A shower, a change, a few fingers through his hair and he was done. Meanwhile, she'd thrashed around in the wardrobe, hunted through her small selection of dresses, had discovered one of her favourite foundation creams had come to a sticky, oozy end on top of a new white tee-shirt, and after cleaning that up, had had no time left to dry her hair. It hung in damp ringlets and she felt like calling it off.

He pulled her into his chest and kissed her. The way he nestled into her made her want to stay at home, in his arms, in bed. 'You look gorgeous.'

She stopped thinking about how she looked and what she was wearing. 'You smell great.'

Lisette was a few years younger than PJ, but Robby and Macka were a bit older. She discovered that Lisette had grown up in a suburb close to the one Mel had lived in with her parents. Jody was late into her pregnancy with her second child and younger than Lisette, but easy company.

'PJ, have you asked Mel to join you for the wind-up dinner?' Lisette's cheeks were flushed with the sparkling wine.

'Would you like to come? I think you'd enjoy it.'

'That's tomorrow night?' Mel still wanted to keep their relationship private, and PJ knew she did. Did it matter?

'Yes.'

'Are you sure? Aren't these exclusive invites for you guys?'

'I have a plus one.'

'Mel, this is going to be a huge night for Bettong and the surfing community down here. You should see what PJ has prepared. You should come. It's going to be one fantastic event.' Lisette put her glass down and stood up. 'I'm off to the bathroom and to check on the kids.'

'What's the dress code?' Mel asked.

'Not like a big formal Perth function, but it's the first one Bettong has hosted so I'm thinking there'll be a bit of glamour. The guys have been told not to wear suits but no denim, and a collared shirt, plain not printed. Ties are optional.' Jody paused to readjust her sitting position. 'Robby, your child's feet are digging into my ribs.' She heaved around on the sofa. 'I won't be staying late tomorrow night.'

Robby leaned forward and rubbed her stomach.

Lisette wandered back into the living room. 'Relax Mel, you're the right size for a heap of beautiful gowns. If you can't find anything, try Camilla's. It's a new store with evening-style dresses.'

'Thanks for the tip. I used to dream about meeting professional surfers when I was a teenager.'

'Now's your chance. PJ knows quite a few.'

Later that night, they hadn't pulled out of Macka's driveway before PJ slid his hand over to find one of Mel's. He brought it to his lips.

At her house, he paused in her driveway.

'I'd love it if you stayed, but I thought you had to be up early for the finals?'

'I do. But I've been waiting to be alone with you all week.'

She undid her seat belt.

'I'll sleep next week,' he said.

They stepped out of the car. She unlocked the front door and felt the beat of his heart through his shirt when it pressed against her back. His hands wandered and rested on her waist and his lips were on the back of her neck. She'd never opened a door like that before.

The next morning Mel woke to find him standing near the window. She watched the tiny hairs on his body glow with the first shafts of pink light. Her entire body suddenly ached for him anew. She didn't think she'd ever feel satisfied living a life without that complete euphoria buzzing around.

'I have to go,' he told her, but not before he slid back into bed for one last kiss. When he left she remained in bed to soak in sensual bliss for another hour.

Mel knew she wouldn't hear from him till the evening. There was only the small matter of a finding a dress.

The morning shimmered as the last pulse of summer bled into autumn and the warmth beckoned her out. Over the last couple of months, Mel started to recognise familiar faces to wave and smile at. It wasn't many, the small smattering of locals she knew, but it made her feel like she was somewhere. She snatched a banana on her way to collect more stock from the few people who'd responded to her emails.

The trickle of tourists turned into a torrent and before long she ran out of the more popular items. Her customers had an unquenchable thirst for tea and for knowledge about land prices, surf spots and activities in the region. She couldn't wait to transform the store.

When Sally shifted her weight in her chair, her blue cotton shirt shuffled around to reveal golden skin. With hands placed around mugs of coffee, they looked out over the bay. Sally's home had an impressive view of the whole of Pelican Point.

'This is truly delicious,' Sally said between mouthfuls. 'I think this will sell.'

They picked through a range of goods Mel had brought to sample.

'These seed crackers are from a new lady not far from Meg's. So, Fairy Godmother, how are your personal stylist skills? I need an outfit for tonight. Why are you grinning at me?'

Sally raised her eyebrows. 'Not for any particular reason, but are you aware how radiant you look?'

'You can think what you like.'

'Sure. If it makes you look and feel that good, it can't be bad can it?'

'No.'

'He's pretty hot.'

Mel tried to stop the red creeping up her face.

'Oh God, don't tell me he's fabulous at everything.'

'Really Sal, I won't be telling you anything.'

'You don't have to.' She looked smug.

'It's been fantastic and we really like each other. I hope no one thinks I'm "an older woman with a younger guy" kind of person.'

'You're both unattached, end of story. It isn't anyone else's business.' Sally paused to flip a slice of local cheese onto a cracker, and with half a mouthful continued. 'You were saying?'

'Do you have any dresses for me?'

'Is that meant to be funny? My wardrobe is my life. We can do a few things to a couple of them to make them fit you. Let's take a look. I kept one or two of my skinny dresses.'

They collapsed into the cushioned chairs on the balcony an hour and a half later with an adjusted turquoise dress and a few accessories, and discussed Mel's business plan.

'You know you're going to have to build a better profile on the web, don't you?'

'I know, and I'll have to use social media even though I don't blog, tweet or hash tag because I don't get the, "Here I am feeding the kids. Here I am reading a book." Really?'

'Don't worry, I have just the guy for you. We've been using his skills to get our caravan parks into the twenty-first century and he's totally professional, but he isn't cheap. Still, it'll get you going.'

'Do you want to come and help me next week, if you have time?'

'Heck yeah, and I want details of the wind-up dinner and dance. That's a very exclusive invite you've got there. Not many tickets went to the locals.'

Absorbed in trawling the web at home, Mel hadn't noticed an accumulation of text messages on her phone. One from Jack made her laugh. *Baby rooms make me want to vomit!*

Lil's text was diplomatic and warm, splashed with love and kisses. Mel prayed for Lil's sweet gentleness to last. Then there were a couple of updates from PJ, both on the competition and his excitement at taking her out to the finals dinner in the evening.

She embraced the profound sense of contentedness that enveloped her. Every other time she felt like that, her life had spun out of control.

Chapter Sixty

Mel took a breath and opened the door.

'Wow, turquoise is your colour. What's the matter?'

'You look amazing and I look like me.'

'Have you looked in the mirror? I came to collect beautiful you. I wasn't planning on going with anyone else. That dress is awesome.'

'Thank you.'

'I don't know whether to take you out or stay in.'

'Let's go, but you don't have to stop the compliments. I need them tonight.'

He bumped her gently with his shoulder. 'You don't need them. You know you look great.'

His all-over excitement whirled straight into Mel that night and made her radiate with far more confidence than she believed possible.

The Uber driver leapt out to open the door.

'Red, you're an Uber driver?'

'Hi Mel. Not many taxis in town and it gets me out of the house.'

When she slid into the seat she sniffed for cat odours. PJ shot her a quizzical look.

'Tell you later. It's nothing,' she whispered.

Red tuned into a local radio station and they settled into the expansive back seats, her fingers threaded in PJ's.

'Are you sure I'm dressed appropriately for this?' She loved the dress and it felt great on, but the colour was fresh and she would usually have worn black for an evening event.

'Seriously? They're all surfers. It stipulated no ties and no suits, relax, you're a dish. An edible one.' His voice came out soft and warm and his cologne was divine. He drew her close and she melted into his arms. Whenever their bodies touched sparks flew, and she wished they could remain in that tantalising state forever.

After half an hour, Red pulled into a winding gravel driveway and stopped at the gates to the function. Mel caught sight of an enormous bright-white marquis outlined by thousands of tiny winking lights. Behind it and off to the side sat an impressive limestone house. Despite the dark, everything glittered and sparkled with masses of tastefully arranged lights.

'Thanks Red.' She tried to look less over-awed than she felt. It wasn't as if she was on any A-list for the to-be-seen-at events hosted in town. It made her want to giggle in embarrassment; for goodness sake she couldn't even surf.

'I'll be back at one unless I hear otherwise.'

'No, that's good,' PJ said. Red waved and drove off.

An attendant at the front checked their identification and gave them each a leather bracelet with a silver ball positioned in the centre to wear. The silver balls had a small number etched on one side and the curve of a wave on the other.

'Who made these?'

'Local artist. Cute, huh?'

'Wow is what I was thinking.' He held her hand.

Each side of the crushed limestone path, tall shrubs in planters glistened with fairy lights, and low flickering lights lay on the ground either side of the path to guide them. Star-like lights shone in the taller trees and swung in the light breeze. People swarmed around the small minibars and food huts dotted around the outside of the marquis, and the faint chords of an acoustic guitar band could be heard above the din of the crowd. Two magnificent sand sculptures adorned the lawn. One was of a surfer paddling on his board, and the other was of a blue whale surrounded by a collection of other marine animals. It was hard to see them in their entirety due to the number of phones snapping photos. She gripped his hand.

They stopped by a food hut serving local abalone in a sea froth concoction spritzed with preserved native finger limes. Each food hut offered a sample of local fare and Mel wanted to try them all. She found it hard not to gawp in wide-eyed wonder at the whole spectacle. Her eyes travelled to the second storey of the house where huge panes of floor-to-ceiling glass overlooked the ocean. No architect could have resisted showcasing a view that ran the length of the stunning surf break where the competition had been held. The incessant pounding of surf reverberated in the air, lending the event an authentic backdrop.

Everyone seemed to know PJ and she couldn't remember half the names she'd been introduced to.

'You want me to get you one of those cocktails?' PJ had a beer but wasn't going to drink much as he still had things to do, he told her. She pretended not to know what some of them were.

'Just a small one, I want to leave room for dinner.' When he slipped away, she felt self-conscious and small, especially compared to the giants of the surf industry, as well as all of the who's who. Although who was who was anybody's guess and she choked back a giggle; she had absolutely no idea who most of the people were.

'Hi.' A tall young woman greeted her.

'Hi, I'm Mel.' Was she supposed to know this very attractive person?

'I'm Andy. I saw you with PJ. Kasey wants to talk to him.' Mel pushed back a stray dark lock and felt like her mother.

'Uh, he's just gone to get me a drink.'

Andy tapped a foot on the ground and glanced around at the crowd. Clearly Mel wasn't the ticketed item. She returned her sunny gaze to light on Mel. 'Are you two together?'

What did she say? She hadn't turned it into an 'us' in her mind yet. 'Yes.' She told herself to stop worrying about what everyone would think. Andy shuffled around and beamed once more at her with perfect white teeth. Mel discreetly poked her tongue between her teeth to extract tiny rubbery pieces of abalone. Hers were a tiny bit crooked and looked okay, from a distance. She smiled back without revealing too many of them.

Like a racehorse, Andy launched at PJ when she spotted him. She wrapped slender bronze arms around him and planted a kiss on his cheek, and remained with her arm trailed around his waist. 'So great to see you PJ.'

PJ extracted himself to place an arm around Mel's waist. 'You've met Mel?'

'Sure have.' A quick dismissive flash of a smile panned out to Mel. 'Kasey would like a word.'

'Come on Mel, let's go chat to Kasey.' If Kasey looked like Andy, she wasn't sure she wanted to go.

'I'll stay here with the cocktail.'

'What? Come on.' He led her through the marquis to where a band of others flocked around a central point like bees to nectar.

'PJ.' A tall tanned blue-eyed man, who Mel immediately recognised as Dwight Manning, holder of the world titles for six years, spun around and grabbed PJ by the shoulders. It knocked Mel's hand and made the cocktail slop over Andy's white dress.

'Dwight!' It must have been his wife. 'Don't worry Andy, Dwight will fix you up for this.'

Andy managed to keep her six-hundred-watt smile firmly in place. Only as she left did she glance over to give Mel a cool look. 'No problem. I'll change.'

'So sorry Andy.' Dwight dropped his hands. 'I'm such a doofus sometimes.'

Mel liked him instantly. 'Why do you call him Kasey?' She whispered to PJ in a stolen moment while the Andy incident scattered everyone's attention.

'It's a code name we use to keep fans and hangers-on from listening in. We have several monikers for him,' he whispered back.

Dwight's wife gave him a quick sign then followed Andy out.

'Mel, this is Dwight.'

Her mouth hung and she darted around in her head for the right words but went clammy and shook his hand, still a little sweaty from a tide of embarrassment.

'You're a very good surfer. Congratulations for your win this round.'

He cocked an eyebrow and grinned. 'Thanks. PJ here, now he's the man. Have you seen his stuff?' He nudged PJ with his arm.

'A bit.' *You're a very good surfer*? Had she seriously said that?

'You're in for a treat tonight.'

She looked at PJ. He shrugged. 'It's nothing much. I got lucky.'

'Yeah right, like I got lucky winning a few world titles. PJ, not many do what you do.'

'The young dudes with go-pros, phones and drones don't do too bad.'

'Anyways, can you come see me next week? We're doing the wine, recline and dine thing before we leave for the east coast.'

'Sure.'

They didn't have time to say any more before the MC leapt onto the stage to ask everyone to find their seats. They were directed to sit at Dwight's table.

'What do you know?' Dwight winked at her.

'We were way at the back. They're not going to love you for that.' PJ said.

'Oh I'm not bothered.' When they took their seats, all of the wait staff suddenly appeared to spread napkins and to pour the first drink. 'I don't even know the Premier of Western Australia.'

Oops, she thought as the champagne bubbled inside.

'That's not our premier,' Mel informed him as she leaned back and let the napkin float gently onto her lap.

'It's not?' Dwight looked genuinely surprised.

'No, the Prime Minister is here for a summit. I think we've taken his spot,' PJ said. They all glanced across the room to where the Prime Minister sat with the runner-up.

'I'll send him a board.' Dwight turned and waved at him.

She tried to imagine the new Prime Minister surfing. She felt shot through with giddiness and wonder. It got better as the night wore on. PJ's clips earned him the applause of everyone and an award for his outstanding surfing footage during the week.

*

When PJ left early, Mel languished in bed with a third cup of tea and considered phoning Sally to fill her in on the evening. A new text bleeped. It took the bubble of joy away. *Dad's bad,* it read, *going to Perth in a few hours. Coming around to see you soon. Love PJ.*

He arrived an hour later, and they lay on her sofa. He drew her close.

'I always thought his early wild years would never catch up with him. He kept himself so well.'

'I don't think this is about his early wild years. This kind of thing happens indiscriminately.'

'I didn't tell you everything. The doctors contacted me and said that most of his vital organs showed the presence of cancerous cells.'

'I am so sorry PJ.'

'He's had a great life, but this isn't fair. I'm going up to spend every day with him. I don't know how much time that will be. I'm taking Dad out when I get to Perth. He used to make me visit all the small museums around the river when we'd go on holidays. He'd take me to catch crabs by the rocks in Fremantle where he'd point out the different sea birds and talk about what the fishing boats were bringing in. I used to think it was boring.' He paused. 'You know, I spent a long time away from Dad until my late twenties, living the kind of life I wanted. In the last few years I've realised what he gave up for me. I hoped he'd be around for his grandkids.'

She trailed a finger over the stubble on his chin and then traced it over the outline of his face.

He leaned over her. 'I love you.'

It made her dizzy. 'I love you too.' She loved the warmth and pressure of his head against her neck, his company and the flood of liquid pleasure she felt being around him.

He would miss one last day of filming where the guys went out for fun. Macka and Robby promised they'd cover for him. Before he left, they lay close and tight, his heart pounded against her chest and he seemed much younger. She ran fingertips over her lips to catch the traces of his last kiss.

Days drifted into weeks and a new postie, Dave, had been appointed to take PJ's place until he returned. Whenever she heard the light putter of the motorbike, Mel half expected to see him. She missed how he would lope off the bike, brush past her and plant a kiss on her lips or neck. He made her feel like she could face down anything. Dave was a local at the tennis club, and despite his cheeriness, she had little to say to him.

PJ texted and sent photos of Thommo; each photo documented his gradual slide. His already slight frame became bony, his tan faded and his eyes grew more milky. The time came when PJ could not take Thommo outside. Thommo had requested that the funeral be in Pelican Point and for his ashes to be cast adrift in the bay.

Mel's mum arrived to help in the shop. Mel grimaced when she watched the finances take a downturn after the excitement of the surf competition, even with the new goods. She knew it was because of a lack of marketing and that she needed a more active website. She enlisted speakers and used the screens to promote as much as possible. As far as business plans went, it was optimistic and wishful.

'You know this is a great little business. I like talking to the locals.' Her mum swept the floors and tidied the shelving before they exited through the back door.

Mel looked into her warm, lined face. 'I don't know if I can survive on tea and biscuits alone, and the goods aren't marching out the door at the moment.' She put her feet up on the outside table and shared the dappled light of the tree with her mother. They both held large mugs of hot chocolate.

'Perhaps I could move down and help you?'

She laughed. 'You know I love you, but we'd drive each other nuts. I wouldn't be that nice to be around when I'm running a business all day, and you love to sit and chat, which of course has its good points.'

'I feel so useless. Georgie has her family and you have your business.'

Georgie had warned her. 'Mum, you are absolutely not useless. You do so much volunteering, you're better than me at crosswords, and you're a great grandmother. Maybe you can enrol in some courses?'

'Time filling, that's all it is.'

They finished their drink.

'Don't worry,' her mother said, 'it's just that I miss you. I'll be fine. I can always come down to annoy you from time to time.' Though she smiled her way through the reassurances, Mel's heart wavered when she took in the soft fall of her mother's face.

They wiped the table and finished with a sudsy hug.

A call came at two in the morning.

Chapter Sixty-one

'Mel, he's gone. He passed away a few minutes ago.'

'Oh PJ.' She paused and heard him breathe. It was harder than she thought it would be. She wiped away her own tears. 'He was my first friend here. You were the best thing in his life. I know he loved you.'

The cremation, PJ told her, had to be in the city as his body was quite deteriorated, but they would have a funeral service the following Wednesday at Pelican Point. People would commune and eat at Thommo's place, and afterwards they would wander down to the water's edge for the final goodbyes.

In the house at breakfast, Mel told her children and mother. Each in their way had a quiet tear. She wept for PJ, for herself, and for Thommo; a friend she thought she'd have for many more years.

All through the week most of Pelican Point dropped by the store. It was the place they most associated with Thommo. Stories and tears ran like the endless teas Mel poured that week and she jotted down what she could remember.

Her mum stayed home with the children when she drove over to PJ's place with her notes.

'Hi.' A small distance had emerged between them. 'You'd be amazed what I found out about your dad.'

'All good I hope?' He held her tight. 'Come and see what I put together for him. I'll show it after the service in the front room, before we go down to the beach. Tell me what you think.'

'I think it's a beautiful celebration of his life.' It made her smile and well up with tears again. 'I thought you might need these words to add, but I don't think they're necessary.'

'I'd like to keep what you wrote in your handwriting.'

She stayed the night.

*

A light breeze was the only thing to disturb an otherwise perfect autumn day and it swept along the bay, bringing with it Beth. Mel was not surprised by the massive turnout. Thommo had been almost an icon and she noticed the difference between the feel of his funeral and others she'd attended in the city.

At the designated time, when the sun hung low in the sky, the entourage ventured down to the bay to farewell Thommo. PJ hopped on his board and said a private farewell. Some distance out he distributed the ashes. No one spoke when PJ paddled back to shore; his expert strokes barely wrinkled the surface.

Chapter Sixty-two

Throughout the week, Mel observed PJ's restlessness and something different ran between them. She wasn't sure it was entirely due to Thommo's passing. Her mum left and the children flew away for their weekend with Tony.

Early in the morning, Mel read a small article about Mitchell Drake in the Perth paper. It mentioned that he'd come out of the coma and was expected to recover some of his mobility, but it didn't mention anything about his intellectual capacities. Mel's heart squeezed for the boy and his family and how they continued to suffer.

'I'd really love to spend all of Sunday together.' PJ pulled her out of her reverie when he entered the kitchen where she was going through the bookwork in an attempt to see if she could summon the forces of the universe to improve her sales sheet. She knew she required something more than creative imagining on a Saturday afternoon.

She pushed stray strands of hair from her eyes. 'Wait a minute, I'll just check my diary.'

PJ looked confused. 'You know you and the kids are my social life.'

Thommo's sickness and death had altered everything about PJ. Mel stood up and rested her hands on his hips. He shifted his weight forward, scooped her up and set her down on the table, where he pressed against her. His kisses were like the PJ she longed to have back.

'I'm going to teach you to surf. Don't look like that, you'll be fine. I haven't drowned anyone yet. Besides, I need you alive.'

'In that case, I accept. Are you coming around this evening, too?'

'It'll be a bit after eight. I have some business to attend to.'

'Sure.' Apart from Sally, she didn't have other friends to visit and enjoy a coffee with. Her life had seemed full enough before, but now she wished she'd found the time to make a few more friends.

On Sunday afternoon, after a great deal of laughter on Mel's behalf, and patient coaching on PJ's behalf, they peeled off rubbery wetsuits to enjoy rare late-autumn warmth on their bare skin. The weather had tipped towards a new season. Her heels dug into the creamy fine sand, specks of shell slivers clung to her feet, and she gazed out over frothy white caps to a faultless turquoise sea.

A persistent wind blew shards of airstream straight from cooler southern oceans. PJ saw her shiver, pressed his warm chest against her back and placed his lips on her neck.

'After the finals,' he said, his voice low and quiet, 'the PR team for Manning and Bells phoned to ask if I wanted to work with them because of the footage they saw in the shop. They told me they loved it and they've offered me an exclusive filming contract. The package is more than decent, but I'd have to fly out next week. They need an answer tomorrow.'

'What did you tell them?'

'I told them I'd talk to my girlfriend and get back to them.'

It was the first time he'd said she was his girlfriend.

'You can't miss this opportunity,' she said, even though she felt a small pocket of emptiness open within her. 'It could set you up for life, you'd never regret it.'

'You don't care about us?'

'How can you say that? You know I do, but my life is all about being a parent and running my business. You have to see what you can do.' What she wanted was to grab him and run.

'You don't know how I feel about you. I haven't met anyone that I wanted to spend so much time with, and I mean it. I love the everyday stuff with you.'

'Because I'm a mum, and maybe women haven't featured in your life all that much.'

'No. You feel right for me. I-could-grow-old-with-you kind of right. I'm not sure that I want to leave you. I need to know how you feel about me.'

Her limited experience had led her to have little faith in long-term relationships, and her immediate future would be all about raising children and working. Could he want that kind of life?

'If we could stay like this forever, my life would be more than complete, but at the back of both of our minds would be the "what if". We both know you need to do this.'

He drew her as far as he could into his arms and pulled her back into the curve of his chest.

'Online buying is eating into our profit margin. Part of my goal is to take our surf store to the world in a promotional package with Macka and Robby. Financially, it's a no-brainer.' He paused to run his free hand through his hair. He'd lost a little of the carefree boyishness she had found so magnetic. 'But I need to hear how you feel.'

'I don't know what's going to happen to us, but I do know that you have to take this on. What we've had so far has been exceptional.'

'That's it? I thought you said you loved me.'

'I did, I mean I do. Do you have any idea how much I'll hate not having you here? But staying with me doesn't compare with what you might be able to achieve in a couple of years, and then there's my children. And relationships change over time.'

'I thought ours would be different. God, Mel, I haven't felt this for anyone in a long time.'

'We can still talk and message daily.'

'I'll be back every three or four months.'

She couldn't speak because he'd locked onto her lips and pressed himself against her. She felt the urgency of his presence and the bitterness of his leaving.

He was something she should have had in her twenties and it terrified her, the reckless sensuality he'd awoken in her, but it wasn't something she could imagine enduring.

During the late afternoon they reviewed their movies and

cooked an early dinner. They discussed how they would keep in touch, but they skirted around the issue of the big gaping hole that was going to come with each other's absence.

Chapter Sixty-three

When PJ left, it was all Mel could do to breathe. Pelican Point became empty and quiet. Her old patterns of self -doubt returned and she couldn't shake off the fear that her business would fail because of her lack of financial finesse. She buried her face in her hands for a moment and considered whether their life was any better at Pelican Point. Had she simply caved in to the urge to hide by moving down south? When she spoke or messaged PJ, it magnified the desolation she felt with his absence, but his phone calls soon became her daily highlight.

The local paper lay stacked on a stand inside the store, and customers helped themselves.

Barbara sat down and flicked through it with a cup of tea. 'Mel, have you read the news about the shopping complex they're building at Bridle Estate?'

'No not yet.' Mel tidied up a couple of display shelves where everything was in a chaotic jumble. Parents allowed their pre-schoolers to do as they pleased and it never failed to astonish her. 'What does it say?' She completed two shelves and dragged a chair to place beside Barbara. No one else had entered the store.

'They've released details of the complex. There was a lot of protest over the original design. They've had to build in more green spaces, build outward-facing shops, plan for water recycling, and create a look more suited to the environment.'

'That's progressive. Most of them look like dumped shipping containers.'

'They've listed the shops,' Barbara added. Mel stretched

out her legs while Barbara read the article aloud. 'These are the shops they say will be there so far: a supermarket, a gym, a chemist, a liquor store, two shoe shops, a newsagent, a gift store, a large franchised hardware store, a jeweller's, four clothing stores, a store selling computers and associated goods, and a post office.'

'What?' Mel blanched. 'Can I take a look?' She took the paper and read on.

'Didn't they tell you?' Barbara frowned at her.

'They told me there'd be shops, not a post office. I'm the post office.' She could feel herself grow clammy. She knew she wasn't a post office though; she was a postal outlet with a review due in eighteen months. She knew what would happen at the review now.

'I thought they would have made it clear to you.' Barbara turned to face her.

'I didn't take it in.' *I do this*, she wanted to shout, *I ignore things because I don't want to see them*. 'I didn't consider the likelihood of anyone replacing this old postal outlet. It makes sense.'

'It won't be ready for about eighteen months.'

'I've been working on other ways to capitalise on the tourist trade and I'm trying to build this place into something unique.'

'It's great what you've done so far,' Barbara rallied. 'The store is so interesting with everything you've brought in. I've booked to hear the talk by the local botanist and I'm going on his weekend hike.'

Mel had hoped to keep the postal store side of things because it gave her a substantial residual income. She balled her fists and gave Barbara a thin crease of her lips. It was as close to a smile as she could muster, but her mind spun with another tear in the fabric of her new life.

She struggled through the day. In the night, her concerns about her financial viability multiplied.

Chapter Sixty-four

Conversations became less frequent. Mel and PJ only had a short time to gather their history, but at night she ached for him, dreamt about him, and carried the loss of him with her.

She lay on her bed after a late dinner and propped her iPad on a pillow to Skype with PJ. 'Hi, what's with the sun lounge?' She did her best to look cheery.

'It's a no-surf day. The waves aren't great but the prediction is for a better swell tomorrow. Then it's a furious tour from here to Spain. How are you?'

'It's getting cold. You never told me how cold it could get. I have icicles instead of toes.'

He laughed. 'Change your ideas on clothes and get some proper socks and boots.'

'Sally suggested the same thing.'

'Hi PJ. You coming tonight?' Mel watched as a slender young woman with long hair wandered behind the lounger and touched him lightly on the shoulder. She could see a bikini through the transparency of the woman's dress.

PJ turned towards her. 'Sure.' Something about the way he said that made Mel bristle. Was she being paranoid? Of course he would be going out and enjoying himself. 'It's Bree, before you ask,' he told her, 'she's part of Manning's public relations team.'

'She's beautiful.' Mel tried to sound matter-of-fact, off-hand, not jealous.

'A real downside of being on the surf circuit.'

'You know—'

'Don't say it,' he cut in. 'You know how I feel about you and I'll be home in a couple of months.'

'But only for a while.'

'I know.'

'I don't know if I can do this,' she said, the emptiness beat around in her heart, and she knew she sounded weak.

'At least let me come home first.'

'Okay. I don't want to hold you back and maybe...'

'Let's give it till I come back. You have nothing to worry about here.'

'I miss you,' she whispered.

'Why don't you come over?'

'I'd love to but you see, there are these little people who've moved into the other two bedrooms and insist on calling me Mum. Not only that, I have to be in a building every day of the week except Sundays, and when I do that, money spits into my bank account. It's all very curious.'

'Another time then, when your business is running so well that you could hire someone to manage it for a couple of weeks, and when the kids are with their dad. You could use my travel points.'

She held out her hand to touch the screen. He held his hand out too, but she had to say it. 'Are you seeing Bree?'

'No. Of course not.'

'Have you kissed her?'

She felt the pause. 'I only kissed her once. We were drunk, we'd had a win.' She would have been hovering, waiting for him to waver, away from his girlfriend, whatever that meant. 'There's a group of us who hang around together. There's nothing in it.'

'Does hanging out together include sex?' She tried to sound casual, like someone who understood that this would happen, but the plaintive tone in her voice betrayed her. She had loved him, and it sounded awful when she thought about it, but she wanted to be the one to end it. PJ had transported her to a time before children, before grown-up responsibilities, to a younger version of herself. She'd enjoyed the indulgence of being consumed by the deliciousness of him. But she knew that what they had would fade with time, and her priority was to be present for Jack and Lil. Still, the humiliation bit and her eyes stung.

'No, and I told her that was it. I'm sorry.'

'Me too.'

'They've offered to increase my pay and finalise the contract. I'm fixed for a few years. I'll still be coming home soon, and every few months.'

'This is your career.'

'I know, but I love you.'

Soft tears fell and she knew she should let him go. He'd already kissed the other woman. Who could blame them when they were so far away from home?

'Don't say that, you kissed her, PJ.'

'Don't go.'

'My life, my heart, it's different to yours.' She shrugged, her lips wobbled and she felt embarrassed at how quickly her eyes ran with tears.

'No it's not.'

'Women will always throw themselves at you, but I'll be here getting older, not prettier, not more exciting. Just go.'

She closed him down.

He rang. She silenced her phone. She knew there'd been more than a kiss; it wasn't that hard to see.

Chapter Sixty-five

Jack and Lil became uneasy about their flights to the city. As a young pregnant woman, Mel remembered being absorbed by the whole process. She didn't envy Leah putting up with Jack's intolerant and caustic tongue.

'Really Mum, I don't care about the latest brain-training films or baby slings. She's driving me nuts! I can't wait for football to start.'

This was news to Mel. Usually, it was all surf and guitars with the twins, Kirby and Tyler. She thought Jack wouldn't be playing football until she found a girls' team, and there weren't many teams in Bettong from what she'd heard.

'Football?'

'Yeah, football.'

'You're playing school football?'

'No. I'm playing for the Under Sixteens at the local club in Bettong. A lot of my friends are in it and I was talent-spotted. Kirby's playing too. If we're good, we'll play regionals. The guys told me this team kills it.'

'I thought you were going to surf through winter?' Does the coach know she's a girl, Mel wondered? Jack had taken to wearing a restrictive band around her slender chest to hide her small breasts.

'I can do both. When I'm playing some of the regional games, I won't be flying up to Dad.'

'He'll hate that.'

'But Dad said he'd try to get down for the games, maybe every second game. I offered him my bedroom.'

Mel raised her eyebrows.

'It's okay. He said he'd rather stay in the caravan park or somewhere. He said he'd rent something big enough so we could stay with him when he comes down.'

There was another advantage for Jack if she played football, she would avoid hormone-laden Leah, and as a bonus, she would have Tony to herself when he came to Pelican Point. Clever manoeuvring by Jack, and she did enjoy football. Jack noticed her grinning as she joined the dots.

'Jack Wilson, you are cunning.'

'Yeah I'm okay.' Jack gave her a cheeky grin.

Tony would relish the opportunity to escape the demands of a heavily pregnant Leah. Tony had loved following Mel around when they were first together, but he'd never enjoyed small babies that much from what she could remember.

'And before you ask, girls can play in the Under Sixteens in club football if they're good enough, but not any higher. I'm the only girl.'

'You're not bothered by that?'

'No. Most of the guys are all right about it. There've been some gender comments.'

Ah, Mel thought, the thing we haven't discussed.

'What are you thinking about your future?' she ventured gently.

'I don't know yet. You know I don't ever think of myself as a girl.'

'We all know that. I only want you to be yourself.'

'I'm not sure about what I'll end up doing. There're a couple of girls like me at school.'

'Really?'

'Yes, and they've been here all their life.'

'Is it okay at school?'

'Yeah. Because I surf and love sports, I'm a bit different to them. I have Kirby and Tyler for friends and they're pretty cool about everything. It's not always easy, but it's okay.'

It was the longest conversation they'd had in a while.

'Jack, you have to be who you were born to be.'

'I know.' Her eyes darted away, and she closed down. Featherings of pain shot through Mel when she saw the emotional wrestle in her daughter's unguarded face. She could see Jack push away the reality of issues that were so close as she skidded towards adulthood. Jack wanted to be left alone to be an adolescent, not an adult.

Mel ached when she thought about what Jack would have to endure to become that person.

Chapter Sixty-six

Over the next few weeks a spate of tourists arrived and told her they'd discovered her shop on the website. The effectiveness of her internet presence meant both the local paper and a local filmmaker working on a promotional clip, had called to interview her. She knew it was because she still had a monopoly in the area.

Even though she didn't have much in the store, everything sold. Everyone wanted something to take away from Pelican Point. She sent silent prayers of thanks as well as loads of texts to Sally and emails of appreciation to her young artists and artisans, telling them the good news. By the time she paid everyone, there was a small buffer left over. She wondered if that would be enough to sustain the business during the quiet times, and how much of her sales were simply novelty value and seasonal. She loaded positive comments from the customers onto her website. There was a gentle wave of excitement and one of the artists, Meg, had become industrious, filling an entire display shelf with her unique recycled frames and storage boxes.

Meanwhile, PJ was desperate to continue communicating with her.

'I think there was more than a kiss.' She saw how the fling with Bree had affected him. He looked too lean.

'It happened once. It was so stupid of me and I apologised to Bree. I was still reeling from Dad and from leaving you. I know it sounds pathetic. I'm sorry.'

'It's inevitable PJ, that's why we can't be together like this. It's too hard and too unrealistic.' She didn't have pleasant thoughts about Bree or PJ at that moment, even though she knew he'd told her the truth because he loved her.

'I'll make it up to you.'

'But I don't think I can do this long-distance relationship. You're so far away, and this is how it'll be for a few years. We didn't have that much time to begin with.'

'I'm coming home in a while.'

'I know.'

'Can we talk then?'

'We can talk, but if something happens, let me know.'

'Same for you.'

'Okay.'

Despite regular contact, their conversation lost intimacy.

*

Beth ventured over on her dinghy more than once to poke around the shop and to have a cup of tea. Lil suggested that Beth was lonely or bored. Mel, however, couldn't picture Beth as anything other than resourceful. Beth liked it if Lil was around and Lil had a special sense about Beth, tramping out to see her when she arrived.

While most of the trees in town were native evergreens, some deciduous trees had been planted in Pelican Point. The leafless trees along with the reduced sunlight, heralded a shift towards a southern winter. Late autumn charged in; rain clouds white-washed the sky and covered the hilltops and islands. Banks of white peaks rolled over the horizon and grey dishcloth clouds wiped the whole town clean until sky and ocean married.

When the sun broke through, it lit up the bay in narrow shafts and spokes of light bounced off the water and flushed bright cheer into Mel's store. Mel and the children found themselves unprepared for the drilling of icy winds that arrived.

Not many tourists ventured down to Pelican Point when winter blew in. Shorter days, cool air, endless grey skies and winter rain kept people at home. Most evenings Mel sat with her head in her hands, going through the insubstantial ledger. She hadn't tried all the things she'd suggested to Sally because carrying them out meant she would have to refurbish and renovate the shop, and she couldn't support more debt. She knew she should have mastered creative accounting long ago.

Tony kept his promise to come down for one of Jack's matches during the football season and was due that morning. He'd taken a couple of days off and she suspected he might have been glad to escape the incessant baby preparation. But maybe she was wrong and he really did want to drive the ridiculous distance down to be with his children. Mel was wiping down the counters when she heard him knock on the door. It was time to open anyway. She was sure the shrill wind he brought in with him had blown straight off the ice shelf. There wouldn't be many customers later.

'Hi Mel.' He entered quietly.

'Tony, how have you been?'

He ran his fingers through his hair and she was shocked by how much it had thinned. Saggy purple sacs lay under each of his eyes and the grey hair had overtaken most of his head. He didn't look like the stud Leah had married a few years ago, though Mel still thought he was a good-looking man for his age.

'Exhausted.' He slipped into a chair surrounding one of her tea tables, threw his shoulders back and let out a sigh.

'It's a long drive down.' And he would have left at five in the morning.

'That too. Leah's finding pregnancy a little hard, now that she's close.'

'To be expected.' Did she really say that?

'Yes of course. You didn't seem to find it hard though.' He smiled up at her, but it was a wobbly kind of smile and she hoped he wasn't going to cry. She could see the strain he was under. A vein pulsed in his forehead and his eyes were laced with thin red lines.

'Here, have a cup of tea. You'll both feel better once the baby is born.' Did he think it would get easier as he got older? Mel wondered why she was playing counsellor.

'I know, but it was a while ago when I last did this.'

'Sure.' And she at least remembered accurately; he never really did it, she did. She quarantined any further antagonistic ex-wife thoughts because she was back into friendly relations with Tony. He was her children's father. 'Jack is so keen for this game. She's been up early, checking over positions. I've never seen her so absorbed.'

'Talent spotters.'

'Again?'

'They're always out there. This is a significant age group for the league to be watching.'

'Yes, but she's a girl.'

'We know that. Jack would love it if they didn't though.'

She sat beside him. 'Lil wants to introduce you to Mina, her horse-riding friend.'

'She seems to like her a lot.'

His interest was fading. She'd never seen him so beat. He picked up his mug and sipped at it, his eyes almost closed.

'Maybe you should fly down next time?'

'Then I'd have to hire a car.'

'You could borrow mine.' What was she saying? 'For the short time you're here.'

'Thanks.'

He didn't move. 'The kids are packed and are ready to go with you to the game.'

'Right.' He looked like he wanted to say more. She didn't think she'd have much more to offer. He stood up and gave her a lopsided smile before he left the store to collect their children.

Chapter Sixty-seven

Mel went down on her hands and knees to scrub the floorboards of the store. Jack was out surfing with Kirby and Tyler, and Lil was horse riding with Mina. The sun broke through the silver-streaked clouds and sent skinny spokes of yellow light through the window. It lit up the whole store. She paused when she thought she heard a voice. When she turned to see who was at the front door, her elbow bumped the bucket of water and it skidded before it toppled over. A considerable amount splattered the bottom half of her jeans and her feet threatened to skate away on the soapy surface as she pushed herself upright.

'Hi Mel.'

'Mark? Hi. What a surprise. Are you here on business again?'

'I'm visiting my mother.'

'Have I met her?' She asked, although she was pretty sure she already knew who his mother was.

When he was happy light glittered in his astonishing eyes. 'You have, it's Beth.'

She smiled. 'I thought so. I saw a photo of a much younger you on her fridge, or at least at the time, I thought it looked like you'

'It's quite an old one.'

She nodded. 'I thought I recognised the features.' He stilled suddenly, and his manner became very serious. 'Is there something I should know?' she asked.

He stepped towards her. 'Stay very still.' In the next second, he flicked then squished a red back spider that had found its way onto her shirtsleeve. The water had dislodged it.

Mel shivered and moved away from it, even though it was well and truly dead. 'Oh God, thank you for that.'

'My pleasure. By the way, I've brought some fish over.'

Mel chuckled. She couldn't help it. 'Do you always bring fish for people?'

'Sometimes,' he gave her a sheepish smile, 'but this isn't from me. I told Beth I was coming over and she asked if I'd give this to you. She caught it this morning.'

'You call her Beth?'

'Since I was a teenager.'

'Tell her thanks. This is an unexpected treat.' She shook out the drops from the bottom of her jeans and invited him to sit at the table near the front.

'Would you like a drink?'

'Not right now, another time. The shop looks a whole lot more interesting. I like the artwork and timber frames.'

'I'm slowly figuring out how to convert it into a profitable business rather than a feel-good store.'

He turned over a small frame of Meg's in his giant hands, made out that he was examining it, then put it down and cleared his throat.

'Would you like to go out to dinner this evening?'

Mark brought her fish yet seemed uncomfortable around her, and Jill had never mentioned what his other issues were. Mel's soul still limped with the loss of PJ, even though things had changed between them.

It was dinner, she rationalised. What harm could there be in eating with the man? 'I'd really like that.'

'I'll pick you up at seven?'

'Sure, perfect.' She watched him through the blinds and noted the lightness in his step. He caught her eye as he slid into the car and she felt the heat rise from her neck. She leaned down to collect the bucket and scrubbing brush but not before witnessing his lips take an uncharacteristic dip upward.

Sally chose that moment to pull in and raised her eyebrows as Mark drove off. 'Mark? You're seeing Mark now?'

'Only for dinner. How come you know him?'

'When is dinner with two singles just dinner?' She saw Mel look at her. 'Oh, I forgot, you're still grieving for PJ. First tell me how you know him.'

'I met him up north on a holiday with the kids. He works on a boat with a friend's brother-in-law at the Banderley Islands. When I was in Perth he'd drop by occasionally and bring us fish.'

'The guy drops in and brings you fish and you didn't think he had a motive?'

'It was a hectic time in my life. But you're probably right, I didn't pay much attention to Mark because another man was in my life then.'

'I never knew you had this secret stash of guys in your life.' Sally crossed her arms against her chest.

'It wasn't nearly like that. I'll fill you in another day.'

'You know the background of his family?' Sally sat down with her iPad. She had come for a business conversation.

'Not really. He told me Beth is his mum, and I pretty much figured it out when I saw an old picture of him at her place..' She squelched over in her canvas shoes and plumped down beside Sally.

Sally switched off her device and gave Mel another one of her looks.

'What? He's obviously a bit different, but I put it down to awkward. You're not going to tell me he was in prison or has thirteen toes or something?'

Sally breathed out. 'You know I don't do gossip, but this isn't gossip. Cassie, my sister, was connected to the Hawthorne boys back in the early days.' She slipped off the chair and grabbed Mel's arm. 'I tell you what, let's walk and talk. There's something I want to show you.'

'Sure. You have a sister?'

'Had.'

'I'm sorry.'

'It's okay.' She smiled at Mel. 'She passed away a while ago. Come on, put the fish away and wear a coat, the wind is freezing.'

She looked down at the soggy jeans. 'And I suggest dry pants or you'll ice up.'

Mel ran into her house and changed both her clothes and shoes.

In communal silence they trotted alongside each other huddled into their jackets. A building wind plucked the lines on the small fleet of yachts and tossed the fishing boats into a cadence of water-slap rhythm, sending out an unmelodic tune. Concert in sea, she mused. She watched Sally. Her countenance was less bouncy, more studied.

Sally, more used to the fluctuating weather as it beat down into a full winter, had a coat. It was a proper coat, she observed, a whole class above her own.

With hands tucked into pockets, they struck up a reasonable pace and tracked around the bay.

'I'll give you a potted version, which is as much as I know. Over the years they've kept to themselves, but there's a stack of stories about them out there. Amongst it all there's a bit of truth. If you get better at reading him, you'll find out yourself. Anyway, this part I do know.'

She found herself warming with their walk and freed her hands out of the pockets.

'Cassie, Mark, Luke—Mark's brother—and Michelle were a unit. Cassie was Luke's on-and-off girlfriend. Luke was a wild young man. Mark and Michelle were a couple.'

'Michelle is Dylan's mother, right?'

'Yes. In fishing, certainly in those heady years, there was always a lot of partying and drinking. Not heavy drugs, but a lot of weed. When the fishing season ended it was such a relief that people took a while off to do as little as possible. Luke was so attractive and so much fun, but he ran incredible risks. One day, at the end of a day out on his dinghy with a few mates, Luke headed up to the shack on the coast to meet Mark, Michelle and Cassie. It's about a half-hour drive south of Beth's place.' She waved her hands in the general direction.

'I'm guessing he was also drinking or something?'

'No, but because of his history everyone jumped to that

conclusion. The truth was that he'd suffered an aneurism to the brain. His mates had driven home and he didn't even have the key in the ignition before it happened. He was found dead in the ute. Beth was angry because it was a while before anyone discovered him.'

'That explains some of Beth's manner.'

'Beth was hard on Mark afterwards. She also said a whole lot more about Cassie, which we feel wasn't entirely warranted. Luke made his own choices. She was just lashing out. Mark and Beth's relationship soured. Mark, as far as anyone knows, never touched weed again. He married Michelle, but she had serious depression. She's been in and out of wellness and support centres at Mark's expense. I heard that even though he divorced her ages ago, he's only now stopped paying for her stints at those places. He didn't want young Dylan to suffer.'

Sally paused and they looked along the bay to where the frothy tops of choppy waves flew up and laced the shore. Salt and dampness rimmed their shoes and sharp tendrils of guano and decaying bait spiced the air into a seaborne infusion. Waving branches made the light flicker from across the bay. Beth was home.

They crunched up the shore. Shell grit clung to their damp shoes. In front of a weathered timber boatshed, Mel stopped. It was no bigger than a double garage and various shades of blue, green and orange paint, each overlaying the other, stuck out in flaky patches. Perpetual dampness had given the remaining paint a shiny hue. Each warped door drooped downwards like tilted rectangles. It was clasped shut with a thick chain and padlock, also victims of the briny air.

Sally rifled around in her pocket. 'I haven't been back here for a while.'

Mel waited while Sally jiggled the lock and hefted one of the doors to swing it open.

'Who owns these canoes?' A strong fug of rubber, mould and dampness hung in the shed.

'A mixture of people in town.' Sally picked her way across the floor strewn with floats, ropes and abandoned oars, above which swung the decaying corpses of life jackets, wet suits and diving masks. 'But these two are mine.' She ran her hands over their smooth curvaceous sides.

Mel leaned into Sally. Sally's hands rested on the canoes.

'Anyway, that's all I know about Mark. I think he's come out of it okay. Cassie was a bit like Luke. Life had to be fast, fun and wild. Rumours flew about her. Mum and Dad tried to ignore them. She moved away over to the east coast, but about five years ago she came back and rented a caravan in our park. A pack of cigarettes a day and her lifestyle had given her a time limit. We took to canoeing as a way to be together. It was the only time she seemed like the sister I knew before Luke. She smoked throughout her treatment and I don't think she ever got over Luke.'

'That would've been a horrible time for your family,' Mel said, feeling the weight of Sally's sadness.

'It was. She lived her life exactly how she wanted and I loved her, everyone did. But I want to go canoeing again.' Sally blinked several times and wiped her eyes. 'What about a group of four of us go out on Sundays? What do you think?'

Mel was still considering what she'd heard about Cassie, Mark, Luke and Michelle. She could feel the stories percolate through the gritty shell-strewn floor. 'I'd love to go canoeing.'

Sally hugged her. It was something, a hug from Sally.

When they arrived back, Sally went through the scenarios for the business again with her. Sally was a doer and she was delighted to see the ideas that had only been tentative become more fleshed out. The additions could be done reasonably, but in Mel's current financial state even that seemed dubious. She didn't want her friend to catch anything but happiness at her help. There wasn't a huge profit margin on the goods. She'd need sales in winter and to draw in more online sales.

'Overall, I think your initial ideas will work. And the sales of everything from the outer regions have been great. You'd be happy about that. You don't look that pleased.'

'I'm not making a lot of money at the moment. I know these ideas could all work, but probably it will take a year to get up and going. In that time, I could lose the business as the bank forecloses on me and you know they're building a post office in the complex.'

'I knew about that, didn't you?'

'I had an inkling, but I thought my store would hold precedence, or that I would be asked about it. I didn't register that as a postal outlet it was within the postal service's right to supersede me with a proper post office.'

'That puts a different light on things. I thought you might have savings or a bigger loan?'

'For an accountant, I've been shocking at managing my own affairs. Honestly, I wasn't that great at being an accountant. I had a lot of debt but scraped out with enough to secure and own a decent percentage of this place, but I need an income to keep us all alive and to run the business, let alone to extend it.'

'Okay, so when you have a crap first year you haven't got a safety net. The first year is always the hardest, and establishing your credibility will take at least that if not more. There has to be an intermediate solution. I'll think about it. There must be an idea we haven't considered yet, but hey, I love the blog. The website's awesome and there's a buzz about the shop.' Sally gave her arm a squeeze.

'That's why you're my friend.' Mel smiled, even though she felt weak in the stomach. Maybe the website and word-of-mouth promotion would work, but it was taking a while, and winter would always be a quiet season.

'We'll be celebrating soon. You've turned this into something amazing already and the internet creates a life of its own.' Sally embraced her one more time and left.

Jack arrived back in the twin's dad's car. Kirby held onto Jack's hand for a couple of seconds. To Mel's shock, he trailed his fingers over the inside of Jack's wrist as she exited the car to untie her surfboard. Mel blinked several times. She hadn't considered Jack's relationship with the twins and what it might mean. Something had changed with her daughter.

Lil texted. *Come pick me up, we're finished now xxx.*

Mel grabbed her keys and reached out to scuff the salt-and-sand-crusted hair of her daughter. 'So, is...?'

'Don't ask. I don't know.'

Lines of confusion flashed across her face. Clearly Jack was still figuring it all out, even though she'd told Mel she didn't want to be gender defined.

'Okay.'

'Don't say anything to Lil or Dad.'

'I won't.'

Anticipating dinner with Mark later that evening elevated Mel's feelings. Lil regaled her with tales about what she'd done at Mina's.

When the time came and Mark's form filled the doorframe, Mel realised she'd forgotten how great it was to have a man drop by to take her out. His build meant that the buttons on the cuff didn't fasten around his wrists, and the shirt he'd chosen wrapped tightly around his chest. After months without PJ, the subtle and not-so-subtle attentions of a man brought about a physical response from Mel she hadn't been expecting.

At the restaurant she wondered how they'd talk because it didn't seem to be Mark's strong point.

'Beth is an amazing woman, living almost off the grid like that,' Mel began.

'She's wilful and strong. Does everything her own way.'

She hoped it wasn't going to be her drawing him out all night. 'Is there some land attached to the shack, only she seems to have a couple of acres over there?'

'She owns the whole headland and a significant amount of land all around here.'

'Oh.'

'It's her way of thumbing her nose up at the developers. They have a blood lust for that land.'

It wasn't just the wine, she was sure his cragginess was transforming into something more relaxed and flirtatious.

'What's her goal?'

'Secure the land for the future and put a caveat on it for no development, ever. She wants all her land to remain in its natural state with only the odd gravel track for firebreaks, or to surf spots. She's always buying additional pockets of land with the same intent. What's yours?'

She hadn't been expecting that, and blossoms of red flourished on her cheeks. She stammered as she spoke. 'To raise my children and run a reasonably successful business, despite the new shopping complex taking over the postal service.'

'Really? Too bad.'

'I have plans, but they could take a bit of money and time, both of which are in short supply. What about yours?'

'Ensure Dylan finishes high school. He wants to study over east so he's on track with his studies so far. Build a house, and fish out of Bettong, both of which I'm doing.' He looked uneasy like he wanted to say more but couldn't find the right words, instead he gave her his first unguarded look, bolstered by the wine, and she blushed. He had layers all right.

'Where are you building?'

'I'll show you when I drive you home.'

'How did Beth come by the land?'

'Beth was the only grandchild and had two sets of grandparents. She inherited a lot, but I never got the business smarts. My dad took off early in their marriage. She's a fierce woman who manages her own business. I think my dad wasn't able to stand her way of doing things.'

They paused to finish the last of their meal.

'If you're building a house and fishing out of Bettong, does this mean you're not fishing up north anymore?'

'No. I've come back.'

Was she mistaken or did he direct that comment to her? She coloured again.

'Your mum will love having you around.'

'I suppose. I plan to spend most of my time helping out the contractor with my house. I designed it myself.'

On the way back in the car, he stopped by a block of land. It was partially cleared and on a slight hill one street back and to the left of her home. It would command outstanding views of the bay.

'You'll be close to me,' Mel told him.

'I bought it years ago. I wasn't planning to build then.'

She shivered in the icy-fresh wind when they stepped out of the car. He drew her in toward him and wrapped his arms around her. It felt natural to lean against him, embrace his warmth and stay like that, close. It's just a friendly hug, she told herself.

When he dropped her off, she thanked him and kissed him on the cheek. She agreed when he suggested they go out again the following weekend.

She knew what she intended to say to PJ when he came back. When she'd told him that she loved him, she knew now that it was the kind of love people said they had for each other when delirious sensations rampaged in their flesh and heart, early in a relationship.

*

Mark was more comfortable around her after their second dinner. When they walked up the hill to look at the progress of his house and then wandered back down to her house, there was no mistaking the intent of his kiss by her front door.

She went inside to consider her situation. All day she hadn't thought about PJ and she'd made a run-and-coffee date with Mark for the next morning. Fishing was off for a month over winter.

When she woke for a cup of tea before her run, she hauled in the paper and read a text from Pete. *I'm sorry.* She'd ignored the text when it flashed on her phone late in the night, thinking it was odd and out of the blue, but that all changed when her eyes fell on an item in the newspaper.

Chapter Sixty-eight

Mel gripped the paper with white knuckles. She cancelled the run and coffee with Mark, saying she felt sick, and she did. On page three were three photos, ordered and connected; each one was damning and provocative and she featured in all of them.

The first photo was different to the usual one of her administering CPR; it was the one normally trotted out for stories about Mitchell's recovery. This one showed her standing on the grass as the ambulance left. It caught her glancing at Cam Robson. It was a photo she'd never seen before. She remembered looking at him, but it was only for a second. She had been exhausted, traumatised, and it was moments before the older lady had walked over to ask for her phone number. The second photo required no caption. It showed her locked in a kiss under a portico of a restaurant with Pete McIver, and she was flattened against him. The third, the one knitting them together in the journalistic spin, was of her learning in towards Daniel Arnott's car window, her face frowning in a knot of pain. It said a street camera at the shops in Shenton Park had captured it over a year ago.

She slipped into her running pants and closed the door. Her cheeks burned before she left. Hard tears settled in the corners of her eyes and her mind shredded.

She struck out on the path that led to Bettong. The cool brisk air rammed into her lungs and she had to take short breaths. Finger trails of mist rode over the ocean and the path was damp with it. Underfoot, plump drops of water pooled and glimmered on the thick leaves of the coastal ground covers. *Breathe.* Her head wanted to explode. A couple of cyclists overtook her. Their thin lights cast strange beams into the surrounding foliage and made her shiver.

After about five minutes of running, she found the junction that took her to a road. She crossed to the other side where she saw the signed entrance to the walk trail. It lay wide with compressed limestone. Small mounds of leaves, black with decomposition, lay along the sides of the path, and fresh green leaves fell with no sound, in a constant drizzle. It led behind the coastal plain and up into the forest; it was slick with the recent rains and quiet, dark. She couldn't find a rhythm.

Spiced with the smell of eucalyptus sap and composting plant debris, the air closed in on her. The beat of the ocean became a vague backdrop, but the clamour of her heart and roar of her mind rang loud. She ran on. After about ten minutes, deep into the track, she found the small traveller's cottage. Three walls of rough-hewn timber, a wide opening where a fourth wall would never be, a tin roof, and off to the side about twenty metres away, a composting toilet. She scanned the area as she paused. Sweat cloaked her body. She could smell herself; self-loathing and perspiration made for an unpleasant odour. Up and down the track, there was not a soul, not a sound, and no one had passed her. She'd heard that since a better track ran along the coast, the only people who took this path were long-distance hikers and teenagers.

Once she stopped, her heart felt dangerous with its erratic beat. A small chorus of birds shrieked their morning calls in the petrichor of the forest. Mel screamed, swore, and pummelled her fists into the timber until her throat was raw. She kept up a tirade of outrage about herself, the media, Pete, and about the flippancy of the internet. Her voice echoed into the bush. She could feel the wave of fury settle into something dark and hard within her.

The planked bench seats were wide enough to take a sleeping bag. She lay down, bunched her legs, and tucked her hands under her arms; it wasn't warm. The cottage had seen its share of teenage rendezvous, but the forest management had kept it reasonably tidy. Her eyes were almost closed when they caught an outline of a figure. It hovered near the entrance. She bolted upright and the sudden movement made her dizzy.

'Hi?' It was a male voice with a trace of an accent. Mel was wildly embarrassed and annoyed. She'd checked that no one was around, and worse, she recognised him.

'Moqutat?' He removed his helmet. A fine trail of sweat dotted his forehead along a red line from the riding helmet. She detected the sound of a horse snort, and the muted clatter of its shoes against the gravelly ground. Her voice, her mind and beating heart, had drowned out all other sounds. She was angry with herself for not finding a more reclusive spot.

'What's wrong Mel?'

She swiped at the tears. 'I'm letting off steam Moqutat, that's all.'

'Do you want me to go?'

'I didn't come here to be with anyone.'

'Of course. I heard screaming and I wasn't sure if someone needed help.'

'Angry yelling, that's all it was.'

'My property backs onto the forest and I follow the trail before heading home.' He didn't leave. 'First thing I do when I wake up is read my online papers, international subscriptions mostly, but I also subscribe to the local state paper.'

'Right.'

'Any wonder you're here and angry. Do you want to talk about it?'

'Not really.' She hugged her arms into herself. She wanted to merge into the timber planks. 'It all happened last year and none of it is how it looks.'

'They're the media, it's a story, a pretty damning story, but they've accessed public photos and they haven't said anything specific about you.'

'Come on Moqutat, I think they've spelled out the intent of the report and it's written so that any idiot can see what's implied, even if it's not the truth. They toy with and devastate lives. It just happens to be mine this week.'

She saw him turn and take a rope from the back of his saddle. He tethered the horse to the stand for mountain bikes outside the cottage, and when he walked back inside, he sat beside her and fiddled with the strap of the helmet. She shuddered beside him. He removed his sweater; a thin pale-blue pure-wool item.

'Here, put it on, I'm warm.'

She went to protest, but took it. Her running shirt was thin and great if you kept running. 'Thanks.'

'Whatever they've written about alleged inappropriate behaviour, it's about the football club, not you.'

'My name is in the article and my face is in all three photos. How can it not be about me?'

'I don't read it that way.'

She bunched up her knees and hesitated, but then she told him everything.

'Surely you see that you're innocent in all of this.'

'I don't think that's the right word. I knew Pete was investigating a few clubs, but he deliberately didn't tell me any details and I didn't want to know. Daniel Arnott, however, believes I knew everything Pete did and that I gave Pete information, spied for him, when I worked for Rockforth Bay. No matter what I say, he'll always think that. The pillow talk with Pete, when I told him I thought Cam had another phone, something I said before Cam admitted it himself, has destroyed any credibility I have with Mitchell's parents and the public, because we're talking about a child here. Everyone lusts to fix the blame on someone, and they wanted Cam. He spoiled it for them by telling the truth. How do I look? Like some desperate middle-aged woman who used the accident to sleep with a reporter, to get a job and to get what I wanted. Cheap, slippery and morally bankrupt, is what I look like.'

'You're pretty hard on yourself.'

She stared out to the frame of trees. The morning sun glanced on the furthest boughs and leaves; they glistened, shiny with the dazzle of raindrops still caught on their gummy surfaces. The view was fuzzed impressionist with her film of tears. 'Some of it is true, Moqutat. I did need a job because my finances were a mess. I didn't want to know if it compromised my position. I had nothing to lose, as far as I was concerned. I wasn't going to spill about Cam, because I didn't think it would make any difference and I wasn't even sure about my memory. I should never have mentioned it to Pete. I was going to admit in court that I might have seen a second phone. That's all. I had no idea they'd use photos of me and spin this story. I'm so stupid.'

'You need to tell your side. I love what you're doing on your website and with your store. You're just caught up in something bigger. Everyone will see what they want to, but the people who have got to know you and your family will understand.'

A shriek of kookaburras splintered into the cool damp air. Mel and Moqutat sat huddled together listening to the reverberation of the comic laugh as it rolled in waves with different clusters of birds joining in the crescendo. Despite his words, her mind ran over the scenes she imagined taking place in Pelican Point at that moment. Papers would be opened; tea would be brought to lips, and faces would pause and gape with slack jaws at the photos. She closed her mind to what she thought they might say to each other. She wouldn't open the store this Saturday morning.

'I'm staying around this week. Mina and I need to spend some time together. I'll take you on Tobias to where the track meets the road.'

'Thanks.' He offered his hand. She took it. He pulled her into a friendly embrace.

'Don't let this get to you. You're strong. My business experience has given me the hide of an elephant. Good people don't let the media decide their opinions.'

'You're very kind, but not everyone is endowed with your sense of justice or empathy.'

'There'll be something you can do, I know it.'

'I wish I shared your conviction.'

'Confidence is a ruse anyone can master.'

'Not everyone.' She watched as he leapt up on the neat brown saddle. Tobias, a glossy-coated stallion, responded to his touch. He made him stand near the bike racks so she could use it to step up. She gripped the horse with her legs and held Moqutat tight around the waist. Everything about the man was impressive.

'We'll take it at a walking pace.'

'Your wife must miss having you around.'

'It isn't easy but we manage. I miss the boys, but this is the best place for Mina. It's a compromise and that's how it's always been for me. I think I'm blessed with my children and wife, although she would like me around a lot more. I'm taking Mina to Europe. We have a property over there and it's where we spend our summer vacation every year. It's very important to us, even if she misses a couple of months of school work.'

'From what I hear, Mina could miss a year of school and still be top of the class.'

'She's smart, but learning about friendships takes time and is a key skill for survival in life and in business. I would like her to be better than me at forging friendships. Women need their friends.'

'Yes they do.' After a few moments of silence, Mel said, 'They say the school has a private benefactor.'

'And you think it could be me?'

'I wouldn't tell anyone.'

'I know you wouldn't. I donate, but I'm not the sole benefactor of the school.'

'Oh.' She imagined his donations weren't insignificant. 'Do you have an idea who is?'

She found his presence and the gentle warmth of the horse and the cadence of the walk comforting. In these last moments she'd shared more with Moqutat than with most of her family, and she'd even taken a while to tell Sally bits and pieces of her history. His confidence in her gave her a small kernel of strength, but she was overwhelmed by the images that flashed into her head. They were on constant replay in her mind. Waves of anxiety hit her about the media frenzy that would now begin, and about what her children would think. She wished she could stay on the horse.

'I do know who she is because she and I have similar philosophies and contribute to some of the same philanthropic causes. We've both put considerable money and resources into ensuring the region of Pelican Point is not available for excessive development and that it retains the majesty and integrity of its forests, rivers and coastal landscape. You can learn a lot from the right people.'

'Beth.' Her name slipped out as realisation dawned.

'I'm sworn to secrecy.'

'I see. I'll never mention it again.'

'Do you believe you can play a role, too?'

'Me? I have no money, no credibility now, and I'm a woman. Added together, these features give me no clout. Glass ceilings still exist.'

'Not so. Not since websites and blogging. They are the undercurrent. A groundswell of people are finding their tribe and finding their voice. They've become a thermometer of trends and an opportunity for people to gather support. Things are changing and you're changing, too. Don't be undermined by this, and I think you have far more to offer than you realise.'

He paused to slide off. They'd reached the point where the track met the road and it wasn't a long jog or walk back home from there. He held the reins in one hand and her hand in the other, as she dismounted. She pulled off his sweater.

'Can I wash it for you since I've sweated in it?'

'No don't worry, and anyway I sweated in it first.'

He leapt back up. 'Come out tomorrow at two if you can. I'll take you for a ride on Jasper and we'll thrash out a few ideas.'

She stood biting her lip. 'Okay, thanks.' What else would she be doing? It was better than sitting around listening to the million phone calls that would be waiting for her. Moqutat could have advice and she needed help; she needed allies. The only thing she had to do on Sunday was to collect the children in the evening. That thought filled her with dread.

Chapter Sixty-nine

Mel found Sally at her front door. Mel didn't say anything except, 'I need a shower.' She raced into the bathroom with Sally following behind her.

The shower made her feel only marginally better, and when she emerged, she found Sally waiting for her in her room. Mel switched off all of the phones and lay in bed. Sally sat on a chair beside her.

'We've got to tell someone. What's wrong with having a relationship and taking on a job, for God's sakes? You were a single woman who needed to support her family.'

'I know Sally, but that's not how they've set up the photos. They've stitched me up and I don't know why.'

Sally paced around the bedroom, her scarf trailing after her. 'This is so wrong.' She slumped back on the chair. 'They can't judge you like this.'

'I did say I saw a phone, a second phone. I worked for Daniel and now they think I'm dodgy. That's how it looks.'

'So what? He already admitted that. You saved Mitchell's life. You worked to pay the bills and you were seduced. They're vile, that's what they are.'

'I wish I'd never set eyes on Pete McIver.'

'Too late,' Sally said.

'Too stupid.'

'You are not. Don't you let them decide that.'

'I'm thinking about Lil and Jack seeing this.'

'But you told them, didn't you? Just in case?'

'Yes, but it's a shock the way I've turned up in the paper.

Imagine what some of their less-friendly school buddies will say.'

'Stop. Don't do it to yourself. Who's the editor who's been chasing you for a story ever since you were in the clip last year? Diana Getty, isn't it? She's the editor of *Women Twenty-four*.'

'I don't want more trash printed.'

'You're wrong. She's tackled a huge range of issues. I think you've got the story that will grab other women. What do you think?'

'I hate it all. I moved here to get away from the disastrous decisions of my previous life. I can't handle this.'

'They don't need your permission so use it for your own benefit. The magazines pay up because this is gold for them, and then next week, a whole new story will run. You have to get your side across.'

She looked at Sally, who pushed her forehead into her hands.

'Sally?' Sally moved off the chair and lay alongside her in the bed. They both stared up at the ceiling.

'Before you came, my life was okay. One day, you walked into my caravan park. From then on I never knew what you were going to do, or what you'd get me involved with, but I loved all of it.'

'Really?'

'When I saw you at the caravan park, I prayed you'd buy the shop. I can't tell you what it is, but you have Mel Factor. Becoming your friend is one of the best things that's ever happened to me, after Brian and Bronte.'

Did Sally see the very tiny flicker of her sparkler?

She leaned in towards her and squeezed her hand. 'I had no idea.' She thought about their friendship, the food and wine, the laughs, building the business and the numerous trips out to source products. She rolled over and propped herself on one elbow, saw the mascara that had streaked Sally's face and was shot through with tenderness for her friend. 'You mean even over your three favourite leading men, you'd choose me?'

'Am I in their bed right now telling them how much they mean to me?'

'I guess not.'

'You're so lucky then.'

'I am.'

'Maybe not Mister Darcy.'

'Diana Getty?'

'You'd better do it. I don't want to walk around defending you to every loose-lipped nitwit in town. Anyone with intelligence will see it for what it is.'

'Not everyone knows and not everyone will see it from that side. They'll harbour their own doubts and draw their own conclusions. Even we could be influenced by what's trotted out by the media if it was about someone else in town.'

Sally sat up in the bed. 'Call her now. She'll be hot for this story. Get her on line. You should offer her an exclusive.'

'Okay.' Mel had no other plan. 'But let's run through the worst kind of questions together and rehearse. I want to know what I'm saying.'

'Of course. It's your turn to put a real spin on this crap.'

Chapter Seventy

On Saturday afternoon, Diana Getty flew from Sydney to Perth in a chartered plane. She took a smaller plane and flew to Bettong early Sunday morning. Cameramen and makeup artists, as well as her personal assistant, accompanied her.

Mel cancelled Moqutat's offer of a ride for the afternoon. The whole interview and story had to be kept under wraps.

Partway into the niceties, Diana began questioning Mel. 'How did you get to know Pete McIver?'

'After the initial interview, he kept inviting me out.'

'Hard to resist?'

'No reason why I had to, we were both single. In the beginning we were friends.'

'Later?'

'We were attracted to each other.' The snake charmer. 'Either way, I fell for him.'

'Hence the photo.'

'Makes you wonder how many cameras are out there bouncing images around of all of us.'

'Plenty. What about the photo of Daniel Arnott and you?'

'He asked me to meet him. He was horrified with Pete's editor pulling out the shelved interview that included me saying I had seen Cam with the other phone. Something I had omitted telling Daniel.'

'Why?'

She'd asked herself this one a million times. 'I didn't want to jeopardise any help he might offer. I had no job and things weren't great. I didn't see that it would matter in the beginning.

Also, I wasn't exactly sure what I'd seen. I didn't know it was definitely a phone. I was too far away.'

'Must have been hard for you?'

'It was.'

'What was he saying?'

'That it was a damning indictment of the club and that I'd lost my job.' Her stomach knotted; the photos, this interview, it all came back.

'A juicy tale for the media.'

'They stitched the photos into a compelling story. There are those who enjoy the public parade of someone else's life and are titillated by the scent of scandal and corruption, whether it's true or not.'

'You know the club is in the clear?'

'I do. I never knew what was going on. I only heard rumours, the same as everyone else.'

'Cam Robson confessed that he accepted the phone. They've now discovered that other young players were also given these phones. It made vulnerable young people highly accessible to certain groups, and it hooked them into gambling sites. It also gave them VIP access to various exclusive events.'

'I didn't know about that, only that he confessed to having a phone when he was in court. I've been too busy running a business to be concerned about much else.'

'The result of the inquiry has led to changes in the management of young players.'

'I presume these reports were a result of Pete McIver's investigations, but they have nothing to do with me. Any parent can testify that events outside of sports and school, let alone being a sole business operator, don't feature on the radar. I didn't want to know because I had enough to deal with at the time.'

'How do you feel now?'

'Outraged at finding three photos of myself in the paper yesterday. I'm astonished at their audacity but not surprised by their lack of empathy.' What she really thought was a whole slather of bad language lower, but her children would see this. 'However, people who read the papers are significantly more intelligent than the media realise and don't rely on what's fed to them. There must be a shortage of newsworthy stories if they keep rehashing old topics.' She'd really practised with Sally. 'I'll be pursuing legal investigations into the influencing tone of the report.' She just threw that line in. She had no funds to do any such thing.

'I hear Cam Robson is working with students in remote communities to build pathways to colleges and to improve confidence in youths through sports scholarships.'

'I read that too. It's a shame that doesn't share more of the limelight.'

'Come on Mel, it's hardly a racy scandal.'

'Exactly.'

'Mitchell's second accident at school has meant that he faces debilitating brain damage. The charge has been reduced to reckless driving.'

'I felt awful for Mitchell when I read about his fall. I didn't know about the charges.'

'Mitchell's parents were content that Cam took responsibility and the charges were reduced. But they're behind the move to ensure the clubs are more accountable for their players. Mitchell's uncle is a football coach. Tell us about your business.'

After another half an hour, they entered the closure piece for the interview.

'It sounds like you've thought this through. I'd love to come down again next year and see what amazing things have happened in this unique business venture.'

'I've had the backing of the local community and some rather special friends. My business and website are all about supporting people through networks and friendship.'

'You've begun a lot of initiatives that will really put Pelican Point on the map.'

'That wasn't my intention. I wanted to build my business into something useful and enjoyable.'

'With your business focus on product provenance, the screens running with demonstrations, and the science and author presentations, I wonder what you'll do next. I really like your "connect and care" idea, too. You've worked hard to provide an authentic view of the region. It sounds like a platform to me.'

'I don't have any political aspirations.' Diana had prepared her to steer the conversation into a new and surprising direction to draw the audience to other issues by the time they'd finished reading or watching. 'I have enough to keep me busy.'

'What are your hopes for the future?'

'To be here for my children and enjoy everything that Pelican Point has to offer.'

'Mel Wilson, thank you.'

'Thank you, Diana.'

At lunchtime on Sunday, the cavalcade left. Mel stood quaking in their wake and wondered about what she'd just done.

Chapter Seventy-one

'She's going to put about five minutes of it in a live current affairs broadcast tonight on that new show and run the whole article in the next edition of *Women Twenty-four*, but that doesn't come out until the beginning of next month.'

'You're kidding. I thought she'd do the interview and put it away for a while.' Sally sat down at the kitchen table after Diana left, and pulled out a warm spinach quiche from a basket, as well as a bottle of champagne. 'Eat up I'm starving, I thought I'd eat with you. Brian and Bronte hounded me to make this, so I made two. Are you going to answer all the texts now and talk to your family? You know I'll stay here with you if you want.'

'I do want you here. This hasn't been an easy decision.' Mel leaned over the quiche and breathed in. 'It smells divine, but I don't think I can do the champagne yet, I have to pick up Lil and Jack this evening and I'll need a clear head with everything they might wish to throw at me.'

'Put it in the fridge. We'll have it when the magazine comes out.'

Despite Sally's attempts at support, the cleansing effect Mel had hoped for from the interview with Diana Getty hadn't occurred. She knew what it would take to get over the sick hollow feeling in her core. She wanted to know that her children were okay with everything and she needed to feel the same level of connection to the community she'd enjoyed on Friday afternoon. She also hoped that Mark would be on her side.

She still had to talk to PJ before she considered anything

with Mark, and everything had become that much harder since her feelings had changed about both men. After reading the paper, she hadn't spoken to Mark and she didn't even know if he wanted to talk to her.

Chapter Seventy-two

Later that evening, Sally brought Brian and Bronte with her so that they could all watch the interview at Mel's house. She gave Mel an excited thump on the arm after the interview was aired. Mel glanced across to see how her children were taking it. When she'd picked them up from the airport, Jack didn't say much except, 'There goes my football career.' Lil had given her several hugs after Jack spoke.

'Connect and care? What the heck is that?' Sally asked.

'I had to make some things up. They're ideas I haven't turned into reality yet.'

'Spoken like a true politician.'

'I wouldn't say it was all empty promises. Did it sound like that?'

'Only to me. The minions will see what's been going on in the store and think you must have all of these other projects lined up.'

'But I do.'

'What were you thinking?'

'The young mums and single parents could do with a helping hand. Pelican Point is overrun with retirees who don't see their own families very much. Connect and care. I just threw the words together. Maybe they could give the mums a break so that they can work on their own business plans, or have a day to themselves. Remember you told me there would be solutions we haven't thought of yet.'

'I was thinking of ones that made you money. Doesn't the local council have those initiatives?'

'Maybe. But it does help me if the young mums feel great and have time to work on their products because the quality and quantity will improve. They could be free to do an increased number of guest talks.'

'Okay. What about the surfboard guys?'

'There are so many older guys with sheds set up with tools that don't get used and skills that don't get shared.'

'I see your plan. Are you thinking that they may commune at your shop?'

'Probably not. What do you think?'

'I think I may have something to offer, too.'

'Sally, you have a lot to offer.'

'Those young men probably don't have a business plan.'

'Taken up surfboard art lately, have you?' Mel teased.

'No, but I'd like to.'

'Brian, your wife is drooling over the washboard stomachs of some young guys. You've obviously given her a taste for it.'

'Did I tell you how perceptive you are Mel?' Brian said tucking into an extra slice of quiche. With his thin frame and short grey hair he was almost the complete physical opposite to Sally.

'It was a washboard and he's still so fit he makes me sick. I cook, he eats and I gain the weight,' Sally thumped him on the arm.

'I love your cooking and just because I paddle every day, it doesn't mean I want you to have rippling abs, Sal. I'd rather come home to your amazing food than to find you'd left me for a marathon.' Brian squeezed Sally's hand.

'Not sure if I'm being complimented, exploited, patronised or all three.'

Jack disappeared into her room after the interview and Bronte wandered into Lil's room so the two girls could watch a movie on Lil's computer. Mel prayed that the light tone of the evening and the clarity of the interview would help offset any trepidation the children felt about the photos and facing their peers at school.

The edited version also included a snapshot of a few other cases where people had been caught up in the sideshow of much bigger investigations. Mel hoped the community of Pelican Point had been watching the segment. It staggered her to think she'd only been talking to Diana that morning.

Despite the presence of Sally, Mel fretted about her children. She wished Jack would say something to her, anything. She felt ill whenever she imagined what might be said to them once they were at school.

Her website showed the number of comments had increased. Sally read out a few and they were all positive.

'For God's sake Mel, keep the store open longer this week. You're going to have a huge week,' Sally said, as the counter on her website clicked over.

Just then, Mark called. Mel mouthed to Sally and moved into the kitchen to talk.

'Hi Mark.'

'How are you?'

'I've had better, less public weekends.'

'I saw. Don't worry, Jill and I chatted ages ago. Do you want me to come over?' Of course he would talk to Jill. It seemed he still liked her.

'Sally and Brian are here.'

'I want to talk to you.' His voice sounded whispery and deep.

She bit her lip. 'I can come over in an hour.'

Sally saw her face and slapped Brian on the thigh. 'Come on let's go, everyone's had a huge weekend.' She hollered up the hallway, 'Bronte!'

'Thanks guys, I appreciate you being here.'

'I'll be around tomorrow Mel. I'll do my bookwork in your store,' Sally told her.

'Let me know if I can do anything too Mel.' Brian grabbed her in a hug and she found her eyes filling.

'Thanks Brian. You don't have to stay all day Sal but I won't say no, I'd rather have you hanging around. I have no idea what's going to happen tomorrow.' A flash of inspiration tore through her.

Meg had said she could come in and she had a friend who could help with the children after school. Every one of her simple, well-made, quirky frames had sold. Mel had observed customers running their fingers over the edges of the woodwork, and often they'd hold it close to breathe in the scent of the oil Meg used. She imagined a hopeful future where she could afford a second-in-charge and thought someone like Meg could fill that role.

Chapter Seventy-three

Mel parked outside the cottage Mark rented. She wondered what he thought about her with all that had happened over the weekend. Clouds of fog came out of her mouth when she breathed. The crystal iciness of the evening made her eyes water and the brilliantly clear night sky was strung with the bling of star clusters. She knocked on his door.

Warm air escaped when he held the door open for her. 'How are you feeling?'

'Like I've gone ten rounds in a boxing ring without gloves. Sick mostly.'

'That great? Come in.'

It was the first time she'd been inside. 'I can't stay long. I only picked the kids up this evening and I promised Jack I'd only be about an hour. It's a lot for them to take in.'

'I understand.' She followed him down the hallway. The smell of wood smoke filled the house and she heard the mini explosions as the fire fizzed and popped in the grate. He took her coat and hung it over a couch.

'Stop frowning,' he said.

'Just so you know, I went public to clear things up, but I hate all this publicity. I can't wait till the whole thing passes.'

'I don't blame you. I want to tell you some things though. I've wanted to tell you for a while.'

She sat on a couch opposite him. He had a chair pulled up by the fire and a whisky tumbler glowed on the table. 'Can I get you something?'

'Nothing for me.'

'Hot chocolate?'

'Except hot chocolate. How did you know?'

'It's winter, you look shell-shocked so the sugar will be good, and you told me you loved them after we had dinner on Friday.'

'I did blather on.'

'I like your blathering.' She grew a little flushed with the warmth and his words.

When he came back in, he told her about Michelle and her depression. He told her that he'd set her up in an apartment in order for Dylan to have somewhere to be with his mother, because she was not able to stay focused for long. Mark owned the apartment since Michelle had spent the proceeds of the divorce long ago. The rest was up to her and her family.

Then he told her about how he had watched her step off the floatplane. He saw her lean over the jetty at the islands and liked how she fooled around with her children. He knew she'd fallen for PJ because Jill told him, and through Beth, he figured she was serious about him. At the time, he'd been wrestling with Michelle to make her move into the apartment.

Mel didn't tell him that Sally had told her some of the story.

He told her that he'd been with other women but hadn't been in a relationship for over a year.

Mel took in a mouthful of hot chocolate. 'You mean you saw my rucked-up shirt that first day? And you noticed that my shorts were on back to front?'

'Yes.'

'And even though I nearly killed my children because I took out the wrong motor and failed to leave a note, you overcame your fisherman prejudice and still liked me?'

'That was a toughy, but yes, I liked you even after that.'

'Even when I blinded you with a Christmas kiss on your eye?'

'Yeah well, then I had second thoughts.'

Mel laughed and she tried to restrain the compulsion to move towards him. There was that conversation PJ still wanted with her. 'Even with the horrible photos in the newspaper?'

Heat radiated off him. He leaned across, bringing his face

close to hers. 'Who,' he whispered, and his lips moved closer, 'gives a fuck about what anyone else thinks.' He paused and lifted his hand to gently remove a few strands of hair from her face. She felt his knees touch hers and she ached for the pressure of his mouth against hers. He stood and drew her into his arms.

'PJ wants to talk to me.'

'Mmm.' He was locked onto her lips.

The kiss was deliciously warm and sensuous, and it took every ounce of self-will she possessed not to dive back in when they pulled apart.

She needed to get back home. She'd promised Jack only an hour and she wasn't going to race into anything this time.

Chapter Seventy-four

When she was a young girl, the holidays meant something completely different to Mel compared with her sister. Georgie would be ferried away for additional sports coaching, whereas Mel would slip down to the river and watch the dawn fill the sky, where the spice of damp gum trees filled the air and the mist hovered. It felt like home to her because it allowed her to daydream.

She'd studied accountancy because she took her parents advice. It was a good job with a future and they didn't really know what else would suit her. She didn't either. It gave her time to think about other things, except she never wanted to be responsible for other people's money. When the first of many lecturing and tutoring positions became available, she took it.

Staring out from the paper one Saturday morning was an old school friend. She had become the chief research biologist on the Great Barrier Reef. Mel dug out all she could about the course work for the degree and thought she could complete that at a later date.

When Jack and Lil arrived, they walked by the ocean, picnicked at parks and played at the beach for hours. Mel watched with an ache when they walked through the school gate a few years later.

Unable to sleep, she researched Christos Angelopoulos for the first time. Even though he'd been dead for a few years, she found tributes from the various boards on which he'd sat. She read one of them. It described his diligence in adopting sustainable agricultural practices and his use of biologically safe solutions to control insects. He didn't want a future, he'd said, for his family that left them with poisoned rivers and soils; he'd wanted his corner of the earth to become safe.

A soft whisper of air came out of her mouth when she read that he had been working with the University of Sydney's research team on biologically safe interdependent practices. He had hope, he had a plan, and he was her real dad.

Maybe she would tell Jack about him one day. Before leaving for Mark's, she'd knocked on her door.

'Jack?'

There'd been a muffled sound. She'd opened the door to find Jack with music, she presumed, filling her ears, and her eyes focused upwards at the ceiling.

'I'm going out for an hour.'

'Okay.'

'You're in charge, Lil's nearly asleep.'

'All right.'

She sat on her bed. 'It's not what is seems Jack.'

'I know. But why were you so dumb?' Her voice came out thick and heavy, like she'd been crying. She looked vulnerable.

'I needed a job. I didn't set out to compromise myself, but I do regret falling for Pete McIver.'

'He's an arsehole.'

'Agreed. I shouldn't have spoken to him.' Jack didn't need to hear how lonely Mel had been, how much she needed someone to say nice things to her, how shattered and fragile she'd felt after losing her job and not having anyone in her life to be there for her.

'I don't want to go to school tomorrow.'

'I understand. Have you spoken to Tyler and Kirby?'

'Yes.'

'And?'

'They're my friends, but I don't want to go.'

What did she say, do?

'Okay, but it'll be harder to go back if you postpone it.'

Jack turned her back to her and flinched when Mel tried to touch her shoulder.

'There's a school,' Jack said.

Mel struggled to suppress the panic that stole through her heart.

'It's a government select school for talented football, netball, cricket, soccer and tennis kids.'

She'd heard about it. Her nephew Clayton had been offered the option, but Georgie had insisted he finished his schooling at the elite school he was attending. Clayton hadn't minded. He had talent enough to pick and choose later on if he wanted a sports career.

'And how do you get in?'

'You're selected.'

'Would you like to go?'

'I'd have to be selected and the scouts are coming down to watch our next game. I've been told by the coach that there's a good chance I'll get in.'

'How do you feel about that?'

'I get to board because my regular address is in the country now. That way I don't have to live with either you or Dad.'

A knife twisted in Mel's gut and the corners of her eyes burned with tiny hot tears.

'Is that what you want?'

'No. I wanted to stay here, until I saw the photos, until I knew everybody would see the photos.'

Mel felt like she kept smashing into walls when it came to her eldest child.

'I love having you here with me, Jack. It won't be what you think. It won't be that big. Other stuff occupies the minds of teenagers, you know that.'

'Right. Everyone around here will be talking about you and the interview on television, all their parents.'

'But it was positive.'

'Still, it sucks. I hate it.'

So did she, but it would pass this blip that felt like a tsunami for Jack. She hated attention and had difficulties enough being a girl who felt like a boy.

Mel went over the interview in her mind and knew it would

blow over. She'd already heard news about a flooding catastrophe on the east coast, and a scandal about a high-profile celebrity who couldn't overcome his foibles. There were photos splashed everywhere of him and his new leading lady. Jack's teenage lens would magnify everything related to her and exacerbate the anguish, even if nothing happened.

'If things go well this year, I'll take us to Hawaii next Christmas holidays.'

Nothing. She put her ear-buds back in.

'Goodnight Mum.' It came out breathy and soft as she closed the door; something to hold on to.

'Goodnight Jack.'

She'd leaned her head against the steering wheel for a good while before she'd driven to Mark's place.

Maybe she'd hold back on the news about her real father till this was well behind them.

Chapter Seventy-five

'So how did it go with PJ?'

A month had passed and Sally had suggested they get out the canoes again. Mel had survived a month of local media attention. She'd had a rotation of artisans and guest speakers in the store, and crowds had signed up for all the meetings and walks; something she attributed to Barbara and Margaret's excellent word-of-mouth publicising. People had latched onto the website and real money rang through the till. It had taken the glare away from the interview and article.

Jack was now speaking to her. Lil had been the recipient of a few stray comments from a clan of girls, but with Mina and Bronte by her side, as well as a troupe of other friends, she had stood up to them, informing them that they clearly hadn't listened to the interview. She was still a little confused by it all but was focused on her preparation for her first eventing experience on a school horse.

After the initial curiosity of the community, things returned to normal, except Mel's business and blog both worked to draw in a constant stream of customers. In one way she'd wished it had been quieter, but the bank account was back in the black. On the Thursday evening of the previous week, when she was securing the back door and setting the alarm, PJ pulled into her driveway.

'Hi Mel.'

'Hi PJ. You're home a week early.'

'Yeah, there wasn't much else for me to do. Anyway, I had to catch up with Macka and Robby. Can you come over to my place, so we can talk?'

With a million beady eyes watching her? 'How about we chat inside here?'

She disarmed the shop and reopened the door. They sat at a table.

'You look great,' she told him.

'Thanks. Following the circuit has its advantages.'

'What we had PJ...'

'Don't say it. I want to ask you something.'

'Of course.'

'Can you forgive me? With Bree? I still love you.' He looked ocean clean, a bit weary, and soft lines ran around his eyes. He wasn't as easy with himself around her. It had been several months.

'I love you too, but you must know it would never be the same. A lot has changed in the short while you've been away. What we had was unique.' Her body didn't respond in the same way. Everything about him felt different. 'I loved every minute of it.'

Tears slid down his face and she ached for him. She caught drifts of his familiar cologne and the thick jumper he wore made her want to hug him.

'I've been having a few dinner dates with Mark Hawthorne, but I've been waiting to talk to you.'

'You don't want to give us a go?'

Her head shook before she spoke. 'It wouldn't be the same, and my life seems to collide into chaos.'

'But that's what I wanted, your life.'

She coloured. 'I know you did. There will be someone exceptional out there for you.'

'I doubt it.'

They chatted quietly for a little while longer, until Mel felt he looked strong enough to leave.

'Bye PJ.'

It had been one of the hardest moments in her life. She couldn't even begin to tell Sally what she'd felt. 'It was tough.' She stared out beyond the breakers to the horizon.

'Some woman is going to be so lucky.'

'Yeah.'

The slosh of the water alongside the canoe and the oily slide of dripping water as it left their raised paddles, were the only sounds that broke the silent minutes.

'Does that mean you and Mark are...?'

'I was waiting till I spoke to PJ.' She liked slow with Mark.

'Hey, keep paddling. He really likes you.'

'And you would know because?'

'It's obvious.'

'Really?'

'You make me sick.'

'If I had a Brian I would feel extremely lucky.'

'He's pretty good. What about we suggest something to the guys making surfboard art?'

'What did you have in mind? You realise this is a business I'm running?'

'Even though you're ticking along nicely now, I thought back to my calendar idea to raise the profile of your business.'

'We could do a calendar of all the artisans and artists with vignettes of what they offer. A brilliant idea.' Mel loved it.

'I had another idea, just with the guys and strategically placed art.'

'You're relentless.' Mel rolled her eyes.

'I just want to see Mrs Dickson's face when she picks one up for her sister in Queensland next Christmas.'

'Now you're just sad.'

Sally splashed her with icy water from her paddle. 'Stop bursting my bubble of joy.'

They paddled around the fishing jetty and surprised a family of pelicans. They both raised their paddles and let their canoes drift silently by.

Further upstream, Mel pulled out the magazine she'd kept inside her coat. 'Here, hot from the office of Diana Getty. We get a sneak preview.'

'What?'

'No one else has seen this.'

'I'm very honoured. Let's have a look.'

They nosed the canoes into a sandy edge and she let Sally read the article. 'She's written a great article. I've never seen Pelican Point and the region promoted like this.' Her voice inched higher and her eyes glittered. 'We're all going to be inundated with tourists. Do you realise what this means? Everyone will want to visit Serendipi Tea now, and Pelican Point. I might have to order extra caravans. I still can't get used to the name.'

'I love it. Kyu suggested it when she came around and I couldn't come up with anything else.'

'I like the by-line you added on your website, "home of goods with provenance". You'll have to stock up because spring is only a month away and a lot of people head down here for holidays.' They reclined in the canoes, savouring the news.

'And I have something else to tell you.'

'What is it?'

'I was really dumb and bought heaps of useless shares as an investment. These ones were five cents each. I purchased one hundred thousand of them.' Mel found it hard to control her voice.

'A whole five thousand dollars? Well done, Mel.'

'In the first two years they slid to two cents. In the third year they rose to five cents. They were the only ones I kept when I sold the house.'

'I'm surprised Wall Street haven't phoned you.'

'Anyway, in the last two years they kept rising in value.'

'No! Don't tell me they're eight cents now?'

'Actually, they finished last month at three dollars fifty. I cashed them in and paid off a large chunk of the loan on the house and business last week.'

'You're kidding! What were the shares in?'

'A biotechnology company. They use seaweed and bacteria to make anything from fuel, to food, to makeup, and they're based on the east coast. It's taken off.'

'That's unbelievable!'

'I know. It still feels unreal. Diana Getty paid me a decent amount for the interview. Are you coming to Hawaii next Christmas?'

'You're kidding?'

'Yes I am. I thought Switzerland first, then Hawaii.'

After they rinsed and stacked the canoes, they discussed the improved financial situation. Sunk low in musty fold-up chairs, they hoed into a small round of local soft cheese and homemade biscuits. Sally supplied the thermos of rich hot chocolate. They looked out through the opened doors of the boatshed to see tiny sparkles of light spin out across the bay; Beth was home. A feeling of buttery warmth spread throughout Mel's body, and it wasn't just the hot chocolate; her application to enrol in a degree in marine science had been successful. It would take at least ten years part-time.

Chapter Seventy-six

On the drive to collect Lil from Mina's, Mel's heart floated like a warm, luminous bubble.

'Hello Mel. Come inside for some tea.' Moqutat escorted her up the sweeping porch steps and into the spare but elegant front room where tea had been set out.

'Thank you Moqutat. Excuse my dress, I've been canoeing with Sally.' She sat on the expansive leather couches while he poured the tea. 'Your tea set is gorgeous.' Everyone had different cups and they were in a riot of colours.

'I have some tea sets.' He moved his slender arm towards a tea chest, where a range of brightly coloured teapots, cups, sugar bowls and creamers sat crowded on the top. 'I wonder if you might have a home for them in your store?'

She flicked him a what-are-you-thinking look, and raised her eyebrows. 'I'd love to have them but I insist on paying.' She walked over and trailed her fingers over the edges of the teacups.

'You can't pay for a gift, but we'll drop by for some company and a cup of tea.'

She couldn't help feeling astonished by him and mouthed an, 'I owe you.' He waved it away and smiled at her.

In the rear-vision mirror she glanced at Lil who held one of the tea sets on her lap. Moqutat had organised to have the tea chest delivered early the following week.

As she rounded the street to her home, a feeling came back to her. Every cell leapt about. With the window down and the sharp cool breeze loosening her hair, she opened her mouth to catch the tang of salt on her tongue. Small sand drifts whorled around the floor mats. It was her car, her store, and her life on the wide rim of an unpredictable coast.

When she turned into her driveway, she saw his big white four-wheel drive.

Mark was deep in conversation with Jack. His arms were loosely folded and one shoulder was pressed against the wall of the store; on the outside table beside him was a belt sander. He'd promised to help her get the back room ready for sealing. She walked over and dead-legged him. He flashed her a private glint. He smelled like wood shavings.

Jack flicked her long fringe and grinned. Light danced on her braces.

Acknowledgements

I was fortunate to receive love, help and support from so many professional teams and divine individuals while writing this book.

My eternal gratitude goes to my outstanding editor, Alexandra Nahlous, who worked tirelessly and gave such astute advice.

Nicola O'Shea who saw the manuscript in its raw and untested form. Nicola provided extremely valuable advice in her rigorous structural edit. From those wise words alone, it grew enormously.

The Fellowship of Australian Writers Western Australia for the variety of courses and conversations with authors they provided.

The University of Western Australia provided numerous excellent world-class courses on writing. It is simply the best location for the Perth Writer's Festival.

Special thanks go to Jay Crisp Crow for her brilliant ideas, enthusiasm and professional work along the way. I doubt I would be here without her.

Nicky Thomas, thank you for your initial coaching and for finding out what buttons needed pushing.

To my family and friends, thank you for your loving support and constant encouragement- you stayed the distance.

For my special friend Deb, for every positive word you said and for every time we laughed our socks off, thanks.

All the cafes along the beach front in Perth—I'll be back!

My children are everything and more. Thank you isn't enough.

About the Author

Annie J Ryan grew up in the suburbs of Perth. She worked as a caretaker of equipment at University while studying. It came as no surprise to her that she was a spectacularly unsuccessful bookkeeper. Thankfully, she hadn't chosen that as her career. For a number of years she was a managing director of a company. She's taught, consulted and lectured in education. Presently, she's involved in innovative education.

She writes continuously. Other things she's written include poetry for weddings, stories for her children, and short stories.

Some of her spare time is spent outside enjoying the enormous Western Australian Coast. She is particularly partial to all of the delicious coastal cafes. On holidays, she flies away to experience other places and heavenly food along the wild Australian shore. She adores her family, friends, reading, sleeping, cycling, learning, eating, and being creative.

She lives in Perth with her grown up children.

Printed in Australia
AUHW011257030519
311804AU00001B/1

9 781925 516432